THE ZION
COVENANT
BOOK 9

P9-DYB-279

Dunkirk Crescendo

THE ZION
COVENANT
BOOK 9

BODIE & BROCK
THOENE

TYNDALE HOUSE PUBLISHERS, INC. • WHEATON, ILLINOIS

Visit Tyndale's exciting Web site at www.tyndale.com

TYNDALE is a registered trademark of Tyndale House Publishers, Inc.

Tyndale's quill logo is a trademark of Tyndale House Publishers, Inc.

Copyright © 1994, 2005 by Bodie Thoene. All rights reserved.

Cover illustration copyright © 2005 by Cliff Nielsen. All rights reserved.

Author photo copyright © 2004 by Brian MacDonald. All rights reserved.

The Zion Covenant series designed by Julie Chen

Designed by Dean H. Renninger

Edited by Ramona Cramer Tucker

Portions of *Dunkirk Crescendo* were printed in *The Twilight of Courage*, © 1994 by Bodie and Brock Thoene, by Thomas Nelson, Inc., Publishers under ISBN 0-7852-8196-7.

First printing of *Dunkirk Crescendo* by Tyndale House Publishers, Inc. in 2005.

Scripture quotations are taken from the *Holy Bible*, King James Version or the *Holy Bible*, New International Version® NIV®. Copyright © 1973, 1978, 1984 by International Bible Society. Used by permission of Zondervan Publishing House. All rights reserved.

This novel is a work of fiction. Names, characters, places, and incidents either are the product of the authors' imaginations or are used fictitiously. Any resemblance to actual events, locales, organizations, or persons, living or dead, is entirely coincidental and beyond the intent of either the authors or publisher.

Library of Congress Cataloging-in-Publication Data

Thoene, Bodie, date.
  Dunkirk crescendo / Bodie & Brock Thoene.
  p. cm. — (The zion covenant ; bk. 9)
  ISBN-13: 978-1-4143-0545-5 (sc)
  ISBN-10: 1-4143-0545-1 (sc)
  1. Dunkirk, Battle of, Dunkerque, France, 1940—Fiction. 2. Holocaust, Jewish (1939-1945)—Fiction. 3. World War, 1939-1945—Fiction. I. Thoene, Brock, date. II. Title. III. Series.
  PS3570.H46D86 2005
  813'.54—dc22   2005006546

Printed in the United States of America

11   10   09   08   07   06   05
7   6   5   4   3   2

With much love for our courageous friends and fellow journalists—
John Waage, Chris Mitchell, Deborah Bunting, Molly Young—
who know what it means to be on the front lines of truth for
America and the land of Israel.

Dunkirk Crescendo is a "Director's Cut,"
including portions of the Thoene Classic *The Twilight of Courage*
and thrilling, never-before-published scenes
with the characters you've come to know
and love through The Zion Covenant series.

❧

1939
September 1—Nazi Germany invades Poland
September 3—England and France declare war on Germany
September 17—Soviets invade Poland
September 27—Warsaw falls

October—"Phony War" begins

December 13—German battleship *Admiral Graf Spee* cornered in
South Atlantic

❧

1940
February 16—*Altmark* incident

April 9—Germany invades Norway

May 10—Winston Churchill becomes British prime minister
May 12—Panzers reach Meuse River
May 13 to 19—Blitzkrieg sweeps across Northern France
May 14—Holland surrenders
May 16—Panic in French government
May 18—Germans capture Cambrai
May 20—Wehrmacht reaches the French seacoast
May 21—British counterattack near Arras
May 26 to June 4—"Miracle of Dunkirk"
May 28—Belgium surrenders

3 0053
00771
5520

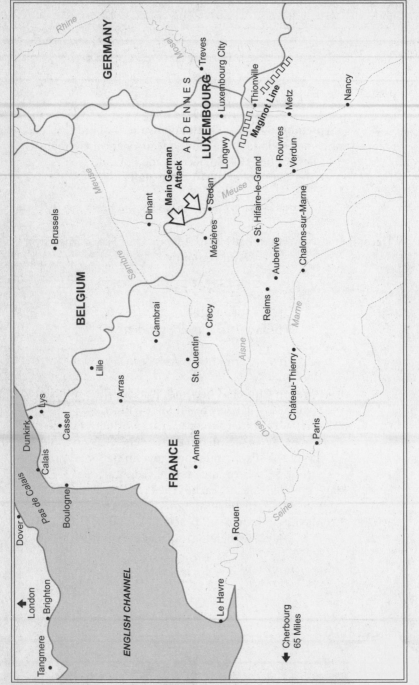

THE WESTERN FRONT

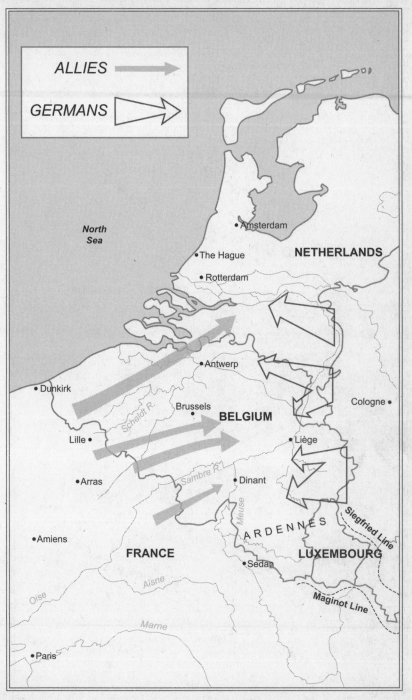

THE DUNKIRK PERIMETER

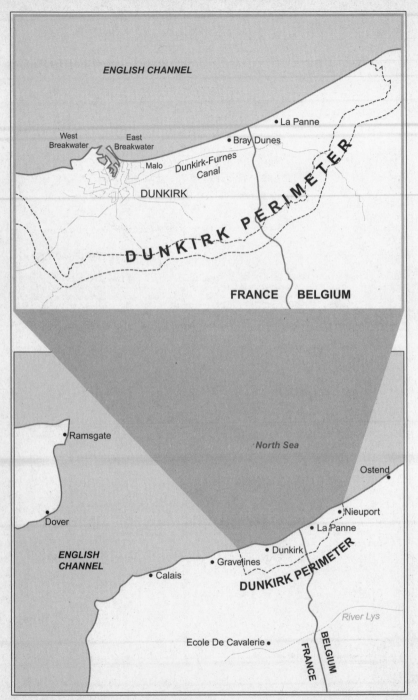

PART I

*It is not by speeches and resolutions
that the questions of time are decided . . .
but by iron and blood.*

> Otto von Bismarck,
> Speech to Prussian House of Delegates
> September 30, 1862

1

The Colors of Spring

All night rain tapped gently on the glass panes above Josephine Marlow's bed. Madame Adelle Watson, the proprietor of the Foyer International on Boulevard St. Michel, had warned the newspaper correspondent against sleeping directly beneath the skylight. It had leaked last year, and Madame Watson was uncertain if the maintenance man, who was a notorious drunk, had fixed it properly. But when the seal had held during the first rain of winter in Paris, Josie had moved her little iron bed beneath the square of glass so she could see the sky at night and the light of morning before the sun arose.

Only then did Madame Watson confess her real purpose in warning Josie about sleeping below the skylight. "Suppose, my dear girl, that we are bombed without warning in the middle of the night? Or suppose those idiot French antiaircraft gunners shoot off a round that misses the Huns entirely and lands smack on you?"

"Even if the round missed my skylight but came through the roof, being in the attic, I would be the first to go. Don't worry, Madame Watson. This way if any Germans fly over Foyer International and aim at my skylight, I will see them and be able to give the alert."

Josie's reasoning satisfied Madame Watson completely.

And when it rained, the rhythmic patter only made Josie sleep more soundly.

Josie was the first in Foyer International to know that spring had arrived. Larks began to build a nest on the windowsill. They chirped and argued with one another about the placing of this twig or that bit of string. When they were finished, Madame Lark laid four eggs.

This morning, from the tall window of her garret room, Josie looked over the wide expanse of the Tuileries gardens. The gravel paths were flanked by color. The chestnut trees were in bloom. The air was fragrant. The cobbles of the street below were shiny after the rain. Vendors rattled their wood-wheeled carts slowly up the lane, selling precious rationed items like milk and eggs and sugar.

War with the Nazis seemed remote—impossible.

Josie had gotten two brief letters from Mac McGrath, the American photographer she had thought she was in love with some time ago. The texts had been run through with the black censor's pen of the French Anastasie. She had learned more about his adventures with the German ship *Altmark* from the newspapers and the wire service than she had gleaned from his notes.

Consistent in both messages was the sense that Mac was very much in love with his Eva. He had met Eva Weitzman, a Czech, during his escape from Warsaw before the Nazis took over the city. Now he wrote Josie dutifully, like a concerned older brother. What was the use of kidding herself? Mac had already made his choice. Josie was no longer in the running.

But then there was Andre Chardon, the man she had met on the train to Paris. Each hour she had spent with him since then was better than the last. He talked openly about his longing to see Juliette, his child, and to get this dreadful war over with and settle back into a comfortable, ordinary existence. To enjoy the spring days of Paris without thinking of the clouds on the eastern horizon.

Josie had fallen in love with the tall, handsome man, in spite of his French colonel's uniform.

⸿

It was a day Josephine Marlow had been looking forward to. The grounds of the Ecole de Cavalerie, the revered cavalry training school in Lys, France, were bright with the colors of spring. The U-shaped, four-story brick structure had a freshly scrubbed look to it after the hard winter. Enormous red crosses had been painted on the roof tiles between the school's dormer windows and its tall rectangular chimneys.

Andre Chardon pointed to the top-story windows of the section that was now a hospital. "I spent the best years of my life dreaming out that view." He laughed.

"When you are not listening, I want Paul to tell me everything there is to tell about you." Josie squeezed Andre's hand.

"That wing is now an isolation ward for measles patients," Andre's younger brother, Paul, observed. The darkly handsome, compact, and athletic man was the chief riding instructor of the school. He inclined his head toward the figure of the head nurse, Miss Abigail Mitchell. "And there is the woman most deserving of isolation."

The tall and muscular Sister Mitchell cast a hard look in Paul's direction, as if she had heard his remark, and then turned away coolly.

Captain Paul Chardon extended his arm to Josie. "If you will allow me, Madame Marlow, I will escort you to the Chardonnet, where the carrousel will take place."

With Andre following, Paul led Josie through the wrought-iron gates with their top rail of gilded spearheads. Past the thickly planted row of tall elms was the grandstand beside the riding arena. After Josie and Andre were seated, Paul excused himself to go to the reviewing box. Standing in front of a microphone, he became the master of ceremonies.

"This arena is called the Chardonnet . . . 'thistle field'? Like your family name?" Josie asked Andre.

Andre smiled. "I think I may have mentioned that our connection with the school goes back quite far. A multigreat ancestor donated this field to King Francis the First for use in jousting tournaments. My forebear was made a baron for his generosity, and he changed his surname to remember the occasion."

"Madames and Monsieurs," Paul announced over the squealing microphone, "the carrousel will commence." Paul waved to two lines of riders at opposite ends of the arena.

With Cadet Sepp leading one column and Cadet Gaston the other, the senior students and their mounts elicited exclamations of approval from the crowd. The horses were harnessed in the gold and purple trappings only used on ceremonial occasions, and their manes and tails were braided with gold silk ribbons.

The boys themselves were also fittingly attired. They wore the brass helmets and shining metal breastplates of the cavalry of Napoleon's day. Each carried a lance with a gleaming brass head, from which fluttered a tiny gold-and-purple pennant.

After a slow pass of the reviewing stand with the lances held stiffly at attention, the two lines of riders completed their circuit of the arena. When they began the second lap, the mounts leaped to a gallop as one. The spearheads flashed in the light as the columns met and swerved aside at the last instant, weaving a high-speed crisscrossing pattern. The slightest miscue would mean a terrible collision or an impaled rider, but such was the precision of the performance that no flaw could be seen. The audience, including Josie, broke into enthusiastic applause.

She watched as the big, muscular Gaston wheeled his troop apart from the others, who retired to the corners of the ring. Under his shouted commands, the group of a dozen equestrians put their chargers through a series of maneuvers that dated to at least the time of King Francis. They executed the *croupade*—that leaping kick backward in midair designed to destroy a pursuer—and the nimble, goatlike jumps of the *cabriole*. When the exhibition was completed, Gaston led his command into a line in front of the stand. Then as the lance tips were lowered to the ground, the row of horses also bowed their heads in a *courbette* in unison.

When Sepp's troop reentered center stage, Josie saw that they had removed their ceremonial costumes and wore their black dress uniforms with the red piping on the collars. Barricades and rails were dragged away from the walls of the ring to form a steeplechase circuit. From a standing start, twelve of the best riders flashed around the loop, leaping over fences, widely spaced bars, and stacks of wine barrels.

Josie added her groan of dismay to the crowd's when Sepp's black horse caught his back hoof on a rail. Sepp tumbled forward over the mane, but he recovered his seat and spurred the mount to even greater speed. With only one quarter lap to go, Sepp caught up with his fastest opponent so the two horses flashed across the final fence exactly even. In the last split second before the finish, Sepp's charger spurted ahead, giving him the victory by a neck.

Josie clapped wildly and joined the others in shouts of "Bravo!"

Andre, smiling, leaned over. "Does it make it more impressive—or less—if I tell you that the entire performance, including the near fall, is part of the act?"

Each year the senior students were allowed to perform a finale of their own choosing. Josie realized that no one, not even Paul, knew what to expect from this display. Curiosity and amusement rippled through the crowd as Sepp and Gaston and their lieutenants carried a table and four chairs into the center of the ring. There they laid out a perfect picnic, including bread, cheese, apples, a bottle of wine, and five glasses.

With expectation growing, Josie craned her neck to watch the action. There was confused laughter as Gaston drew the cork of the wine bottle with a flourish and poured four glasses of red Bordeaux. In a loud voice, he proposed a toast to the Ecole de Cavalerie. His three comrades stood and raised their glasses.

At that exact moment, Cadet Raymond leaped on a charging bay over the wall at the far end of the arena. He spurred directly at the table, as if he did not even see it. The horse neither swerved nor shied. At the last possible second, the four boys sat down in their chairs just as Raymond urged the bay into an enormous leap. Horse and rider sailed over the group of cadets, who made a great show of clinking their glasses under the horse's belly.

And then, when a gasp of relief had already gone up from the crowd, Josie saw Raymond pull up the mount at the far end of the field and spur back again. As the cadets calmly ignored the thundering horse bearing down on them, they again toasted each other with the red wine.

Gaston refilled the glasses and this time also filled the empty fifth goblet. Timing his movement to match the jump, Gaston stood and thrust the glass into Raymond's hand. The cadet captain downed the liquid before the hooves of his mount crashed again into the soil of the arena.

The four young men at the table rose as Raymond circled his horse to come up behind them, and all faced the reviewing stand. Wineglasses in hand, they saluted Captain Chardon and their guests. In a resounding tone, Gaston said, "We hope you agree, Madames and Monsieurs, that this year is a truly excellent vintage possessing style and grace!"

On April 16, two months to the day after the captured British sailors were rescued from the holds of the Nazi prison ship *Altmark*, Mac McGrath was in Greenwich, on the Thames east of London. He was there to visit the former *Altmark* prisoner Trevor Galway, to check up on the young officer's recovery.

Lt. Commander Galway was seated on a lawn chair, his lap draped in a blanket. Although he was clothed like an invalid, his physical appearance was greatly improved since Mac had last seen him emerging from the *Altmark*'s hellhole.

"What have they been feeding you?" the American cameraman asked as he crossed the wide expanse of green. "You look like you've gained thirty pounds."

"Two stone, to be precise," Galway corrected, smiling. "Two kilos heavier than before I enjoyed the hospitality of the Nazis." He stood up in his bathrobe and slippers to shake Mac's hand.

"Don't get up. You'll get me in trouble with your nurse."

"Never fear." Trevor laughed. "I'm quite recovered. So well, in fact, that I go back on active service next week. I've been assigned to the destroyer *Intrepid*."

"Congratulations! Does that mean you'll be going to Norway?"

"I can't really discuss that, sorry. But speaking of nurses, here comes mine now."

Mac turned to see a pretty, red-haired young woman with a radiant smile. Accompanying her were a balding older gentleman and an enormous Saint Bernard. "Team of specialists, too?" Mac questioned.

"Mac McGrath, meet my father, John Galway, and my sister, Annie.

The long-haired horse there is Duffy." Duffy lay down on the green grass and rolled over like a puppy, for all of his two hundred pounds.

Annie, Mac found out, really was a nurse. "My applause, Miss Galway. Your brother looks fit. Your care must suit him."

"Pooh!" she scoffed. "He is the worst, most uncooperative patient ever. If he gets well, it is in spite of me. But I must thank you, Mr. McGrath. Trevor tells me that you are the man who pulled him out of that dreadful hole."

"Aye, that's why I remember the name. Give us your hand again, then," demanded John Galway. His fist engulfed Mac's and pumped it vigorously. "I'd still like to lay hold of them Nazi—" He caught himself.

"Easy, Da," Trevor and Annie both cautioned.

"Besides," Trevor added, "I'll be doing my own paying back after next week. My orders have come through and I got *Intrepid*."

Annie looked worried. "Ah, Trev. Back to the war so soon?"

"At least it won't be to Norway you'll be goin'," John Galway muttered, waving his meaty fists in agitation. "A hopeless muddle! Jerry has troops at Trondheim and Narvik and Oslo, and we can't budge 'em. Too little, too late, I say. You mark my words: Our boys'll come home with their tails betwixt their legs, and it'll be the end of this Prime Minister Chamberlain and his mealymouthed bunch of—"

"Da," Annie scolded with a wink at Mac that her father did not see, "you must not get Trev excited now!"

"Do you really think this failure will bring down the government?" Mac asked. The Phony War had already claimed French Premier Daladier as a political casualty. Was Chamberlain next? A movement on the hill behind the navy buildings at Greenwich caught Mac's eye. The red time signal ball was hoisted to the top of its staff.

"Has to, laddie," John Galway concluded in a calmer tone. "The PM has been wrong once too often, and this time our people have suffered for it. He'll have to go. It's just a matter of when."

On the top of the cupola of the observation tower, the red ball descended from the peak, accompanied by the firing of a signal gun. This signaled noon on the prime meridian, setting time for the entire world.

2

An Elementary Calculation

It was the first of May. A warm, pleasantly balmy day bloomed over Paris, like the unfolding of a delicate flower. But no matter how hard he tried, Andre could not dispel the obsessive sense of gloom and anxiety that weighed on his thoughts.

There was a German invasion coming; he could feel it. The rains had stopped, and the fields were drying rapidly. Soon there would be no barrier to the free movement of tanks and armored vehicles—no fear of their bogging down.

Even worse, military and political figures alike were distracted. The High Command was not focused on France. They were bemoaning April's debacle when the Wehrmacht had swept over Norway. After delaying a week, giving the Germans ample opportunity to land troops all along the Norwegian coast, the Allies had sent too little help. In ten days the campaign had been lost, and those who were not dead or captured returned home. Chalk up another victory for the undefeated Führer. How much longer would he hold back Blitzkrieg from France, which had declared a state of war against Germany on September 3? And what reason had the Western Allies shown to make him hesitate? None!

The French generals blamed the French politicians for not committing to help Norway sooner. The politicians blamed the generals for their ill-prepared troops. Both groups blamed the British. After all, Norway involved maritime forces and the landing of troop ships. Wasn't that the subject in which the Royal Navy claimed unmatched expertise?

The upshot was that French politics was in one of its perpetual crises. Prime Minister Reynaud was rumored to be fed up with General

Gamelin and his cohort Daladier, no longer France's prime minister but now defense minister. But if Reynaud fired those two, it would certainly bring down the new government. Meanwhile, English Prime Minister Chamberlain was also on thin ice for the failure in Norway. It appeared that both administrations might collapse within the week. It could not have come at a worse time. Everyone was already bored with predictions of a German invasion that never really materialized. Now it was impossible to get anyone in authority to listen.

Andre was more of an outcast than ever, since he was still convinced that the main Nazi threat would not come from where the aging leaders from the Great War claimed it would.

He sat on the second-from-the-bottom tread of the stairs leading down to his basement and studied a back view of the brilliant but quirky Richard Lewinski. The carrottopped engineer was enmeshed in the bowels of his reconstruction of the Nazi code machine, Enigma, as if the giant machine were swallowing him. It was difficult to separate the wild explosion of wiry hair from the profusion of tangled wires that encircled the cabinet where he worked. If it were not for the thin, khaki-clad legs that protruded below the circuitry, Andre could not have disassociated Lewinski from the machine.

It was a decision born of months of frustration that made Andre call out to Lewinski, "Richard, are you making any progress?"

The Polish Jew's form did not change position, so it was as if his backside were answering the question. "Of course. I now know the wiring of the first three wheels. If there were only three, we would be done."

"Can you do anything to . . . speed up the process?"

Now Lewinski emerged, looking childishly peeved. His face puckered into a pout. "I am working as hard as I can, Andre . . . all alone and from memory. Can you think of a way for me to work harder?"

Andre waved his hands to soothe his friend and head off a potential tantrum. Then he reached inside his coat pocket and removed a pair of twice-folded sheets of paper. "Richard," he said at last, "I am not supposed to have this, let alone show it to you. But desperate times call for desperate measures."

Lewinski came over to sit beside Andre on the step. His bony knees stuck up so that he resembled a stork awkwardly perched on a wire. "This is a coded transmission. Where did it come from?"

"Where is not important. In fact, the reason you did not—could not—know about this is that if you were . . . it is just better for you to not know any more than you need to."

"So, spy games and paranoia. What is this?" Lewinski asked.

"These are intercepts of two Wehrmacht radio transmissions from last September—the first page of each. A team of cryptanalysts has been studying them for patterns to find clues to the settings of the dials."

"Is there a starting hint?"

"Not really—just a guess. The British think that the Germans use rhymes or clichés as test messages. If they were so stupid as to use the same test phrase more than once, we might catch the repeat . . ."

"And be able to unlock the settings of the dials," Lewinski finished. "Andre, I should have seen these long ago. Now, what common German sayings are short enough?"

Lewinski was already lost in thought. Like a child absorbed in a riddle, he pored over the pages, squinting at the meaningless words and counting letters. "Four, five, three . . . and over here four, five, three . . . no, that's no good. The next word is six on one, three on the other."

Scanning the documents with the intensity of a hawk soaring over a field that contained a hidden rabbit, Lewinski suddenly pounced. "Ha! Here it is. It is the same sequence, only backward on one page."

Andre peered over his shoulder. "If it is backward, how do you know it is the same?"

Giving his friend a withering stare, Lewinski asked, "Do you think the radio operators have time or intellect enough to make up new phrases every day? Of course not! Now, let's see, what proverb is six, six, three, five, five . . . oh, how absurdly simple."

"What?" Andre said breathlessly, unable to believe what he was hearing.

"You know how the Deutschlanders like to hang posters and paint slogans? Well, I could hardly miss this one. It was printed in red and black letters over my workbench in Berlin. Look here." Lewinski pointed a crooked forefinger at a line of type. "This can be nothing but *'Morgen, morgen, nur nicht heute, sagen alle faulen Leute.'* 'Tomorrow, tomorrow, never today, say all lazy people.'"

"That is it? Just like that?"

Lewinski looked offended.

"Not that I doubt your brilliance," Andre hastily reassured his friend. "It is just that . . . the others have been working for months. How did they miss this?"

"Were they Poles?"

"Yes," Andre cautiously agreed.

"That explains it, then. When I worked in Germany, I forced myself to *think* in German. Besides, they have probably never studied gematria."

"Gematria?"

"The Jewish practice of numerology. It helps one recognize patterns like nothing else."

"And now?"

"Now I go to work seeing how the patterns changed from one paper to the next, and I will know how to set the wheels. Can I get more of these? Something current, so we can test the hypothesis?"

"Anything you want." Andre jumped to his feet and ran up the stairs. "You are a genius!"

Hugging his knees, Lewinski rocked with a satisfied grin. "I know."

"You see," Lewinski said later the same morning to Andre and Colonel Gustave Bertrand of French Military Intelligence, "once you find a pattern in the way the coding changes, you can deduce the method to predict future changes."

"And have you done that?" Bertrand insisted. "Can you decode all the messages? Tell us how it works!"

Lewinski looked disappointed. Andre knew the engineer wanted to spin out this yarn in his own way, milking to the fullest the story and his role in the discovery. But Bertrand was no-nonsense.

"Yes." Lewinski sniffed. "I took as my premise that the change from one day to the next would have to follow a simple model. That way the superiors of the field operators of the Enigma machine would always know the correct settings for the wheels. Just think, if they had to follow an instruction book for each day's changes, what would happen if that book was lost or stolen? It is much simpler for a communications officer at, say, the division level, to have the guide memorized and radio the new setting as the last message encoded on the old setting."

"Yes, yes!" broke in Bertrand impatiently. "Get on with it!"

Andre laid his hand on Bertrand's shoulder, silently urging him to contain himself. Temperamental geniuses could not be rushed. He said soothingly to Lewinski, "You are explaining this so well, Richard! Please go on."

"It is simple, really. The shift of the dials depends on the date, the day of the week, and the cycles of the moon. I just consulted a simple almanac, which I got from the newsstand at Place St. Michelle, and there it was."

Bertrand appeared stunned. In a low tone he said, "Are you telling me that the Germans change the wheels based on an elementary calculation? that you can decode their messages?"

"Not only can, I already have," Lewinski said proudly. "My machine, though not as polished-looking as theirs, is every bit as functional. See for yourself: Here is something I fed in this morning."

Bertrand gave Andre a sharp look. Lewinski was not supposed to actually decipher communications. His role was only to reach a conclusion about the encoding pattern.

"I felt there was no time to waste," Andre said by way of explanation.

"All right, what do these messages say?" Bertrand asked.

Andre took over at this point. "Most are routine transmissions regarding resupply and logistics—except for this one. It reads: *'Fall Gelb will commence 10 May. Sichelschnitt must reach Meuse by 12 May.'*"

Bertrand exhaled. "Plan Yellow and the Cut of the Sickle? It still does not tell us anything."

"Yes, it does!" Andre insisted. "I have studied the maps. The only operation of any kind that can reach the Meuse River in two days is an armored attack through the Ardennes!"

"We must see Gamelin at once," Bertrand replied, his face white.

Lewinski brightened. "Do you suppose I will get a medal?"

"Richard," Bertrand said kindly, "you cannot go. It is more important than ever that you be protected. You can imagine how valuable this information would be to the Germans. They would change the whole system if they knew. Not only would all your work be for nothing, but you would personally be in great danger."

Lewinski deflated. If compared to a balloon, he had never resembled more than a very skinny one. Now he looked like the remains of one after it had been popped. "Find me a new project then," he pleaded. "I am already bored."

☙

"I am really sorry, Chardon, but the C-in-C cannot see you today after all. He is incredibly busy with really important matters." Colonel Pucelle's tone laid a thick stress on the word *really*.

"When *can* the general see me? It is extremely important!" It was just after lunch, and Andre was ready to punch General Gamelin's assistant in the mouth for his superior attitude and manner.

"Why do you not just give the message to me, and I will deliver it to the general."

Andre exchanged a glance with Gustave Bertrand. The very last thing the two intelligence officers wanted to do was to put sensitive material in Pucelle's hands. Lewinski's breakthrough was too important to be filtered through a man whose most prominent ability was currying favor.

Maybe there was still a way. "Look, Pucelle," Andre tried, "you remember the earlier discussion about where the focus of the German attack would be? We have new evidence that the invasion of Holland will primarily be a diversion."

"Oh no!" Pucelle groaned with dismay. "Not again! Really, Chardon, this horse will not run. The general has studied all the possible invasion routes from the Sedan gap to an airborne offensive on Rotterdam. No more idle speculation, please!"

"Pucelle," Andre insisted, "just suppose there is something to this. Suppose the Germans *are* planning an attack through the Ardennes. If you suggested to General Gamelin that he reinforce Corap's Ninth Army and Huntziger's Second Army by shifting over part of Conde's force, you would look like a genius."

Pucelle's face twitched. It was a feline expression, like a cat narrowing his eyes when he spots a bird within reach. Andre knew Pucelle never wanted to disagree with anything on which Gamelin held convictions. But a chance to pull off a strategic coup and get all the credit would be too good for Pucelle to pass up. Even so, he was not about to stick out his neck too far.

"Since you will not reveal your source," Pucelle said haughtily, "I have nothing on which to base such a suggestion except your opinion. Get me some concrete evidence that you are correct, and I will consider broaching the subject with the general. Now I really must go, gentlemen. You will have to excuse me."

3

An Unlikely Refuge

Rocking the plane from side to side enabled American pilot David Meyer to see over his shoulder as the flight of Hurricanes proceeded up the valley of the Meuse River toward Belgium. The swaying motion used up more fuel, but it was necessary as a means to watch for enemy fighters that might be sneaking up behind.

Only two days earlier Benny Turpin, a new boy with the Royal Air Force's 73 Squadron, had not paid careful enough attention to the six o'clock position astern. Benny had ended a promising flying career in a ball of flame at the hands of an ME-109. It only marginally lightened David's thoughts to recall that he had personally dispatched the Messerschmitt just moments later.

David's mood was also darker than usual because of the plane he was flying—or rather, because of the aircraft he was *not* flying. *Annie*, named for red-haired Annie Galway, the woman he had fallen in love with, had taken a bullet through the oil cooler in the engagement with the German who shot down Turpin. She was out of service for another day, so David was flying a spare ship. He felt no connection with this aircraft. It almost seemed that the controls were not as responsive to his touch, even though the mechanic assured him that it was all his imagination.

Hewitt's voice barked over the radio. "Cluster of black dots at my two o'clock high."

"Roger that," Simpson agreed. "Could be Heinkels. Let's go."

The three RAF pilots took their planes into a steep climb to position themselves above the intended targets. The number of enemy bombers seemed to be increasing as the Hurricanes got closer.

"I count twenty," Simpson reported. A moment later he amended the number to thirty and then again to forty.

Black dots appeared to materialize out of thin air. The range closed rapidly as Simpson prepared to initiate the dive that would lead the three fighters swooping down on the intended victims, when suddenly he announced, "What a duff play this is."

From his position guarding the rear of the formation, David had not yet figured out what Simpson meant.

"Flaming onions," Hewitt growled. "Take a closer look at our targets. Those are ack-ack bursts."

And so it proved. The magically increasing numbers of enemy bombers turned out to be the black puffs that marked the explosions of anti-aircraft shells.

"Let's get out of here before someone throws one of those our way," Simpson ordered.

"They must be shooting at something," David observed, scanning the sky as the Hurricanes turned back to their original course. His view from twenty-five-thousand feet covered a lot of territory. "And there it is," he continued. "Dead ahead. A flight of Dorniers at angels twelve. Two pairs of ME-110s flying cover. All heading northeast, back to the Reich."

"Full bore now," Simpson said.

"Even into Belgium?"

"Didn't stop the Nazis, did it? We'll chase them into Germany if we have to. Hewitt, you and I will take the two on the right. Meyer, you have a go at the other pair. If we can scatter them, we'll come back after the bombers. Let's go."

The RAF plunge took the German fighters completely by surprise. Although they were not as maneuverable as the ME-109s that Germany also used, these twin-engine ME-110 German fighter escorts were nevertheless tough to knock down. When they were in service with General Franco during the Spanish civil war, they were known as "destroyers," and with good reason.

David's attack slashed toward the inside of the two German planes from an angle on its stern. A short burst from David's machine guns was followed by another, longer stream, as the 110 broke to the outside. The line of David's fire sawed through the rudder of the craft, tearing part of it completely free. A portion of the tail surface was severed as well. The German pilot banked sharply, trying to control his now erratically plunging machine. David followed in a tight spiral, hoping that a final salvo into the nearside engine would finish the battle.

That was the instant when David chanced to look groundward. The aerial combat had carried him very near the German border. And what a view of Western Germany it was. On the roads leading back from the border were countless parallel rows of German tanks, armored cars, and half-tracks hauling artillery pieces. They were nose to tail, like elephants heading for a watering hole.

For a second David thought about the significance of this sight. Then there was an enormous explosion, and his plane began to shudder and lose altitude rapidly. Over his shoulder, David could see the pursuing form of another Messerschmitt. It was the partner of the one David had just downed. David's fighter had taken a blast of 20 mm cannon fire at close range.

He went into a steep dive, twisting the damaged Hurricane around and heading it back toward France and home. The maneuver successfully evaded the Messerschmitt, but the right wing was making a whining complaint. Worse, the craft felt sluggish and heavy, as if lifting more than its accustomed weight. When the engine burst into flames that hungrily licked at the cowling, David knew it was time to kiss the airplane good-bye. This was the first time he was glad he wasn't flying *Annie*.

David eased the ship out of its dive and hoped that any other nearby German pilots had better things to do than chase parachutes. He opened the canopy just as the engine conked out. Once clear of the radio cable and the oxygen tube, the pilot dove over the side into space.

When the chute popped, the sudden uplift yanked him away from the fighter. It dipped its nose and raised its tail, almost as if waving good-bye.

David had barely had time to observe his surroundings before his hurried exit from the aircraft. But drifting silently toward the ground, he used the opportunity to examine the forested hillsides below, confirming his earlier suspicion. It was the wrong side of the river that seemed to be slowly twisting below him. He was coming down in Belgium.

As David watched from his floating perch beneath the canopy of the parachute, his Hurricane streaked earthward. It was headed toward the church steeple of a village on the horizon. Now trailing a column of thick, black smoke, the aircraft was a flaming arrow on a colossal scale. David held his breath. The fighter struck the ground a couple miles from the village, and a fiery pillar shot into the air. The dull roar of the explosion followed a few seconds later.

As grateful as he was for the safe descent, David wished that it would get over quickly. The detonation and the bonfire blazing above the territory of the Ardennes Forest would attract some unwelcome attention. The Belgians, as citizens of a still-neutral nation, were not at all happy about the Germans and the Allies using the skies above their country as a battlefield. They not only shot at the airplanes of both sides; they interned captured pilots for the duration of the war. David didn't plan on being one of them.

The Belgians, like the Dutch, were being very shortsighted and ungrateful, David thought. After all, the presence of the Allied army was keeping the Führer off of their necks. With all the German armor poised on the edge of Belgium, the security gained by Belgium's fragile neutrality was not going to last much longer anyway.

Perhaps David could parlay information about the terrifying buildup into freedom and safe passage to France. But he couldn't very well surrender and then ask the Belgians if they would please let him go. Better to stay out of their clutches and save the barter plan for a last resort.

He was now drifting onto a timbered hillside. There were no buildings in sight, except for a farmhouse on the far side of the knoll. A clearing with a creek at the bottom presented itself as a likely possibility. So did a patch of bare grassy slope covered in white and pink wildflowers. No such luck. The light swirl of wind chose that instant to die away completely, lowering David directly toward the tops of the pine trees that crowned the hill.

Trying to coax the chute into another course by pulling on the straps met with no success. Plunging between two sixty-foot pines, the edge of the silk bubble caught on one side, swinging David across the open space. Partially tearing, it dropped his shoulders while his feet swung up again like a pendulum. He was hanging almost upside down, one leg tangled in the shrouds, suspended six or so feet off the ground.

Groping awkwardly in a zippered pocket on the leg of his flight suit, David searched for the small knife he carried for just such an emergency. If he could saw through the cords in which his leg was caught, he might be lowered enough to cut himself free from the rest of the parachute. He could fall the short remaining distance.

David removed the knife and opened it, taking care not to drop it because of the strange angle at which he was working. Half of the lines were severed when he first heard a dog barking. The sound of the animal's deep voice echoed from just over the hill toward the farm. It was still far away but definitely coming closer. He began to saw even faster, anxious to get down and find a place to hide.

The dog bayed again—a real bloodhound noise David knew from his own childhood year in Arkansas. Not a good sign if the beast was accompanied by the Belgian police.

Two cords remained to be cut when the knife slipped from his fingers. David made a frantic grab for it as it fell but only succeeded in batting it into a high arc. The knife gleamed in the afternoon sun, then dropped earthward, sticking upright in the grassy soil. It mocked David from six feet below.

The barking dog was still coming. David began to yank on the almost detached leads. Once more he gave a hard tug, and the strap parted. His weight pivoted on the remaining tether and swung him sideways at the same instant the rent in the parachute tore larger.

Just as the hound crashed through the brush surrounding the trees, David's head smacked into the trunk of the pine. Despite his leather flying helmet, the impact stunned him. The animal was almost on top of him, and there was nothing he could do about it.

Then into David's upside-down view bounded the biggest black dog he had seen since his childhood companion, a Newfoundland named Codfish.

"Good dog," he called, trying to keep his voice calm and friendly.

The dog's tone changed to a suspicious growl. Its hackles rose, and it walked stiff-legged toward the strange apparition hanging in the tree.

"Good dog," David tried again. "*Bon chien*. That's it, *bon chien*!"

The dog continued to snarl menacingly.

"*Gute Hund! Gute Hund!*"

The coal black shape made a leap that carried it directly up to David. The pilot put up his arms in an effort to protect his face from the mauling he was sure was coming. He felt the animal's hot breath on his neck, and then it began to lick his ear.

Cautiously David inched his hands apart and peeked out. The dog, still regarding him with curiosity, was wagging his tail. "*Gute Hund!*" he repeated, heaving an enormous sigh of relief. "Now if you could only help me get down from here."

"Are you speaking to the dog?" asked a gruff voice in French. "Have you always been crazy, or does it happen when you fly planes?"

David pivoted again and focused his eyes on a pair of rough country boots. From these he scanned upward over heavy, corduroy-covered legs, a bulky torso, muscular arms, and a face framed by a salt-and-pepper beard. One of the hands was holding a pitchfork.

"Can you get me down?"

"You are English?" the farmer asked.

"American flying for the RAF."

"That was your air machine that crashed over by Couvin?"

"Yes, I am sure it was. Could we discuss this after you cut me loose?"

The farmer pulled an enormous jackknife from his pocket and sliced the remaining shroud lines in one stroke.

Tumbling free, David scrambled to his feet. "Thank you, Monsieur. Where is the French border?"

The grizzled farmer shook his head. "The police will be searching for you. You must hide until nightfall, when it will be safer. They do not want to find you, you understand. It is not as if you were *German.*" He spat out the word as something incredibly distasteful. "But there are those in the village who favor the Nazis. They would make trouble if the police found you and then let you go free. You must come with me. I will hide you until dark."

"Good idea," David agreed. Then a worrisome thought crossed his mind. "Tell me, why does your dog understand German and not French?"

The man looked amused. "He is a refugee. Showed up on my door-step two years ago. Ask him, Monsieur. He hates Nazis."

David spotted his pocketknife sticking in the ground. Picking it up, he offered it to the farmer. "I am grateful for your kindness. May I give you this knife to say thank you?"

The man scowled. "I take no pay for helping someone who fights the Boche! But perhaps I will make a trade." The two men and the dog started over the hill toward the farm. "My knife for yours?"

"Done. But your knife is so much bigger and sharper. What will you do with mine?"

Winking at David, the farmer said, "Give it to my grandson for a toy."

When they reached the Belgian farmhouse, David saw that it was modest but built of stone and sturdy looking. It nestled in a ravine be-tween two shoulders of the hillside and overlooked a marshy pasture in which a few tawny milk cows were placidly grazing.

"I will show you where to hide," the farmer told David, "and then I must return to my chores. If I am not at work at this time of day, the au-thorities will find it suspicious."

"Fine," agreed David. "In your barn or in the house?"

"Neither will serve. The police may wish to check them. But there is a place that I can vouch for as safe. Come with me."

On an incline at the edge of the pasture stood a wooden structure whose appearance left no doubt as to its function. David hesitated at the doorway. "How long will I—?"

"Get in quickly," the farmer urged. "I'll come back later and take you into the house." Whistling at the dog, the man shut the door behind Da-vid and turned toward the field.

If the farmer intended to betray David to the authorities, then they would all have a good laugh when his location was revealed, David thought. It was a warm day, and the atmosphere in the hideout was ripe.

It was not long before the issue was decided. The black dog barked a warning, and soon the jingle of a bicycle's bell announced an arrival. Peeping through a crack in the outhouse wall, David saw a blue-coated gendarme waving to the farmer. The policeman was accompanied by a second bicyclist, a fat man in knee britches and a waistcoat.

"*Bonjour*, Dennis," called the gendarme to the farmer. "Did you see the crash of the airplane?"

"You mean the machine that went over my house like a duck with its tail feathers on fire? Of course I saw it! Scared my cows with its great roaring sound. Probably soured their milk. What brings you out here, Joseph—you and Monsieur Navet?"

The fat man, wiping his flushed face and panting to catch his breath, answered for the gendarme. "Did you see a parachute near here? We have heard that one floated down in this direction."

"Do I have nothing better to do than watch the sky for falling Englishmen?" Dennis scoffed.

"How did you know he was English?" The fat man pounced on the farmer's words like a cat on a mouse.

"German then, or French. What is it to you, Navet?"

"It is a matter of extreme importance! Just last week two English airmen escaped from the jail at Dinant. How long do you think Belgium's neutrality will be respected if we aid the Allies?"

"And how long even if we don't? Go away, Navet; you annoy me. Search if you wish, but why would a man who has just fallen from an airplane run to where he would be captured? Don't you think he would remain up in the hills until dark?"

"Come along, Monsieur Navet," the policeman urged. "Dennis is right. We must start hiking if we expect to locate the flier."

"We should search the house and the barn first!"

"Fine," the farmer agreed. "Search away."

The fat man motioned for Joseph to follow him as he bustled importantly into the farmhouse and reemerged moments later, looking disappointed. He then examined the barn and came back covered in dirt and with straw in his hair.

"Sorry to have bothered you," the gendarme apologized.

Monsieur Navet glanced around suspiciously. His eye lit on the outhouse. "Wait. There is yet one more place to look."

David tensed at the words and braced himself to make a run for it.

Dennis shrugged. "It's a good idea. Leave nothing unchecked. I would not want you to come back later and accuse me of something, Navet."

Navet's eyes narrowed in his fleshy face, disappearing into swinelike folds. "I think you are toying with us. Why are you being so agreeable?" He squinted at the sinking position of the sun. "Let's go, Joseph. We've wasted enough time here already."

Dennis turned his back and continued tending his cows. Several minutes passed, and then he went into the barn and brought out a sack of grain. He fed the hens, tossing handfuls of corn on the ground, and wandered toward the outhouse. In a low voice, with his head down as if addressing the chickens, he said, "That Navet! He is a Gestapo agent, that one. Fat pig! I hope he busts something pumping his bicycle up and down the hills!"

"When can I come out?" David pleaded.

"Not before dark. Be patient."

❦

As soon as the shadows of the surrounding pines lengthened enough to cover the little valley in the Ardennes, David was released from his odorous refuge and brought into the comfort of the farmhouse. Dennis provided fresh water for bathing and a change of clothing, then sat the pilot down at a rough-hewn plank table in the kitchen. The farmer produced a heaping platter of *jambon ardennais*—smoked ham—a half-dozen boiled eggs, an entire loaf of fresh bread, and a pitcher of cold buttermilk. David protested that it was too much but proceeded to devour it all anyway.

Then it was dark and time for David to be leaving. During the long hours of waiting, he had heard the sounds of passing aircraft overhead. He thought about his buddies, who would not know what had become of him, and how some raw recruit would soon be filling his spot, flying *Annie*, if he didn't make it back fast. It was time to rejoin the war.

"The border is ten kilometers southeast from here," the farmer explained. "I will give you my bicycle for the journey. As long as you speak to no one, you will be safe. Your accent is atrocious! When you come to the river, get off the road. You should have no difficulty finding a rowboat that you can borrow, and then you will be back in France. But if you cannot cross tonight, find somewhere to hide and try again tomorrow night. There are others, like Navet, who volunteer to guard Belgium's neutrality by watching the border crossing for escapees. Trust no one!"

"I want to thank you again, and the best way I know is to warn you: The Boche are coming. I have seen a huge army forming just across the frontier. They will be coming straight at you."

The farmer shrugged. "The Germans have come before, twenty years ago, and earlier than that, in the time of my grandfather. The Spanish against the Dutch, the French against the English, the Romans against the Franks . . . the armies of many nations have found it convenient to fight their wars on our soil rather than on their own. But, you see, the good God is very good indeed. We remain."

"It will not be like any other war in history," David warned. "From what I have seen, if the Nazis break through, they will go all the way to the Channel."

The Belgian looked sad. "Then, my friend, it will be a long road back. May God protect you until we meet again. Now go."

One of the spokes on the bicycle was broken and made a continuous clicking sound. The handlebars were loose, and the frame wobbled from side to side. David had to struggle to keep from either shooting abruptly across the center of the lane or crashing into the ditch. But the country road had no turnings and was easy to follow even in the inky blackness. The cool night air was scented with flowers.

When he came to the village, everything was still. A dog barked as he clicked by, but all was in darkness. David stopped at a fork in the road just outside the town and struck a match to examine a road sign. One fork led toward Mariembourg; the other indicated Rocroy. Neither pointed the way toward the river and France. As he stood studying the problem, the noise of an automobile engine reached him. The car was coming at a high rate of speed.

Bare, grassy swards fell away from the highway on both sides. There was no place to hide. Running across the fields was out. All David could do was go on, as if he had a perfect right to be cycling down a road in Belgium.

Remounting the bicycle, David peddled stoutly toward Rocroy, with his back to the oncoming car. As he came within its headlight beams, the vehicle slowed momentarily, as if looking him over. Then it picked up speed again until it pulled up alongside and passed him without stopping.

Breathing a sigh of relief, David set himself once more to the task of keeping the bicycle on the road when suddenly the car braked at the curve ahead. The gears clashed as it shifted into reverse and began to back up toward him.

"Do you need a ride? I am going to the border crossing," called a nasally voice from the dark interior of the car. The question was followed by a sneeze.

The voice was familiar. *Navet!* David realized. *The Gestapo agent who visited the Belgian farmer.*

Thoughts of sitting out the war in a Belgian prison raced through David's head. His French was bad; there was no way he could be mistaken for a native. What to do?

"I said, do you want a ride?" came Navet's strangled-sounding voice again, impatiently.

"Sorry, I do not speak French," said David in English.

The car, which had been pacing David's progress, squealed to a halt.

"Who are you, and what do you do here?" questioned Navet, replying in the same language. "You are—" the man sneezed again, loudly— "American?"

David nodded.

"I thought so! I pride myself on how well I can distinguish accents. Tell me—did you see anyone else along the road? An Englishman, a pilot, perhaps?"

David shook his head. "Nobody but me. Why?"

"The impertinent British think they can fly over our country to make war on Germany. But we always catch and imprison their fliers when they are shot down. I myself have been searching today for just such a one. We are very careful of our neutrality. Do not many in *your* country favor the French and the English?"

"Most folks figure Hitler for a bully and a blowhard. Personally, I don't pay much attention to politics. I do like a place where everything works, though. I hear the Germans are very efficient."

"You have not been to Germany in your travels? You would like it. Of course, it is difficult at present to get freely across the border. But soon it will be put right again."

When Navet offered a ride again, David knew he would have to accept. To not do so at night might bring him under suspicion. Abandoning the broken bicycle at the side of the road, David opened the passenger door and climbed in.

Navet and David passed several minutes in one-sided conversation, with the Belgian explaining how the West should be grateful to the Nazis for standing up to Stalin, and how it was only the Communists, the Jews, and the English who had forced France into a war.

Finally, around a curve in the road, the headlights gleamed on the flow of the river. The lights of the bridge and the border crossing were visible a half mile ahead.

"Say, would you mind stopping? Need to answer a call of nature." David was already opening the car door, so Navet instinctively slowed down.

"Just be a minute," David called, hopping out and jogging into the bushes that covered the slope of the riverbank.

Where were those boats that the farmer had described? David slipped and fell on the muddy incline, kicking a rock into the stream with a splash.

"Are you all right?" called Navet's voice from the road.

Then David saw the rowboats. The first was chained to a log. The second had no oars. The third was half full of water, and one of its oars was broken.

"Where are you?" Navet asked again. "Have you injured yourself?" The sound of another sneeze boomed down from the road and echoed along the water.

The last dinghy in the line was tied to a tree stump. The oars rested in the oarlocks, and it was clean and dry. David yanked out the jackknife he had received in the trade and slashed the rope. Pushing the boat into the fast-flowing stream, he jumped in and began to row for the far shore. "Good-bye, Monsieur," he called to Navet. "Thanks for the ride. Maybe the RAF will give you a medal for your assistance."

4

Cloak-and-Dagger Acts

Following the instructions he'd received from Military Intelligence, Andre Chardon boarded the *bateau mouche* named *Vert Galant* at the platform below the Hotel DeVille on the Right Bank of Paris. He stood near the bow, letting the warm breeze flow over him with its scent of peaceful renewal. The little steamer was not crowded at this hour of mid-morning. The clerks and shopkeepers who used the river for their commute to work had long since arrived at their destinations.

Scanning the few other passengers, Andre saw no one he knew, nor did anyone seem to be showing any particular interest in him. The boat passed under the bridge adorned with the carved leering caricatures said to be Henri IV's comic revenge on his ministers. It swept downriver to its stop below the Louvre, where most of the travelers exited and a handful of others got on. There was still no attempt made to contact Andre, and he was getting impatient.

The steamer released its moorings for what was only a short move farther downstream to the wharf leading to the Tuileries. At the last moment before casting off, when the stern line had already been released and the gangplank slipped ashore, Gustave Bertrand jumped aboard. He spotted Andre at once but strolled nonchalantly around the ship before joining him in the bow. He asked Andre for a match to light a cigarette, as if they were total strangers.

"What is the meaning of the cloak-and-dagger act?" Andre quizzed. "Could we not have met at my home or your office, and without all the theatrics?"

Bertrand looked wounded. "Do you think that I do this for fun? I have been followed, Andre. Gestapo, I think. It would be extremely dangerous for your houseguest and his work if I was to be shadowed to your home, or if you were pursued after meeting with me. Believe me, this is necessary."

The top of the obelisk in the Place de la Concorde slid by as Andre considered the weight of what Bertrand had said. "Perhaps I need to move Lewinski out of Paris. To Vignolles?"

Bertrand nodded thoughtfully. "That may be the answer. We'll look into it as soon as you return."

"Return? From where? Not another trip to England, Gustave? Paul cannot be recalled from his duties just now to babysit Richard."

"Calm down, Andre. This is not another trip to England. In fact, you will be back the same day. And it *is* vitally important."

Sighing heavily, Andre said, "There is no escape, I suppose. What is this about?"

"I knew I could count on you. I want you to go to Mezieres, to the aerodrome there. There is a young English fighter pilot, David Meyer. He was shot down on a mission a couple days ago, but he says just before bailing out, he spotted an enormous buildup of German armor—tanks and troop carriers."

"How does this involve us, Gustave? Shouldn't it be reported to General Headquarters?"

"That's exactly the point. It already has been, and no one is taking him seriously. You see, the area over which he was flying is the Ardennes."

Andre gripped his friend's arm. "You mean that what we have feared is coming to pass?"

"It appears so. Now you understand. I need someone with your reputation to talk to this Meyer. If, in your judgment, he is correct, there is still time to shift some of our forces to meet this threat. But only if we hurry."

"I will leave tomorrow!"

"I thought you'd say that. Here are your tickets."

The *Vert Galant* pulled alongside the quai at Pont de l'Alma, with its stone figure of the soldier in the uniform of a Zouave. The water swirled around the knees of the statue's baggy trousers.

"I will leave you here," Bertrand said. "It would be best if you ride another stop or two before you disembark." He took a step toward the gangplank, then paused and gestured at the statue. "You know how Parisians watch the level of the river? If it reaches to his waist, there will be a disastrous flood. Let us hope the rest of our army is in no such danger."

☙

Frank Blake, Associated Press Paris bureau chief, was cranky.

"So! What do I find this morning? A wire from New York. From Larry, no less! *'Come on, Frank,'* he says. *'Send us the war!'*" Frank blew his nose loudly and kicked the overflowing trash can beside his desk. "Like I can control this! Like I can inspire Hitler to get moving! That's it! I'll just send der Führer a wire:

"DEAR HITLER,

PLEASE ATTACK AT DAWN.

THE AMERICAN PUBLIC IS BORED WITH THE WAR!"

Alma Dodge leaned over Josie Marlow's desk and whispered, "A little too much *ooh-la-la* for Frankie last night. Quite a little tart from what I hear. She stole his wallet."

Josie nodded and continued typing as Frank went on with his tirade.

"This is the most boring war I have ever—" he stopped midsentence and turned toward Josie—"hey! Marlow! Yeah, you! What are you working on?" Without waiting for reply, he snatched the paper from her typewriter and held it up to the light. He began to read: "'Champagne is now added to the ration list. It is available in Paris only three days a week!'" He screamed out the lines, then pounded his fist on her desk. "Do you think this matters to the American people? Champagne is rationed! Who cares? You know how many Americans have champagne three times in their whole dreary little lives? Let alone three times a week! Is this appropriate? What possible difference can it make how many bottles of champagne—"

Furious, Josie stood and squared off with Blake. "Frank, you are a cretin. You are the one who gave me this lousy assignment yesterday, and now you may take your bottle of champagne and place it wherever you feel is most appropriate."

There was applause from a half-dozen other reporters at their desks.

Blake sneered and spun around to glare back at every face. "Mutineers!" he spat.

More applause. The chorus chimed in:

"You're a really scary guy, Frank."

" . . . when you have a hangover."

"Or when some French beauty steals your wallet!"

Much laughter.

Blake actually blushed.

"We ought to send you to Berlin. You'd get the war going in no time!" added another reporter.

Blake blew his nose and tossed Josie's lead paragraph back onto her desk. He rubbed his forehead and plopped down hard in his chair. "Okay. Gimme some help here, fellas. And Madames. What I need is some American story. I mean, this place is the morgue. We got ladies knitting socks for the poilus. We got little collection boxes on the bar at the Crillon for the Help Beautify the Maginot Fund!" He shook his fist in frustration. "Somebody gimme some human interest, or I'll be on the next boat back to New York for a permanent position doing obits on a daily!"

The telephone rang. Alma passed it to Josie with a shrug.

Madame Rose Smith was on the other end of the line. Josie could hear the happy shouts of children echoing off the courtyard walls of No. 5 Rue de la Huchette, the orphanage and refugee center.

"Josie, dear! Dear, dear girl! Good news! Your adoption papers are complete. You must—*must*—pick up your baby boy on the eighth of May. Do you understand, my dear? The stamp specifically designates the eighth of May."

Josie considered the implications. The papers of the Jewish child Yacov Lubetkin would be smuggled into the Reich beneath the endpapers of a German book. But it was imperative that the child's documents be stamped ahead of time with the forged imprint of a Reich visa and the date, as though he had crossed the border into Germany at Wasserbillig Bridge with her at the same time. This narrowed the possibilities for her own journey into Germany. This opportunity to save one member of a doomed Polish-Jewish family was so important to Josie that she set aside thoughts of danger to herself.

She repeated the date. "May eighth. Yes, I'll arrange it. Should make a very good story." She replaced the handset and smiled at Frank Blake, who was still grousing. "Well, Frank, I've got your war for you. I've been invited to see the German Siegfried Line firsthand."

Blake's jaw dropped. He considered her with grave suspicion. "How did you do that?"

"I've been working on it for some time."

Two hours later, after the office emptied out for lunch, Josie sent a wire to AP Amsterdam, to be conveyed to Bill Cooper at AP Berlin, who would then pass the date to Josie's German coconspirator Katrina von Bockman, as arranged beforehand and set down in Cooper's instructions to Mac McGrath.

The message said simply:

Happy Birthday, Bill.
Hard to believe you are 58.
Signed, Jo.

Of course Cooper was at least ten years younger, but 5 was the number of the month and 8 marked the day of the month when Josie was to cross the Wasserbillig Bridge from Luxembourg into Nazi territory.

ᏸ

The next day Andre Chardon studied the young freckle-faced American wearing the uniform of a pilot officer in the RAF. "I realize that you have repeated this story fifteen times, but tell me again exactly what you saw."

David looked disgusted. "Will it make any difference? All right, here it is. I was engaging an ME-110 that was flying escort to a squadron of Heinkels returning to Germany from a raid."

"And this was . . . ?"

"Just north of Luxembourg, where the Ardennes Plateau crosses from Belgium into Germany."

"So you were over Belgian territory?"

"Yeah. We are spread so thin, we can't catch all the bombing runs on the way in, but we don't like to let them get back to Naziland unpunished."

"And were you alone?"

"No, my section mates—Flight Lieutenant Simpson and Pilot Sergeant Hewitt—were there, too."

"Did they see anything like what you report seeing?"

David shook his head and frowned. "No, unfortunately not. They were busy. But that doesn't change what I saw," he finished belligerently.

"Calm down, Meyer. I didn't say that I doubted your word."

David sagged visibly in his chair. "Sorry. It's just that no one seems to take me seriously! I even volunteered to fly a recon mission myself to get proof. They said no! Said for us to stay away from Belgian territory after this." The flier stood abruptly and pointed to a map on the wall. "Right there—not a hundred miles from where we are right now. I'd say at least two divisions, maybe more. Tanks and all the support equipment to go with them."

"And how do you know the objective is the Ardennes? Perhaps they were being moved farther north, where the main body of the German force is known to be."

David pounded his fist on the topmost point of the triangular outline of Luxembourg. "Aimed straight into Belgium! Not loaded on railcars, either. Those big gray monsters were on their tracks, Colonel. I may not know much about tanks, but unless somebody gets in their way with a lot of firepower, those babies could be in our laps in about two days."

"And you realize the importance of this information?"

"You bet I do!" David tugged at his sandy, tousled hair in frustration. "We've already been told that our unit will be pulled back when the Germans launch their attack. Problem is, the High Command says the invasion will come through Holland . . . two hundred miles in the wrong direction!"

⌘

The day after his return from Mezieres, Andre slammed the door of his study and paced the room as Josie explained about Yacov Lubetkin and the planned rendezvous in the German city of Treves on May 8.

Andre was angry with her. "You will get captured and killed!"

"It is already arranged," Josie countered, stiffening. "I am going with or without you, Andre."

"I forbid it!"

"Forbid?" Her eyes narrowed. "What right have you . . . ?"

"You will not cross the French frontier into Luxembourg if I put a stop to it!"

"And if you do, I will catch the clipper and fly out of Paris and out of your life tomorrow!" she stormed.

He took her arm and spun her around. "Listen to me! I lost one woman I loved to the Nazis—"

"You lost Elaine through your own . . . *stupidity*!" she shot back. "You lost her long before the Gestapo got hold of her. And they killed her for the same reason you let her walk out of your life. The same reason, Andre! You let some bigoted old man ruin your life and hers. Destroy your love. You let it happen!"

He stepped back as if she had struck him. "What do you know about it?"

"Only what you talked about. And your brother, Paul."

"What did he tell you?"

"Everything. About your grandfather. About you being more afraid of that wicked old man than losing the woman you loved and losing the right to be a father."

"This has nothing to do with you crossing the Wasserbillig Bridge on the eighth of May! It is too close!"

"Too close to what?"

"You think the Germans are camping out over there for fun? There will be several hundred thousand Wehrmacht, SS, and Gestapo between you and that baby in Treves!"

"I have faced them before."

"Not on the eighth of May!" he roared. "Not Luxembourg! It will be the Nazi high road into—"

Josie glared back at him. She tossed her head defiantly. "You have a *daughter* in Luxembourg. Have you forgotten?"

Parting the curtains, Andre raised his eyes slowly toward the twilight gathering east of Paris. The Eiffel Tower stood silhouetted against a backdrop of lavender hues. Like the watercolor painting of a Montmartre street artist, the pastels faded to purple and then to black.

So few hours remained before the darkest nightfall. . . .

"Juliette," he said softly, all the fight gone out of him.

"What do you think the Nazis will do to the half-Jewish daughter of a French colonel when they march across the Wasserbillig Bridge into Luxembourg?"

"You know what they will do."

"Yes, I do know. And there is another Jewish baby waiting for me in Treves. All he needs is for one of those Aryan hags to change his diapers over there, and what do you think will happen to him? And to the people who care for him?"

"You do not even know him." His argument was feeble.

"And how well do you know Juliette?"

Andre was beaten and he knew it. "Then we will go to Luxembourg together. You cannot—must not—go alone, *ma chèrie*. If they should attack . . ." He nodded, arguing with himself. "Across the bridge on the eighth. Back the morning of the ninth. You must promise me."

"Yes. And while I am gone, will you speak with Abraham Snow about Juliette?"

"Even if he will not see me, I will make certain my daughter will not remain behind in Luxembourg to face the Nazis."

⨌

Mac McGrath and John Murphy, head of Trump European News Service, took their seats in the reporters' gallery of the House of Commons. The two friends viewed the hall from above and behind the Speaker's chair at the north end.

Murphy had been tipped off that the debate offered on Saturday, the seventh of May, would be important—perhaps even critical—for the Chamberlain government. Only three weeks after the British mobilized to combat the Nazi invasion of Norway, the battle was lost and the troops had been withdrawn. Just as Papa Galway had predicted, Mac remembered.

Prime Minister Neville Chamberlain entered the House of Commons. He was greeted with unenthusiastic applause from his allies and scathing rebukes from his political enemies. Mac heard someone call out, "Missed the bus!" Other voices took it up, until the oak-paneled chamber rang with shouts of "Missed the bus! Missed the bus!"

Mac knew that the wisecrack came from an unfortunate remark made by Chamberlain himself. The prime minister had told the House that Hitler could have attacked France right after Poland, but now the Allied positions were too strong, so Hitler had missed the bus. Now that the campaign in Norway was a disaster and a clear-cut German victory, Chamberlain's quote came back to haunt him.

Mac wondered who would replace Chamberlain if the government fell. He hoped it would be Churchill, but Halifax and David Lloyd George were also possibilities. One thing was certain: Chamberlain was fighting for his political life . . . and he might be the only one who didn't know it.

Neville Chamberlain opted to speak first. He droned on at length about how the country really did not want war, how the people were unconcerned and complacent about events outside England. He got roundly hissed for that. As Mac laughed to himself, Chamberlain gave a very prissy, effeminate gesture of exasperation. "I still have friends," he pouted, and the hissing turned to jeers. "Now that Germany controls harbors in the North Sea, I fear that our country does not realize the gravity of its peril," Chamberlain suggested.

"Do you?" mocked a voice from the back bench, and a new round of catcalls and "Missed the bus!" erupted.

Chamberlain sat down, looking dejected and tired.

Clement Atlee, head of the Labour Party, and Sir Archibald Sinclair, leader of the Liberals, both gave speeches criticizing the handling of the war. But in Mac's opinion, the fireworks didn't really get started until Labour Member of Parliament Josiah Wedgwood gave a speech in which he accused the Royal Navy of cowardice.

Just as Wedgwood was finishing, Murphy nudged Mac's elbow and pointed. Into the chamber walked Admiral Sir Roger Keyes. Someone Mac did not recognize handed a note to the highly decorated officer.

The face of Keyes got as red as the ribbons of the medals on his chest. This naval hero of the Great War demanded and was granted the right to reply immediately to the insult. "I have repeatedly offered to lead a fleet of warships into the fjords," Keyes said, "and just as repeatedly have been told that the army had the situation well in hand. How can our troops be expected to advance along a narrow shoreline under constant and undeterred fire from the German ships? It is not a lack of courage with the sailors! It is a failure of leadership in this government!"

Cheering from the Opposition Party was greeted with stony silence and deep frowns from the government side of the House—Sir Roger had been one of their own.

Mac wondered if Churchill, as First Lord of the Admiralty, would get tarred with the same brush as Chamberlain.

David Lloyd George, the Opposition statesman who had led England during the 1914 war, rose to speak. Adjusting his pince-nez, he theatrically ran a hand through his mane of silver hair and attacked. "This country is in greater peril now than during the whole of the Great War. What is the good of sea power if it is unused?"

A chorus of "Hear, hear!" sounded from both sides of the aisle.

"But I do not think that the First Lord is to be blamed for the mistakes," Lloyd George continued.

Churchill popped up from his seat beside Chamberlain. His brooding pose had made Mac think that Winston was scarcely following the debate, but this sudden spring proved that idea false. "I take my full share of the responsibility, sir," Churchill said.

"Admirable," Lloyd George replied, "but I hope that the First Lord will not become an air-raid shelter to keep splinters from hitting his colleagues!"

Applause followed these words.

It was unexpected support. Maybe Churchill could surface from the sinking ship after all.

Leo Amery was called on to speak next. It was Amery who had attacked Chamberlain's conduct of the war clear back in September; his views had not moderated since then. "We must have men in government who can match our enemies in fighting spirit, in daring, resolution, and thirst for victory."

Mac saw Amery study the faces of the Members of Parliament, obviously thinking about what he was about to say, judging its timing. "I quote certain words of Oliver Cromwell spoken to a government he judged no longer fit to rule. I do this with reluctance, because those to whom it applies are old friends of mine. But this is what he said." Amery stopped and stared squarely at the top of Chamberlain's bowed head. "He said, 'You have sat too long for any good you have been doing. Depart, I say, and let us have done with you. In the name of God, go!'"

As the Speaker called for order to be restored, Mac thought that there was no longer any question whether Neville Chamberlain would remain prime minister. The resultant vote of confidence on the conduct of the war produced a Conservative victory, but only by a margin of eighty-one votes. Every single uniformed member of Chamberlain's party deserted him and voted with the Opposition. Clearly, it was time for him to go.

On May 8, as instructed, Josie left the Brasseur Hotel carrying only her passport, twelve dollars' worth of Luxembourg francs, and the precious volume of Goethe's *Faust* with the travel documents of Yacov Lubetkin sealed beneath the end sheets. Nothing else.

Driving the car from Luxembourg City into the village of Wasserbillig, she parked at a Bierstube whose windows overlooked the river and the bridge into Germany. She gave the dubious barkeeper a slip of paper instructing him to turn the automobile over to Andre Chardon, who was staying in Luxembourg, if she should fail to return from her trek into the Reich.

A charge of excitement went through her as she walked onto the Wasserbillig Bridge. Below the metal girders she could see the slow-moving river that divided Luxembourg from Germany. Pontoon bridges were built halfway across from the German shore. Terminating in the center of the languid current, the pontoons punctuated the border at one-hundred-yard intervals both upstream and down. Even if the little army of Luxembourg blew up their half of the Wasserbillig Bridge, how long would it take the Nazi engineers to slip the rest of the pontoons into place for the crossing? Then how long would it be before the panzers would overflow the Luxembourg side of the riverbank?

Midway across the Wasserbillig Bridge was a gatehouse and customs office festooned with warning signs and capped with the swastika flag. A handsome young Wehrmacht sentry stared through Josie without curiosity as she approached the barrier. He stopped her with stiff formality and demanded her passport.

He seemed unimpressed by the American document but not at all surprised that an American journalist was walking on his bridge and entering Germany. "Your destination, Fräulein?"

"Treves."

"Purpose?"

"Sightseeing." This she said in a matter-of-fact tone, as if the Siegfried Line were not between her and Treves . . . as if she were a tourist out for a day trip, and there was not a war on.

Without comment, the youth directed her to an anteroom in the customs office, where the Nazi officials took on a much more sinister tone and appearance. The manner of the questioning was far from friendly.

A poster bearing the likeness of the Führer glared down on a small assembly of civilians: two men and three women who had crossed the bridge ahead of Josie. They were returning to Germany by order of the Reich. They all seemed unhappy about it. One portly, middle-aged woman wept continuously without any attempt to hide the reason for her tears.

"She is sad because we have to leave our little grandchildren," her pale, frightened husband kept explaining over and over to the interrogators. "She will feel better when we get back home. We have not been there in ten years."

The resident Gestapo agent was unimpressed. In his eyes something was definitely wrong with a German citizen who had stayed away from the Fatherland so long and who wept so copiously at the prospect of returning. As Josie waited in line behind the woman, she watched the official tear through the couple's luggage. He ferreted out a bar of chocolate, held it up in triumph, stripped it of paper, and broke it into tiny pieces as the woman's weeping became louder.

"Do you not know it is illegal to smuggle contraband chocolate into the Reich?" He roared his displeasure as if her crime was a personal offense. With a wave of his hand he summoned a white-uniformed Nazi matron, who forcibly hauled the unhappy woman into an examination room while her meek husband was escorted to a second room.

The woman screamed as the door was closed. Then it was Josie's turn at the declaration counter. Oblivious to the howls of the captive, the officer snapped open Josie's passport and examined it without comment.

Cold eyes pivoted to study her press uniform. Then back to the passport photograph. Then to her face and the press badge on the shoulder of her jacket.

"Fräulein Marlow, is it? An American journalist, are you? Anything to declare today, have you?" He smiled, but his eyes were dull and hard, like the eyes of a copperhead snake Josie had nearly stepped on as a child in Arkansas. The impression given was that he could kill her without a twinge of emotion simply because she put her foot down wrong.

"What is the purpose of your visit to the Reich, Fräulein Marlow?"

"Sightseeing." She tried not to look at the conspicuously posted sign that listed the names and photographs of foreign travelers who had been convicted and executed as spies in the last twelve months.

He closed the passport. "Have you anything to declare?"

"Thirty Luxembourg francs. Nothing else."

"Empty your pockets."

She did so. The copy of *Faust* was placed on the counter. Heaping coins and cash onto the cover of her book, she slid it across to him.

He picked up the bills one by one, as if checking for counterfeit currency. Stacking the cash neatly to one side, he retrieved the volume of Goethe.

The rush of Josie's blood pumped in her ears. She focused her eyes on the small rectangle of Hitler's mustache as the agent examined each page with the same intensity with which he had checked the bills. What was he looking for? A code? Some message pricked into the paper with the point of a pin?

"What is this, Fräulein?"

"A copy of *Faust*."

Suspicion hardened the line of his mouth. Josie resisted the urge to turn and run out the door—to escape back into the safety of Luxembourg.

"Why do you carry Goethe's work into the Reich?"

She shrugged. "Something to read on the ride into Treves. *Faust* is not among the banned books. Germany is quite fond of Goethe, I understand."

He thumbed through it as the wailing of the woman prisoner in the examining room diminished to a whimper. Beads of sweat formed on Josie's brow. The prickle of fear crept up the back of her neck. Her mouth tasted like iron.

Would he notice the thickness of the baby's forged papers sealed beneath the end sheets?

"Why exactly did you choose this volume, Fräulein?"

"Because I was certain I would not be inconvenienced if I carried approved reading materials into the Reich. If I was wrong, then keep it for yourself." She glanced accusingly at the splintered slab of chocolate. "You can see I have come here empty-handed to avoid any waste of time at the crossing. One volume is not worth it. I can buy myself a dozen more just like it."

He furrowed his brow and silently read through a passage. "It is not to my liking." Snapping it shut, he passed it back to her, along with the neatly stacked bills. "Heil Hitler." He thumped the stamp down on her passport and dismissed her, turning his reptilian gaze onto a sallow old woman who brooded in line behind Josie.

As Josie emerged into the spring warmth, the old woman was arguing with the official without fear of Hitler or his splendor or his might. The words were bitter and loud. Josie could hear the curses as she walked unsteadily toward the German end of the Wasserbillig Bridge.

A taxi driver was waiting for her on the German side of the Wasserbillig Bridge. A squat, muscular little man with swarthy skin and big ears protruding from beneath a Jäger's hat, he smiled broadly with gapped teeth and waved at her approach. He leaned against the bent fender of an ancient taxi. Tires were worn down to the fabric. Windows were cracked, but they had been polished. Yet the taxi was clean. The metal of the fenders shone through what had been black paint.

"You are the American. *Ja!* It is plain to see. *Guten Morgen*, Fräulein Marlow. I am Hermann Goltz," the driver said joyfully as he opened the back door for Josie and bowed slightly like a chauffeur as she entered. He waved happily at the sentries, who stared at the scene from their posts on the bridge. "You see; I promised I would be here. Although I had to wait. I thought perhaps you would not come, but I waited here all the same. Where do you want to go?"

"To Treves. Porta Nigra Hotel." Josie gestured broadly eastward where the forward blockhouses of the Siegfried Line were in plain view.

"Very good, Fräulein. As we travel I shall point out all objects of interest along the way. Americans like to see the sights. I have always enjoyed guiding Americans. They do not come here often enough these days." He closed the door and hurried around the car to slip in behind the wheel.

Josie believed that she was quite possibly the first American that he had seen in many months.

The taxi lurched into motion. The engine had a knock that made the vehicle shudder like a dog shaking water from its fur as they turned off the main highway to Treves. Instead, their route followed a secondary road that skirted a high bluff and led away from the river. This road was clogged with military traffic. Motorcycles roared past. Armored cars and troop lorries rumbled off along snaking side roads to isolated blockhouses and rows of mobile artillery set to face France as well as little Luxembourg.

It was clear to Josie within minutes that she was seeing what she was not meant to see. She pictured the poster commemorating the execution of foreign spies by the Reich. She imagined her own face smiling serenely out at future travelers. She felt the sick chill of apprehension.

"How is it you are able to get a pass to move so freely through this zone?" she dared to ask.

"A pass?" He chortled. "I have no pass, Fräulein!"

"Then how . . . ?"

"They do not ask me. Who would be here unless they were allowed?" Another laugh ended in a contented sigh. Then he continued pointing out items of interest while Josie sat grim and pale in the rear seat. "Americans enjoy the back roads. Unusual sights. I know this well. How else will you see unless I guide you? This first line is six miles deep," instructed the taxi driver over the clacking engine. "The second line behind Treves is much deeper. Many more troops. Much more going on. But you can see. They are all moving forward!"

This information was expressed with the same enthusiasm Josie had once heard in the voice of a Beefeater conducting tours of the Tower of London. But this military zone was no tourist trap, no point of interest to be found in a guidebook. Josie knew she was witnessing some terrible and momentous force being set in place, like the pieces of a chess game. And yet the taxi moved with absolute freedom through the forbidden region of the German West Wall!

Hermann Goltz greeted military sentries cheerfully. He expressed to them his delight in the beauty of the day. They smiled back. Perhaps it was his audacity that kept him from being stopped and challenged. No one driving such a contraption could be a spy.

He pulled to the side of the road as a convoy of troop lorries blocked the way in front of them. Through the spiderweb pattern of the cracked glass, Josie looked out on an erratic field of green concrete barriers that traced the folds of the hills and valleys on and on into the lovely spring haze. A sentry beside a roadblock fixed his gaze on the taxi. But he did not move forward to question Hermann.

"This," the driver exclaimed loudly and within hearing of the sentry, "is a tank trap. The French call them asparagus beds. The French are very amusing." Hermann laughed.

The sentry laughed, too.

Only Josie remained unamused. Her mind was racing with the dreadful implications of what she was seeing. Enormous artillery pieces on carriages with rubber wheels were being hauled toward the Meuse River, toward Belgium, toward Luxembourg. Not toward France.

She had observed enough to be shot as a spy a dozen times over. She would tell Andre everything she had witnessed, but she did not want to see any more. Her only desire was to get the baby and then to get out of the way of the Nazi steamroller poised to flatten everything on the other side of the river.

"Is there a quicker way to Treves?" she asked.

"*Ja*. But very uninteresting. Americans like to see the sights."

With that they were waved on through the chicane by the sentry. The highway ran parallel to an obviously occupied trench punctuated by a series of large gun emplacements.

"Fräulein Marlow! Look there," shouted Hermann as he pointed to a cliff wall that rose from the side of the road. A half-dozen sentries observed him with fascinated curiosity but made no move to stop him. "It is a fort. You see there where the colors change from green to brown? Very good, is it not?"

And then Josie saw that the rock was no rock at all but a heap of concrete piled up and painted to match the cliff face. No reconnaissance plane could pick it out. It was nearly invisible, even close up. The Nazis had intended that this place be kept a secret; otherwise they would not have gone to all the trouble of making it a secret.

Josie averted her eyes. "Please, Herr Goltz. Take me to Treves now. The shortest route."

He was disappointed. The tour had only just begun in his eyes. Still, he agreed and pointed the taxi toward the city. There were still plenty of sights if one knew where to look, he explained. There were antiaircraft guns in haystacks—88 mm artillery pieces concealed inside steep-gabled little farmhouses and barns.

"Just think," the fool said brightly as they passed a house that resembled something out of *Snow White and the Seven Dwarfs*, "what the French air force would not give to know that there is an 88 mm long rifle hidden under that roof! When it begins to send its shells into the French troops, the French generals will not even know where to look for it. They will not know where to drop the bomb to stop it, will they? The French will be very sorry they did not drop their bombs first." He turned and winked at Josie. "I think it will begin very soon now, Fräulein. Perhaps within days. The 'Sitzkrieg' is about to become the Blitzkrieg."

❧

"Monsieur Snow is not at home, I tell you!" the elderly butler insisted.

But Andre Chardon had come too far and was on too serious a mission to be stopped now. He hadn't been able to do anything about Elaine Snow's death. He was determined not to let the same thing happen to her child—*their* child.

He pushed past the butler into the spacious foyer of the steel magnate's Luxembourg mansion. "Then I will wait for him."

"You must ring for an appointment, Monsieur Colonel," the man pleaded. He glanced nervously over his shoulder at a pair of heavy mahogany double doors.

"His office?" Andre asked.

"No, Colonel." The man stepped between Andre and the doors. "If you do not leave at once, I shall regretfully be forced to telephone the—"

The panels slid back, interrupting the threat. Abraham Snow, a dignified presence with white hair and a drooping mustache, wearing a suit and waistcoat from another era, stood framed in the arched doorway of the study. He viewed Andre for a long moment and then glanced up at the landing of the grand staircase.

Andre followed his gaze, hoping to glimpse Juliette, but the stairs were empty.

"Thank you, Pascal. You may show the colonel in. That will be all."

The servant bowed, clicked his heels like a Prussian aristocrat, and stepped aside. Pivoting with military precision, he hurried down the corridor.

Silence reigned as the two men contemplated one another for the first time. An enormous grandfather clock counted the seconds.

"You are Colonel Chardon." Snow nodded once. "She has your eyes."

"I had to speak with you."

"We may be a very ancient house, but we do have the modern conveniences. You might have telephoned."

"Like the last time? To give you opportunity to go to . . . where was it?"

"Belgium." Snow's eyes narrowed. "We will be able to speak more freely in here."

Andre entered the large, high-ceilinged room with tall, Gothic windows overlooking the Petrusse River. It was lined with bookshelves that surrounded an alcove where three original paintings of haystacks by Monet were hung side by side to capture the full effect of the changing light.

On the wall behind an enormous, ornately carved desk was a full-length portrait of a woman in a long, yellow gown of Victorian fashion. She resembled Elaine. Andre's eyes lingered on the woman's features.

"I see you are a man who appreciates beauty," Snow said gruffly.

"She looks so much like—"

"She was Elaine's mother. She passed her perfection along to my daughter. And ultimately to your daughter as well."

"Monsieur Snow," Andre began, "I must speak to you about Juliette."

"She is at school, or I might have had you arrested at the door. You have been here before; have you not? Standing there on the riverbank?"

"Yes." Andre glanced at the light streaming through the window. Snow had watched him from here.

"Won't you sit down, Colonel Chardon? I suspect I know why you have come." There was resignation in his voice. He took a seat in a tall wingback leather chair opposite Andre. "I hear that the Nazis are collectors of great art." His gaze lingered on Monet's haystacks. "Hermann Göring, is it? He has had a palace built in Berlin just to house the paintings he has stolen." He inclined his head, as if bowing to the inevitable. "Did you know the haystacks in the fields just across the river from us in Germany now conceal machine-gun emplacements?"

Andre inhaled deeply with relief. It was true that Abraham Snow had good reason to hate the man who had impregnated his daughter then not married her, but he was a realist. "That is why I hoped to speak with you today."

"Of course." Snow smoothed his mustache. "We in Luxembourg are protected by an army of three hundred and fifty soldiers, Colonel. I am no fool, although others in the Grand Duchy may be. How long do you think we have?"

"It is spring. The ground is drying out."

"I drove to the Meuse yesterday. The Germans are observing our neutrality in a peculiar way. They have built their pontoon bridges halfway out from their side of the river to the center of the stream." He gave a bitter laugh and reached for a box of cigars on his desk. He offered one to Andre, who refused it, then took one for himself. "You are a soldier, Colonel. How long would it take them to construct the other half of their bridges into Luxembourg if der Führer is so inclined?"

"No doubt the parts are prefabricated."

"How long?"

"An hour."

With much thought, Snow trimmed the end of his cigar and lit it. "A single hour. And Luxembourg would go up in smoke."

"It could be. Yes. And that is why I came. If the Germans come through the Ardennes and Luxembourg—"

"If?" Snow interrupted. "Is it not inevitable?"

"There are some who think not."

Snow laughed. "Well, then, they are in for a surprise, are they not, Colonel?"

Andre did not express his own certainty. "I am concerned for your welfare."

"And the welfare of my granddaughter?"

"Of course."

Snow let the ash on the end of his cigar grow. "It has occurred to me, of course, that I may be at some disadvantage considering my social status. That is, if Hitler turns his eye on Luxembourg." He held up his fingers, ticking off logical reasons for danger. "I am, first of all, a Jew. A very unpopular thing to be in the eyes of the Nazis. Secondly, I own the highest-producing steel manufacturing plant in the Duchy. And thirdly, of course, I have a collection of fine art that would be highly prized by Hermann Göring."

"Good reasons to get out of the way. Just in case."

"I considered Switzerland. But it is rumored the Nazis will move against Switzerland at the same moment they strike Belgium, Holland, and our little corner of the world."

"I cannot speak to that. Only to the fact that Luxembourg is likely to be a very busy intersection in a long German highway before long."

Abraham Snow tapped the cigar delicately on the edge of the ashtray. "All of this does not mean that I do not despise you for what you have done. However, even in your folly you accomplished one good thing in your life. There is Juliette. My last real treasure, Colonel. The Nazis do not like Jewish children any more than they like steel magnates and art collectors, I am told."

"Then let me take her to Paris, to my home," Andre urged. "You will both be welcome . . . safe there. Two million French soldiers stand between Germany and Paris, Monsieur Snow. I cannot think that line will be broken. And . . . I will not . . ." He faltered, unable to finish.

"You will not tell her who you are?"

"It does not matter. Her safety is my only concern now."

"In that we see eye to eye. Otherwise you would not be here. When will you take her?"

"Tonight. But you will not be coming with her?"

"I will follow later. If there is a later."

6

Momentous Events

With a promise to pick up Josie at seven o'clock the next morning, Hermann Goltz let her out at the ancient Black Gate in Treves. The Porta Nigra Hotel, named for this Roman wall, was a grand old pile built in the Victorian splendor of the 1890s. But now swastika banners draped the gingerbread cornices. Tall, arched windows looked out on a quaint square that bustled with men in uniform.

The staff cars sporting the flags of officers from the German High Command arrived one after the other in front of the hotel. Josie recognized these men from photographs and her brief stay in occupied Poland. Arriving first was the chief of Army Group A, von Rundstedt, and his army commanders, Busch and List, as well as Army Group B's chief, von Bock, and his subordinates, Reichenau and von Kuchler. Following these were the lesser lights: division leaders Erwin Rommel and Heinz Guderian.

Josie watched them enter the Porta Nigra with the sense that she had somehow stumbled into the hub of the Wehrmacht universe. There was a tangible excitement in the atmosphere. This gathering of eagles held the portent of momentous events.

Not one head turned her way as she ascended the steps and entered the hotel among the less vaunted members of the General Staff. Josie brushed shoulders with the plainclothes Gestapo agents, uniformed secretaries, and young adjutants all crowding into the lobby. Like a school of tiny scavenger fish, they swarmed after the sharks, oblivious to everything but the proud backs of their masters.

No one checked her documents. Would she be at the Porta Nigra without permission from Berlin? Impossible!

Josie hung back as they tramped en masse down a wide corridor to the double doors of a meeting room. Was Major Horst von Bockman among them? she wondered. Who of all these sycophants would have the courage to bring a Jewish child into the midst of such a congregation?

The undertone of conversation sounded like a gaggle of geese. Coats and gun belts were hung on a long polished coatrack in the hall. Here was proof of the superiority of the German nation; was it not? No one in the Reich would dare to steal the gun or the coat of a general.

The doors banged shut. The roar subsided to a murmur. Josie remained alone in the foyer and was at last approached by a wizened little doorman in the long, green coat of a turn-of-the-century hack driver.

"May I direct you, Fräulein?"

"I have reserved a room."

With this revelation, he handed her over to the desk clerk, who confirmed the fact that American journalist Josephine Marlow was indeed expected and most welcome in Treves. So far so good. He picked up a dusty book entitled *Rules for the Entertainment of American Tourists* and rang the bell to summon a porter. When Josie pointed out that she had no luggage, she was escorted to her small hotel room, where the red fabric of the Nazi flag blocked the view out onto the square. There, as instructed, she settled down to wait.

◦◦◦

Wehrmacht Major Horst von Bockman emerged from the German staff meeting at the Porta Nigra Hotel in the late afternoon. The ever-present Gestapo agents lounged in overstuffed chairs in the lobby. They pretended to read the *Frankfurter Zeitung* as they observed the comings and goings of everyone who was not one of them. Wehrmacht officers made quiet jokes about Himmler's goons, citing the fact that this race of weasels had completely disappeared when the real action had started in Poland. They had only resurfaced when the bombs stopped falling. Soon enough they would scurry back to Berlin and hide in the Chancellery bunker once the offensive against France began.

In the meantime, they were here in Treves and were as dangerous as an 88 mm long rifle. Horst resisted the urge to climb the stairs and knock on the door of No. 221. He had spotted the tall, chestnut-haired Josephine Marlow instantly among the crush of the crowd this morning. The American had arrived safely at least and had moved easily through the confusion of the meeting as Horst had hoped. But things were quiet now, and he dared not push their luck. He decided to wait until after supper to go to her room. By then most of Himmler's agents would be full of sauerbraten and half drunk on good Münchner beer.

He escaped the cloud of tobacco smoke, emerging onto the steps of the hotel. The morning had given some promise of warmth, but now there was a chill in the air.

Thousands of soldiers strolled along the twisting lanes of medieval Treves. They cluttered the sidewalks and bargained for mementos to send to their families back home. Inkwells, cheap fountain pens, lead paperweights fashioned in the form of the cathedral all bore the legend *Souvenir of Treves*. By tomorrow night, Horst knew, they would be called back to their units in preparation for the offensive. By the end of the week, it was quite possible that the fresh-faced private waiting patiently to purchase a pink comb for ten times its worth would no longer have a head.

And all the while, on the other side of the line? French and British soldiers, destined to die, were also being lovingly cheated by the merchants of their homelands. Just boys, all of them. Horst could not help feeling pity for them. The day was so beautiful. How many beautiful days did the world have left? He could count what remained of peace in hours now.

Horst inched his way through the throng and turned up an alleyway in a shortcut to the house of his wife Katrina's aunt. The echo of youthful laughter pursued him. The living voices of the condemned already seemed a distant memory.

By tomorrow afternoon the shops will be empty. . . .

The windows of the half-timbered home on St. Helena Strasse were open wide to let in the fresh air. Katrina was playing Aunt Lottie's piano. Horst could hear the music of Beethoven's "Für Elise" as he rounded the corner of the medieval lane. Window boxes overflowed with red and yellow blooms.

By tomorrow afternoon Katrina will be on a train to Berlin and I will be gone. . . .

He quickened his pace. He was grateful that the baby had given her reason to come to Treves. Pastel banners in the sky began to deepen to lavender and purple as he looked up through the steep gables. He took the stairs to the front door two at a time.

Katrina was here, he knew, but it seemed like a dream. Reality loomed, terrible and dark, over the beauty of Treves. How many years would it be before there was another spring day like this one in Europe?

Katrina and Yacov were alone in the house when Horst entered the small sitting room. She did not look away from the piano until the baby playing happily at her feet squealed and crawled quickly to Horst.

Horst stood awkwardly gazing down as Yacov reached to bat his reflection in the highly polished boots.

Katrina stopped playing. She smiled at the scene. "Pick him up,
Horst. He wants you to pick him up."

The tall man scooped up the child and raised him high overhead.
Yacov chuckled a deep and rollicking baby laugh that made Horst smile
in spite of all the news he had heard today.

"You should be a father," Katrina said wistfully.

He held Yacov in the crook of his elbow and sat in a delicate petit-
point chair beside the window of the bric-a-brac–cluttered room.
"When things are different, we will have children. When our world is not
controlled by madmen and morons and sadists."

"When will that be?"

He ignored her question. "Where is Aunt Lottie?"

"I took her to the train station. She will stay at Aunt Margaret's until
. . . I don't know how long."

"We are alone, then."

Yacov drove his finger into the side of Horst's mouth as if to disagree
with the last statement.

"Almost alone," Horst corrected himself.

"Yes." Katrina folded the sheets of music. "You did not tell me if the
American came."

"She did."

Katrina lowered her head. "I see."

"You are sorry she came."

"He is a good baby, Horst." She did not look at her husband or the
child. "I was hoping—"

He interrupted. "He is not a lost puppy."

She straightened. "That was a harsh thing to say. Please, I only meant
that I will miss him."

"I suppose his mother feels the same. If she is still alive," he remarked bitterly. He hated the fact that he wanted to argue with her, even
when it was not her fault.

She glared at him. "What happened to you between this morning
and now?"

He rubbed his forehead, attempting to push away the ache. "We are
all being called up. Every unit. You know what that means."

Her eyes lingered on the baby. "It means . . . he must go with her.
Must." Then her gaze flitted to Horst's face. "It means this is our last
night. It means . . . let's not waste what few hours we have left. Not argue.
Look at me, Horst. Please."

He nodded and stretched out his hand to her.

She came to him and cradled his head.

"I am sorry," he whispered. "For myself. For you. For this child and ten million others. For everyone. And there is nothing more I can do. There is no changing anything."

⟨∞⟩

The interior of the Snow mansion was built in the grand style of the nineteenth century. A formal staircase led up to a large sitting room with Louis XIV furniture and a massive concert piano in the corner. French doors opened onto a broad balcony that overlooked the Petrusse River.

It was nearly 8 PM, but the sky was still light behind the rain clouds when Andre arrived and was directed by the sad-eyed butler up to the sitting room.

At the top of the stairs was a portrait of Elaine in the blue dress Andre had so loved. She smiled down at him. Her tranquil gaze followed him with the same tolerant amusement he had seen in her eyes a thousand times when they had been together.

"You have been a fool, Andre," she seemed to say. *"You missed the best of everything. You lost me and nearly lost Juliette! But now you have another chance. Take it!"*

Those words thrummed in his head with every step: *Another chance! Another chance! Another chance!*

He entered the pale yellow room that displayed the stamp of Elaine's good taste. Monsieur Snow stood beside the piano that Elaine had played. He wore a dark burgundy smoking jacket. The dourness of his expression and the darkness of his form and clothing seemed to clash with the brightness of the space.

Andre's breath was coming fast as he scanned the room for Juliette. The little girl was not here.

Snow did not move as Andre entered. He pivoted his head slightly in acknowledgment and nodded to the butler in some unspoken signal that the two men understood.

The servant gave Andre a half smile, as if to indicate that he had kept his promise from Andre's first visit and given the doll to Juliette. Pascal was an ally, silently cheering Andre on with his warm brown eyes.

"You are very prompt, Colonel," Snow said stiffly.

"I hope not too early."

"Juliette is not yet here." Snow inclined his head slightly. "Ballet class. Like her mother at that age." There was infinite sadness in his voice. "We are losing our whole world. But little girls must have dancing lessons."

How to reply? Should he promise that Juliette would forever have ballet lessons? piano lessons? ride the carrousel in the Tuileries every Sunday? Should he tell Monsieur Snow that his granddaughter would live in a world as perfect as if there were no war?

Finally he said, "Shall I collect her luggage before she comes back? Perhaps it will make the parting easier."

"There will be time for that. My servant Grundig will see to it."

"How did she take the news that she is leaving?"

"She does not know yet." The old man's shoulders sagged for just an instant. "I could not bring myself to tell her everything today. Only that she would be leaving with a friend of her mother's for a short visit."

It was clear in his expression that Snow did not believe he would ever see the child again. This was more than just a temporary parting for him. It was a final farewell.

Andre took a step nearer and extended his hand, palm up, like a supplicant begging for forgiveness. "Please. You must come with her. Elaine would approve if—after everything—we were to become friends. Please come to stay in my house in Paris until this business is over."

The old man stiffened, refusing to take Andre's hands. "We will never be friends, Colonel. We may be allies out of necessity for this time, but we will never be friends." His cheek twitched with emotion. "Why was it you were unable to marry Elaine?"

Carrying two brandy snifters, the butler entered the room, interrupting Andre's reply.

Snow raised his glass. "Napoleon brandy." He swirled the amber liquid. "From 1860. I was saving the bottle to share with the man who married Elaine. If it might have been. I will have to content myself to drink with the father of my grandchild."

The servant left and closed the double doors behind him. "Now you must explain to me," Snow insisted. "Why did you not marry my daughter?"

Andre studied the brandy. This was the question he had dreaded. "My grandfather threatened to disinherit me if I—"

"If you married a Jewess?" Snow finished and inhaled deeply on his brandy. "Is that correct, Colonel?"

"It is." Did Andre's voice betray the depth of shame he felt in that admission?

Snow raised his brows slightly in a gesture of understanding. He looked from Andre to the faint light emanating through the window. "Ah, well, it does not matter after today, does it? Our lives, our individual folly—all evaporate after today."

"This war—this Great Folly—is made up of insignificant foolishness, Monsieur Snow. Each minute evil committed or allowed by ordinary men has evaporated into the air like water in the hot sun. We thought it did not matter," Andre said passionately. "But now it has come back in a cloud to cover us with darkness—with storm and flood and thunder. My little sins? Joined with those of other men, they may now wash us all away." Andre placed his snifter on the table. "I was wrong, Monsieur Snow. Terribly wrong. And others have suffered because of my cowardice. I know that now. I am a better man for the knowing." He bowed his head. "I hope to be a worthy father."

"In that case, pick up your glass, Colonel. I will drink with you. I should have liked you, I think, if there had been time."

They drank together.

The servant knocked softly on the door. "Mam'zelle Juliette has just arrived, Monsieur Snow."

"Thank you." And then to Andre, "Have you seen her?" Snow held back the curtain and let Andre look down on the street.

Andre watched as a gray-uniformed chauffeur circled the car and opened the back passenger door. Reaching in, he extended a gloved hand to assist his passenger. Several seconds passed, and then a five-year-old girl emerged. Miraculously, she held the doll—Andre's mother's doll, which Andre had left for her so many months before.

Juliette was dressed all in blue: blue coat, hat, and toe shoes. Very pretty, and yet she was a picture of the unhappiness she surely felt.

The child was not in a hurry to climb the steps. As she turned her oval face up toward the house, Andre could see she was frightened. She blinked as drops of rain began to fall like tears. Turning to the open door of the vehicle, it seemed as if she would step back in.

The chauffeur bent at the waist until his face was level with hers. He smiled, gestured toward the house, then took her hand. She nodded and, with only one downward thrust of her chin, walked slowly up the steps beside the chauffeur.

"She is small," Andre said under his breath. "So small."

The bell rang. Andre watched his daughter enter the house. Conversation drifted up the stairs. The too-cheerful voice of the housekeeper asked the chauffeur about the weather and the roads. She asked him how his seven children were doing and then about the dance class.

"I almost missed you standing there behind fat Rene, Mademoiselle! Pardon!" the housekeeper teased. "Come here, Juliette. Let's have a look at the costume. Ah, very fine. Beautiful, wouldn't you say, Rene?"

Rene agreed with a laugh and then excused himself to get the young lady's valise.

Andre's throat constricted as he and the old man stepped out of the sitting room and stood on the landing to listen. The child's voice was soft. Some words were lost to him. Andre peeked over the banister but could not see her face. She seemed even smaller beside Rene's six-foot-three frame. She blended into a sapphire square of marble on the checkerboard floor of the foyer.

Boot heels clicked on the polished tiles. For an instant Andre wished his brother, Paul, were here. Paul may have envied Andre's ability with women, but Paul was a master with children. Dumb animals and innocents were charmed by his cheerful nature and openness. Andre had always considered those traits to be foolish, but today, for the first time, he envied his brother.

"I will go down first," said Monsieur Snow in a forced tone.

Evidently hearing the old man's voice, the child replied hesitantly, "How do you do, Grandpapa?"

"I am very well indeed, despite the rain. Our guest has come."

So she had come home to meet the old friend of her mother. She had come to meet Andre, who was standing frozen above them on the landing, wishing he were elsewhere.

Monsieur Snow looked up. His eyes locked on Andre's face.

Andre was surprised to see a flash of compassion there. And a question, too. Was Andre coming down? Andre nodded curtly, drew a deep breath, and hurried down the broad, curving stairway.

"Here he comes now, I think, Juliette." Snow put his hands on her shoulders and gently pivoted her toward the staircase.

For an instant her eyes flitted upward toward Andre.

Brown eyes. More like milk chocolate than dark. Like my own eyes.

Juliette looked quickly at the toes of her shoes. Her cheeks were flushed. She had dark eyebrows and long lashes. Andre could not see her hair color beneath the snug-fitting cap, but she appeared to be a miniature version of her mother. She was darker of complexion perhaps, but there was no doubt that this was Elaine's child—a beautiful child.

He and Snow exchanged looks over the child's head.

"*Bonjour*, Mademoiselle Juliette." Andre extended his hand, palm up. Still unable to meet his gaze, she touched her tiny fingertips to his.

He quickly kissed her hand and then stepped back.

"*Bonjour*," she whispered.

"I am . . . I was . . . I knew your mother very well, Juliette." Andre caught his own reflection in the gilt mirror. Today he looked older than his thirty-two years. There were dark circles under his brown eyes. His normally elegant and erect, over six-foot frame seemed a bit stooped. He had shaved, yet his face seemed dark. "I am sorry about what has happened to your maman."

Juliette did not answer. Her chin trembled. She stared at his highly polished shoes, at his gold cuff links, at his hands and manicured nails, but never at his face.

Had Elaine told the child about him . . . about them? he wondered. "Do you know who I am, Juliette?"

"Yes, Monsieur. You are Monsieur Andre Chardon. You were ma mère's friend a very long time ago. And I am to stay at your house now for a short time. Grandpapa says so."

So she was unaware. It would make it easier for Andre if she did not know. Then there would be no messy sentimentality, no expectations. He began to talk as though he were discussing the sale of a thousand cases of wine.

"Very good, Juliette. Monsieur Paul and I and a fellow named Richard have a room prepared for you. We are three bachelors in a very big house and know very little about children. Monsieur Paul, my brother, is an officer at a military school . . . and away from Paris much of the time. I have duties with the government now. And there is a gentleman, Richard, whom you will meet, who is a guest there. You may think he is odd. He may seem to ignore you, but he is very bright and only thinking all the time. He may not even know you are there. A very beautiful lady from America will ride with us to Paris."

Juliette looked up at him fiercely. "Maman kept your photograph on her dressing table." The statement was an accusation.

Andre could see the questions in her eyes. Why had he never come to see them? If he was such a good friend before, why did he not help Maman when she needed a friend?

Juliette's eyes brimmed. She bit her lip to hold back tears.

Andre grimaced inwardly. He was not handling this well at all. "I was sorry to hear about your maman, Juliette. Truly I was. She was very beautiful. Bright and happy when I knew her." Andre dropped the business-like tone.

Silence reigned in the room.

"Are you hungry?" Andre asked. "Have you eaten? I made a reservation for supper, and then tomorrow we can go to Paris. There is a carrousel at the Tuileries if you like."

Silence again. Juliette clasped her hands and eyed the enormous front door as though she wanted to run away.

Thankfully Snow put his hand firmly on Andre's shoulder in a gesture of support. "Juliette, it was Colonel Chardon who gave you Giselle, your doll. You will enjoy being with him. Rene will drive you to your hotel."

Juliette clung to her grandfather's hand. "Will you not come too, Grandpapa?"

The old man shook his head firmly. "We have been over that. I have business." Although Abraham Snow's tone was abrupt, Andre saw the shine of moisture in the man's eyes. He stooped and embraced the child briefly, then turned wordlessly and climbed the stairs to pass out of her life forever.

7
Waiting Game

W*hat if nobody comes?*

The thought occurred to Josie a hundred times as the evening deepened into night. It was after nine o'clock. She was hungry, but she dared not go down to dinner. She sat beside the window in the unlit room and tried to peer into the square. The breeze caught the red banner and lifted it, then let it fall again.

Tinny music from a phonograph playing military marches penetrated the walls. Voices and footsteps passed in the corridor. No one knocked. Would the German major bring the child to her? The instructions had seemed so simple:

Enter Germany through Luxembourg over Wasserbillig Bridge. A taxi will be waiting for you there. Bring nothing but your passport and American documents for the child. Treves. Porta Nigra Hotel. A room will be reserved in your name. Wait there.

And so she waited. She had waited for hours. She had not yet cut away the end sheets from the book to remove the child's identity papers. She would not do so until she had the baby safely in her arms. To be arrested with forged identity documents and no infant to go along with them would be proof of intention to defraud the Reich. The volume of *Faust* and her passport remained on the night table.

Now it occurred to her that perhaps there was no more German major, no Jewish baby from Warsaw. All this might be an exercise in futility. A German officer determined to risk his safety for the sake of one child might already be tucked away in one of those prisons the Western democracies kept hearing about. If that was the case, she would simply meet the taxi driver in the morning and head back to the Wasserbillig Bridge.

She was about to kick off her shoes and climb onto the bed when soft rapping sounded on the door.

She did not switch on the lamp but stood in the darkness with her hand on the doorknob and her heart beating a tattoo as she remembered the Gestapo agents downstairs. She wondered if her ride through the Siegfried Line had somehow caught up with her.

"Who is it?" she asked stupidly in French.

"Frau Marlow?" The response was whispered, urgent.

She opened the door to the dim blue light of the corridor. A tall, lean German officer pushed past her, shut the door behind him, and snapped the bolt in place. She could not see his face. He did not attempt to turn on the light.

"Horst von Bockman. *Guten Abend. Bitte*, take off your clothes, Frau Marlow." He was already unbuttoning his tunic.

"T-take off my—," she stammered and backed away. Either this was some kind of joke, or the major was drunk. She could see the outline of a bottle in his hand.

"I have been followed," he said urgently. "Gestapo. Do as I say, Frau Marlow, or we are dead! Take off your clothes and get into bed." She fumbled at the buttons of her jacket and blouse. He flung his tunic carelessly across the back of a chair and kicked off his shoes, then pulled the blackout curtain tight across the window, mussed his hair, and turned back the sheets. "He may come to this room. You and I have been lovers since Warsaw."

She obeyed him, stripping to her camisole, and climbed into bed with her skirt on. She pulled the blanket tight around her chin and lay there with her teeth chattering. He left his trousers on and stood barefoot in the center of the room to wait.

The blare of the military march seemed a strange counterpoint to the pounding of her heart. Why had he been tailed?

Only seconds passed before a fist hammered on the thin wood.

"What do you want?" Horst bellowed angrily.

"If you please," came the polite reply. "A message for you, Herr Officer."

"I am busy! Go annoy someone else!"

"It is most urgent, I assure you," the voice whined.

Horst leaned close to Josie. "We met in Poland, you and I. Remember, we are in love."

Then Horst cursed loudly for the benefit of the intruder and fumbled with the bolt before he opened the door a crack.

Blue light spilled in, followed by the rough shove of a man in a long leather coat. There was an instant of struggle in the blackness. When the light was snapped on, a gun was at the head of Horst von Bockman.

"Well, well. Heil Hitler." The Gestapo agent beamed at Josie. "Two birds with one stone, it seems."

"What is the meaning of this?" Horst growled through clenched teeth as the muzzle of the weapon steered him toward a chair and guided him to sit.

"Come now, Major von Bockman." The dark-eyed man seemed very pleased with himself. "While every other member of my force has been scampering after the great men, I alone have been observing. It was you who arranged for a taxi to be at the Wasserbillig Bridge this morning, was it not? That half-wit of a taxi driver told me everything."

No use denying the fact, Josie thought.

"So what?" Horst said harshly.

"So, you bring this American woman here through the western defenses. You take me for a fool? She is a spy. And you are a traitor."

Horst stiffened at the accusation.

The hammer on the pistol clicked back.

"Does this look like we are involved in treason?" Horst waved the brandy bottle clutched in his fist.

The Gestapo agent pivoted to consider Josie, who peered out with wide, terrified eyes at the scene. She attempted to blurt out the words from the impromptu script the major had given her, but she could not speak.

"A little pleasure with your business, Herr Major?" The agent smirked.

"Americans are neutrals, or have you forgotten?" Horst remarked coolly. "And you are taking your idiotic games too far for the approval of the Reich or the Führer or your own superiors." He gestured toward his tunic, which bore the decoration earned for bravery in Poland. "You call me a traitor? I will see you are shot for this, Herr whatever-your-name-is."

"Herr Müller," replied the agent with a click of his heels.

Clearly he would not be easily convinced.

"Then, Herr Müller, I would suggest you remove your weapon from my head and telephone General Rommel to ask his opinion of my loyalty. He is staying in this hotel."

For the first time Josie saw the fixed smile of Herr Müller twitch with doubt. "The general should not be bothered with matters of security."

"He will wish to be consulted in a matter so serious; I assure you. A matter involving harassment and false accusations against one of his frontline commanders."

Müller stepped back from Horst, still keeping the barrel level on his head.

"Shall *I* call the general then?" Horst demanded.

Müller's smile vanished. The taint of fear crept into the diminuitive man's expression. He took another step back.

"Please summon the general, Herr Müller. I insist you do, unless you wish to be strung up by piano wire. Frau Marlow and I have known one another since Warsaw. You may check that if you wish." Horst von Bockman's rebuttal was hard steel and ice, the voice of a leader not to be questioned. "Frau Marlow is an American journalist. She was trapped behind the lines in the siege. We met and have been good friends since that time. Her documents are quite in order." He reached over and snatched up her passport, opening it to display the visa stamps of Poland, then the Nazi-occupied territories of Poland, after that the Third Reich, and finally the stamp of the customs officials at the Wasserbillig Bridge. "All in order, Herr Müller."

Horst tossed the passport to Josie. It fell on the bed beside her. She merely nodded. She remained mute.

The Gestapo agent was also struck dumb. He lowered his weapon a fraction; it seemed Horst had defeated him. Then he threw a hard look at Josie's jacket and blouse. His mouth curved in a half smile. He reached out and tore the blanket off the bed, revealing that Josie was still wearing her skirt and her shoes.

He threw back his head in laughter at the attempted deception. "Very good! I was almost convinced. In quite a rush, Major?" He pressed the gun hard against Josie's temple. "Get up, Frau Marlow," he said in a menacing tone. "Gestapo headquarters will be interested to hear you explain that Americans make love with their shoes on. I remain unconvinced, however." He ogled her form, leering at her as if her obvious terror heightened his own pleasure. "You are both under arrest for espionage and conspiracy against the Reich. Heil Hit—"

The heavy glass of the brandy bottle crashed down on the back of Müller's skull. The force of the blow propelled him face-first into the wall at the head of the bed. Josie clamped both hands on her mouth to stifle her own scream. The gun flew up in the air and landed on a pillow as Josie rolled across to the opposite side. Müller fell heavily across the bed. His mouth hung limply open and a heavy, sonorous sound rolled from it, as if he were sleeping off drunkenness.

Josie pressed against the farthest wall, wide-eyed and panting. She clutched her jacket to her like a life preserver.

As Horst examined Müller, he still gripped the brandy bottle by its neck in readiness.

"Well, Frau Marlow." Horst's words were calm, but Josie could see his eyes darting around the room, keeping pace with his racing thoughts. "We are very fortunate . . . all things considered. The gun did not go off, the bottle did not break, and we do not have a dead Gestapo agent in your bedroom to explain."

"But what will we do now?"

Horst uncorked the brandy and splashed some on the recumbent Müller. "I have a car in the alley behind the hotel. With your help I think we can take our drunken friend here for a ride. It is too dangerous for you to remain in Treves until morning," he warned Josie as he began to sift through Müller's pockets. He shredded every scrap of identification and proceeded to flush the paper down the toilet. "We must take you directly to Wasserbillig. Do you have the documents for the baby?"

She held up the copy of *Faust* in reply. "Here."

"Listen carefully." He took her arm, and his eyes pierced hers. "You must not take the child back to France."

"Belgium or Holland then?"

"No!" He emphasized his vehemence by gripping her arm painfully. "Get him off the Continent. To England first. Do it immediately. Do you understand me, Frau Marlow? After tomorrow it will be too late. Take a train from Luxembourg, then a neutral ferry to England from Ostend. Soon there will be no neutrals."

"But Holland—"

"You witnessed Poland. I need not tell you more. Get him out of Europe!"

His warning was so stern and frightening that Josie knew instantly there was far more at stake here than the life of one child. *"Not Holland! Not Belgium! Soon there will be no neutrals!"*

Horst checked to see that the corridor was clear. Then, supporting Müller between them, Josie and Horst staggered down the back stairs of the Porta Nigra. A Wehrmacht staff car waited in the alley.

The blackout in Treves facilitated their moves. Horst bound and gagged Müller, then crammed him into the trunk of the vehicle as Josie climbed into the passenger seat.

The soft voice of a woman startled her. "He is a good baby, Frau Marlow. No trouble. You will see."

Josie gasped and whirled to peer into the dark shadows. She could see only the vague outline of someone directly behind her. "Who are you?"

"I am Katrina von Bockman. The major's wife. I have brought Yacov to you."

Josie wished her mastery of German were better. There was so much she wanted to say, so many questions to ask, but the words escaped her.

In an instant Horst was behind the wheel, and they were inching through the narrow lanes of Treves.

"There was trouble," Horst explained to Katrina.

"Gestapo?"

"Yes."

Katrina was calm. "He is dead?"

"Not yet."

"What will we do?" If she was worried, the tone of her voice did not betray it.

"It is tragic how many drunks stumble in the dark," Horst replied. Then to Josie he said, "It is time now to take out the travel documents of your son, Frau Marlow. You have been a delightful guest for me and Katrina. We hate to see you go."

Josie peeled back the end sheet on the copy of *Faust* and removed the dated document for infant Daniel John Marlow. They rode in silence for several miles, finally coming to a roadblock guarded by a drowsy sentry who shone his flashlight in through the window at each of the occupants. This was the first glimpse Josie had of the baby who was supposed to be her son. He slept in the arms of Katrina. He was fair-skinned and plump. A blue knit cap covered his head. He sucked his thumb in contentment. A beautiful child.

With seemingly detached boredom, Horst passed their documents to the sentry, who gave them a cursory glance and then waved the vehicle through. A number of rumbling lorries pulled up to the gate behind them. Horst sped up and drove for a while, finally turning onto a side lane beside the berm of a rail line.

Switching off the engine, he sat in silence for a moment. "Herr Müller is about to attempt to stop the train to Luxembourg." With that he set the hand brake, retrieved a tire iron from beneath the seat, and left the car.

The baby sighed in Katrina's arms. The sweet scent of flowers drifted in through the window. Josie heard the trunk lid open and the moan of Müller through the gag. This was followed by what sounded like a metallic *clank* against a ripe melon. Then there was silence. Horst von Bockman had left nothing to chance.

Josie felt ill.

Katrina von Bockman defended her husband in a hoarse whisper. "He has done what he must, Frau Marlow."

The vehicle swayed a bit as the major pulled the heavy body of Müller out of the trunk. And then above the calls of the night birds was the sound of the body being dragged through the gravel and up the berm to be deposited on the tracks.

How cool von Bockman seemed! He returned to the car. His demeanor was as unruffled as if he had just stepped on a cockroach instead of killing a man! Josie was not sure she liked him. She knew she should thank him for saving her life. She should admire him for rescuing the baby.

"I-I am . . . grateful," she stammered unconvincingly.

"Do not waste pity on a creature like Müller," Horst said flatly.

"You are efficient," she replied. It was his efficiency that disturbed her most about all of this.

He replied to her unspoken question. "I know it is hard for you to understand, Frau Marlow. Perhaps later you will see it is necessary. When an unpleasant task is necessary, then emotion is a waste of energy. Perhaps even dangerous. You will be safe now. And this baby will be out of reach of a man like Müller for the time being. That is what matters."

He turned the key in the ignition and pulled away. "The train to Luxembourg is due to pass here in ten minutes. Chances are the authorities will never know who he was. Better for us. The offensive begins immediately, so who will even think of a drunk on the railroad tracks after that?"

Minutes later they were back on the main highway, driving through the darkness toward Wasserbillig Bridge.

8

Upon What Small Hinges . . .

The sky was backlit with the glow of predawn pastels by the time Horst, Katrina, Josie, and the baby reached Wasserbillig Bridge. Across the river the hilly outline of Luxembourg appeared peaceful as Horst and Katrina escorted Josie into the customshouse.

Perhaps it was the sight of the Knight's Cross on the uniform of Horst von Bockman that made the customs officials and sentries step aside as Josie and the baby were waved through the barrier. Yacov Lubetkin, who had been well dosed with cough medicine beforehand, slept through the inspection.

Continuing the charade, Josie embraced Katrina von Bockman as if she were a family member. She kissed the major awkwardly on his cheek and thanked him for the enjoyable time.

In an exuberant voice Horst explained to the early morning shift that Frau Marlow was an American cousin and that the trip with her small son was their very first into the Reich. "She has seen the miracle of National Socialism," he announced solemnly, "and she will carry the good report back to America."

The officials nodded with pleasure. They did not doubt that National Socialism was the eighth wonder of the world. They simply wanted the world to agree with them.

What Josie had to recount upon her return, however, was far more sobering than a glowing account of the Nazi miracle. The details of the Wehrmacht's plan she was carrying back, along with the contraband baby, were enough to have her executed a hundred times. She knew it. Horst von Bockman knew it. The weight of it made her resent the cheerful conversation and the too-long good-byes on the German side of the barrier on Wasserbillig. But for the sake of authenticity, they acted out their family farewell to the last detail.

"Take care of the little one." Horst touched the cheek of the sleeping child. Then he lowered his voice as he leaned close to her ear. "Remember. Do as I told you."

There were tears in Katrina's eyes as she stooped to kiss Yacov. "He will not remember me," she whispered quickly against Josie's hair. "Such a good baby. Mention us to his grandfather, will you, Josephine? Tell him . . . I pray for the baby's mother. I wonder . . ." Then, "Pray for us." The words were no mere scene being played for the Nazi onlookers.

"I will." Josie nodded stiffly. *"Danke."* She knew she should say something kind—leave some good word with them. But she could think of nothing but the car parked at the Bierstube on the other side of the bridge. She wanted nothing except to put as much distance between her and the miracle of National Socialism as possible.

It was as if she could feel the earth already rumbling from the rolling tracks of thousands of German tanks. What would this place look like by the next dawn?

"Auf Wiedersehen."

The striped barrier pole was raised. The young sentry saluted Horst. Eyes flitted to the Knight's Cross. Then the young Aryan chucked the Jewish baby on the chin as Josie passed by and strode the few paces into Luxembourg.

She tried to control her urge to jog the remaining length of the bridge onto the soil of the Grand Duchy. She heard the *clunk* of the barrier falling into place behind her. Turning to look back, she saw Horst and Katrina von Bockman gazing after her wistfully. Soon enough the major would be crossing some other neutral border, Josie knew. She did not want to be there to greet him when he arrived.

They waved. The sentry waved. And Josie waved.

◍

Richard Lewinski stared at Gustave Bertrand with disdain.

"What do you mean, you can't read them anymore?" Bertrand snapped.

Lewinski shook a bony finger in Bertrand's face. "Was I not speaking plainly enough, Colonel Bertrand? I mean, the pattern for setting the wheels has changed. It no longer follows the formula I deduced on the first of May, over a week ago."

"Could you have miscalculated?"

Lewinski gave Bertrand a withering look. "I never miscalculate. I *never* miscalculate! What this must mean is that the invasion is really on for to-morrow. It makes sense to change the pattern when strategic orders are about to be replaced by tactical ones. You know, when a division commander calls for help or some such operation, if your enemy has even the slightest clue about what you are up to, then it would be disastrous."

"I know!" Bertrand exploded. "Like this alteration is disastrous for us! How long will it take to uncover the new procedure?"

Lewinski's look changed to one of pity. "I suppose that depends on what they changed it to; now doesn't it?"

"Could this mean that they know we've cracked the first setting?"

"Possibly, or perhaps they had always planned this change to occur simultaneously with the invasion. But there is one sure way to tell."

"What is that?" Bertrand asked, desperate for a ray of hope.

"If they know that we know, they'll change the routine so drastically that it may be months—even years—before we crack the new one."

◈

"Tell me everything you saw, *ma chèrie*! Everything the major said!" Andre gripped the hands of Josie as she recited the details of what lay beyond the West Wall.

"Thousands of soldiers . . . and he told me I must not go back to Paris."

"They mean to bomb Paris then."

"He told me to take the baby right on to England. The train from Luxembourg to Ostend today and then the ferry across the Channel tomorrow."

Andre glanced at his watch. "We've missed the train. The next is not until tomorrow." He raised his gaze through the double doors of the suite in the Brasseur Hotel, to where Juliette played on the floor beside the baby boy. She was happy for the first time since they had left the home of Abraham Snow yesterday. Had he found her only to let her go so soon?

Josie must have recognized the anguish in his eyes. "Come with us, Andre," she whispered urgently. "Come with us to England."

Considering her with a sad smile, he shook his head. "It was you who spoke of courage, *chèrie*. Could I run away for the sake of love?"

"Yes!" Her vehemence surprised him. "Please, Andre! There is Juliette to consider now . . . and me! I don't want to say good-bye again! You once said you had found something worth living for—someone worth living for. We can marry. Go to America and—"

The telephone rang. Andre picked up the receiver and held it to his ear. Who would be calling him here? He recognized the voice of Bertrand instantly.

"We have passed Lewinski's information to the Belgian king in Brussels. German fifth columnists disguised as tourists are pouring across the borders of Belgium and Holland. They are being mobilized at this instant. You are needed at our embassy in Brussels tonight."

Did Bertrand not realize that the telephone lines might be tapped? Andre wondered. That to mention the name of Richard Lewinski was not only foolish but dangerous?

Bertrand did not wait for Andre to respond. "Do you understand?"

"*Oui.*"

"Go now. Tomorrow will be too late. Good luck."

The line clicked dead. What additional news had Lewinski gleaned from the dispatches that had made the always careful Gustave Bertrand throw caution to the wind? Andre replaced the receiver in its cradle.

"I will drive you as far as Brussels," he told Josie. "Then you must take both children to Ostend by train. Then the ferry across to England—"

"But, Andre!" she protested.

He cupped her chin in his hand. "My sweet hypocrite. I cannot go with you. I do not know if I am honored by your request for my desertion or insulted that you really thought I might go."

"Then I'll stay with you," Josie insisted. "Stay in Paris. The Nazis will never get as far as Paris."

Andre directed her gaze to the children. "Have you forgotten Warsaw, *chèrie*? Warsaw, where perhaps the parents of that baby have been murdered. Paris will be bombed. Look at them. They are your duty. Yacov. Juliette."

She embraced him. Tears stung her eyes. "But to leave you, Andre! Knowing that maybe . . ."

"To think of maybe will make us both cowards. The hour has come for France. Some to fight. Some to say farewell. I will not say which is harder. But as for us, we will follow whatever course is charted for us."

⥂

Nazi Gestapo agent, Russian-born Nicholi Federov, nodded and tapped his patent-leather shoe in time to the tune. Mozart was one of his favorites, and the Paris student ensemble performed most credibly.

Having offered to cater the light refreshments for the noontime recital, the supposed wine merchant was naturally offered a seat in the front row. The Église de la Sorbonne, where the concert was being held, was a pleasant setting, especially with the white marble tomb of Cardinal Richelieu providing the backdrop for the string quartet.

The midday gathering was well attended, despite the restrictions imposed by the war. Federov was certain that since the majority of those in attendance were either poor students or underpaid instructors, perhaps the refreshments were as big a draw as the music. Sugar for fancy baked goods and German Rhine wines to accompany them were almost impossible to obtain at any price. Several of the university officials made a particular point of thanking Federov personally.

"Completely my pleasure," Federov acknowledged to Professor Argo of the mathematics department. "But tell me, are we missing a few familiar faces?"

"Ah yes," Argo agreed, smoothing back his white hair and stroking his pointed white beard. "The Americans have all gone home, as have the Swiss and the Belgians. It seems that our colleagues of the neutral nations have scurried away."

"Well, it has happened all over because of blighted politics," Federov pointed out. "Fascist beliefs and intellectual life cannot coexist, it seems. Of course, some consequences are more drastic than others. Look at what happened to university life in Warsaw." He shook his head. "Tragic." Then as if a thought struck him, he snapped his fingers. "Say, I wonder whatever happened to that eccentric genius who was Polish. You know the one I mean . . . what is his name? His father was a professor here, and he is a wizard at numbers."

Professor Argo thought a moment. "You must mean the Lewinskis."

"That is it, exactly. What do you suppose happened to him?"

"It is odd you should mention him," Argo said. "A promising advanced-level student of mine—female, great mind for numbers theory, higher order equations, that sort of thing—where was I?"

"Lewinski," Federov encouraged, trying not to let his impatience show.

"Yes, well, this student, who had heard Lewinski lecture on his arcane theory some years ago—something about a universal machine that can speak to other machines—anyway, this student thought she encountered Lewinski and mentioned it to me."

"Encountered him where?"

"Here—that is, in Paris somewhere."

"What did she mean, she *thought* she met him?"

Argo held the tuft of his beard as if squeezing the recollection out of it. "It has been some time ago now, but I think she said hello to a man, thinking it was he, and this fellow denied it. Still, she mentioned the shock of red hair. He is rather unique looking, you know."

"Did she mention where this occurred?"

"No . . . that is, I cannot remember. Is it important?"

Argo, for all his bumbling ways, had a sharp mind. Federov was concerned that he not make the issue seem significant.

"Not at all," Federov said. "Curious how people pop into your mind at odd times, is it not?"

"I can only spare a moment, gentlemen," Winston Churchill intoned in his office in the Admiralty Building on the afternoon of May 9. "I am dining at eight o'clock with Mr. Eden and Mr. Sinclair."

John Murphy looked at Mac McGrath, then asked the question he had been waiting for two hours to pose. "First Lord," Murphy said, "I wonder if you would care to comment on the rumor that you are about to become prime minister?"

"A politician may be in the position of starting rumors or even of being their subject, but he should never comment on them."

"Understood, sir." Murphy grinned. "Perhaps you would just comment as to the accuracy of some . . . statements others have made about the present situation."

"I believe you have phrased it delicately enough now, Mr. Murphy. Frame your statements."

"Is it true that Clement Atlee and the Labour Party have declared that they will participate in a National Coalition government only if Mr. Chamberlain is not the head?"

"I have heard something to that effect, yes," Churchill agreed.

"Furthermore, they specifically reject Mr. Chamberlain's handpicked successor, Lord Halifax."

"As to that," Churchill said, "I do not know. However, Halifax has mentioned that he does not feel he can lead effectively from the House of Lords."

"Meaning he is taking himself out of consideration?"

Churchill pursed his lips and shrugged. "Meaning no more than he intends to mean, I am sure."

"Doesn't that suggest that you are the logical choice? that tomorrow you may be prime minister?" Murphy pressed.

Churchill smirked. "I fear we have wandered back into speculation again, Mr. Murphy. Now if you and Mr. McGrath will excuse me."

"Just one more thing, please, First Lord," interjected Mac.

Murphy held his breath. He knew what Mac was going to ask, and Churchill was the one person whose answer was worth hearing.

"Is it possible that if you are prime minister, it will be because of the *Altmark*?" Mac asked bluntly.

Picking at some imaginary lint on the sleeve of his jacket gave Churchill a moment to phrase his reply. "You are very astute, Mr. McGrath," he said at last. "I have been debating the same chain of events myself. If the *Altmark* had not been run to earth in Jossing Fjord, then perhaps Herr Hitler would not have stretched out his angry little hand against Norway, or at least not at the time that he chose. In such a case, the present cabinet crisis might not exist, and all the speculation about its outcome would be moot."

Churchill withdrew a cigar from a leather case and studied it as if he found a message written there. "It is strange, is it not, upon what small hinges great events often turn?"

9

Moving Out

Young Jerome Jardin received word that the patients at the Hospital de la Charité were to be evacuated south so that space might be dedicated to the future victims of bombing in Paris. If there were any.

His blind Uncle Jambonneau was very pleased, he told Jerome. Uncle Jambonneau had always wanted to spend time in Southern France with its balmy climate and vineyards and such. He dictated a message of farewell:

> *Perhaps I shall learn to paint! A new experience for me! Landscapes by a blind man. Ah well, maybe not. Next to seeing the sun, the best thing is to feel the sun warming one's face. . . .*

Promising to send notes often, Uncle Jambonneau gave the address of the sanitarium for soldiers of des Grandes Armee outside Marseilles. As a parting gift, he even bequeathed his "dog," the rat Papillon, to Jerome forever. It was very touching, especially since Jerome knew how much Papillon meant to Uncle Jambonneau. Jerome was glad that Madame Rose and Madame Betsy wouldn't mind Uncle Jambonneau's dog staying with them on a more lasting basis.

And today there would be a special celebration. There were ninety children staying at No. 5 Rue de la Huchette on May 9. Madame Rose Smith had managed through the assistance of friends in high places to obtain tickets to the matinee performance of *Snow White* for everyone.

Jerome Jardin had been to only one movie in his entire life, and of all the impossible things that Madame Rose and God had arranged, this seemed the most miraculous of all.

Columns of children passed to the Right Bank of Paris over Pont Neuf. Pushing his friend Henri's wheelchair, Jerome pointed out his former home—the barge *Stinking Garlic* moored below. The boat looked very fine now. Madame Hilaire and her associate thief had fixed it up. There was a *For Sale* sign on the end of the gangway. The rudder was in place. The sails and rigging were repaired and tied off neatly. Smoke from the engine sputtered up as the Thief worked on it.

"My sister and I used to live there," Jerome told Henri.

"Why do you not live there now?" Henri looked at the boat and then down to admire the shine of his riding boots. Another miracle of Madame Rose and God.

"It was stolen from us. But it does not matter," Jerome replied. "It was a good thing they stole it because my sister, Marie, now has glasses, and we are very happy with Madame Rose and Madame Betsy. I think when Papa comes back from the war and meets the sisters, he will see what a good thing it is we did not stay with Madame Hilaire while he was gone."

Jerome meant what he said. He did not even feel angry about the *Garlic* anymore. He had friends and lots to eat these days. He did not have to worry about Marie. He was going to see an American motion picture with dwarfs and witches. And it was spring. There would be flowers blooming at the Maginot Line for his papa to see. Soon the war would be over. How much better could life be?

⌒∽⌒

The sun was high above the hills and canyons of Luxembourg as Andre took the road north across the frontier into Belgium.

Yacov perched wide-eyed and attentive on Josie's lap. Juliette Snow sat sad and solemn in the backseat of the Citroën as the familiar sights of the Grand Duchy fell away. Andre's papers were checked by a single sentry at the Belgian frontier. They were quickly waved through the barrier to enter the pine forests, rocky promontories, and deep valleys of the Ardennes.

The Ardennes—Belgium's natural Maginot Line. Swift rivers ran past castles and tiny slate-roofed villages. Summerhouses, stone-walled inns, and taverns lined roads that reached out from Liege like the thin strands of a spiderweb. But the idyllic, storybook beauty could not conceal the vision of coming horror in Andre's mind as he sped through lonely forests and past high cliffs that dropped away into the river valleys below.

This vacationer's paradise, this seemingly intractable wilderness, was Hitler's biggest secret weapon. Behind the peaceful woodlands,

Hitler's Panzerkorps waited for the signal to explode across the border into Belgium.

There was little sign of any Belgian military presence on the serpentine highway. A Belgian motorcyclist roared by, followed by a group of young men on bicycles, who pedaled toward the heart of the forest. Were they among the thousands of German "tourists" Lewinski's decoded messages had said were being sent across the neutral frontier of the Ardennes in advance of invasion? Dressed in camping clothes suitable for an outing in the area, they were nonetheless grim-faced and hard-looking. They did not look like young students out for a holiday.

Andre did not express his suspicions, but he pressed his foot down harder on the accelerator.

Josephine must have felt his urgency to reach Brussels, yet for the sake of Juliette, she pretended that this was nothing more than a lovely excursion. Yacov had fallen asleep in her arms as she taught the child American songs: "Bye, Bye Blackbird" and "Happy Days Are Here Again!" The latter seemed a ludicrous sentiment to Andre, considering that this might well be the last happy day in Europe for a long time.

They stopped at an inn and purchased sandwiches made from famous Ardennes ham. Juliette picked out a half-dozen pastries to take along with them. That and a bottle of cold, fresh milk provided the makings of a picnic. But they ate their meal as Andre drove too fast along the treacherous highway that led into the lowlands.

ᦒ

There was in all the world nothing so wonderful as *Snow White*, Jerome thought. He conceded that his Communist papa would consider the Seven Dwarfs greedy little capitalists who should have distributed all those jewels from their mines to the poor, but Jerome liked them all the same. He hoped that one day the Dwarfs would meet up with Madame Rose, and their hoarded wealth would become potatoes and shoes and eyeglasses and even tickets to the cinema.

He would like to be around to see it!

The air-raid siren erupted just as Jerome pushed Henri's chair onto Pont Neuf. There were a few squeaks and squeals from the girls. Everyone craned their heads to search the sky for German bombers. Madame Betsy was calm. Madame Rose was calm. A few German bombers? Nothing to worry about. Walk to the nearest shelter and wait till the all clear.

Below the stone wall of the bridge, the piercing voice of Madame Hilaire echoed: "*Mon dieu!* Hurry! To the shelter! We must run to the shelter. You know what the fireman has said! The Boche will bomb boats on the quai to block the river first of all."

Jerome leaned over the rail. He peered down at the woman he called a crazed anteater—one of those hideous creatures who sucks helpless ants out of their houses—as she ran in circles and waved her arms at the Thief, who moved slowly, wearily, toward the gangway. She dragged him toward the stone steps that led up to the street level.

Poor fellow, that Thief. He thought he was only stealing the *Garlic*, and he ended up with Madame Hilaire. A fate worse than death. She was louder than the siren, Jerome thought as he pushed Henri's chair toward the nearest shelter.

ᥫᩣ

The sun was setting as Andre, Josie, and the children swooped out of the foothills. Here they came upon a long line of rumbling troop lorries and camouflaged trucks, followed by small artillery pieces mounted on rattling tractors.

Only now did Josie dare to compare the Belgian defenses with what she had witnessed on her journey through the German lines facing Luxembourg. She looked at Andre. "Is this the best they have?" she asked him with dread.

"It is," he replied curtly. "And it is headed away from the Ardennes, as you see. Entirely in the wrong direction."

ᥫᩣ

Andre drove into the parking area of the Brussels North Train Station just after nine o'clock on the evening of May 9. The city was brightly lit in spite of the fact that Belgian military mobilization was in full swing. It was a strange contrast to Paris and London, and proof that, in spite of intelligence information to the contrary, most Belgian civilians did not believe Hitler would dare violate their neutrality.

Inside the hall of the terminal echoed with soldiers and crowds of men and women who had come to see them off. Andre left Josie with the children on a stone bench beneath the clock and hurried off to purchase passage to Ostend and then on to Dover. He returned a half hour later with tickets but also with grim news.

"No trains to Ostend tonight." He picked up Juliette, who had been sleeping on the bench. Cradling her against his shoulder, he brushed his lips against her cheek.

"My daddy used to hold us like that," Josie said gently, lapsing into English. "On the way home from barn dances my brothers and sisters and I would pretend to fall asleep in the back of the pickup. All six of them and me. Just so he would carry us into the house."

What a time to think of such a thing, she realized.

She put a hand to her head and chuckled. "I must be remembering someone else's life. It could never have been so easy."

"It is not supposed to be this hard, *ma chèrie*," Andre replied wearily.

How long had it been since he had slept? she wondered. "She is a beautiful child, Andre. Really. And someday—"

"I cannot think of someday." He shot a hot look at the huffing train that was packed with soldiers leaning out the windows and shouting their farewells. "I can think only of tomorrow—of you and Juliette and the baby safely away from here. The next train leaves at nine in the morning. It is nearly sold out . . . second-class tickets only. It seems a number of wealthy Belgians developed a sudden desire to see England. I should drive you to the Channel myself except . . ." He sighed.

"Except you may be needed here tomorrow."

"I am needed here tonight. At our embassy. Paris telephoned ahead. They are expecting me there now. A meeting with the military attaché to the king. I would like you to tell him what you saw in Germany. They will make up a room for you and the children to stay tonight. As for the morning? We will just hope the train leaves before the arrival of the Luftwaffe."

It was just after midnight when Sergeant Fiske shook Horst by the arm. Horst bolted upright, reaching for his Luger in the holster that hung over the back of a chair.

"It is me, Major. Fiske. Coded Enigma message from headquarters."

"So? What is the time, Fiske? Could this not wait till morning?" Horst switched on the light beside the bed and groped for the wristwatch that he had knocked onto the floor.

"It was marked *Urgent. Highest Priority*, sir."

"All right, Fiske. I am awake now. Where is the dispatch?"

"It did not seem necessary to bring a copy, sir, for just a one-word message."

Horst felt a chill even though the room was warm. "What is it?"

"The word, sir, is *Danzig*."

"Wake the company commanders," Horst commanded. "Tell them to order their troops to fall in and stand by their machines. Have the men draw rations for three days. Then tell them I want them here, reporting complete readiness, in twenty minutes."

When Fiske had saluted crisply and left on his errand, Horst slipped into his uniform and pulled on his tall boots. He was buttoning his tunic in front of the mirror when he stopped and studied his reflection in the glass. So it had happened. The signal to launch Blitzkrieg against the

West had come. Horst knew he would be summoned to General Rommel in a very short time to hear how soon his units would be rolling across the border to engage the Belgians.

He felt oddly calm. Now that the order was given, the time for introspection was past. He owed it to the men—*his* men—to offer them the best leadership possible. No second thoughts, no troubling doubts. They were counting on him to help them survive, to live through today and the days that followed, until the ordeal was over. . . .

An hour later Horst was sitting with the other officers of Seventh Panzer as their division commander briefed them. General Erwin Rommel was impeccably dressed in his best uniform, his boots polished to a high gloss. With a Leica camera hanging around his neck, he looked more like a wealthy Berlin staff officer on holiday than a field commander preparing to go into battle.

"We push off at dawn," Rommel informed the group. "The spearhead of each of our assigned routes will be a reconnaissance team, accompanied by Brandenburgers to deal with any demolition charges the Belgians may have left behind. The main body will follow. Keep the formation tight, gentlemen! I will sack any commander who does not keep to schedule. I have personally promised General von Rundstedt that the Seventh will reach the Meuse River before any other unit in Army Group A. I intend for us to keep that promise."

Colonel Neumann, one of Rommel's tank commanders, raised the question all of them were thinking. "And what weight of opposition do we expect to encounter from the enemy?"

"At the same time we move out, General von Bock's Army Group B will move into northern Belgium and the Netherlands. Their attacks will race toward Rotterdam and Brussels. These actions, together with airborne landings behind the enemy lines in Holland, will convince the Allies that we are doing exactly what they expect and repeating the frontal assault of 1914. Therefore, they will weaken the forces facing us to reinforce the north. To answer your question, Neumann, there will be no serious opposition until we reach the Meuse, and we will be there the day after tomorrow. That will be all, gentlemen. Be ready to move out at 0500."

10

The Waiting Is Finished

Hotel des Flandres on the Place Royal in Brussels, Belgium, was listed as the second-best hotel in Mac's *Baedeker's Guide*. The establishment that received the highest ranking was the Bellevue, noted in the guidebook as "frequented by royalty and the noblesse; high prices." Even the location of the two hotels seemed to reflect this snootiness. The Bellevue and the Flandres were adjacent, but the more expensive lodging preempted the view of the park.

All of which mattered very little to Mac. After a late arrival on the boat from England and a midnight train ride into Brussels, he was merely pleased to have a place to sleep.

He was up in the early morning hours of the tenth of May, poring over a map staked out between a silver coffeepot and a creamer on his breakfast table in the dining room. Mac was plotting a route that would take him to the Belgian fortress of Eben Emael east of the town. His assignment was to film the Belgian counterpart of the Maginot Line at what was reported to be the most modern defensive work in the world, completely impregnable.

The white-uniformed waiter appeared to take Mac's order for toast and marmalade, bacon, three eggs, and a grilled chop. With a raised eyebrow the waiter asked, "And how many will be joining you for breakfast, Monsieur?"

Mac waved him away impatiently and returned to studying the map. Newsreel cameramen, like old soldiers, learned to eat whenever the opportunity existed. For who knew what would happen between this sure thing and another meal?

The distance to where Mac expected to find his story was not far. The map's inch of space translated into no more than sixty miles.

The bacon, eggs, and toast had arrived at Mac's elbow, but the chop had not yet appeared when the air-raid alarm on top of the Bibliotheque Royale began screaming out its warning. Mac's waiter dropped a cup of coffee into the lap of a fat man at a nearby table, adding a different note to the wail of the siren. The service staff all dropped whatever they were carrying and disappeared through the doors to the kitchen, leaving a dumbfounded group of diners staring at each other.

The *crump* of bombs falling in the distance joined the clamor of the alert. The bass-voiced bells of the cathedral across the park were harmonized by the tenor accent of those at the Church of St. Jacques around the corner.

Mac was already under the table, cradling his precious stack of Eva's letters. "Get down!" he urged the obese man who was still standing, cursing the waiter, and mopping his trousers with his napkin. Other early diners appeared to be more concerned with looking foolish than being protected.

"Surely this hotel cannot be threatened," remarked a tall, aristocratic woman who had not budged from her tea. She sounded as though the Germans had a better sense of social propriety than to bomb the second-best hotel in Brussels.

"Get down!" Mac said again as he crawled away from the windows and toward the kitchen entrance. "The Boche may be hitting the airport, but their aim is not always perfect!"

As if to punctuate his words, the antiaircraft guns on top of the nearby Palais du Comte began their rhythmic pulse. A second later the drone of airplanes was heard and then the whistle of bombs.

The first explosion in the downtown area hit a building only three blocks away. The sound of the detonation was followed by a rushing wind, and the plate glass facing the blast blew in. Shards from the broken windows scattered across the dining-room floor, and the concussion knocked down an entire shelf of stemware with a crash that was the loudest noise of all.

Mac scooted across the tile and into the kitchen, where he discovered stairs leading down to a basement pantry. He sprinted to the shelter, finding it already populated with the cook, waiters, and dishwashers. Right behind Mac came the heavy man, the society woman, and the rest of the breakfast guests.

"I hope you turned off the stove," Mac said to the cook. "I do not want you to burn my chop." Then addressing the assembled group he added, "Ladies and gentlemen, say good-bye to the Phony War."

℘

Was it a nightmare? Once again the too-familiar dreams of Warsaw returned to trouble Josie's sleep. She struggled against the images of carnage; then she sat bolt upright in her bed, eyes wide.

It was not the drone of Heinkel engines that tore her from a sound sleep at the French Embassy in Brussels but the wail of little Yacov Lubetkin. This was no dream!

Like Josie, the baby had heard the rumbling before. It was followed by the undulating scream of air-raid sirens and the distant whine as a stick of bombs was released. Finally the dull *crumps* rattled the windows and jingled the prisms on the lamp shade like sleigh bells.

Juliette, asleep on a little bed on the far side of the room, miraculously did not stir. Josie grabbed Yacov and held him close to her. In spite of the clamor in the streets, she sat on the edge of the bed and rocked him in an attempt to calm him. Did he feel her trembling?

Shouts of other occupants of the embassy sounded up and down the corridor. She could hear the patter of bare feet on the polished wood floors.

"L'Allemand attaque! The Germans are attacking!"

There followed a light, yet frantic, knock at her door. Paralyzed, she could not force herself to answer or call out. Yacov, red-faced, was blue about the lips because the force of his sobs kept him from drawing a deep breath. He pushed against her as if in instinct of flight. To hide. To shut out the terrible sounds! What must this tiny person have witnessed in Poland?

He would not be comforted. Juliette did not wake up. Unable to move, Josie sat with the baby in her arms.

A long, long whistle and a deafening explosion nearly shook the windows from the frames. The knocking was drowned out. The door flew open. Andre, barefoot and with only his trousers on, stumbled in as plaster dust fell from the ceiling. He picked up Juliette as a bomb pierced the roof of a three-story building across the park. The walls puffed out, hung in midair for an instant, then spewed glass and wood and stone and people into the manicured lawn of the little park.

Juliette screamed and buried her face in Andre's neck. He grabbed Josie by the arm and jerked her to her feet. "To the cellar!" he shouted over the roar of Heinkels and explosions.

Then Josie's every nerve awakened. She grabbed her robe and dashed out the door with Andre as the bedroom window shattered from the force of a bomb at the center of the block. They reached the cellar and slammed the door shut.

The smoke and the terrified cries of the servant girls were all something Josie remembered too well. It was all happening again, she thought as the masonry walls of the cellar cracked and swayed, and a curtain of dust covered the crouched occupants.

"The war is finally here!" A pale, dark-eyed secretary laughed hysterically. "The waiting is finished!"

⟨QD⟩

It was eight in the morning, and the leading elements of Seventh Panzer were already fifteen miles inside Belgium. The resistance had not been light; it had been nonexistent. Despite the enormous buildup of German forces, or perhaps because of it, the expected opposition by the Belgian troops had failed to materialize.

Horst stood in the hatch of his Kfz 231—a fast, agile, six-wheeled armored car. The morning sun was warm on the back of his neck and the day had a pleasant feel. Below him the radio crackled to life, and a moment later Sergeant Fiske called up to him, "Major, Captain Grühn reports a group of men with weapons at the highway intersection in Pepinster, about a half mile from his present position. He wants to know if he should open fire."

"Ask him if the men have bicycles."

Fiske knew better than to dispute his commander's questions, no matter how odd they might sound. He relayed the inquiry, then said, "Grühn says yes, all have bicycles."

"Tell him to advance without firing—cautiously, of course. If the cyclists neither shoot nor flee, then they are ours."

So this much of the plan had worked completely. For several days before the launch of the invasion force, groups of German "tourists" had cycled peacefully into Luxembourg, Holland, and here in Belgium. Since dawn this morning they had been holding key intersections in advance of the Panzergruppen.

Horst saluted the infiltrators as his command vehicle rolled through Pepinster. The men threw off their civilian clothing and, now wearing Wehrmacht uniforms, stood proudly at attention. One of them waved a red *Baedeker's* guidebook at Horst and grinned.

The Belgian civilians, awakening on an ordinary market day, looked at the parade of motorcycles and armored cars with astonishment. Horst studied a group of women and children standing near a table displaying strawberries. They huddled together in a frightened knot, intimidated by the German onslaught and not knowing what to expect.

"Pull up in the market square," Horst ordered.

He got on the loudspeaker and in his most authoritative tone issued an announcement: "Attention! All civilians are warned that this city is a military target. It will be bombed. You have one hour to gather your belongings and depart to the west. Do not disregard this warning; we do not wish to harm you, but leaving is your only chance for safety."

There was a moment's hesitation, like a frozen frame in a newsreel, then pandemonium. Mothers screamed and snatched up small children, who an instant before had been playing in the dusty street. Larger children were dragged away by their wrists or herded into houses with sharp words and slaps.

Doors slammed shut and the street was deserted—a conjuring trick. The citizens of Pepinster began to reappear almost at once, bearing precious things and loading them into wagons and wheelbarrows.

Sergeant Fiske tugged on Horst's pant leg. "Begging the major's pardon. Do we have the authority to order an air strike on a purely civilian target?"

"No." Horst shook his head. "But if they believe me, Fiske, and flood the roads across the border in France, preventing the Allies from counterattacking, perhaps it will *save* their town from being bombed for real."

‍⚬‍

The early morning wedding between Miss Bremmer, the English nurse from Jersey, and Jules Sully, the chemistry professor, took place in the chapel of the Ecole de Cavalerie.

Father François Perrin, the priest from the village of Lys, conducted the ceremony. The cadets provided the honor guard. Sepp, Gaston, and Raymond led the troop in a military salute.

The marriage had the same effect, Paul Chardon thought, as some ancient royal union of children from warring nations. Here at the Ecole de Cavalerie, at least, France and England were finally friends!

Blessed event.

There was a lovely reception in the gardens, which were blooming with red roses. It was attended by the British Expeditionary Force medical staff from the surrounding countryside, as well as by French cavalry officers.

Paul, surrounded by Sepp, Gaston, Raymond, and six other cadets, was discussing the possibility that there could be a negotiated peace if the Phony War rocked along many more months. All of the cadets were outraged at the thought of such a thing.

And then came Sister Mitchell. She had not spoken three words to Paul except of necessity since that cold night in the stable some months before. She had attempted to convince Paul not to approve the marriage of Miss Bremmer and Jules Sully. She had claimed it was not fitting. Now she raised her champagne glass slightly and gave an almost Gallic shrug to indicate that he had been right and she wrong.

It was gratifying. As she approached, the cadets murmured, bowed stiffly, and dispersed. Paul supposed that they were afraid of being rounded up to collect the dirty dishes or help the caterers distribute hors d'oeuvres.

Paul was left to face her alone.

"A lovely wedding, don't you think, Captain Chardon?"

"If one likes weddings. Which I do." He sipped his champagne.

"So do I." She raised her chin as if to challenge him to dispute her.

He narrowed his eyes. "Only a cold, unfeeling individual with anti-septic in her veins could—"

She stopped his jibe with a hand on his sleeve. "Please, Captain. There is no person with whom I have so enjoyed conflict as you. Animosity between us has been quite . . . stimulating. However . . ."

"I see what you mean. Something exciting to think about during the long, lonely hours in the empty and sterile CCS?"

"Something like that." She looked past him to where the happy couple was being congratulated by the cadets. "I was wrong. About a lot of things. I wanted to apologize."

"In that case"—he raised his glass in salute—"I will tell you something I wanted to say since the first moment I saw you."

She grimaced. "It sounds terrible."

"Yes. Terrible, only because you do not let anyone say it to you."

"Then say it."

"All right. You are beautiful."

She laughed and put her hand self-consciously to the top button of her uniform.

"You are beautiful," he continued, "and—" he leaned close to her and inhaled—"today you smell like Chanel."

"Borrowed."

"You should have a bottle for yourself. It is much better than camphor."

"I suppose I should say thank you."

"Yes."

"Thank you." She lowered her eyes shyly. "Is that all?"

"No. Some months ago I considered asking you to dinner. But I was afraid you would inspect the kitchen of the restaurant and scrub the cook before we ate. So I did not ask."

"If I promise to behave myself?" A smile twinkled in her eyes.

"Then we should be friends," he announced. "Or we should dine together at least once to see if it is possible for one so English and one so French to remain civil for an entire evening. Yes?"

"Yes."

"In that case I must ask you if you possess anything to wear besides the scarlet cloak. I am a bit intimidated by it, you know."

Abigail Mitchell's response was interrupted by a sudden droning overhead. All the military personnel ran outside to watch as the sky darkened with flight after flight of German bombers.

11

Targets of Opportunity

The fanlight window above the door of the French Embassy lay shattered across the sidewalk as Josie and Andre loaded luggage and children into the Citroën. Juliette was frantic about her grandfather in Luxembourg. The Nazis were coming. Were they not the same men who had taken her mother away?

Andre assured her that Monsieur Snow was likely on his way to Paris. But she must go to England and be safe and happy when he came. This comforted her. Clutching her doll tightly, she did not cry. But Josie thought there had never been such sad and knowing eyes in a child.

Except for broken windows and the bellied-out building across the square, there was very little damage evident in the streets of Brussels. Red Cross ambulances clanged by, heading in the direction of the airport. For the moment there was no news of the North Train Station. Had it escaped the raid unharmed? Would the train to the Channel still be running?

Josie secretly hoped that the train would be delayed or canceled altogether. She wanted to go back to Paris with Andre when he left this morning.

But that was not to be. North Station was untouched by German bombs or stray Belgian antiaircraft fire. It resounded with the babble of confusion as panicked citizens pushed toward the green train that chuffed impatiently at the siding.

Andre carried Juliette on his shoulders, safely above the crush. He parted the sea of bodies ahead of Josie by using a suitcase as a shield. Coming at last to the open door of a second-class car, he held other people back and jerked a frightened French poilu from his seat.

Once Josie and her charges were safely seated, Andre gave the man a shake and threw him from the train. "The war is in the opposite direction," Andre called harshly. "French deserters will be shot!"

The soldier scrambled to his feet and, the instant Andre turned back to Josie, skittered off into the packed crowd.

The train whistle shrilled. Andre stooped to kiss Josie.

"You always were good at controlling riots in train stations." She touched his cheek and tried to smile up at him. "The first time I ever saw you . . ."

"Be safe. Remember I love you," he replied, kissing her again. Then to Juliette, lodged between Josie and a hefty gray-haired woman with a green parakeet in a cage, he said, "Well, Juliette, I hope we will meet again very soon."

"*Oui*, Monsieur." She nodded. "Maman used to say I have your eyes, Monsieur Chardon. Your eyes are so very sad when they look at me."

"It is only because . . ." He could hardly speak. "My eyes long to look at you always because you are so beautiful."

She smiled shyly at his compliment.

"But you see, Juliette, sometimes we cannot have everything we wish. And so I am sad," he concluded.

The child threw her arms around his neck and embraced him. "Tell my grandpapa when you see him in Paris I am having a very exciting time. I have never been to England. Tell him I will see him soon."

"I will do that, *ma chèrie*."

The whistle shrilled a second time. The shout of the conductor sounded over the racket. Andre squeezed Juliette's hand one last time, then backed out of the car and slammed the door. He watched as the train chugged slowly out of the station.

ᴑᴑ

Andre's black Citroën rounded a curve at high speed. Blitzkrieg had released the terrors of war on the population of western Europe, but everyone experienced the horror in a little different form.

Now that Josie and Juliette were safely headed out of harm's way, Andre's panic was one of failed duty. He had put his personal concerns above his obligation to France, if only briefly. Richard Lewinski was alone in Paris. Lewinski, who might hold the key to unraveling the German plans and stopping the Wehrmacht steamroller.

Pressing harder on the accelerator, Andre raced out of Brussels toward Lys and the cavalry school. There was still one more personal duty that could not be ignored. He wanted to see Paul, to tell him that it was past time to get the boys away.

He was within fifteen kilometers of the town when the first flight of

Heinkels went over. A squadron of twenty of the stubby, twin-engined planes passed overhead, followed by another group of twenty. Andre ignored them. He suspected that their target was in fact Armentieres, just ahead of him on the road, but there was something he could do about that. He veered to the east to take a country lane around the town, planning to regain the main highway after he had passed the zone of the bombing.

Topping a hill, he could see smoke rising ahead, though he was still too far away to hear the thunder of the bombs. A flight of French Morane fighters streaked into view from the south, climbing to intercept the German bombers.

Not able to help himself, since the show was right in front of him, Andre's eyes flicked upward. His attention was drawn to the aerial combat; then he glanced quickly back to negotiate the curves of the narrow, two-lane road.

The overhead display got more interesting by the minute. A cloud of tiny black dots that were airplanes at a very high altitude began dropping out of the sky. Suddenly the blue canopy was filled with white streaks as ME-109s engaged the Moranes.

A French fighter, streaming black smoke, dove away from the battle. A parachute popped open, the canopy rocking as the pilot floated earthward. Two more 109s circled another Morane. A wing was torn from the French warplane, and the crippled fuselage spun crazily out of control.

Andre's eyes snapped back to the roadway just in time to avoid crashing into an oncoming convoy of trucks. The three-quarter-ton army vehicle in the lead was well over the center, leaving a tiny space on Andre's side. He jerked the steering wheel hard to the right. The wheels of the Citroën dropped onto the shoulder of the road, spurting gravel from under the tires. The rear of the car fishtailed, heading toward the ditch.

Jerking the car back to the left, Andre overcorrected the skid. For an instant it seemed that the auto would straighten out, but the sideways momentum of the slide was too much for it to hold the road.

Andre felt the loss of control. Through the windshield, the world started to spin. Instinctively he lunged toward the passenger side, forcing his body into the tiny space below the seat. The driver's side flipped upward, and everything went black.

ᙆᗠ

The medic in the passing convoy watched in horror as the Citroën rolled over, bounced in the air, and rolled again. It came to rest right side up, just off the shoulder of the road.

"Stop!" the medic called to the driver of the truck. He hurried out of the truck and toward the wrecked Citroën.

The man inside was unconscious, trapped in the tiny space in front of the passenger seat. The medic was amazed the man wasn't dead. He whistled when he saw the insignia of rank designating the bleeding man as a colonel.

A truck was detailed out of the unit to act as an ambulance, carrying the colonel to the military hospital at the Ecole de Cavalerie at Lys.

◎

In spite of the cramped accommodations, the trip from Brussels to Ostend proved to be an interesting one for Josie. Twenty kilometers west of Brussels, the train was shunted onto a siding as a troop train sped by, headed in the opposite direction.

Juliette and Yacov did not mind the delay. Both were fascinated with the green parakeet named Petit Chou, or Little Cabbage. Petit Chou chirped in the small cage that was held by its portly owner named Madame Hasselt. To Josie's delight, the old woman entertained the children by putting the cage in front of her moonlike face and pretending that she was trapped inside the bars like the bird.

When she chirped and cheeped, Petit Chou responded. Even little Yacov laughed a great baby belly laugh, but Josie noted that his eyes were still swollen from a morning of hysteria.

There was no tea trolley on the train and no dining car, but Madame Hasselt shared her black bread and cheese. Josie tried to pay her for the food, but she would not have it.

She was going to Ostend to catch the ferry to England, where her son worked in a Belgian shipping firm. She had been planning the journey a long time before today, so it was an unpleasant surprise when the Germans finally broke their long silence. But Madame Hasselt believed with every certainty that the Boche would be turned back this time, that they would not have their way with Belgium as they had done in the last war. Madame Hasselt did not like the Boche, she confided to Josie. They were dark-hearted beasts. But she would not say more lest she frighten the little ones.

As the train finally lurched forward again, Madame Hasselt allowed Juliette to put her hand in the cage. Petit Chou perched on her finger. Little claws tickled her knuckles, and she giggled. When Juliette laughed, so did Yacov. His joyous howls were infectious, making Juliette laugh harder. This was perhaps the first happiness in an otherwise dreadful day, much to the delight of all the other passengers in the compartment. It was assumed that the two children belonged to Josie and the French colonel. Everyone commented that most certainly this pretty little Juliette looked like her father. There was no mistaking, they noted, that Juliette had the eyes and coloring of the handsome Frenchman.

"My maman always said that also," Juliette agreed, although the implications of that statement did not seem to register with her.

And as for Yacov! Madame Hasselt said she had never seen such a good-natured baby. And after such a terrible day!

Josie agreed that Yacov was a delight and silently wondered what desperation must have forced the child's mother to send such a remarkable little boy so far away.

The playful atmosphere onboard the train came to an abrupt end with the arrival of a German Heinkel. Returning to its base from having completed its bombing mission, the warplane was evidently looking for targets of opportunity when it spotted the train.

Josie barely noticed a dark shape heading for the tracks like an arrow flashing toward its target. She had glanced back at Yacov as he burst out with another peal of laughter, when the significance of the onrushing plane crashed in on her.

The bomber opened fire with its machine guns, raking the length of the train forward from the compartment just ahead of where Josie and the children were riding. The sound of shattering glass and a loud pounding noise, as if someone were swinging a hammer against the metal of the train's skin, mingled with terrified screams.

The Heinkel roared over, pulling up on the far side of the tracks. The train engine's whistle gave a long, drawn-out cry, as if the iron beast had felt the damage inflicted on it.

The bomber made a lazy turn, in full view of the passengers, then swept back toward the train again. Josie pulled a sobbing Juliette down to the floor and covered the girl and Yacov with her own body.

This time the bullets clattered into the car just behind Josie's, killing two people and wounding a third. When the Heinkel climbed into the sunlight after the second pass, it soared away toward Germany.

Incredibly the brakes on the train squealed and the forward movement slowed, even as all the passengers were urging it to speed up and get them away from the killing zone. A pair of conductors came through the cars, asking for doctors or nurses to help with the wounded.

"But why have we stopped?" Josie pleaded. "Can't we go to Ostend and find medical help there?"

"Regrettably, Madame, what you suggest is not possible," said one of the trainmen. "Attention, everyone," he continued in a louder voice. "The train has stopped because the engine has been damaged. It is impossible for us to continue onward. Everyone must get off."

"And what will we do then?" Madame Hasselt asked.

The conductor shrugged. "I myself will walk back to Brussels. I suggest that you do the same."

PART II

It's jolly to look at the map
And finish the foe in a day.
It's not easy to get at the chap;
These neutrals are so in the way.

A.P. Herbert,
Punch *magazine*,
April 1940

12

The Arrival of Blitzkrieg

David "Tinman" Meyer's squadron had moved to a new aerodrome near Reims, in part to provide air cover for the headquarters of the Advanced Air Striking Force that was located there. The transfer had only been completed late on the night of the ninth of May, and A flight was supposed to have the morning to sleep.

It was with irritation that David found himself being awakened. "What's the idea, Corporal?"

"Beg pardon, sir, but the balloon's gone up. Jerry is attacking in force, and the squadron is ordered to cover our bombers."

Shortly afterward two flights of Hurricanes climbed through a thick mist to twenty thousand feet, heading northeast toward the Meuse River. The shadows cast by the early morning light and the swirling ground fog made picking out landmarks difficult.

As the sun grew higher and the mist cleared some, David could see the bend of the river and the town of Sedan on the east bank of the Meuse. He could also see an enormous formation of tanks and artillery that cluttered the main road into the city and stretched back to the far horizon. This had to be the same panzer formation he had seen eighty or more miles away when his plane had crashed. They had crossed all of southern Belgium and were now across the border into France.

"Where are those Blenheims we're supposed to be protecting?" Hewitt questioned over the radio transmitter.

"Perhaps they didn't like the odds and went home," Simpson replied. "No matter. We'll find plenty to occupy ourselves. Dorniers at twelve o'clock, angels five."

"Cheeky buggers, flying so low," Hewitt muttered. "Don't think much of French antiaircraft fire, do they?"

The formation of forty pencil-shaped bombers was plastering their target, the French artillery emplacements west of Sedan. David scanned the skies, locating the fighter cover he was sure accompanied the Dorniers. "Two flights of Messers flanking the Does, angels twelve."

"Roger that, Tinman. And more fighters at angels thirty orbiting north of the town and just waiting to pounce on us."

In all there were more than a hundred enemy aircraft facing a dozen Hurricanes. "Slash and run is the ticket," Simpson ordered. "B flight to engage the 109s flying low cover, A flight to bust through and have a go at the Dorniers. Good hunting, chaps. We're off!"

In contrast to the tactics practiced earlier in the war, the enormous disparity of numbers meant that the RAF rarely had the luxury of ganging up on a single German bomber with a whole section of fighters. As soon as David's section swooped into the middle of the Luftwaffe formation, it was every man for himself.

David selected a Do 17 to attack. He curved in toward it from above and commenced firing at three-quarters' deflection. The angle of his assault propelled *Annie* over the bomber from its port side. The Hurricane's machine guns drew a double line across the German plane's left engine, which began spewing a white cloud of vaporized glycol coolant.

David's pass carried him toward the tail of the next bomber in the formation, which had seen the attack coming and was turning away, climbing into the sun. He had just an instant to loose a burst into its tail surface before he was below the elevation of the Dorniers and had to regain some altitude.

The Hurricane pulled out of its dive and mounted upward when the ME-109s jumped him. A pair of the fighters attacked *Annie* from above, and a burst of machine-gun fire jolted the fuselage in back of the cockpit. The first enemy plane flashed past him, and the second came in fast. David kicked his fighter into a climbing turn. He could not get around quickly enough to face the oncoming Messerschmitt, but the move got him out of its sights. By now, however, the first attacker had reversed its dive and was on David's tail.

Bullets whistled by the cockpit as David banked sharply left, then dove, attempting to shake off his pursuer. The Hurricane's slower speed meant that it would take superior maneuvering to get away, and it had to happen soon or the partner of this pair would return. The two Germans could play him like a pair of foxes driving a rabbit back and forth between them.

"Tinman!" came Hewitt's urgent voice. "On two, break hard left. One! Two!"

David was in no position to question Hewitt's instruction. As soon as "Two!" was pronounced, he yanked the spade grip over, pulling the fighter's right wing up and throwing his plane into a tight left-hand turn at the same moment. This gave an instant in which he was free of the 109's guns and provided Hewitt, who was on the German's tail, a clear shot.

Hewitt's gunfire converged at the optimum range of 250 yards, raking the fuselage of the Messerschmitt from its tail all the way forward to its engine. The Luftwaffe plane rolled over and dove, belly-up, toward the Meuse River.

Hewitt laughed over the radio transmitter. "You're my witness, Tinman. Scratch one Messer, and you owe me a—"

He never had a chance to utter the word *drink*. Pulling out of his spiral, David saw the second 109 rejoin the battle from below. The Messerschmitt's gunfire tore the right wing off Hewitt's Hurricane. It dropped sideways out of the sky, like a duck falls after being blasted by a shotgun.

"Get out of there, Hewitt!" shouted David.

There was no response. David never saw the hatch open. No chute appeared as Hewitt's plane dwindled to a falling speck.

David and the remaining Messerschmitt fired at each other twice more as the aerial combat carried them far north of Sedan. Then David's guns were empty. He put *Annie* on the deck and swept toward the base to rearm.

○○

The arrival of Blitzkrieg on Mac's doorstep changed his plans some. He was stuck in Brussels all day on the tenth, unable to get transport toward the front, as the trains were all requisitioned for troop movements and the roads were packed with military convoys. The Belgian authorities would not give him a pass to ride with their soldiers.

The news Mac heard on the morning of the eleventh of May, as he finally managed to hitch a ride with a passing BEF troop lorry, was good and bad. It was good because the Wehrmacht was doing exactly what they were supposed to do. According to the Allied plan, which had not changed since 1918, the French and British troops would advance rapidly into Belgium to meet the invaders head-on.

But if the good news was good, the bad was fearful. The Nazis were slicing through Holland like a sharp knife through Dutch cheese. And the mighty fortress of Eben Emael, which had been Mac's destination a short time before? Its unprotected roof had received a gliderload of

German paratroops, who blasted their way in. The fortification had already surrendered.

Mac was not even sure how the Allied advance was progressing.

"We was held up crossin' the border from France into Belgium," remarked a private who wore the unicorn emblem of the Fiftieth Northumbrian Infantry Division. "Them border guards wasn't told that we was invited!"

"How'd it work out?" Mac asked.

"Sergeant Major Quinn pointed a Bren gun at the guards and told 'em that the lorries could either go around 'em or over 'em—their choice. The barricade got moved double quick!"

The area assigned to the BEF was a length of the Dyle River just east of Brussels. The troops were supposed to arrive there in one day, but with the road packed with fleeing refugees, it did not look like that could possibly happen.

There was a roar of airplane engines over the highway. Mac's experience in Poland made him jump up, ready to stampede from the lorry into a nearby ditch. The Northumbrians pointed at him and laughed. "What's the matter, mate? Got the wind up already?"

The heavily lumbering warplanes were not Messerschmitts or Stukas. They were Fairey Battle bombers and Blenheims belonging to the RAF.

Mac's face was red as he sat back down, but his mind was still churning an observation. Why wasn't the Luftwaffe challenging the Allied advance? Where were the dive-bomber attacks that had so paralyzed the Polish military movements? It was almost as if the Germans were allowing the Allies an opportunity to get moved into position. Such consideration on the part of the Nazis worried him.

⊙

Josie and Madame Hasselt had started their trek toward safety in tandem and had remained together through the first two harrowing days. Juliette, clutching her doll in one hand and carrying the cage of Petit Chou in the other, tried to keep pace but tired quickly. Their little group split off from the larger group, seeking shade beneath the leafy plane trees. In a ditch beside the road they found a child's wagon, and soon Juliette and Yacov were being pulled along among the hundreds of thousands of civilians attempting to flee Belgium. But where to go?

All the ports of Belgium and Holland were under heavy attack from the Luftwaffe. Ostend had been bombed. The ferries to England were sunk with many drowned, refugees reported as they streamed back from the coast. And Brussels? Bombing had increased at such a rate that those fleeing the capital predicted it could become another Warsaw. Auxiliary train routes were being systematically smashed to halt the movement of troops and equipment.

The Nazi strategy of civilian panic was working with complete success. After the initial advances, French, British, and Belgian troops on the highways slowed to a crawl as they faced hordes of frantic people on every lane. Little Luxembourg had vanished into the Nazi maw. Grand Duchess Charlotte had already fled to France.

It was this final news that shifted the movement of the frightened herd of refugees south toward the border of France. The human tide along the main road swelled and overflowed.

⸙

The roads into the interior of Belgium were filled with traffic going in both directions. The troop lorry of artillerymen in which Mac hitched a ride stopped on the road from Brussels to Leuven when a Bren-gun carrier in front of them broke down. Bren-gun carriers always reminded Mac of toy tanks with the turrets torn off. As capable as they were at crossing fields or traversing marshy ground, when the tracked vehicles stalled on roadways, they were almost impossible to push by hand.

The four soldiers who traveled in the small, open-topped machine jumped off. When their attempt to shove the machine was futile, they appealed to the men in the truck with Mac for help.

"One try, mates," the artillery lieutenant warned. "Then we use the lorry to push her out of the way."

Besides the British troops moving toward the front, heading the opposite direction was a family of refugees. Their dusty shoes were no strangers to the unpaved dirt lanes. They threaded between the troop lorry and the stalled Bren carrier.

Leading the group of civilians caught amid the warring armies was a young man carrying a baby. The youth might have been in the army himself; he looked old enough. As he passed, he yanked his cloth cap low on his forehead and turned away, as if fearful that the soldiers might challenge him for being out of uniform.

But the attention of the Bren-gun crew was focused on the second figure in the eastbound parade. A pretty blond woman in her early twenties pushed a four-wheeled pram loaded with blankets and clothing. She looked tired but determined. The British would have loved to offer her a ride; they hoped that the fellow carrying the baby was her brother and not her husband.

That this family had been prosperous before the war was demonstrated by the figure who came next. The head of the household, wearing his best suit coat and tie, also pushed a baby carriage loaded with belongings. This pram sported a double-chrome bumper and a satin lining, but its rightful occupant had been displaced in favor of a gramophone and a mahogany mantel clock.

Beside the man walked a woman in a heavy, expensive coat, even though the day was warm and the May sun bright on her grim face. Mac wondered how far they could have walked in the two days since the war started and where they would end up before they were through.

A pair of servants in plain black dresses completed the cavalcade. The cook and a maid perhaps? They carried carpetbags over their shoulders and toted two suitcases apiece as they trudged along. From the sour expressions on their faces, it seemed that they had started to wonder whether they would still be paid for all the extra effort.

A whistling sound suddenly screamed high overhead, and a German artillery round blasted a crater in the vineyard beside the road. The shell exploded with a roar, and Mac's three-quarter-ton ride leaped forward as its driver popped the clutch.

"Time's up, lads!" the lieutenant shouted.

The troop lorry rammed the Bren carrier as the soldiers trying to shift it tumbled out of the way. "Come on! Get aboard!" the officer ordered. It took no further suggestion to get the soldiers to move as a second and third high-explosive shell slammed into the roadway, bracketing the travelers. The refugees scattered into the vineyard, throwing themselves away from the highway and deserting their possessions.

Mac swung onto the truck as it backed up hastily from its collision. The soldiers jumped for the running boards, using the motion of the vehicle to swing themselves up, like trick riders in a rodeo. The lorry roared off, carrying four new occupants.

When Mac looked back, he saw no bodies lying in the road. Maybe there were no casualties this time. One of the prams was overturned in a ditch. The other had been crushed by the wheels of the truck. Pieces of smashed mahogany clock and splintered gramophone littered the ground in silent company with the abandoned Bren-gun carrier.

That the Germans were close enough to shell the road to Leuven meant that they were already across the Dyle. Whatever defensive positions the British finally adopted would surrender a huge chunk of Belgium to the Nazis.

⟨♋⟩

The last of the tinned milk was used, and Josie and Madame Hasselt were making little progress. With only a word of agreement between them, they left the main highway and, entering a wooded glen, came upon a dirt track that led to a deserted barn. That night they slept in a hayrick, where the war seemed to be only a bad dream. The star-streaked sky and the scent of hay reminded Josie of her childhood back home. Madame Hasselt prayed quietly and sang the children to sleep. Josie drifted off with them. . . .

Before dawn Josie was awakened by the munching of an abandoned Jersey cow whose udder was swollen with milk. There was a halter on her head, and a lead rope dangled from the leather buckle. What had happened to her owner?

Josie simply reached out and grasped the line, and the cow was captured. As Madame Hasselt held the grateful animal and Juliette stroked the velvet muzzle, Josie milked her. The foursome breakfasted on sweet, warm milk shared from a small tin pot Madame Hasselt had carried with her. The old woman still packed a variety of fine cheeses, two pounds of ham, and chocolate, which she had intended to present to her grandchildren in England.

"A few miles across the border in France there is a boys' cavalry school," Josie said. "I know the chief riding instructor, Paul Chardon. He will help us get to Paris if we can make it that far."

"It will take us several days if we stick to back roads. You see; we are alone here. But look." Madame Hasselt gestured to a thick plume of smoke that billowed up over the treetops a few kilometers to the east. "If we are careful, our provisions will last." Madame Hasselt soaked her feet in a shallow stream at the edge of the pasture. "And this cow? She is sent from heaven." The old woman winked at Juliette. "My dear child, how would you like to ride to France like a princess, on the back of a pretty brown-eyed Jersey cow?"

Juliette conceded that she would like it very much, and so she and her doll were placed atop the sweet-tempered creature. Yacov was perched in front of her. Juliette wrapped her arms around his middle. The cage of Petit Chou was set between the jutting hip bones of the cow. The bird chirped back at other birds in the trees.

"Very well!" the old grandmother declared, cheerfully loading the rest of their belongings into the wagon. She pointed at the dirt lane that meandered through the pasture and into a deep wood. "France is that direction; I am certain."

13

A Harvest of Destruction

The view of the Meuse River valley was anything but encouraging to Horst von Bockman as he stood beside his half-track north of the Belgian town of Dinant. Since his reconnaissance teams had first arrived at the river, French artillery had been bombarding the east bank. Horst had no weapons powerful enough to silence the guns and had ordered his men to pull back while he studied the scene and mentally prepared a report for General Rommel.

On May 12, after two days of offering no opposition to the Wehrmacht's sweep across Belgium, the German forces had finally reached a position that the Allies intended to defend. Small-arms fire crackled from the far shore, shattering the peace of the Sunday afternoon. The Belgian and French soldiers were dug in along the water's edge and prepared to deny any crossing by the Panzer unit. The bridge across the river had been dynamited—a fact Horst was not looking forward to recounting. Rommel had wanted that crossing taken intact. He needed it to keep his vow to von Rundstedt that Seventh Panzer would be first across the Meuse.

Without the bridge, the Meuse in spring was no small obstacle. Draining waters from the Langres Plateau in France all the way to the North Sea, the Meuse at Dinant was deep enough and broad enough for commercial vessels. Tanks got bogged down in marshy ground; in water higher than their treads, they sank like stones.

Horst signaled for a fast scout car to pick him up for the journey rearward to locate General Rommel. The driver took off at high speed, expecting to find the division commander back near the center of the Panzer column advance that stretched for five miles back from the river.

Instead Rommel's specially equipped command vehicle, bristling with radio aerials, was sighted before Horst had traveled even a mile. Unlike most division commanders, Rommel wanted to see the battle-front firsthand.

"Report, Major," Rommel ordered tersely.

Horst explained the situation regarding the bridge and the French artillery, then waited while Rommel pondered.

"Engineers and infantry to the front," Rommel said at last. "We will attempt a crossing by rubber boats. Major, you send a company upstream. See if there are any other suitable openings. Speed is important, and not only because of our present need. Great things are happening. Our paratroops have landed in Rotterdam, and the fortress of Eben Emael has been taken. We must not miss our share of the glory. We must have at least one unit across the river tonight!"

⟨꙰⟩

On the French-held side of the Meuse, north of Dinant, a rifle company commanded by Captain Hugo Ney was dug in beneath the willows overlooking a flood-control weir and an island. The rushing water was soothing, and the shade made this a pleasant place to wait for the war.

Papa Jardin, whose head was too small for his helmet, resembled a turtle peering out from his shell. He leaned back against his cumbersome pack and lit a cigarette as Captain Ney paced and lectured and gestured in the direction of the booming French artillery.

"Listen, men! It is the sound of French victory! Two miles from where we sit, our armee is beating back the Boche. History in the making! And here we sit!" The captain, who claimed to be a distant descendant of Napoleon's great General Ney, was a strutting, irritating young fellow. Every man considered him a fool. Today the Grand Captain Ney was unhappy that his company was missing the glory of battle.

Jardin leaned close to his friend Furfooz, whose eyelids were heavy in the warmth of the day. "This is what I do not understand," Jardin whispered. "Why is it that a French poilu is paid only fifty centimes a day and the English soldier is paid seventeen francs a day? I have two small children in Paris who must live on such poor wages. Do they eat less than the English brats?"

"It is the British who got us into this war, and they sent only ten divisions!" Furfooz jerked his head at the ranting Captain Ney. "And for that we must endure this!"

Jardin nodded. "Our Grand Captain," he scoffed. "Even seventeen francs a day would not be pay enough for this!"

Ney raised his hand and pointed at the weir. His voice was tremulous with lust for battle. "Perhaps we will not miss everything! If we are lucky, we will be able to pick off a few stray Boche. If they would only try to cross the river here! They shall not pass!"

Jardin shrugged. "They shall not pass? That is what they have been saying at the Maginot Line. On the Maginot the poilus sleep indoors. They eat hot food at tables. They have huge guns pointed down the throat of Germany. But this is not the Maginot, Furfooz. This is a river. Suitable for fishing. For eating a picnic. For making love with a woman beside the rushing waters. But I do not fancy shooting across it at someone who might shoot back."

The eyes of Furfooz narrowed into hostile slits as he eyed Ney with contempt. "I tell you who we should shoot first. . . ."

Ney took a stance imitating the great Napoleon: head lofty, legs slightly apart, fingers slipped between the buttons of his tunic. "We shall hold the Boche here, men!"

"He is posing for a bronze," Jardin remarked. "He hopes to die a hero's death."

"Paris has too many statues already," Furfooz commented.

Ney's eyes were alight with imagination as he spoke to the backdrop of the distant booms of artillery and the fire of conflicting tanks. "I say to you, loyal French patriots . . . they shall not pass!"

"He is repeating himself."

The volume of Ney's speech increased. His eyes were wild. His face was flushed with patriotic ardor. "We shall stand our ground here! We shall die to the last man before we let the Boches get by our rifles! France shall revere our memories."

"That is a new thought," Furfooz said glumly. "Now it is not only that the Boche shall not pass, but the Grand Captain adds that we are supposed to all die to stop the Boche from crossing the Meuse."

Jardin wagged his head beneath the shade of his helmet. "I am not for that part of his plan, Furfooz." He drew deeply on his cigarette. "What is the point of that, after all? If we die for France, then what good is France to us?"

Ney stood on a fallen log. ". . . and so, my brave soldiers, remember what it is you fight for! *Vive la France!*"

☙

The scream of a French artillery shell made Horst duck inside the hatch. The concussion of the explosion rocked the armored car as it sped away.

North of Dinant, the river gorge was narrow, with no possibility to deploy the division in strength along a wide front. The terrain west of the river was higher in elevation than that held by the Germans. Allied artillery could, by raining down from behind the shelter of the far line of hills, make it impossible for the column of tanks to remain.

"Pull up," Horst told the driver. Through his field glasses he inspected a flood-control weir built across the Meuse. The rock dam was topped with a skinny path. It led from the near shore to an island midstream and then carried on across a still-intact bridge to the far side. It was far too small to support vehicles, but it might work for men. If enough firepower was moved quickly across the stream, a bridgehead could be established from which infantry could circle behind the French artillery.

Horst radioed Rommel to explain his plan and request that additional motorcycle troops be sent forward. "Approved," Rommel's voice crackled back in agreement. "Pass the coordinates, and we will lay in some mortar fire."

"Any chance of Stukas?" Horst asked, remembering the effectiveness of the dive-bombers in the Polish campaign.

"Negative," came the reply. "I already asked. Enigma transmission from von Rundstedt says the air support has all gone to General Guderian. Even so, I depend on you, Major. The first wave of inflatable boats has been thrown back. Get across!"

Below a concealing rim of willow trees, Horst assembled his troops. A great spiral of 750 cc BMW motorcycles gathered in a clearing, like the coils of a lethal snake preparing to strike. The men were armed with rifles, Mauser machine pistols, and MG-34 light machine guns.

"There will be no further reason for reconnaissance if the division doesn't get over the river," Horst said. "So we are going to dismount and make a dash for the island. Once there, we'll dig in and probe the defenses on the other bank. There is only room to go single file; who will volunteer to be first?"

Captain Grühn raised his hand. "I claim that privilege, Major."

The explosions of the French artillery shells continued from downstream. It was plain that the direct attack by boats was not going well, and the day was winding down toward late afternoon.

"Go!" Horst shouted.

Grühn led off, Mauser in hand. He was followed by five men carrying a pair of machine guns and ammunition boxes. Horst himself led the second wave. The old stone weir looked like a rotting jawbone with some teeth sticking up and many empty sockets. Horst felt naked as he tried to hurry across the slippery rocks, watch his footing, and keep an eye on the far shore—all at the same time. With every running step he ex-

pected the rattle of machine guns and thought he would see the west
bank of the river erupt in a blaze of rifle fire.

Amazingly, no shots were fired at all. Horst's men slipped into the
scrub brush and trees that marked the halfway point. They set up MG-
34s at the far ends of the rocky island and another pair behind an old
lock gate that controlled the outflow of water past the weir.

At a signal from Horst, Grühn waved his arm for his men to follow
him across to the other shore. The instant Grühn stood up on the edge of
the riverbank, a machine gun began to chatter from the French-held
side, and he was cut down without making a sound.

The battle of the weir was joined. A line of bullets stitched the
ground beside Horst, and he flung himself behind a pile of boulders at
the water's edge. He fired his Mauser through a gap in the rocks until the
clip emptied, then reloaded and emptied it again. Fragments of stone
rattled off Horst's helmet as the French fired back.

The first rush of firing stilled as both sides realized that their targets
were well concealed and protected. Horst studied a map and scribbled
some coordinates on a piece of paper. This he handed to Sergeant Fiske,
who had been at his elbow throughout the assault. "Get this to the mortar squad."

Fiske jumped up and ran back across the weir. He jogged from side to
side as bullets traced his progress, slapping into trees and kicking up dirt
beside his path. When he disappeared from view, the firing stopped
again. Horst watched him go, turning when Lieutenant Gelb spoke to
him from behind the wall of the lock gate. "Major? Grühn is dead, sir."

"What other casualties?"

"Two wounded, neither serious. What next?"

"Sit tight and wait. We'll see if some mortar rounds won't stir things
up a little."

Five long minutes passed; then a shadow flitted back to Horst's side.
In the gathering darkness the returning shape of Fiske drew only a single
shot that ricocheted against a rock and whined off down the canyon.
"Fiske! I did not tell you to come back across!"

The sergeant grinned. "You didn't tell me not to, Major. Where else
should I be?"

The deep cough as the first mortar shell launched was joined by others in quick succession, until that noise was drowned out by the detonations of the high explosives as they landed among the French positions.

ᘓ

The Grand Captain Ney continued to exhort his company as another
round of German mortar fire found its mark on the French side of the

Meuse. Willow trees exploded, flinging huge splinters that impaled soldiers to the embankment. Earth and rocks rained down to cover the
men. A machine gun on its tripod soared like a rocket into the air.

Jardin burrowed beneath his pack and pressed his face into the
ground as though trying to crawl beneath it.

"Remember France!" shouted Ney. *"Vive la France!"*

Between deafening detonations the scene was still not silent. Furfooz
covered his ears with his hands and let out one continuous scream,
pausing only to fill his lungs with cordite-thickened air.

"They shall not pass!" Captain Ney shrieked. "Stand like men!" He
stood among his crouching troops. "Get up! Open fire! Hold the Boche!
For France!"

Furfooz, clutching his rifle beneath him, turned on his side, took
aim, and fired. The Grand Captain, his hand still high in the air, opened
his mouth and eyes as if in amazement. His knees buckled, and he fell to
the ground.

"Save yourself!" Jardin howled as he turned his back to the river.
"Sauve qui peut!"

At least twenty men joined him and Furfooz in the mad retreat up
the embankment.

Bullets nipped at Jardin's heels. To his right, four men shrieked in agony and fell back. Ten paces ahead, Furfooz clawed upward. Spinning
around, he stretched his arms out as if in appeal, then tumbled past
Jardin and slid back to land on the body of Captain Ney.

Jardin clutched his helmet to his head and strained toward the top of
the hillside. Behind him the others scrambled over the bodies of their
companions in their headlong flight from the Boche and the River Meuse.

෴

Horst saw the French fighters running up the far slope of the canyon.

"Now!" he yelled. "Machine guns open fire! Rifle squads, across the
river!"

Twenty minutes later, four companies of Seventh Panzer were
rounding up French prisoners and planting their machine guns in new
defensive positions. Horst radioed General Rommel that the division
had its bridgehead on the west bank of the Meuse.

14

The Long and Hard Road

By the thirteenth of May it was clear that the German thrust into Holland and northern Belgium was a device to keep the Allies pinned in a corner. Meanwhile, the real major offensive was hammering at the gates of France, having successfully navigated the Ardennes and crossed the Meuse.

The Allies gave ground grudgingly in Belgium, but the clear danger to their southern flank meant the necessity of withdrawing to a less exposed position. There was never any chance of breaking completely free of Wehrmacht Army Group B and going to the assistance of the embattled French troops in the path of the panzers.

But Mac had no difficulty withdrawing from the battle line. He saw more clearly than the French High Command that the real story of the war was developing between the Belgian town of Dinant and the city of Sedan in France.

He paid a thousand francs for a fifteen-year-old Delfosse sports car. It had no top and the seats showed more of the springs than the leather, but it also had a 3500 cc engine and the ability to cover four hundred kilometers on one tank of petrol. By driving all day, all night, and the next day, Mac hoped to be back in Nancy or wherever the action was on that side of the German advance.

His travel took him south from Brussels to Reims, where he stopped to gulp down some food before going on. The little auberge where he pulled over offered *coq au vin* and an ancient radio that whined and squawked like the ghost of the chicken in the stew as the proprietor attempted to tune in a recognizable sound.

In one of the passes up and down the cracked dial, Mac heard an

English voice announce that they were repeating the words of new Prime Minister Churchill's address to the House of Commons.

"One moment, Monsieur," Mac requested. "I would like to hear what Monsieur Churchill has to say."

The measured tones and carefully chosen phrases of Winston Churchill crackled through the warped, dusty speaker, but the power of his character was unmistakable:

> "I would say to the House, as I said to those who have joined this government: I have nothing to offer but blood, toil, tears, and sweat. You ask, what is our policy? I can say: It is to wage war by sea, land, and air, with all our might and with all the strength God can give us. That is our policy. You ask, what is our aim? I can answer in one word: It is victory. Victory at all costs. Victory in spite of all terror. Victory, however long and hard the road may be; for without victory, there is no survival."

◌◦

The movement of soldiers and a harsh warning about mines placed along the Lys River toward France put Josie's little entourage back on the main highway. The Jersey cow now carried five small children and the parakeet.

The Ecole de Cavalerie was fifty kilometers downriver and across the border in France. Josie looked at the slowly flowing stream that cut across the flatlands and imagined that this same water would be flowing past the Ecole at the exact moment she greeted Paul Chardon. The thought made the journey somehow more bearable.

They passed what remained of the town of Olsene, which had been bombed the night before. The metal girders of the rail bridge across the Lys was twisted like a giant pretzel. Warehouses, homes, and businesses still smoldered. Old people stood in the doorways of their windowless houses and watched with blank faces as the endless stream of people coursed through their main street. Some citizens of Olsene, with carts and little bundles tied on their backs, joined the great exodus.

Automobiles, with mattresses tied on their tops to stop bullets, bullied through the mass. And then there were the bicycles. Endless thousands of men and women and children who had cycled from Holland caught up with the flow just beyond Olsene.

But no mode of transportation was so fine as the Jersey cow. She not only carried the children but fed them as well. Yes, the creature moved slowly. The Dutch cyclists rushed past. But each evening she was led onto some grassy place and allowed to feed. By morning her udder was near to bursting again. Two pails a day were filled. Dozens of little ones were fed. She was a four-legged miracle coveted by all.

A few miles from Olsene the long-suffering column was met by shrieking flocks of British motorcyclists in goggles and leather helmets. They rumbled past, beeping their horns. Giving the thumbs-up sign, they shouted and waved at the children on the Jersey. Startled, the cow gave a low bellow and a little hop, sending all her passengers tumbling onto the ground.

Josie and the Belgian mothers gathered them up again. Set them on the cow. They were not hurt. It was nothing at all. What was a little tumble onto the road compared to the horror happening around them?

In Rotterdam thirty thousand died in one day of bombing. In Brussels fifty schoolchildren perished in one instant when a Messerschmitt emptied its machine guns into them. Beside the travelers the fields were littered with shallow graves of the nameless dead who had done nothing wrong except be there at the wrong time.

The conversation invariably drifted to the proper position to assume while being strafed. To lay outstretched on the ground meant more body surface exposed to the bullets. Best to stand upright, it was decided. Best to lead the cow and its passengers beneath the shade of a poplar tree and wait calmly.

Minutes later a white ring of smoke above the trudging column identified a Messerschmitt circling like a hawk. The fighter plane fell from the sky in perfect mimicry of a raptor's attack, and the crowd on the road scattered like rabbits.

Bicycles were hastily abandoned in crumpled heaps as their riders took cover under hedges. Mothers, trying to track flocks of children, shooed some away even while calling others back. A car careened out of control and knocked down a man pushing a wheelbarrow even before bullets began to plow a harvest of destruction.

Trembling all over, Josie tried to sound calm as she grabbed Yacov so he would not take another fall and led the Jersey off the road and under the tree. She motioned for the children riding the cow to plug their ears with their fingers, as if this were all an elaborate game.

Standing perfectly still, with the Jersey behind the tree trunk and out of sight of the carnage on the road, Josie nevertheless peeked around it herself. An elderly couple, separated by the initial panic, tottered toward each other from opposite sides of the dusty lane.

The bullets of the ME-109 knit them together even as they touched, and as Josie ducked her head and squeezed her eyes shut, they fell into the embrace of death.

∾

Only days after the fighting began, the students of the Ecole de Cavalerie were witnesses to an unusual event. They were turned out of their bunks at dawn and told to form into companies and march to the train station.

"I knew it!" Gaston exulted. "France needs us! We are going to the front!"

"Being sent away, more likely," Sepp said, shaking his head. "They are not going to let us fight."

A special train was on the siding at the rail platform. The cars were lettered *8 Chevaux Ou 40 Hommes.* "Eight horses or forty men," Gaston read. "We are going to the war in horsecars?"

But it soon proved otherwise. When the sliding doors to the railcars were opened, down the ramps came two dozen proud, nervous horses. Following the cavalry steeds, a tiny pony was also led down the walkway.

"What is this?" Gaston wondered aloud. "Are we getting fresh mounts to ride into battle? Who gets the pony? Raymond?"

"Be quiet, you idiot," hissed Sepp as a man dressed in the uniform of a Belgian cavalry officer saluted Captain Chardon. "These are not for us. This is the stable of the royal family of Belgium. Look! That is King Leopold's stallion right there."

The boys were detailed in pairs to walk the horses back to the cavalry school. "Brussels is not safe for them anymore," Sepp said, "so they have been evacuated to stay here."

"Fine thing," Gaston muttered. "It is not right for trained horses or trained men like us to hide back where it is safe. Captain," Gaston called to Paul Chardon, "will we be exercising these animals for the king?"

"Oh no," Paul corrected. "This is just a rest stop for them until this afternoon. We will be sending them on, just as soon as more cars are coupled to the train to take our own broodmares."

"Take them where?"

Paul eyed his young officers. "Farther south. Where it is safe."

∾

It was Juliette who found her. She was only six, and she was weeping in the field beside the body of her mother. Her name was Angelique, and she did not know where they were going, only that they had come a very long way from Ghent.

The mother, who had been a pretty young woman in her late twenties, was buried by an old farmer who had an army spade tucked into the pile on his wheelbarrow. And Juliette, who knew about such things as dead mothers, mothers killed by all varieties of Nazis, let Angelique hold her doll.

Now the Jersey cow carried six children on her back. She did not complain. Josie thought of the two sisters in Paris and remembered the joyous laughter of the children at the orphanage at No. 5 Rue de la Huchette. Surely there would be room for one more little girl who would need to learn to laugh again.

How long would it be before Josie would feel happiness again? She could have wept easily. Raising her eyes from the hilltop, she looked across the miles and miles of road that wound down from Belgium to the border of France. There were the young and the very old, the very rich and the poor, the feeble and the strong—mingled together in one un-broken tide of terror. Numbering two million, this migration of fear marched against the Allied armies, blocking their road to battle more ef-fectively than an enemy artillery barrage.

She glanced back. There seemed to be no beginning to the line. And forward: There was no end to it.

As Josie looked, she could see that Death, the very thing they were fleeing, marched patiently beside them all.

ᘒᗡ

There was no missing the Red Cross symbol painted on the roof of the U-shaped, four-story, brick Ecole de Cavalerie. That is what the cadets and medical personnel said as they dug through the shattered right wing of the building after the lone Heinkel dropped a single bomb that col-lapsed two floors and left a gaping wound in the brick. Two hundred wounded were now dead. One British doctor, four nurses, and two or-derlies had also been killed. But Andre Chardon, Paul's brother, who was still recovering from his automobile accident wounds, had lived.

Paul Chardon dug through the rubble with Sister Abigail Mitchell and several hundred angry cadets, who took the attack as a personal insult.

The operating theatre was moved to the chapel. Summoned from the village by young Gaston during the emergency, Father Perrin and seven-teen nuns from the church at Lys arrived to take the places of the fallen medical staff. There were no more refugees passing through the village. Now it was only the soldiers moving inexorably toward the coast. The ci-vilian population had mostly fled to Paris, Mother Superior told Paul and Sister Mitchell. Was help needed to fight the unmerciful Boche with mercy?

There was no need to ask. Father Perrin was already busy administer-ing last rites. The sisters helped salvage supplies and set up a treatment room. Raymond, his youthful face showing grief beyond his years, formed a burial squad and helped to lay out the dead in long rows.

That afternoon a doctor from Ghent, who had followed the river back to the village by boat, arrived at the docks in front of the town in hopes of acquiring provisions. When Sepp examined his papers and found that he was a physician, he brought the doctor to the chapel at gunpoint.

"But I am an obstetrician!" the man declared.

Sister Mitchell drew herself up in her most formidable pose. She spat the angry words out in English for Sepp to translate in French.

"The most esteemed Sister Mitchell says that you learned to set bones in medical school, Monsieur. You are Belgian, and many of the wounded are your countrymen. You will go to work with the rest of us or this young man—by which she means me—may suspect that you are a Nazi spy and will shoot you as a fifth columnist."

Sepp jabbed the muzzle of his rifle in the doctor's back for emphasis. Soon the Belgian obstetrician was delivering shrapnel from the bodies of French poilus as if he had stopped at the Ecole for that very purpose.

⟨Ѡ⟩

The battle Mac witnessed seemed to demonstrate that the Allied High Command had not been wrong in their assessment of French military muscle after all. After the German tanks rolled out of the forest and through the little town of Longwy, they were met with concentrated fire from the French cannons.

Mac stood beside the forward artillery observer, a calm, middle-aged man with a gray mustache and quick, darting eyes. "New coordinates, 75-10 to 78-4," Captain Druot said into the field telephone. Then to Mac, "I'm sorry, Monsieur. Where were we?"

"I was saying that the accuracy of the French artillery is certainly being verified here today."

"Ah, yes," replied the officer modestly, taking credit for the entire operation but showing humility at the same time. "The Germans cannot advance into such a conflagration."

It was true. The eye of Mac's camera registered three PzKw-IIIs turned to flaming wreckage in the field outside the town. The others turned about and scurried back toward cover as fast as their clanking treads could carry them.

The barrage of sharp, angry sounds from the 75 mm cannon continued cracking. As Captain Druot whispered into his mouthpiece, the sights of the bombardment lifted. The fountains of dirt from the rain of shells pursued the German machines with an effect that was almost comical.

"But of course, artillery cannot do it alone." Druot waved toward an echelon of French tanks that had emerged from around the base of the hill. "Our guns can keep the Boche from taking a position and can even retake an objective. But cannon shells cannot hold a position all alone, you see." He spoke of the 75s with great affection and seemed to be apologetic for the fact that artillery alone could not win the war.

The French armored unit, a mixed force of fast-moving Somuas, tiny two-man Renaults, and one gigantic, lumbering 32-ton Char approached Longwy. They opened up with their machine guns, chasing a pocket of German riflemen out of cover. The Char, carrying a 75 mm weapon of its own, launched a round of such force that the clock tower of the city hall was demolished with one blow.

The German tanks, trying to regroup on the far side of the village, were still being routed by the French artillery. "We have superior artillery and, as you have noted, Monsieur McGrath, clearly equal quality of armor. The courage of our foot soldiers is undoubted. In what respect are we not the match of the Boche?"

The first Stuka dropped out of the sun, followed by three more. Single-minded weapons that carried men on their backs, the dive-bombers fell toward the formation of French tanks. Pulling out of their swoops much lower than the approved height of three thousand feet, the German pilots risked being caught in their own detonating explosives, but the effect was one of firing at point-blank range.

The Char, standing out on the bare field like the Eiffel Tower stands above the skyline of Paris, was singled out first. A five-hundred-pound bomb, released at a thousand feet above the tank, impacted directly on the cannon of the Char. The French machine disappeared in a roar of smoke and flame. When the shower of debris had fallen and the fumes cleared, nothing remained but the barrel of its weapon and a pile of charred metal.

In quick succession, the other Stukas attacked the tank formation. Then it was the turn of the French armor to run for safety. But there was no safety. From their aerial perspective, the German warplanes could pick out the tanks wherever they fled. Unlike the artillery barrage, it was not possible for the French machines to retreat out of range. The dive-bombers pursued them wherever they went.

Mac saw the German troops and their armor advance back into the town recently vacated. Druot, still calm and matter-of-fact in the face of the reversal, issued new coordinates to the guns.

As soon as the French 75s opened up again, new waves of Stukas dropped toward the white streamers from the firing cannons. As if tired of chasing tanks, the dive-bombers unloaded their deadly eggs on the French gun emplacements instead.

One after another, the barking noises of the 75s ceased. Although Druot cranked the telephone and called each of four batteries in turn, he received no further response. A Stuka, returning from having destroyed the pride of the French artillery, spotted Mac and the captain in their exposed position on the hill.

The gull-winged warbird flattened out its dive, skimming the hilltop with its machine guns blazing. Mac threw himself into a slit trench as a furious line of bullets stalked him.

When the gunfire stopped, Mac risked a glance out of the trench. The artillery observer's body reclined on the ground as if he had chosen a pleasant afternoon to watch the passing clouds. In his fist Captain Druot still grasped the handset of the telephone. His sightless eyes stared upward, registering forever a lesson harshly learned: the part of the war in which the French were no match.

☙☙

It was a tiny village with some unpronounceable Flemish name. Josie did not attempt to say it. Traffic was snarled in the center of the square around a fountain and the statue of Jeanne d'Arc. Josie felt an amused revenge against the loaded vehicles that had streaked past them on the main highway earlier in the day. Their horns blared to no avail. They were stuck, while Josie and Madame Hasselt led the little Jersey in and out of the mess with ease.

Some of their larger group had broken off, taking their children with them on a different route to France. Now there were only the cow, Josie, Madame Hasselt, Juliette, Yacov, and solemn little Angelique still clutching Juliette's baby doll.

There were shops open in this unpronounceable place. A miracle!

The provision of Madame Hasselt's ham was gone, the chocolate consumed. The cheeses in her pack were moldy. Here was opportunity to obtain food enough to get them to the border at least. It was worth braving the traffic and the reflected heat off the cobbles.

Josie headed to the cheese shop, which still displayed enormous red waxed wheels in the window. Madame Hasselt was left in charge of the bovine and the children. She removed the three little ones from the back of the cow and let the beast drink slowly and with great satisfaction out of Jeanne d'Arc's fountain.

The queue at the cheese shop was long, but the great rounds of cheese would last awhile yet. The proprietor, in fairness to all, allowed only two pounds per customer. Out of fairness to himself he charged exorbitant prices. People paid him willingly, gratefully. Better to sell the stuff now than to let the Nazis have it, the proprietor remarked. At this, men and women eyed one another uncomfortably. Could the old fellow really mean he believed the Germans would get as far as his cheese shop?

Josie took her place at the end of the line. Progress was slow. Past the red waxed disks and through the plate-glass window, she could see little Angelique sitting on the lip of the fountain with the doll. She appeared cool in spite of the hot sun. Her brown eyes were looking down affectionately at the porcelain face. It was a grubby porcelain face by this time, but Josie figured it would clean up as easily as the live children when they all arrived in Paris. The question at that time would only be if Angelique could be parted from the doll. Josie determined then and there that she would take the child to La Samaritaine and buy her any doll she wanted in the entire store.

But where was Madame Hasselt? Josie cast her eyes around the square, finally spotting the old woman with the cow and Juliette and Yacov standing in another long queue outside the public toilet.

Josie had just gotten to the counter and Madame Hasselt had just tied off the cow and entered the toilet stall when the shriek of an air-raid siren split the air.

Instantly the square had the look of an anthill stamped on by the foot of a giant. Men and women dove out of their automobiles and fought one another to run to shelter in basements and shops.

Then Josie saw Angelique. Fearless, oblivious, the little girl embraced the baby doll and remained on the fountain. Josie cried out and sprinted in an attempt to get to her. But the panic of the mob pushed her back. The snarl of Heinkel engines and the long whistle of bombs were almost drowned out by the screams of the terrified throng. But there beyond the window and the red wheels and the terror was Angelique.

Josie reached the door, only to be thrown back onto the floor as a large man charged in and dove for cover.

The first bomb exploded. Glass shattered, pocking the counter where she had stood. Buildings in the square unfolded like they were made of playing cards. The statue of Jeanne d'Arc collapsed, and tile from the church portico slid down onto it. The second bomb fell a block away, rocking the shop.

And then there was silence, as profound and terrible as if Josie had gone deaf. No moans. No cries for help. Was it over so quickly?

"Is everyone all right?" the cheese man asked feebly.

A dozen people got up slowly. Josie struggled to rise. The door of the public toilet opened, and Madame Hasselt, shaken but unharmed, emerged with Juliette and Yacov into the bright sunlight. The cow had broken her tether but stood serenely chewing her cud a few paces away.

And there was little Angelique . . . still beside the fountain . . . still clutching the doll. So very still.

She was dead, of course. Josie knew it before she stumbled, weeping, across the rubble to the girl's body. Sinking to her knees, she picked up the doll and clutched it to her.

A small crowd gathered around her. Someone asked if Josie was the mother of the dead child.

"No."

"What was her name?" a gendarme asked gently.

"Angelique."

"Her surname?"

"I do not know. Her mother was killed on the road. There is nothing else I can tell you."

From around the corner came a blind man, frantically tapping his way across the square with his cane.

"God pity the blind," said the gendarme.

"The blind are blessed," Josie replied.

15

A New Offensive Line

Since Seventh Panzer had broken out from the bridgehead across the Meuse, it had covered over fifty miles. Not content to be the command that breached the first Allied line of defense, Rommel pushed his men to remain in the forefront of the Blitzkrieg.

The French troops reeled backward in confusion, tangling the reinforcements that were rushed up to stem the rout. The French High Command wanted to draw a new defensive line along the Sambre River.

But the panzer advance followed so closely on the heels of the French retreat that key bridges were still intact. Such was the case when Lieutenant Shultz reconnoitered the highway that led to the river crossing at Aulnoye, just beyond the little town of Avesnes.

Horst assembled his company commanders, including Lieutenant Borger, who had replaced Captain Grühn, for an afternoon conference in Avesnes. "Just think, gentlemen," Horst urged his officers, "Paris is only a hundred miles or so in that direction." He waved his hand toward the southwest. "At our present pace, we could be in sight of the Eiffel Tower in four or five days."

"Does the major think that will happen?" Borger asked.

"Unlikely. In my opinion, OKW wants to make the French *think* our objective is Paris in order to freeze troop movements while we actually strike westward. If we can completely cut off the Allied Army and trap them between us and our force in Holland, the war will be over in two weeks."

A scout car roared into the village square, and an agitated Lieutenant

Shultz jumped out and ran to the group. "Major, the bridge . . . the bridge is still intact!"

"Slow down, Shultz. Borger, give him a drink of water."

When the excited outrider had recovered his breath, he explained that he had encountered no enemy soldiers before reaching a point from which he could see the Sambre. "I backed away as quickly as I could to come and tell you," he said. "I did not want to use the radio in case the French intercepted the transmission."

"How many defenders?"

"Only a handful."

"Any tanks?"

"None that I could see. There was a line of trucks crossing the bridge that I think were full of retreating troops. They must not know we are so close or they wouldn't be so unconcerned."

There was no time to reflect, not a moment to lose. Horst could not even relay to his superiors what he intended. At any moment the French defenders would get news of the German advance and demolish the bridge. "Shultz, you take the lead. Borger, I will ride with you. Gelb, you send all your motorcycles with us, while you find General Rommel and inform him about this opportunity. Tell him that I will attempt to seize the crossing. Request that he send reinforcements at once. Everybody move!"

෴

"I assure you, Monsieur McGrath, this was all foreseen. It is a most well-planned and orderly retrenchment." The captain explaining the fine points of how the French army had intentionally given up half a hundred miles of territory sounded convincing. His performance was somewhat diluted by the fact that he kept looking over his shoulder in the direction of the bridge.

"Then you would not mind if I filmed the movement of troops returning across the Sambre?" Mac studiously avoided using the word *retreat*. He had been warned that even a suggestion that the French army was in flight would mean the confiscation of his camera and possibly get him barred from the front.

"The passage of trucks is not . . . edifying. Why do you not wait until the Boche come to foolishly throw themselves against our defenses? That will be something to witness."

"And when do you expect this battle to take place?"

"Not for two or perhaps three days. Everyone knows that an army cannot advance without artillery, and it takes many hours to move and set up the big cannons. No, Monsieur, the Germans cannot reach here before day after tomorrow. But then, I promise you, there will be something to see!"

"I notice," commented Mac to the thin officer with the prominent Adam's apple, "that your troops are setting up machine guns and wiring the bridge for destruction."

"Ah yes," agreed the captain. "Our engineers are very thorough. All will be in readiness long before the Boche arrive."

～∽∞～

When Horst's column of armored cars and motorcycles arrived at the edge of the hill overlooking Aulnoye, the situation had drastically changed. A pair of machine guns flanked the near end of the bridge, and the ominous snout of an antitank weapon poked out of some brush on the far side. A half-dozen men emerged from the shadows beneath the bridge, each carrying a spool of wire. The strands were joined into a single braid, and one man began backing across to the western side.

The same tall figure who had stretched the final strand of the demolition cord returned across the bridge and spoke to the gunners. The machine-gun crews broke down their weapons and hefted them to carry over.

The armored car of Lieutenant Shultz raced forward, spraying bullets from the gun in its turret. One of the French machine-gun crew turned toward the oncoming Germans and was shot down; the others dropped the tripods and weapons and fled.

The French antitank gun roared, and a shell shattered a tree trunk beside the road. Horst's column was closing rapidly on the bridge, with less than two hundred yards to go. Rifle bullets pinged off the armor on the scout cars. A motorcyclist near Horst threw up his hands and crashed as a slug hit him in the face.

The antitank gun fired again, and an armor-piercing shell sliced through Shultz's vehicle. The armored car slewed sideways in the roadway, then rolled over and over until coming to rest upside down.

"Jog left," Horst ordered Borger at the controls of what was now the lead car. The maneuver was intended to spoil the aim of the antitank crew and spread out the targets. The Kfz 231s took advantage of an open area in front of the bridge to move apart, flanking the approach to the span.

The machine guns of the German attackers replied to the rifle fire. The antitank gun fired again, a high-explosive round this time, with deadly effect. The shell missed the front rank of German machines and landed in the middle of a group of motorcycles, killing three men.

The armored car to the right of Horst cut back into line with the roadway, attempting to make a crossing while the antitank crew was reloading. Halfway over, a high-explosive round took it squarely in front, flipping the vehicle over backward in a great gout of flame. Now the bridge was blocked.

⊙

A bullet went through Mac's camera case where it sat on a tree stump. He dove for cover behind a wood fence, then hastily abandoned the spot when more bullets sailed between the gap in the rails to kick up small explosions in the dirt behind him. Crawling on his belly and pushing the camera ahead of him, Mac wormed his way to the reassuring shelter of a rock wall.

The French rifle fire that responded to the German MG-34s sounded puny by comparison. There was no chance for the poilus to reassemble their machine guns. The only effective weapon the defenders possessed, it seemed, was the 25 mm Hotchkiss antitank gun. It was keeping up a rapid and potent barrage that had already destroyed several vehicles in the charge down the hill.

Mac's DeVry camera poked over the stones like the periscope of a U-boat. He continued grinding frame after frame of the activity around the scene, which his escort had dismissed as not edifying. Mac thought that the film would prove very educational. How was it that the Germans had arrived twenty minutes after the captain had pronounced that it would be at least forty-eight hours? And no artillery barrage had preceded this attack. The German motorcycles and armored cars that flung themselves against the defenses of the bridge were staking everything on the speed of their assault.

How had French intelligence failed so badly? Or was it a failure of imagination? The French General Staff had not been in Poland, nor had they been interested in discussing the tactics of Blitzkrieg. General Gamelin and his cohorts believed that the strength of the French army could resist the initial German offensive, after which the war would stalemate again until the Allied stranglehold on the German economy dragged them to the peace table.

That idea seemed as likely to explode as the armored car that had reached the midpoint of the bridge before being blown into a heap of flaming rubble. That was the whole picture, Mac decided. The antitank gun, like the French strategy, was adequate only if the foe did exactly what you expected. But German tactics, like the armored cars now spreading out across the town square and pouring their flanking fire into the French positions, were not so predictable.

As Mac peeked through a gap in the stones that he hoped was too obscure for a bullet to find, an odd footrace developed. On the near side of the Sambre, the engineer who had been in charge of the demolition detail grabbed a rifle and sprinted onto the bridge. Across the river, another armored car slewed to a sideways halt, and a figure in a German uniform emerged to challenge the Frenchman for possession of the bridge.

◇

"Knock out the gun!" Horst ordered Borger. He jumped out of the armored car to lead an attack on foot. Horst expected the bridge to disintegrate in front of him at any second. Surprise was lost and the delay was too great.

That was when Horst spotted the French officer in charge of the demolition detail sprinting toward the center of the bridge. It could mean only one thing: The charge had failed to explode electrically and the man was going to try to set it off by hand.

Horst fired his Luger and missed, then was forced to duck behind the stonework of bridge abutment as a stream of bullets sought him. When the shooting stopped, he jumped up. The French officer leaned over the center of the trestle, aiming a rifle at the charges below. Horst fired again, hitting the Frenchman in the leg and spinning him around. The man sagged against the railing but squeezed off a shot that passed between Horst's arm and his body.

Tossing the now-empty pistol aside, Horst leaped for the French officer's throat. The two men wrestled on the roadway, while the French antitank gun roared above their heads and the German machine guns chattered back. Another armored car exploded.

Horst hammered his fist into the Frenchman's face. The wounded man swung his rifle up from the ground, and the barrel hit Horst in the side of the head, knocking him away. The French officer rolled on top of Horst and pressed his rifle across Horst's throat.

A pool of burning gasoline spread out from the destroyed armored car. Horst could see the puddle of fire running closer and closer to his face. He could feel the heat as he struggled to breathe, to dislodge the weight pressing him toward blackness.

Flinging up his legs while grasping the Frenchman's rifle as a pivot, Horst planted both boots in the man's midsection and kicked. The force of the jolt broke the tug-of-war for the rifle and propelled the Frenchman through the air. He landed in the pool of fiery gasoline. His uniform blazing, the man jumped up, screaming. He climbed over the railing of the bridge and flung himself into the river.

The antitank gun exploded in a shattering roar. From back up the hill, a German PzKw-38 tank fired again, and its high-explosive round annihilated another pocket of French defenders. Two more PzKw-38s, made in the captured arms factories of occupied Czechoslovakia, moved out of the woods and flanked the scene, their machine guns tearing up the remaining cover on the west side of the Sambre.

A bit of ragged white cloth appeared on the end of a French bayonet. "Enough," cried a poilu. "We surrender. *La guerre est fini.* The war is done."

∽✥∾

Mac continued filming as the 37 mm shells landed only a hundred feet or so in front of him. But when the tank commanders started walking the shell fire even closer to the stone wall behind which he had taken refuge, it was time to leave. The captain who was his chaperone was already back in the car and waving for Mac to hurry.

"Rejoin your units!" the officer was saying to a group of poilus who surrounded the car. They were demanding to be driven away from the Germans. "Find your commander at once!"

"What for?" one of them growled. "The officers are all either captured or dead already. I have no wish to join them. But you may, since you are so heroic!" The burly soldier grabbed the scrawny captain by the neck and, dragging him out through the car window, threw him to the ground.

"This is desertion! You . . . ," the captain began, subsiding when three French rifles pointed at his bobbing throat.

"Be very still and we will not have to shoot you," the chief of the mutiny promised.

"Hold on a minute," said Mac, hurrying up. Two of the rifles swiveled to cover him. He displayed his camera. "I am not an officer, and I need a ride. How about it?"

"Why not?" the ringleader agreed. "It is time someone reported the truth about this debacle."

"You are betraying France!" shouted the captain in a brave tone, although he had not moved from the round.

The poilu shrugged. "Our ignorant generals betrayed France first. We are only following their lead."

16

In the Path of the Advance

The distant *crump*s of artillery sounded like thunder booming out of a clear sky as Josie and Madame Hasselt led the Jersey cow through the ancient stone gate of the Flemish town of Courtrai on the fifteenth of May. Courtrai was situated along the River Lys. Across the border and a few miles downstream was the Ecole de Cavalerie, but the school seemed very much out of reach to Josie this afternoon.

Before the war, Courtrai had been famous for the manufacture of lace and table linen. Today it was the last major Belgian stop before the frontier crossing into France.

Now little Courtrai was overflowing with human flotsam. Old men and women and children all slept in the cobbled square and drank and washed in the public fountains.

The airfield had been bombed on the first day, as had the train station. But though the roar of battles was clearly audible, the ancient Flemish town itself was miraculously unharmed. It was clearly in the path of the advance, however.

For now, St. Martin's Church, opposite the sixteenth-century belfry of the town hall, opened its doors to feed the hungry. The Church of Notre Dame was now a BEF Casualty Clearing Station, being filled hourly by freshly wounded soldiers from the front. In the chapel behind the choir men were being operated on beneath a Van Dyck painting called *Raising of the Cross*. The picture of suffering seemed appropriate in such a place, Josie thought when she was told about it. Rumor was that the Belgian army was being crucified by the panzers. The Germans had broken through the line at the Meuse, and a pall of gloom hung over the place.

Madame Hasselt had a sister in Courtrai. By this she meant that her sister was a member of a lay sisterhood called the Beguines, who lived in a gray cloister across the square. Could they stay the night and rest in real beds before pushing on?

Madame Hasselt knocked on the centuries-old gate, asked to see Sister Madeline, and was admitted while Josie and the children were asked to wait.

Ten minutes passed, and an aerial dogfight took place overhead. Josie could not tell which planes were Allies and which were Germans. Two spiraled downward in flames and exploded in the flax acreage beyond the walled city. Others made white, smoky circles above Courtrai, as if to mark its location for bombers.

Yacov was cranky from a slight sunburn. Juliette, who was quite ragged now, stretched out on the back of her cow and watched the distant air battle without emotion. She held up the cage of Petit Chou and poked her finger through the bars in boredom.

And then the gate opened on the serene courtyard, and the orb of Madame Hasselt's face beamed out. "Come in! Come in!" She motioned to them. "Bring the cow!" She applauded herself happily. "There is a BEF medical officer here to discuss the care of additional British wounded at the cloister! I have traded the milk cow to his hospital for a ride across the border to Armentieres for you and the children. I will stay here in the convent with my sister."

❧

Gustave Bertrand was waiting in the study when Andre finally arrived home. He seemed not to notice the bandage on Andre's head. After all, what was one little head wound when all of France was getting its brains kicked out?

"It took you long enough." Bertrand was irritable.

"As you can see. . . ." Andre put a hand to his head.

"I hope this does not mean you will not be able to think straight. They have changed the codes again, you know. At the most critical time. And Lewinski with his miracle machine cannot seem to figure out the riddle this time." Bertrand was clearly impatient with the fiery-haired scientist. "I've got to get back to Vignolles." He stood, then remembering something, dug in his pocket and handed Andre the yellow envelope of a telegram. It was open.

"What does it say?" Andre asked with a hint of sarcasm.

"Our Anastasie intelligence service has chopped it up pretty good, but it says that Josephine arrived safely. At least I think that's what it says." He snatched his hat from the coatrack and jammed it onto his head. "Now, if that lunatic in your basement comes up with something, you know where I will be. In the meantime, the new British prime minister is flying into Paris tomorrow for an enlightening meeting with our fearless leader, General Gamelin. Be there. For the historical interest it is not something you would want to miss, at any rate. Our senile old general lecturing Churchill, who predicted every wrong turn our government has taken over the years!" And then, in a grieving voice, "Why did our soldiers not hold the line at Meuse, Andre? How did we let the Meuse be crossed? Is our honor dead?"

"Only sleeping," Andre remarked bitterly.

"Yes. Well. We may lose Paris and France because of this little snooze. Good day, Andre. I know my way out." With that, Bertrand hurried out of the house and sped away in his staff car.

Alone, Andre sat down slowly behind his desk and slipped Josie's telegram from its envelope. The paper was filled with black marks— words crossed out by the censors until only the barest essence of the message remained.

> DIFFICULTY CROSSING TO THE . . . ALL SAFE AT . . .
> COMING SOON TO . . . SEE YOU . . . LOVE, JOSIE

Filling in the missing pieces, Andre read the message as he assumed she had written it: She had experienced difficulty crossing the Channel. She and the children were finally safe in England. They were coming to . . . someplace . . . maybe London?

"Thank God they are out of here." Andre sighed. His head was throbbing.

～☾♡☽～

The next day Andre met the Flamingo light plane when it arrived at Le Bourget Airport, carrying Prime Minister Churchill and his staff assistant, General Hastings Ismay. Andre's head was still wrapped in bandages, and he was afraid he would look foolish.

"Andre, dear boy!" Churchill exclaimed. "How good to see you up and about. I heard about your injury. Clemmie and I were very concerned for you."

Andre grinned ruefully. "Tell Clemmie that she and I now have something in common, and tell her that she did much better with her automobile accident than I did with mine."

The reason for Churchill's decision to fly to Paris had hinged on an impassioned phone call from French Premier Reynaud. "All is lost,"

Reynaud's voice had gasped in Churchill's ear. "The Germans will be in Paris in two days!"

"Tell me the truth, Andre," Churchill urged as they rode in the limousine toward Quai d'Orsay. "Is it as bad as all that? This attack began only six days ago."

"There has been a breakthrough near Sedan," Andre said. "But I am sorry to say that I was not made privy to the details. I will be as much a student at this lesson as you."

Churchill snorted. It was evident the idea of sitting while General Gamelin lectured chafed him.

The spacious consultation room on the ground floor was occupied by Gamelin, Premier Reynaud, and Defense Minister Daladier. Near the fireplace was an easel bearing a map of the French northeastern provinces.

"Mr. Premier," Churchill addressed Reynaud, "how sad that our first official meeting as heads of our respective governments should come at such at hour."

The diminutive man with the features of Mickey Mouse wrung his hands. "It is worse than sad. It is tragic!"

Gamelin lectured with all the pomposity Andre had expected. "This black mark I have drawn on the map represents the front line."

Churchill nodded his understanding, as if the chart were not self-explanatory.

"And this bulge," Gamelin continued, "represents a breakthrough of German tanks in the area of Sedan."

"How big and how deep a penetration?" Churchill asked.

Gamelin looked unhappy at being interrupted. "As I was about to say," he said peevishly, "the gap is one hundred kilometers wide and one hundred kilometers deep."

"And has it been contained?"

Gamelin nodded. "Surrounded, sealed off. I am afraid our esteemed premier has exaggerated the danger."

Andre thought that if Gamelin was not worried, that fact by itself was tremendous cause for concern.

Reynaud was certainly not reassured. "The German tanks are exploiting the gap. They are racing toward Amiens . . . Arras . . . even Abbeville on the coast. Or perhaps they will turn south and strike at Paris."

Churchill tried to sound reassuring. "But surely, Mr. Premier, a counterattack launched against the flanks of this corridor would prove efficacious." Turning to Gamelin he asked, "How many divisions are there in reserve for such a counterthrust?"

"There are no reserves," the commander in chief replied blandly. "Oh, eight or nine divisions can be withdrawn from elsewhere, and I can order another eight or nine sent from Africa in . . . two weeks, perhaps three."

Churchill and Andre were alike stunned at the news. No reserves, and the French reeling back before the hammer blows of the Panzerkorps? Churchill pursed his lips and asked judiciously, "And what assistance are you seeking from us?"

"Planes!" Reynaud interjected. "Fighters to deal with the terrible menace of the Stukas and the other German bombers. Our artillery can deal with the tanks if we do not have to face bombers."

Churchill pondered a moment, though he had come prepared for this request. "I can offer four additional squadrons."

"It is not enough!" Reynaud pleaded. "We need more."

Gamelin actually looked pleased at his leader's discomfiture.

"I will seek approval to release an additional six, for a total of ten," Churchill said at last. "But that is the absolute limit. The rest must be *reserved*—" he laid extra stress on the word, staring at Gamelin as he did so—"reserved for defense. You understand."

Reynaud was almost pathetically grateful. "Thank you! That will make the difference. We will turn the tide now; you will see."

Churchill approved of the return of confidence in the premier, but he also wanted to know how the French really planned to deal with the German thrust. "And the counterattack?" he quizzed Gamelin.

The commander shrugged. "We have inferior numbers . . . inferior equipment . . . inferior methods. . . ." The rest of the sentence expired in the air and fell to the floor. This was the response from the man who had presided over the training and equipping of the present French army.

"I am sure you will find a way to cope with the situation," Churchill said, but his expression showed he was dubious. "And now I must go telephone my cabinet in regard to the fighter squadrons." Passing near Reynaud but close enough for Andre to overhear, Churchill muttered to the premier, "You must get rid of him."

Reynaud bobbed his head nervously and hurried out of the room. Gamelin covered the map with a cloth. He wore a satisfied expression, as if a successful lecture equated to a successful military victory.

Churchill paused before exiting the room as a square green object hurtled past the window of the conference room to explode like a bomb in the courtyard. Another followed and another. A cloud of smoke drifted upward in front of Churchill's view, carrying fragments of burning paper on the rising drafts. "What is that?" Churchill asked. "What is going on?"

"The government office upstairs," Daladier said. "We are burning the secret files . . . as a precaution."

Fish in a Barrel

It was the second pullback in three days. "Don't return after this patrol," Wing Commander Brown told David's flight. "Too much chance of being caught on the ground by another raid. We're moving back again. Your personal effects will come by truck. Good luck and good hunting."

David's Hurricane was orbiting at twenty-five-thousand feet when Simpson's voice clicked over the radio.

"Right," Simpson said. "A half-dozen Heinkels without escort at angels twelve, twenty miles north. Tallyho!"

It was a situation tailor-made for a fighter pilot: slow-flying enemy planes without fighter protection too close by to miss and too much lower in altitude to escape. Covering the distance was a matter of three minutes. David scanned the space below him for the group of bombers. Then suddenly there they were. "Fish in a barrel," David muttered.

"They've seen us," Simpson reported as the Heinkels began to break formation and scatter. "I'll take the leader. Jones, yours is the next clockwise; Meyer, the next to port. Watch your six."

David's first pass on the Heinkel 111 shattered the top turret's Plexiglas and silenced the machine gunner. He came back on the clumsy aircraft from its opposite quarter, just as the German pilot was attempting a roll-away from his attack. The stream of fire from David's eight machine guns converged on the underside of the Heinkel. As David rocketed past, a ball of flame and a concussion shook the Hurricane. It was obvious that these bombers had been intercepted before delivering their payloads. Five thousand pounds of high explosive had detonated, disintegrating the German plane in midair.

David's altitude was now down to eight thousand feet, so he put *Annie* into a steep climb to regain some height. As soon as the nose pointed skyward, David gasped at what he saw and got on the radio. "Simpson," he called urgently. "Forty more Heinkels on the way in from northeast. They have top cover, too . . . looks like twenty . . . no, make that thirty 109s."

"Roger that," Simpson responded. "I'll try to get us some more for our side. Pick out a partner; looks like the dance is in full swing!"

David roared at the Heinkels from underneath this time, loosing a burst at the port-side wing of one as he swept upward. There was no time for a return pass; the accompanying Messerschmitts had seen him and were already beginning their pounce.

At a severe disadvantage because of his lower elevation and slowed by the climb, David could do nothing but meet the enemy head-on. As the range toward the swooping German fighter closed to under a quarter mile, David fired a short burst and then another. The Nazi pilot was firing back, but was more intent on not colliding with David than on his gunnery. The two planes jerked violently apart at a distance of mere yards, without damage to either.

When David came out of his bank and roll, two more Messerschmitts were on his tail. He ducked away from one, using the Hurricane's tighter turning ability. The first enemy attacker hurtled by, and David was able to turn toward the other in another headlong rush.

He took more deliberate aim this time and saw the line of his bullets converge on the 109's nose. An instant later David was rewarded by an eruption of black smoke from the Messerschmitt's engine. It fluttered from side to side, like a dog shaking its head, then dropped away.

David followed, loosing another short stream into the tail of the enemy fighter. After a final burst, his ammunition was exhausted. This was no place to be without a weapon. The Heinkels had taken the opportunity to disappear, but the sky was still full of dogfighting Hurricanes and 109s. Obviously Simpson's call for more players on the side of the RAF had been answered.

One of the latecomers was in trouble. David watched a Hurricane ten thousand feet above him get into a losing tussle with a pair of Messerschmitts. David was streaking for home himself, but he kept an eye on the damaged British plane as it tumbled like a leaf out of the fight. The Germans must have figured it was done for, because they left off pursuing it and took out after another Hurricane.

When the falling aircraft reached David's altitude, it regained some measure of control. The pilot was able to level out, even though the plane was trailing smoke. David moved *Annie* to join formation with the injured one. He recognized the numbers on the craft as belonging to the First Squadron, together with the identification letter *K*. Who flew the plane designated *K* in First Squadron? David could not remember.

The injured Hurricane seemed to be able to fly all right, but David could see what part of the difficulty was: An oil line had been shattered and covered the windscreen with a thick black layer. On the radio David announced, "Hurricane K, this is Meyer. I am formatted on your left wing. I can see your problem and I can help. I'll guide you home. What's your engine temp reading?"

"I . . . I . . . don't know," replied a voice that betrayed near panic barely under control.

Suddenly David remembered who it was that flew the airplane in First Squadron with the letter *K*. He recognized the voice. It was David's longtime nemesis, Badger Cross!

"What do you mean, don't know?" David asked, trying to keep the contempt he felt out of his voice.

"When the hot oil . . . I opened the canopy . . . my eyes and my hands are . . . help me, Meyer! I'm blind!"

"Pop the hatch and hit the silk," David urged Badger Cross. "Get out of there!"

"I tried!" Cross' voice screamed through the earphones. "The hatch is jammed! It won't open any farther!"

"Hammer on it!" David shouted back as though the two men could hear each other through the twenty yards of air that separated the two planes.

"My hands are burned. Burned! Do you understand? All I can do is hang on to the stick!"

Swallowing hard and trying to think what to do, David got back on the radio. "All right, Cross. I'm with you. Just do exactly as I say, and you'll be all right."

David knew what had happened. When the Messerschmitt's bullets had pierced the oil line on the Hurricane, the hot oil streaming over the engine manifold had filled the cockpit with smoke. Cross had cracked the canopy to clear the fumes, but the slipstream had sucked the boiling lubricant over his hands as they reached up to open the hatch and directly into his face. Now with the canopy jammed, it was impossible for the man to bail out.

David began searching for a suitable field. Without being able to get a picture of the oil pressure and the engine temperature in the stricken craft, there was no way to tell how soon the engine would seize up. It was essential to get down as quickly as possible.

"Meyer!" came Cross' anxious voice. "Where are you? You can't leave me!"

Gritting his teeth, David replied, "I'm right here, Cross, and I'll stay right here. Keep it steady and level for now. I'm just hunting for a clear space."

Over rolling hills and forested terrain they flew, each passing moment decreasing Cross' chances of survival. Not that they had ever been good. How to talk a blind, crippled flier down from ten thousand feet while hurling through the air at three hundred miles an hour in a machine about to break at any minute was not in any course of instruction David had ever had.

There was a field coming up. It looked flat enough, and there were no obvious ditches or rocks sticking out. "Okay, Cross," David radioed. "There's your field coming up now. We need to kill some altitude, so when I count to three, I want a nice easy dive and a gentle bank left."

Through the oil-streaked glass of Cross' canopy, David could barely make out the hunched-over figure of the pilot. "Relax," David said. "Pretend this is back in the old Tiger Moth training days, and I'm sitting in the backseat telling you what to do next."

The gradual circuits of the field brought them down to fifteen hundred feet. David maintained a running monologue about routine things, keeping his voice even. "Bring the nose up a touch, Cross. That's it; you're doing fine." If David let so much as half a minute go by in silence, Cross began yelling over the radio. The man seemed certain that David would abandon him.

David moved the *Annie* into a direct line astern of Cross. "All right now, pay attention. You are lined up perfectly with the field. When I say to, cut your engine. Don't move the stick or rudder, and you'll glide right in. Got it?"

Silence from the other plane.

"Cross, did you hear me?"

A very meek voice replied, "Don't kill me, Meyer. Don't let me die. I'm trusting you."

"Cut your engine now! Now, Cross, do it! You'll overshoot the field! Trust me, Cross, cut it now!"

The engine of Cross' fighter stopped, and it began to drop away from David toward the ground.

David put his Hurricane into another gentle circle of the field to observe the result of his coaching. He held his breath as Cross swept down toward the pasture below. The extra moments of power caused by hesitation carried the plane farther out than David had planned.

At the far end of the grassy area were a hedge and a row of trees. As David watched helplessly, the other aircraft touched down, bounced, and ran on at high speed toward the end of the field. "Brake!" David ordered sharply. "Brake again! Now kick it around to port, Cross. Do it!"

The Hurricane ran headlong into the hedgerow. David could not tell if Cross had ever applied the brakes or had remained frozen in place. When the Hurricane connected with the brush, the tail flipped into the air. The fighter plane collapsed sideways toward the ground and ended the crash upside down.

"Cross!" David radioed. "Cross, do you read me?"

There was no response.

David's fuel gauge showed that he had enough fuel to make Auberive, but just barely. He circled the downed plane a final time, looking for any sign of life, and then flew off toward the west.

⌒

"Are you completely clear on your orders, Major?" General Rommel's question was very pointed. With many other commanders a subordinate would have been intimidated into acquiescing whether he understood or not. But Rommel was different, a natural leader. He had personally directed river crossings and had stood his ground while artillery shells rained down, killing men as close as a few feet from him. If there was a remaining question, he would not ridicule a man for asking it.

"No, sir," Horst admitted. "That is, I am clear on the order, but not the intent. I am to spread my entire command into six columns at the extreme left flank of the division. On your signal we are to thrust north and then east around the town of Cambrai. The columns are to remain separated by one-hundred-yard intervals, and we are to make as much dust as possible. Is that all correct, sir?"

"Perfectly," Rommel agreed. "Do you know the history of Cambrai, Major?"

"Just what I remember from the war college classes, sir . . . in fact, I believe it was in one you taught. Cambrai is the site of the first major tank engagement ever. It is recorded as a British victory in the Great War, although they were unable to hold their gains."

"Very good, Major. Highest marks. From that battle came the standard doctrine that tanks must always accompany the infantry and never operate as independent units. The French and the British still believe this, which is why there are no true armored divisions such as our panzers among the Allied forces."

"I am sorry, sir, but I must be failing this class. I don't see the connection between the history and our present plan of attack."

"The chief benefit of tank attack is fear, Major. Fear of being overwhelmed. Fear of facing a steel-hided beast, while you are armed with a popgun. The British General Fuller had the right idea, but he was before his time. His tanks could travel at only five or six kilometers per hour.

Ours can do close to fifty! Today we will see what intimidation can really accomplish. Go on now. We move out in one hour."

Armored cars in the lead, flanked and followed by motorcycles, Horst ordered the drivers to weave as they drove among the plowed fields and country lanes, stirring the dust into plumes.

~∞~

Mac's view of the countryside around Cambrai was excellent, since he and the city's mayor were standing in the belfry of the cathedral. From his perch he could look down on the walls of chalky white stone that distinguished the ancient city of Cambrai from its redbrick, industrial-age neighbors.

The mayor pointed out the gateway called the Porte de Paris, built in the 1300s. "And 150 kilometers south *is* Paris," explained the short man with an ill-fitting toupee and a warlike attitude. "A great many of the cowardly among our citizens have taken that road in the last week, Monsieur."

Mac scanned the sprawling municipal plaza, over which hovered the cupola of the Hotel de Ville, the city hall. The large square was crammed with people thronging the pavement, gawking at the exotic Oriental statues on the clock tower, and leaving behind their discarded garbage. "But your population does not seem to have shrunk, Monsieur the mayor."

"They are not *our* people," replied the official, shaking his fist. "They are Dutch refugees, Belgian refugees, even—" he paused to load his words with disgust—"deserters among the crowd, Monsieur. Men who should be at the front defending France from the Boche!"

Mac panned his camera over the plaza, giving his viewers a high shot of the mass of humans who had run before the Wehrmacht. The truth of the mayor's words was apparent. There were a number of French soldiers in the throng. Some had discarded half their uniforms and their equipment; none seemed to have weapons. Over his shoulder to the mayor Mac remarked, "What is the plan for the defense of the city?"

"Defense?" the administrator repeated, one hand holding his hairpiece against a gust of wind. "We have a garrison of infantry here, Monsieur, who will fight to the death. No tanks, no cannons, no planes. But we are a bulwark of the southern line of our army. We will hold the Germans here and give our forces time to launch the counterattack. We will arm the citizens for the love of France!"

Mac raised the camera's lens and swung it slowly around the horizon, then turned to study the little man. "I think you'll soon get your chance, Mayor. Take a look there." He indicated the rising pillars of dust that grew in the south and crept closer, encircling the city from the west. Black masses of moving vehicles could be seen below the swirling columns.

"*Sacre bleu!* They are supposed to go west! They are not supposed to come here. Not today!"

Mac had pivoted the camera from the approaching German forces to record the mayor's reaction—warlike, defiant. What he got was the back of the man's coat as he retreated abruptly down the stairs and a shot of a forlorn toupee, blown off by the wind and lying on the stones.

ᴄᴐ

As soon as the German advance swept toward Cambrai, hundreds of civilians began to appear. They carried baskets of clothing, pushed carts loaded with furniture, toted bottles of some precious vintage wines. Among the throngs that walked with heads down, not looking at the invaders, were weaponless French soldiers in dirty uniforms.

Horst studied the dispirited faces. One French soldier glanced up and caught Horst looking at him. The man quickly turned his head to the side, moved to put a horse-drawn cart loaded with children between himself and the major, and shuffled even faster away from Cambrai. Horst thought that for that man and the others, the war was over. He could imagine what the effect would be on French morale when they saw the number of deserters, and they had not even fired a shot.

Nor did the Germans. The mayor of Cambrai advanced to meet the encircling force with a bedsheet as a flag of truce. It was longer than the little man was tall and threatened to trip him about every third step. "*Mon general,*" the mayor addressed Rommel. "Will you please spare our city? When the garrison saw the immense size of your force and we heard it was the Phantom Division, with your terrible and unstoppable tanks, we knew that resistance was futile. We surrender completely. Only please do not unleash your tanks on Cambrai."

ᴄᴐ

Mac moved northward away from Cambrai with a mass of others who did not trust the goodwill of the Germans enough to either remain in the city or try to cross the battle lines by heading south. North was where the Allied Army lay and some hope of stopping the Germans before they reached the Channel.

As Mac hiked along the dusty road toward Lille, he fell in step beside a man wearing the uniform trousers of a poilu. The man had no tunic, no helmet, no weapon. He looked at Mac without interest, then returned to staring at his shoes, as if seeking something in the dirt.

"What is your name?" Mac asked casually.

"Jardin," the man said without looking up.

"Where is your regiment?"

"I do not have any idea."

"Are you trying to find it?"

"What for?" the man asked suspiciously.

There was no reply to this that did not sound antagonistic, and Mac remembered the quick tempers of the deserters who had fled the battle at the Sambre. "Your rifle?" he said instead.

"Too heavy for this hot weather," Jardin replied. "Besides, it was rusty. And there are plenty more." He pointed to the side of the road where discarded rifles, cartridge belts, even a French machine gun lay alongside grenades.

"Did you fight the Germans?"

"Proudly," said the man in a voice of bitterness and no pride at all. "At Dinant, on the Meuse. And later, at . . . I forget the name."

"After Dinant, did you *see* Germans?"

Jardin frowned. "It was not required. We know they are unstoppable. Someone yelled, 'Save yourself,' and . . . that was all."

"And now?"

Jardin finally looked at Mac. "It was not supposed to be this way, Monsieur. All I wanted was some money to send home to my children and a pension for my old age. What will happen to them? The politicians have betrayed us. They did not tell us the truth about this war, which they said was no war at all."

᭞

"Phantom Division. I like that," Rommel remarked to Horst at a conference after the town of Cambrai had capitulated. "How little they know about the accuracy of that statement."

"Sorry, sir. I guess I still do not follow."

"It is all right, Major. No reason why you should, but I can explain now. You see, your battalion was the 'immense force.' My tanks are still back east of the town, waiting for fuel and ammunition to catch up with us. Intimidation is a very real and effective weapon."

By the time Blitzkrieg was in its ninth day, the Allies were falling back everywhere, giving ground, abandoning defensive positions. On May 17, Colonel de Gaulle had counterattacked near the fourteenth-century battlefield of Crecy. It was a brave attempt to break the Nazi momentum but failed for lack of coordination. One hundred fifty French tanks were ambushed by, in de Gaulle's words, "a forest of antitank guns." The promised infantry support failed to materialize. The air arm of the French forces could not hold off the Stukas. In the end, the panzers brushed de Gaulle aside and swept onward.

On the eighteenth, General Guderian's Second Panzer took the town of St. Quentin before eight o'clock in the morning. Forty of the precious few French warplanes that remained were somehow caught on the ground near Cambrai and shot to pieces. And Cambrai itself had surrendered to Rommel without a struggle.

It was clear that by the end of the day on the nineteenth, all Hitler's panzers would be in place for the final push to the Channel. General Weygand, a feisty old campaigner, was reportedly in Paris to replace Gamelin as French commander in chief. But what any one man could do to stem the tide was impossible to say.

The mood around Andre Chardon's home was one of unrelieved gloom, despite the fact that Lewinski had deciphered the change in the Enigma settings. It had taken the genius only ten days to figure out the new substitution, but it was almost too late to matter.

It was anticlimactic. The movements of Guderian and Rommel were not exactly secret any longer. And with the speed of the advance, the panzers were outstripping their own orders. How could any message de-coded in even one day be valuable when towns were being overrun in a matter of hours?

Andre, Lewinski, and Bertrand pondered what was to be done. All knew that the information they possessed was valuable only if it could also be made timely.

When the Wehrmacht reached the sea, as would likely happen in a day or two at most, the Allied forces would be cut in two. The French and British armies that had advanced into Belgium when the conflict began would be surrounded and pressed against the seashore.

The three friends pondered. "When the Nazis went into Poland," Lewinski recalled, "the only thing I could think about was getting out."

Andre nodded, then shrugged, uncertain how that observation helped. "We may all wish to be somewhere else soon. Especially the sol-diers caught in the pocket at the Channel. And they *will* be caught unless they can walk on water." He slapped his hands together, punctuating the importance of the thought. "It is the only solution, of course."

"Evacuation?" Bertrand said.

"Certainly! The British navy might be able to rescue a hundred, maybe even two hundred thousand men, to fight again."

"But no one in our High Command talks anything but nonsense. They are convinced that the British army is not trying hard enough to break out. It is almost as if they have been watching some other war and are still trying to draw a line and dig some trenches!" Bertrand snorted his derision. "I do not think Weygand will have any better ideas, either."

"I bet the British General Gort would listen," Andre said.

"Even if he did, how could we get the Germans to stop rolling over everything? Can we say to them, 'Excuse us, but would you please stop shooting long enough for us to rescue a couple hundred thousand troops?' "

"What if a major counterattack punched a hole in the weakest point of their lines?"

"At least it would slow them down, make them blink," mused Bertrand aloud.

"And Enigma can tell us where that fragile link is found!" said Andre with rising excitement. "Look at this!" He read over the most recently de-ciphered messages. "It tells Rommel to expect to be joined on the east by a newly formed SS infantry division."

Bertrand caught the idea at once. "New ground troops, coming late to an operation where the experience and the heavy armor are in ad-vance of them. Rommel's division is already stretched thin and is the closest to the Allied forces." Then Bertrand's enthusiasm waned. "You know the High Command will never go for this."

"I know," said Andre, "but Gort will. His eyes are open to reality." Then to Lewinski, Andre urged, "Decode any remaining intercepts and keep doing it as they come in. It is critical that we have the most current information possible about the positioning of the SS troops."

When Lewinski had retreated back down the stairs, Andre drew Bertrand aside. "I know that I am the one who will have to go. And even if our plan succeeds, I will not be able to get back across the lines. Take care of Lewinski for me, will you, Bertrand?"

Bertrand grinned ruefully. "Why do you get all the easy jobs?"

Josie and the children rode from Belgium to the Ecole de Cavalerie in the front seat of an ambulance. The officer roared over the road like a demented taxi driver.

Outside Armentieres, he crossed the Lys River on a bridge that was already wired with explosives and barricaded on both sides. Which side of the river would the Germans attempt to cross . . . if they came?

"It is a precaution only, Madame," the officer said. "The Boche will never get this far."

But Josie wondered about it all the same.

Yacov slept soundly in her arms as if he had toddled all the way from Belgium and now could not keep his eyes open one moment longer. Juliette, her stubby legs jutting out toward the gearshift, slept against Josie's arm with the same exhaustion.

Josie and the officer talked about the Americans. Would they again come to the aid of France? Josie remembered the songs the veterans had sung at Fourth of July picnics at the Fort Smith Electric Park beside the Arkansas River. *"Oh! Madamoiselle from Armenteer, parlay-voo . . ."*

This time the Yanks weren't coming. The old songs would not be sung on the banks of the Lys in 1940. Roosevelt had too much at stake with a third-term election coming up to enter a war.

The ambulance passed ragged pilgrims with their battered luggage and their bent birdcages and their crying babies and the old people in wheelchairs. All had tear-swollen faces and bewildered eyes. They looked up enviously as the ambulance sped by. What they would give for a lift to anywhere, Josie knew.

A short time later, the high, elegant walls and the red roof of the Ecole de Cavalerie loomed above the budding poplar trees. A line of lorries and ambulances was stopped at a checkpoint manned by a dozen armed youngsters who wore the dark tin hats of the poilus. They took their duty with a seriousness Josie had not seen anywhere else in her long journey. Beneath the brim of their helmets, their beardless faces were solemn as they narrowed their eyes and studied the documents of each ambulance crew and lorry driver. Teams of youths opened the backs of the vehicles and, rifles at the ready, peered in to search for secreted enemy who might wish to take the hospital and the school by treachery.

It was an oddly comforting ritual. Even with the ever-present threat of Stukas appearing overhead, she felt almost safe for the first time since the bombs had fallen on Brussels. How many days ago had that been? Or was it years?

"And this is Madame Marlow." The driver indicated Josie with a jerk of his thumb. "American."

"Papers, please." This boy had a scruffy attempt at a goatee sprouting on his chin. His eyes were dark and earnest.

Josie passed him her precious documents and those of Juliette and the baby. The thought occurred to her that the young cadet might wish to frisk the baby before he was finished.

"I am a good friend of Captain Paul Chardon," she added.

The boy's goatee jutted out with new interest. He smiled. "Ah yes! I remember now! You are the . . . the . . . very, very good friend of our commander's brother; is it not so? I am Sepp." He tugged his beard. "You see. It has grown; has it not?"

Josie laughed for the first time in days. "It" seemed no fuller than last time, but she agreed that it was a most wonderful beard and that he was certainly doing well at his post.

And they were waved through cheerfully.

Paul, looking anything but cheerful, was in his office when Josie knocked at the door. He was on the telephone to Gort's BEF headquarters. He patiently discussed the importance of evacuating the wounded because there were new casualties arriving each hour. There were no more beds and only a few hundred cadets to defend the perimeter if the Germans should make their swing toward the coast.

Juliette, clutching the doll, stood at Josie's side. With Yacov still sound asleep in her arms, Josie waited until Paul replaced the handset with a frustrated clatter before she spoke.

It took a moment for Paul to register who she was. Then, "Josephine?" He rose quickly to embrace her.

She began to cry now as the dam of emotion finally burst. She leaned against him, and he patted her back in a clumsy attempt to comfort, like he was patting the neck of a good horse after a grueling race. *Dear Paul.*

"I was going to Ostend. . . . Andre sent me. . . . Juliette and the baby . . . the train was . . . oh, Paul!"

"Yes, *ma chèrie*. All the way from Brussels you have walked?" He asked this in English and then led her to a chair.

Taking the hand of Juliette, he knelt before her and brushed a strand of hair back from her face. "And you are very pretty, Mam'zelle Juliette." He lapsed back into French.

She was ragged and dirty, but the eyes of Andre in miniature gravely considered him. "How do you know my name, Monsieur?" she asked.

"It is a name that fits someone so beautiful, and you are the most beautiful little girl I have seen in a very long time." He laughed as poor Josie continued to weep with relief. "I will kiss your hand, *chèrie*."

He did so, which brought a slight smile to the child's lips. Her face was smudged with grime.

"My name is Paul, and you are quite safe now. I have a chocolate in my desk. I was saving it for someone so beautiful as you are. Would you like it?"

She nodded eagerly. The ordeal was finished.

"I will see that you are well cared for here at my school. And soon we will see you to Paris."

❦

73 Squadron had experienced so many combat losses by the nineteenth of May that David was made Acting Flight Leader of B flight. But he led a unit that consisted of only four Hurricanes. Even worse, the other three pilots were all new replacements, with only limited combat experience.

Jimmy Small was American, like David. Tay Churchman was Australian, and Jeffrey Cameron was a Scot. Small had once attacked a Heinkel off the Thames estuary. Of the other two, Churchman had only seen German aircraft from a distance. Cameron had never seen one at all, only pictures.

Cameron had not even expected to stay in France. He was a ferry pilot, bringing over one of the preciously allotted replacement fighters. Simpson, now the squadron leader, pressed him into service as a combat flier.

"Do you like that Hurricane you brought us?" Simpson asked as Cameron was invited for a drink in the squadron mess.

"Yes, Squadron Leader. It's a fine machine."

"Any problems to speak of?"

"None. I would say that it is in tip-top shape."

"You had better hope you're right, my lad, because as of right now, it's yours. Tinman, meet your new pilot."

Despite Cameron's protest, David's only discussion with Simpson involved seeing that Advanced Striking Force HQ was notified. "You heard the same story I did," David warned, "about the ferry pilot who got recruited into Number 1 Squadron and was sent up that same afternoon."

"What about him? What happened?" Cameron broke in.

David exchanged glances with Simpson. "He bought it in the first engagement," David explained. "But no one could remember his name, and since he had not been properly enrolled, well . . ."

"Don't worry, lad," Simpson reassured the Scot. "I'll see to it that you are properly listed as one of us."

Cameron still looked worried an hour later when the squadron was scrambled to provide cover for a mission of Blenheims. The British bombers were attacking the German advance at the crossing of the Oise Canal. The intent was to protect the French town of Le Cateau.

Because of the inexperience of his flight, David was to fly high cover only. They would assist if A flight got in trouble and then retreat to a high vantage point.

"You'll be all right," David told Cameron. "You fly on my wing and keep an eye on six o'clock and you'll do fine."

What else was there to say? Even experienced pilots like Hewitt and Cross had bought it. It was a fact of war.

Orbiting at twenty thousand feet, the squadron saw neither Blenheims nor enemies for almost an hour. "Stood up again," Simpson broadcast on the R/T. "Pack it in, chaps. Let's head for home."

Clouds extended down to ten thousand feet, and it was while passing a gap in a pair of the towering columns of white mist that Simpson spotted the formation of bombers at last. There were twenty of them, heading east, and they were flying below the base of the clouds.

The whole squadron dove to form up on the bombers, but when the maneuver was only halfway completed, Simpson announced a change. "Correction," he radioed calmly. "Those are Heinkels, not Blenheims, and they seem to be unescorted. Tallyho, chaps."

Simpson ordered a formation that swept the Hurricanes back in a diagonal line from Simpson at the leading left-hand end of the line. Because there were no German fighters around, David's flight joined in the attack.

The squadron pounced on the HE-111s and caught them unaware. The first pass sent one Heinkel breaking out of formation and spiraling downward. Another was left slowly losing altitude with one dead engine. None of the Hurricanes were hit.

But on the second attack, the Germans changed tactics. The V formations of bombers fought as units, rather than as individual ships. They concentrated their fire on one Hurricane at a time. As the leader,

Simpson drew an especially large share of tracers. He shot down another HE-111; then white smoke began trailing from his airplane.

"Rotten luck," David heard him say. "Caught one in the engine coolant somewhere."

"Can you make it back?" David radioed.

"Don't think so. Engine's overheating. I'll try to make Le Cateau."

The squadron had racked up three definite kills and possibly five when they broke off the attack and headed for home. David was now leading both flights, and he intended for them to stay with Simpson until reaching the nearby airfield.

"There it is, and none too soon," Simpson radioed. "I'll rejoin you just as soon as I can. Simpson out."

From the formation altitude at ten thousand feet, David watched his friend's gentle descent toward Le Cateau. It looked smooth until Simpson's Hurricane reached five thousand feet, when black puffs of flak began to appear all around him.

"Pull the override and get out of there," David demanded over the R/T.

"It's no good," Simpson responded. "No power. Get the chicks home safely, will you, Tinman?"

A cluster of four bursts of antiaircraft fire erupted directly in front of Simpson. Pieces of his engine cowling and canopy flew off as if the Hurricane were shedding. Then the airframe shattered completely, raining fragments of the British fighter over the airfield of Le Cateau.

When David got the rest of the squadron back to base, he reported the downed Heinkels and Simpson's death. "How could those French gunners be so stupid?" he asked angrily.

"Don't blame the French," he was told. "The Germans were already across the canal and captured Le Cateau before you ever got there."

19

Refugees at Gare du Nord

Josephine was at least clean when she stepped from the train at Gare du Nord. That was more than could be said for the masses of refugees who had accompanied her and the children on their journey.

Josie remembered how empty and gloomy the station had been when she had returned to Paris last fall. *A few ragged porters. Old women in felt slippers pushing wide brooms across clean, uncluttered floors . . .*

It was instantly clear that Paris had been changed to the very core after only a little more than one week of war. The great station resounded with suffering. Dutch and Belgians and French—so many tragic and innocent faces. Faces reflecting confusion and bitterness and loss and rage and weariness now filled the cavernous hall of departure.

Thousands slept beside their baggage on the once-spotless floors. Quaking old grandparents with parchment skin watched over small children. Mothers rested or stared blankly at the gilt clock face as if it could tell them what the next hours would bring. Where were the fathers? And where were the sons?

French Boy Scouts provided some order to the chaos. They helped people off the trains and stacked bicycles and issued claim checks for so many thousands that the true owners of the cycles would never be found. Bicycles overflowed the check rooms and lined the walls to tower over the clusters of refugees who had grown together like little villages becoming one vast city.

There were Red Cross stations at either end of the Gare. Long queues were formed for the bathing and dressing of blistered feet and the patching of wounds and the feeding of the multitudes.

There, in the eye of the storm, was Madame Rose Smith, washing the bloody feet of an old peasant woman while she instructed a young, wealthy Parisian volunteer with soft hands to go out and find nipples for the baby bottles and bring back diapers, too.

Josie caught her eye and waved, pointing at Yacov, who gaped wide-eyed at the confusion around him. Madame Rose gave her the same thumbs-up sign Josie had seen among the soldiers at the front.

"Come by later," Rose mouthed. There was too much going on to stop even for a minute, so Josie headed for the exit of Gare du Nord and the taxi stand.

Once again Josie had no luggage. She carried Yacov on her hip. Juliette, her little fingers hooked in Josie's belt, trailed along. No children were allowed in Foyer International, so Paul had given Josie the key to the Chardon house on Quai d'Anjou. No doubt Andre would be off some-where with all the other men of his age. They were all somewhere else.

The taxis were also gone. They had been confiscated by the army, it was explained, on the same day that Paris had been declared a part of the Zone des Armees.

So they rode the train to Notre Dame Station, the closest metro to the Chardon house. Hoping that Andre would miraculously be home, Josie decided to knock first.

The flustered face of Colonel Gustave Bertrand appeared at the door. "Josephine!" He seemed startled by her appearance. "We thought you were in London!"

"As Chamberlain said, I missed the bus, Colonel Bertrand. Now, will you let me in or must I stand here in the hot sun until the Germans come?"

Flustered, he stepped aside. "Andre is gone off to the front, wherever that may be. The servants have gone south. I have to get to Vignolles. You must stay with Lewinski for the sake of France!" Not waiting for her to reply, he hurriedly scrawled out his private telephone number and gave it to her. "Keep him in the house until I come for him."

"But when will Andre be back?"

"Who can say?"

"When will you—"

"I will telephone. You are leaving Paris as well then?" He glanced at the children, as if it was no surprise she had two little ones in tow. *"There are strays everywhere in the city these days,"* his expression seemed to say. "The Boche will begin bombing soon; we are certain of it. Most of Paris is sending the children away. You might want to think of doing the same . . . wherever they come from, they will be better off elsewhere. Get them on a train if you can." He called down the stairs to Lewinski, "Madame Josephine Marlow is here to stay with you, Lewinski!"

"Good!" Lewinski shouted up. "Finally a red rose to look at instead of a croaking toad!"

Bertrand grimaced. It was clear the two men did not get along. "Too much! Too much! He is a madman! Good luck, Josephine." And then he was gone without explanation or apology.

◌〰◌

Jerome Jardin and the five Goldblatt brothers, Jewish refugees from Austria, were not Boy Scouts, yet they were given Red Cross armbands by Madame Rose, and they worked hard at the bicycle racks in Gare du Nord.

Blue-uniformed gendarmes swung their nightsticks and walked casually among the refugees as if they were strolling through the Tuileries gardens. But the station was no garden. It did not smell of flowers. The gendarmes were checking and rechecking the papers of all the refugees because clever Hitler had sent in many fifth columnists with them, it was rumored.

Jerome felt sorry for the refugees. Even on his worst day he had not been as bad off as these pitiful creatures. It had occurred to him many times that he could steal one of the better bicycles and get out of Paris.

Eleven-year-old Georg, the eldest of the brothers, said as much out loud. "You know, we could each steal one of these bicycles and pedal off to the south of France."

Jerome surprised himself with his reply. "Madame Rose would not like it."

"So what?" Georg tossed another tagged bike on the heap.

"That would be stealing," Jerome said. He felt himself pale at such unexpected words, for how many times had he done just that?

"Who would know?" Georg put his hands on his hips.

"God." The Name just blurted out! No stopping it! He had definitely been around Madame Rose too long!

Georg wiped his nose on the back of his hand and gave a slight snarl. He looked very tough. Jerome thought that it was too bad the Germans did not like Jews because Georg would have made such a fierce soldier. They had missed a good thing, those Nazis.

"Well, well! God, is it?" Georg picked up a bicycle off the vast heap. "You see this? The Nazis melted down all the bikes in Austria after they came so they could make them into bombs! Ha! So what do you think those Stukas are dropping on our heads now?"

"Bicycles?" Jerome chirped. *An amazing thought.*

"My bike, to be exact! You think we should leave them any more to drop and kill people?"

"Probably not. If you put it that way."

Georg whistled long and loud and made a *boom* sound. "Gears and spokes and handlebars! *Ker-pow!* It is immoral!"

Georg was talking himself and his brothers into taking those potential bombs and defusing them by riding off to the Riviera. They might all have done so if it had not been for the sudden wailing that erupted from the young woman holding a baby not far from the stack.

A gendarme was speaking quietly to her, trying very hard to take the baby. "But the child is dead, Madame," the policeman pleaded.

"*No!*" she wailed. "You cannot take him! You must not take my baby!"

It was a pitiful sight. Others gathered around and tried to talk her into giving up the dead child. She insisted he was not dead. But Jerome could see plainly that he was. Very gray. Very still. His tiny arm hung awkwardly from the blanket.

Now the mother kicked out at the officer. She drew a knife and held it to her own heart. He stepped back. It was very sad. The five brothers forgot all about the temptations at their fingertips.

"Poor thing," whispered Georg. "Poor lady."

"Get Madame Rose," Jerome said. And he and the brothers ran the length of the terminal to fetch her.

With a grave expression, Madame Rose left her station. Like she was marching to war, she came with the boys to the scene of the tragic confrontation.

Somehow the crowd of onlookers knew at her approach that she was someone who could help. They parted for her instantly.

She turned on them all and growled, "Get back to your own business! All of you!"

What fierce and angry eyes she had. Even though there was no business for anyone in Gare du Nord to get back to, they all pretended to have other things to do.

Jerome and Georg and the brothers returned to the bicycles. They fussed with the hubs and observed the scene through the spokes.

Madame Rose stuck her lower lip out and waved her hands as though she were shooing away a bunch of dogs. And then she turned and knelt before the wild-eyed woman. But at a distance.

Jerome could not hear what the old woman said, but all the gruffness melted away. Now she was the Madame Rose who rocked the little children to sleep and told angel stories to the ones frightened in the dark.

The fear on the frantic face of the mother melted. She looked at her dead child.

Grief!

She looked at Madame Rose.

Help me!

Madame Rose stretched out her square and calloused hand. She shook her head and looked up toward heaven.

Could it be?

The mother touched the infant's cheek. She buried her face against the tiny body.

Madame Rose, on her knees, came close enough to put her big, strong arms around the mother. The woman leaned against her just like the children at No. 5 Rue de la Huchette did. She sobbed and sobbed, and Madame Rose let her cry as long as she wanted.

It was a long time. And then it was over.

Jerome read the lips of the young woman as she passed the child to Madame Rose.

"Take him then. He belongs to God."

ᥫᦔ

Lord Gort, commander of the British Expeditionary Force in France, tightened his thin lips into a disapproving line. The visit of Colonel Andre Chardon was an interruption.

Even in the pale, early morning light of the twentieth of May, Gort was already hard at work. All around him on the floor of his headquarters were discarded maps of Northern France. Each was marked with troop movements and enemy positions; each had become outdated and useless in a matter of hours. The speed of the German Lightning War made the concept of a static front line obsolete.

"I believe you are who you claim to be, Colonel. Otherwise I would have had you arrested. But why haven't you approached your own High Command—General Georges or General Billotte—with this information?"

"I tried to, sir. I am either ignored or not believed. In the case of the new commander in chief, Weygand, I am told that he is too busy getting the 'big picture' to be bothered with 'tactical details.' No one else wants to make a decision this important without testing it for the approval of Weygand, so on and on it goes."

Gort was a hearty, bluff man. Straightforward in his speech and actions, he also was angry with politicians who played at things military and generals who had political motives. He put his hand to his square jaw and pondered a moment. "I can understand your frustration, Chardon."

The new French Commander in Chief Weygand, age seventy-three, had been recalled from the Near East to replace General Gamelin. Since his appointment to the Supreme Command, he had issued no new orders and spent his time "acquainting himself" with what was a rapidly deteriorating situation.

"All right, Colonel. What is this urgent secret news?"

"The German drive will pivot north tomorrow. Guderian will continue on to the seacoast near Abbeville. Rommel will swing toward the Channel at the Belgian border to cut off any port of resupply and reinforcement. Wehrmacht Army Group B will pinch in from the northeast."

Gort swung his chair around to study the map that remained on the wall behind him. "At the rate they have been gaining ground, we should begin pulling back immediately to save any Channel port at all," he mused, "even for evacuation." Then, despite Andre's presence, he said, "It makes sense. They have us in a bag, and they would like to draw the string around the top. You must know that a rescue operation may be our only remaining option."

Andre nodded. This was exactly the situation he knew Gort would recognize and the reason he was willing to exceed his authority in sharing the secret Enigma message. "Here is one piece of good news from the same source: Rommel's division is stretched quite thin in the vicinity of Arras, General. And behind him in the line is a brand-new, untried SS infantry division."

Gort saw the opportunity. "I could order General Franklyn to attack south, try to break through at Arras. But to do so will mean weakening our forces engaged in supporting the Belgians. How can we be certain that your information is correct?"

"I've thought of that, sir. According to our intelligence, Guderian is about to divide his forces. First Panzer will aim for Calais and Second Panzer for Boulogne. This separation will confirm that our intercepts are true."

"And what is the identity of the new unit joining Rommel?"

"They are called the *Totenkopf*—the Death's Head Division."

"Very well, Colonel. If your predictions are confirmed today, then I will order an attempt to break the German advance at Arras. Perhaps we will force our way out of this box."

20

Determining Factors

On the twenty-first of May, Seventh Panzer was just south of Arras, the capital of the French province of Artois. Only sixty miles separated it from the English Channel. Rommel was ordered to turn north. The movement would cut off the retreating Allies from possible reinforcement or evacuation through the ports of Boulogne and Calais. The general was not happy about the order because it meant that Guderian's force, heading due west for Abbeville, would reach the coast first.

Seventh Panzer was running low on fuel and spare parts. The tanks in particular were being kept in operation by a supply line that stretched over two hundred miles back to Germany. It was the Luftwaffe domination of the skies that allowed the Junkers transports to keep pace with the advance of the Wehrmacht. Otherwise many of the machines would have broken down. As it was, Rommel's forces were a thin string that encircled the southern boundary of the shrinking area still occupied by the Allies.

Horst was at the front of a column of armored cars and motorcycles, reconnoitering for the tank battalions. Behind the tanks were the rest of the Seventh and the newly arrived motorized infantry of the SS Death's Head Division.

It was midafternoon when the British launched their counterattack, using a mixed force of light and medium tanks. Some of them were the new Matildas with heavier armor plating. Two British columns emerged from the forest in a surprise movement that struck the line of SS transports.

Horst was ordered to go immediately to the assistance of the infantry. His armored car crossed a hilltop toward the assault, just in time to see a high-explosive shell from a British Matilda tank make a direct hit on a troop carrier. The truck exploded with a roar, scattering bodies below a billowing cloud of flame and black smoke. Everywhere over an area of several miles, there were prostrate bodies and burning vehicles.

Pulling up below the brow of the hill, Horst was next to an antitank battery. The lieutenant in charge was feverishly working his men, demanding that they reload and fire: *"Schneller, schneller!"* Even the skinny cannons seemed to be in a hurry as they barked out their eighty rounds per minute.

A line of men passed ammunition up to the Panzerabwehrkanone. The weapon coughed its defiance of the British tanks, and an instant later the 37 mm rounds scored two direct hits on the front armor of the Matilda. The tank paused, like a lumbering bear that has been hit by a tree limb. Then it clanked straight ahead again, its machine gun mowing down more German soldiers.

"The shells bounce off!" the antitank lieutenant exclaimed in despair. "We have scored six times on that same machine, and still it comes on!"

The impact of the shell against the tank's steel skin had scarcely damaged it but seemed to have angered it. A high-explosive round from the Matilda arched over the German guns, bursting in the grapevine-covered hillside. A second shot followed, detonating on the ground immediately in front of one of the antitank weapons. The gun barrel twisted like a strand of spaghetti, and six crewmen lay in shattered pieces.

There were at least fifty British tanks in sight, and more were appearing over the northern horizon. The danger was immediate. If the Allied flank attack was successful, a larger rupture would pierce the German advance, splitting the tanks from the weaker elements. If a way south was opened for the Allies, it would trap the forward component of the panzers between the enemy and the sea, instead of the other way around.

"General," Horst radioed Rommel, "we need Stukas, and we need them now!" Quickly Horst explained the situation and its urgency.

Two more antitank weapons were destroyed before the first dive-bombers appeared. In further exchanges of fire, two tanks of the SS division that had joined the battle were also reduced to flaming pyres.

At last black dots appeared high overhead. They fell screaming out of the sky, releasing their deadly burdens. The first wave of four Stukas attacked in a row, like a formation of diving pelicans. Each released a pair of bombs that threw up eruptions of earth, showering the tanks with debris.

One of the British machines took a direct hit. Horst watched the bomb release, saw it arc toward the target, saw the impact. The explosion blew the Matilda apart as if it had been made of tinfoil. Horst blinked at the instant of the burst. When he looked again, only the two treads, looped like giant discarded ribbons, gave any sign of where the tank had been.

But the BEF crews could not hear the sound effects that had been so terrorizing to the Polish and French infantries, and they took no notice of near misses. Even after several waves of planes had destroyed two squadrons of the British tanks, still they rolled forward.

Horst again contacted Rommel.

The general seemed unruffled. "Duly noted," he said calmly. "Do you know the whereabouts of the closest antiaircraft battery?"

"I passed one about a mile back, General. But we have not seen any Allied aircraft, except a few of their fighters. No threat to us."

"Bring the battery to the front, and have them engage the British armor," Rommel ordered.

Horst sent Lieutenant Borger back to locate the battery and bring them up at once.

The ungainly Fliegerabwehrkanone weapons had long barrels and cumbersome mechanisms for achieving the elevation needed to shoot down warplanes. Flak guns looked like a poor choice for the flat shooting required to engage tanks. Horst hoped that Rommel's plan was not one borne of desperation.

The arrogant captain of the antiaircraft unit was eager to show what his section could do. "Step aside, Major," he said, with scarcely any deference to Horst's rank. "Watch what something with some muscle can accomplish."

The 8.8 cm shells were more than twice as big as those for the antitank guns, but at one-fourth the rate of fire, Horst was still skeptical. The first shot fired ripped the left-hand track off of an advancing Matilda. The crippled machine shambled in a clumsy circle as its undamaged tread tried to move it forward. A second shot impacted just under the Matilda's stubby gun, tearing the turret completely off the tank.

But the British armor continued to advance. Their gunners loaded and fired with precision, and they stayed constantly in motion, making them difficult targets for the slower-firing German cannons. They were making for the center of the line of troop transports, German trucks and half-tracks filled with members of the SS Death's Head Division.

The SS troops had cheered the Stukas. They had applauded the results of Rommel's novel use of the antiaircraft guns. Now they were stunned. The German army was unbeatable; was it not? The SS in particular thought of themselves as the elite, the unstoppable, the invincible.

A high-explosive shell landed in the middle of a circle of SS trucks. The canvas covers were shredded, and so were the men inside. All along the line, SS soldiers were hiding in ditches, taking cover behind half-tracks, bailing out of burning vehicles. They stared in dumbfounded horror at the approaching tanks; many did not even bother to reload their rifles. Horst was unpleasantly reminded about the lesson of Cambrai: Terror and intimidation were fully as powerful as the cannons of the British tanks.

As Horst looked on, the SS division wavered, then broke and fled. Streaming to the rear, their retreat opened a gap in the German line. For the first time since the war began, Blitzkrieg was in jeopardy.

⌒

The third wave of Stukas that came over released their bombs short of the line of tanks. Whether by accident or design, the explosives fell in the woods from which the British advance had emerged and in which more units were waiting.

The terrible screaming of the dive-bombers made Mac keep close to a ditch or a particularly solid-looking tree. He lay in the bottom of a creekbed now, cinching up his helmet strap with one hand and hugging his camera with the other.

Mobile artillery. That was how the Wehrmacht used the Stukas. It was the reason the Germans did not have to wait for their heavy cannons to arrive before launching an attack. It was the factor that had negated the Ardennes as a defense. The planes were used with surgical precision and were almost impossible to shoot down. Mac had never seen one crash because of ground fire, and he had seen no Allied fighters all day.

When the aerial assault ended, Mac was behind a British tank-destroyer unit being moved into position. It gave him a panorama of the battlefield of Arras. He could see the spearhead of British Mark I and Mark II tanks rolling over the German opposition in spite of the Stukas and the German antitank weapons.

"Why haven't you Brits done this before?" he asked a gunnery sergeant.

"Blimey, guv, that's what I'd like to know. Mind now, the day ain't won just yet. Them Jerries will be jumpin' on us with their own bloomin' great tanks. Our job is to keep 'em off long enough for our boys to open a big 'ole. Then we can celebrate."

Mac filmed the scene of burning German equipment. Smoldering bonfires made up of troop transports and half-tracks littered the nearer fields. At the far edge of the scene he could make out Nazi soldiers running from the advancing tanks.

"See there," said the sergeant, pointing a greasy finger toward the farthest hill. "Them dark spots is Jerry tanks. They aim to 'it us in the flank, same as we done them."

"Couldn't you use some more tanks to get in and mix it up with the Germans? I understand that they don't like to fight tank-to-tank battles."

"Right you are. But the problem is, you're lookin' at all we got just now. Cobbled together on short notice, don't you see."

"Aren't there any French tanks available?"

"I'm sure I don't know the answer to that. You 'ave to ask the Frogs. In my opinion, it's best to leave them out of it anyway. The Froggies got no radios in their tanks. You can't tell them where they are needed. Once they get started, it's just like windup toys . . . they keep rollin' and firin' till they get blown up or run out of things to shoot."

∽∾

Horst watched the SS soldiers streaming away from the Arras battlefield. He felt a curious sense of satisfaction at their precipitate retreat, as if every doubt he had about their vaunted courage was confirmed. Himmler had insisted they be included in the conduct of the Blitzkrieg so they would share in the glory. Evidently Reichsführer Himmler had thought the campaign was so well in hand that his untried troops could not fail. Instead they now jeopardized the entire operation.

Colonel Neumann, commanding a Seventh Panzer tank battalion, arrived on the scene. He stood upright in the turret of his PzKw-IV tank, commenting to Horst on the scene before them. "Look at those dogs run! It seems that enthusiasm for the party one week does not make for heroic actions the next. They would run all the way back to Germany, and perhaps we should let them!"

Neumann was waiting for an intelligence report from Horst's motorcycle patrol before leading his tanks in a flank assault of his own. He was to strike the center of the Allied line, split it, and then chew up the broken halves. The problem was the light. It was nearing seven o'clock in the evening—already too late for more Stuka attacks and soon too dim for tanks.

Neumann did not seem concerned. "We will pierce the line; then we will pinch the first half into a pocket to destroy at leisure. The rest will certainly retreat." He said something to his driver, and the deeply rumbling engine revved up.

"Do you not want to wait for my lieutenant to get back from recon, Colonel? We don't know what else is behind those Matildas in the cover of the trees."

The colonel squinted at the setting sun, then shook his head. "We can deal with whatever it is. Right now the determining factor is daylight." Neumann gave the order to his column of tanks to attack, and the PzKw-IV ground into forward motion, its tracks clanking. He was wasting no time. The muzzle of the 75 mm gun was already swiveling, seeking its first target.

The tank plunged down the hill. At almost the same moment, Lieutenant Borger arrived beside Horst. "Recon report, Major," he said, saluting. "Warn Colonel Neumann that there are a couple squadrons of French Somua tanks concealed behind the farthest hedgerow and two or three tank destroyer units just emerging from the woods. I do not know if they are French or British."

Horst turned to the handset of the radio that Sergeant Fiske was already offering. Still in Horst's line of sight, Neumann was no more than a hundred yards forward. The tall colonel was still standing; he had not yet buttoned up the hatch.

The first round of antitank fire struck the PzKw-III that was immediately behind Neumann's tank. The projectile shattered against the sloping armor, but the burst reached out in a deadly star-shaped pattern to embrace the colonel. His back was riddled with shrapnel. When he slumped over the hatch, his body pivoted limply and he hung on the edge of the turret. Other rounds began striking the German line. Two tanks exploded in flames.

The entire column halted. Horst ran forward, catching Neumann's body as it slid to the ground. He pulled the colonel's lifeless form out of the way and jumped up on the hatch. "Go," he shouted to the driver. "You cannot stay here. The advance will be cut to pieces if you do not destroy those guns."

The radio operator looked shaken. "The colonel did not have time to tell us his plan. The second in command has just been reported killed as well. What do we do?"

Horst had never directed a tank in battle before, let alone an entire column of tanks, but he had a clear picture in his mind of the terrain and the reported location of the Allied weapons. He jackknifed into the commander's seat. "Radio," he ordered. "Squadrons three and four attack the center of the British line as planned. In column, high speed, fifty-meter intervals. Squadrons one and two form two waves, fifty meters between tanks and one hundred meters between waves, and follow us!"

The inside of the tank smelled of fuel, hot oil, and unwashed bodies. Machine-gun bullets pinged off the steel armor. The sound reminded Horst that if the enemy antitank gunners selected this particular PzKw to target, his career as a tank commander would be very brief.

"Pivot left thirty," he ordered the driver. The man operating the machine gun was firing short bursts, distracting the antitank crews as they sought cover for themselves. But so far the main gun had not fired. "What are you waiting for?" Horst demanded.

"Not in range yet, Major," the gunner replied. "This 7.5 cm gun throws a seven kilo shell, but it doesn't throw it very far."

"Radio, tell tanks two and four in each wave to drop back fifty meters from their present positions. I want to make us as hard to hit as possible."

"Acknowledged," returned the radio operator. "Major, second squadron reports that tank four is out of action with a track knocked off."

Through the periscope, Horst could make out the edge of the woods ahead and the row of antitank guns. He instinctively flinched at a muzzle flash and braced himself for an explosion, but the shot was long and burst behind them.

"We have range now, Major."

"Target left forty-five."

"I have him."

"Fire!"

The high-explosive round landed short of the mark, but the concussion cartwheeled the tank destroyer gun twenty feet in the air. Even so, there was no time to exult in a single well-placed shot.

"Target right ninety."

The gunner had picked up the next location as quickly as Horst, and the turret pivoted smoothly the instant he finished speaking.

All the rounds being launched were high explosives, since their targets were not other tanks but men and equipment without steel covers that required armor-piercing shells. Horst was so impressed with the competence and skill of the crew that he was already searching for the next objective even before the last shot had been fired. Just after the gun roared again, Horst commanded, "Reload with HE. No! Check that! Hard right! Load armor piercing, target right forty-five!"

What Horst had seen was a line of French Somua tanks emerging from behind the thick row of hedge across the field. The purpose of the panzer attack was to break through the British line of armor. Even if it meant sacrificing himself, his battle group had to now counter this new threat to the main German thrust.

Somuas were the best tanks the Allies possessed: faster than the German panzers and, even so, more heavily armored. They did not mount as large a cannon but had almost twice the muzzle velocity with greater range and striking force. The only positive thing Horst could think of was that he saw only four of them.

"We are within their range already," the gunner reported to Horst, "but not ours."

There was nothing to do but charge ahead, zigzagging in the hope of escaping a lucky hit until able to shoot back.

The leading Somua's muzzle erupted in flame, as did the second and the third. Once again, Horst prepared for the expected shock, but no blow fell.

"Major!" the radio operator said with excitement. "Second Squadron reports that the Somuas are firing at their own tank destroyers!"

21

A Two-Pronged Attack

Mac's camera watched the approach of the German tanks. He saw them divide their force into a two-pronged attack, one of which aimed for the heart of the British charge. The other was coming right toward him, straight down the throat of the tank-destroyer unit.

The British gunnery sergeant was very methodical as he went about the business of loading, aiming, and firing. At each recoil, the antitank gun jumped up on its rubber tires like a warhorse rearing in the excitement of battle.

With an enemy approaching head-on, there was no need to adjust for the speed of the quarry; it was enough to steadily reduce the elevation as the oncoming panzers roared straight in. The two-pound shells were having a dramatic effect. A PzKw-III burst into a ball of fire. It continued rumbling forward for a time, trailing a flag of thick, black fumes. Orange flames shot into the evening sky. Eventually it rolled to a stop, and the pursuing cloud of dark smoke caught up and enveloped it completely. No one emerged from the pyre.

A second tank was hit low in the left-hand track as it was at the edge of a slanting culvert. The sudden loss of half its footing made the PzKw-III roll over sideways. As Mac watched the machine ponderously revolve, it occurred to him that a viewer seeing this film would assume that it was captured in slow motion. The tank came to rest upside down, its tracks still futilely turning, like an enormous turtle flipped on its back and helpless. Moments later three men emerged from the carcass. One of them was shot down at the edge of the culvert while the other two huddled below the lip of the ditch.

An approaching PzKw-IV fired a shell that fell short in front of the tank destroyers. The sergeant smoothly redirected his weapon to take on the new challenger. The first round sailed over the tank. The sergeant was calmly readjusting the height when another incoming projectile exploded into the British line from the side. Two more followed, tearing through the antitank weapons like a scythe through a handful of wheat stalks. The impact tore the first gun into ragged chunks of metal that spun across the intervening yards.

"Flank attack!" the sergeant yelled to his remaining squadron of guns.

The next detonation flung Mac into a cavity left from one of the first shells to reach its target. On the theory that lightning would not strike twice in the same spot, Mac stayed in the shallow depression, operating his camera over the lip of the crater. The camera lens and the top of his helmet were the only things that protruded above ground level. Mac thought that an observer could now compare *his* appearance to a turtle.

The tank destroyers fired in a continuous staccato popping. Against the muzzle blasts of the tanks, it sounded weak and almost silly, but when Mac cautiously peered into the eyepiece, he could see that it was effective. One of the attacking tanks was stopped dead, a gaping hole torn in its front surface. Another was still firing its machine gun, but its main weapon was broken off short and contorted from taking a direct hit.

There was something odd about its shape. Mac studied the outline. German tanks from the smallest PzKw-I to the new model IV had a similar profile: The turret was mounted directly above the level of the tracks. These machines were built in three stages: tracks, body, and then turret perched on top. They were . . .

"It's the bloody Frogs!" the sergeant bitterly cried. "Our allies have busted us to pieces!"

"Cease firing," Mac yelled, as if he were an officer instead of an onlooker.

"Cease nothing!" corrected the sergeant. "We can't stop shooting unless they do or we'll be blown to kingdom come!"

❧

The view through Horst's periscope showed an amazing scene. The newly arrived French armor was blasting away not at the German tanks but at the detachment of British antitank guns. The British, not knowing the identity of their new attackers, pivoted their weapons and replied to what was for them a much nearer danger than Horst.

"Turn!" Horst shouted. "If they keep each other occupied, we will hit the British Matildas from behind!"

Squadrons three and four of the German column were mixing it up with the English tanks in tank-to-tank combat. The Brits were still trying to maintain order and complete their breakthrough of the SS division, but the new strike from the rear surprised them.

Horst knew tanks were not well protected at the back, and the older British units were especially vulnerable there. The first blast of Horst's 7.5 cm gun tore a Mark I in half, scattering debris over half an acre.

The second Mark I targeted received an armor-piercing round that must have struck the ammunition hold after penetrating. The turret lifted straight up in the air like the lid of a teakettle. The chain reaction of exploding shells then ripped the tank to pieces from the inside out.

Horst was indicating the position of the next Mark I when a shell hit the panzer from behind. The solid shot burst low in the bowels of the tank, killing the driver and the machine gunner instantly. A shrapnel spear sliced into Horst's upper arm. Jagged metal protruded from both sides of his bicep. He stared at it stupidly for a moment, remembering the splinter of metal that had struck his hand during the shelling in Poland. Then he passed out.

When he came to, Horst was lying on a stretcher next to a row of German antiaircraft guns. They were lowered to flat trajectories and blazing away. General Rommel hurried from gun to gun, personally directing the target search of each. He acted as if he wished he could hold each cannon to his shoulder like a rifle.

Rommel paused beside Horst, where a medic was swabbing his wound with something that smelled terrible and burned even worse. "So, you are awake? And what do you have to say for yourself?"

Horst was certain that he was going to be shot. Now that the excitement was over, Horst knew that he had exceeded his authority and botched it. He was sure that he had led the German tanks into a trap and that he would be court-martialed. "Herr General," he began weakly, "I do not know what to say."

"Say nothing!" Rommel grinned. "Save your strength. After your brilliant attack, you have left me nothing to do but mop up the stragglers! There will be a Knight's Cross for you in this, Major, and a new job, too!"

⟨ಞ⟩

Andre was in Lord Gort's headquarters, waiting for word about the outcome of the counterattack at Arras. Gort was late getting back from a meeting with Supreme Commander Weygand, the Belgian king Leopold, and French general Billotte.

When he finally returned, he was in a foul mood. "Did not even wait for me!" Gort stormed into his office and threw down his cap with disgust. "Gave me no notice of this conference until it was too late to reach it on time, then departed before I even arrived! God spare us from allies such as these!"

Noticing the presence of the French Intelligence officer did not make Gort apologetic. "I'm glad you waited, Colonel, so you can take a first-hand report to somebody. General Billotte was killed tonight."

"Bombing raid?"

"Killed when his car skidded into a truckload of refugees moving on the highway at two miles an hour! He was the only other officer besides King Leopold who knew Weygand's plans. And I'm not sure how much longer Leopold can be relied on to hold. How can we coordinate any counterattacks now?"

Andre waited patiently while Gort unbuttoned his tunic and settled into his chair.

Finally Andre asked, "Is there any news from Arras?"

"Yes, the only positive light in this miserable tunnel. Two columns of our armor hit Rommel hard, scattering the SS division."

"Did they achieve a breakthrough?"

Gort shook his head slowly. "No, but they have punished the German flank and accomplished, I think, part of our purpose. Herr Hitler is full of boundless enthusiasm for war, so long as he is winning. Even a small set-back worries him, makes him rethink his plans. Now he will worry about overextended supply lines. He will order his panzers to slow down for consolidation. He might even force them to halt temporarily."

"And you will withdraw Franklyn's force?"

Again Gort shook his head, even more ponderously, as if a great weight were pressing him into his seat. "Not yet. If they remain where they are, the Germans will have to consume another twenty-four or thirty-six hours mopping up. If Franklyn's force is seen as expendable, it will make the Nazis believe that we have more armor than we do. That deception can buy us some time—time we desperately need." The general pivoted his chair to stare up at the map. "Did you know that Guderian reached Abbeville on the Channel? Boulogne and Calais are next."

Andre followed Gort's view to a tiny corner where the French and Belgian frontiers met—a small city and a harbor named Dunkirk. The eyes of the two men met.

"Colonel, there is more you should know. You have greatly exceeded your orders in bringing me valuable information and could be in severe difficulty with your own High Command. That I cannot permit."

Andre's gut tightened. "I don't understand what you mean, General."

"I have backdated a request to Commander in Chief Weygand, ap-pointing you my new liaison officer. Welcome to my staff, Colonel."

The meeting was buzzing with excited speculation. After the two-day battle at Arras, Seventh Panzer had been ordered to halt for repair, resupply, and reinforcement. With the race to the sea already won by Guderian, even Rommel admitted the wisdom of such a move. After all, his tanks had taken 50 percent casualties, counting dead, wounded, and equipment out of action.

His newest tank battalion commander, Horst von Bockman, had also been grateful for the chance to recuperate. His arm was healing well, though it hurt like the devil whenever he tried to lift anything heavier than a piece of paper.

Horst had tried to dissuade Rommel from giving him the new command. He had pleaded ignorance of tank operation and tactics, but the general was not swayed from his decision.

"Anyone who is as good an instinctive leader as you cannot be allowed to go to waste," Rommel concluded. "You handled the columns like an old-time Prussian cavalry officer. It was beautiful."

Horst could hardly plead ignorance of cavalry tactics. So here he was, officer over twelve of the new PzKw-IVs, together with all their men and machinery.

For over two days the division had rested. Now, on the twenty-fifth of May, it was ready to jump off again. The speculation in the meeting of brigade and battalion leaders ran the gamut of possible next moves. Richter, the senior tank officer present, held out for an immediate attack on the BEF troops at Hazebrouck. Colonel Eckberg, the chief of the division's artillery, was certain that the target would be Lille, where the remaining French forces in the north were said to be concentrated. Horst, feeling very junior to the rest, kept his mouth shut, but privately he believed the Seventh would pivot directly toward the Channel. He had heard some rumors from interrogated French prisoners that the British had gotten a bellyful and were ready to call it quits. If true, they would certainly fall back toward the coast to attempt an evacuation.

All the men stood when General Rommel entered the room. Horst could tell the general was seething with anger before he spoke a single word. Rommel's jaw was clenched and his face drawn in a very uncharacteristic frown. He waved the officers to their seats, but it was some seconds before he could allow himself to speak.

"We are *ordered* to halt for two *more* days. The division will not advance. Our units that have already crossed . . . *already crossed*," he repeated, as if he could not believe the words, "the canal will be pulled back. That is all, gentlemen."

As soon as Rommel stalked out, the rising flow of conjecture over-flowed its banks. "It is Göring's fault," Eckberg complained bitterly. "He wants to cover his flyboys with some glory, now that we have done all the work. When the Allies in the pocket surrender, we will see that the Luftwaffe gets all the credit."

"I disagree," Richter said. "The ground ahead is marshy—much more so than what we have crossed already. It is belated caution setting in. Or perhaps the armored units are just being saved for the next phase of the campaign. After all, it is about time the infantry do some work, too."

Horst remained silent. But he knew there was more to this than met the eye. When you have an opponent on the ropes, you finish him as quickly as possible. Otherwise you risk letting him escape or get his second wind. Making the Allies a present of the time to regroup was not something that Rommel would have permitted. And neither would Tank Battalion Commander von Bockman.

⌘

Together with British troops from the Second and Fifth Gloucester Regiments, Mac found himself on the road to the Channel. Two thousand men were ordered to defend an important stretch of the southern perimeter of the Allied defenses, centered on the city of Cassel.

Mac watched a young lieutenant, who spoke no French, trying to explain to a baker and his wife that their home was needed as a fortification. Eventually they were persuaded to leave, but Mac felt sure that they did not understand fully what was happening. The message became clear to the couple only after the lieutenant ordered a squad to knock a hole in the wall of the ground floor to make an emplacement for an anti-tank gun.

When Mac asked them how they felt about the war, the baker shrugged and said nothing. But the wife took off like a rocket. "What has happened to the Phony War?" she demanded. "What has happened to the Maginot Line? What do the politicians say now? And the vaunted British—is this what they call 'coming to our aid'? L'Anglais ou L'Allemand . . . je ne saisis pa la nuance. British or German, I do not see the difference."

Cassel was a hilltop town only eighteen miles from the coast. It was also in the middle of some of the flattest, best operating country for tanks between the Germans and the sea. That both sides regarded it as crucial was no surprise.

So it was back to business as usual, as Mac saw it. The story of this whole campaign for the Allies had been dropping back and trying to hang on to a strongpoint. Arras had been the best shot at changing all that, but here it was again.

The lieutenant continued in his efforts to carry out orders. He had another squad of men build a barricade. Soon a pile of milk cans, a horse-drawn plow, and an overturned manure spreader blocked the main road. As a work of art, it would have been titled *Nineteenth-century Farming*. Mac was sure that it did not belong in twentieth-century warfare.

The work of fortifying the town of Cassel was as complete as imagination and muscle power could make it. Several homes besides the baker's now sported holes in their walls from which machine guns protruded. A Bren gun sat picturesquely on top of a commandeered chicken coop, and the men at the barricade counted a Boyes antitank rifle among their arsenal.

"Fat lot of good it is, too," remarked the sergeant who had charge of it. "Shells bounce off the Jerry tanks."

"Don't you have anything else?" Mac asked.

"Sure we do," replied the sergeant sarcastically. "Here, Castle. Take this gentleman and show him the heavy artillery."

Mac was led to a fenced depression behind the front row of houses. By its smell the previous occupants from whom it had been requisitioned were pigs. The center of the low spot was occupied by a three-inch mortar and a crew of three men. The soldiers took turns leaving their position and going to the edge of the hill for fresh air.

At midnight the hum of airplanes was heard coming from the northwest. Mac guessed that there was very little chance they would be friendly. Cassel's position on the highest knob of land in the area was particularly attractive to bombers. Long before the sound of the planes had arrived directly overhead, Mac and all the soldiers had taken what shelter they could find in cellars and slit trenches.

Mac was crouching in a recently dug hole next to his tour guide. Lance Corporal Castle may not have been a religious man, but he kept up a constant litany just the same. "Here they come. We're gonna catch it now. We surely are. What's to stop 'em? They're right on top of us. Here they come. . . ."

Mac found himself wishing that something would happen, just to provide a change from Castle's monotonous refrain. When the steady drone of the engines neared the hilltop, Mac and the corporal ducked below the level of the slit trench. Mac's world was suddenly reduced to a space scarcely more than one foot wide and three feet deep.

The chatter of machine guns welcomed the German planes—not that anybody expected to actually down one. It just felt better to pretend to fight back.

A whistling noise announced that the bombs were on the way, and even Castle got quiet. Mac had been through this enough before to know that everyone held his breath until the first explosion. After that you either waited it out, or you took a direct hit and had no more breath to hold.

Mac counted to ten by patting his breast-pocket stash of Eva's letters. His marking time was interrupted by a clanging noise, as if the Germans were dropping milk cans like the ones in Cassel's rampart. Then he heard a fluttering clamor, like a thousand pigeons taking off all at once.

Mac discovered that he was still holding his breath, way past time for the first blast. Cautiously he poked his head out of the trench and looked around. Thirty yards away was a new dark lump, sticking in the ground at an angle. And falling through the trees were objects that floated like falling leaves.

Ducking back much faster than he had popped up, Mac thought about unexploded bombs. But this object did not look much like a bomb; it looked more like a milk can. Did the Germans have a new type of delayed-action weapon, designed to lure people out of safety before it detonated?

Castle still cowered in the trench. He was no help in analyzing this development. Mac reviewed what he had seen. There had been no explosions, only the harmless-looking cylinder and drifting scraps of something white.

All at once Mac stood up, embarrassed with himself. "Come on, Corporal," he said to Castle. "We've just been attacked by a volley of leaflets."

The canister that had failed to open was full of squares of paper, and the ground around the knoll of Cassel was littered with them. Reading by the brief light of a flickering match, they saw that each carried the same message, repeated in both French and English:

> *Allied soldiers: Look at this map. It gives your true situation. Your troops are entirely surrounded—stop fighting! Put down your arms!*

The map illustrated a tiny pocket around the Channel town of Dunkirk, encircled by a wide bank marked *The Germans*.

Lance Corporal Castle gathered a handful of the propaganda sheets.

"What are you going to do with those, Corporal?" Mac asked.

Castle's voice in the darkness had a smile in it. "Latrine duty."

Mac decided that he really liked the corporal after all.

22

Last Mission

Boulogne flashed past below. Black puffs of German antiaircraft fire reached up toward the pitiful flight of three Hurricanes. Boulogne had fallen the day before, and 73 Squadron was flying its last mission. What was left of the group had been recalled to England to reform. After today, RAF missions over France would be flown only by Spitfires and Hurricanes operating from Kent.

David found it hard to believe that the entire north coast of France was in Nazi hands. The Wehrmacht invasion had begun only sixteen days earlier. Now the last, best hope was to save as many Allied soldiers as possible. There were those who spoke of holding an enclave on the Channel, of resupply and reinforcement. The truth was a bitter pill: Northern France was lost.

Still, David was proud of 73's performance. For the first six months he had flown *Annie*, the squadron had shot down only thirty enemy planes. In the last two weeks they had accounted for over one hundred. But hardly anyone was left to share the memories. His old friends Hewitt and Simpson were both gone.

"Close up, Tay," he broadcast to Churchman on his right wing. "Stay tight. You all right back there, Jimmy?" Small was flying as "arse-end Charlie," above and behind the other two, keeping a wary eye out for Messerschmitts.

The instructions for the three pilots had been very simple:

> *"The British Expeditionary Force is being withdrawn from France by way of Dunkirk. Give them all the help you can today, and tomorrow you'll be back in England."*

Swooping in over Dunkirk now, David spotted thousands of men assembling, waiting to be removed. The roads heading into the evacuation area were packed as well. Though outlying units fought rearguard actions as far away as Lille, forty miles inland, the defensive perimeter established around Dunkirk was only twenty miles long and scarcely five deep.

Already the area was being pounded by the Luftwaffe. A flight of Heinkels was unloading thousands of pounds of high explosives on the fortifications and the warehouses. Billowing columns of black, oily smoke curled upward into the sky, towering over the five-thousand-foot elevation of the Hurricanes. David thought that the pillars of pitch-dark fumes must be visible from the seashore of England.

Ready to order an attack on the bombers, David stopped when he saw the harbor. A hospital ship, marked with giant red crosses on each side of its funnel and on its deck both fore and aft, was tied up at the Gare Maritime, loading wounded. Six ME-109s were taking turns strafing the ship, diving in from the east and shooting up the length of the vessel.

"Right. Messers at twelve o'clock." David tried to keep his words steady, but his anger rose in his throat, almost choking him. His voice quivered with fury. "Catch them as they pull up from a run," he ordered. "Send them all to hell!"

The timing was perfect. One ME-109 was still reaching for the top of its ascent. The second Messerschmitt was just climbing away from the hospital ship. And a third was beginning its machine-gun attack. The other three were only starting their runs. The Luftwaffe apparently believed that their superiority over the air of Dunkirk was complete. They had left no high cover for themselves and had posted no rear guard.

The three RAF fighters dove out of the sun. David and Churchman aimed directly for where the German fighters were the most vulnerable: pulling out of the attack. Jimmy Small was instructed to get on the tail of the last ME-109 in the line and follow him wherever he went.

David charged the lead Messerschmitt. Some flash from the attacking Hurricane must have reached the German pilot, or perhaps he had a sudden premonition. Across the intervening two hundred yards, David could see the man raise his hand to shield his eyes against the glare. At that same moment David squeezed the trigger, loosing a burst of .303-caliber fury. He watched the bullets penetrate the glass of the cockpit.

One down.

Rolling sharply left and reversing direction, *Annie* roared past where Churchman had shot the tail off his target. The pilot of the second 109 pushed open his canopy and jumped away from the out-of-control plane.

Two down.

David dove into the face of the German fighter that had just completed its attack on the mercy ship. The Hurricane's sudden appearance panicked the Luftwaffe pilot, who rolled his craft into the stream of bullets.

There was no chance to see what the lucky burst had accomplished. David was plunging almost straight down toward the bow of the ship. As the next 109 cleared the deck, David fired again. The line of tracers tracked exactly into the fuselage of the fighter. It may have been massive damage or perhaps just panic again, because the German fighter dove to escape, despite its lack of height, and plunged into the sea.

Three down.

An excited yelp came over the R/T from Jimmy. "Scratch one for me!"

Four down.

Pulling out of his dive, David circled back over the Channel, looking for the remaining two Messerschmitts. He spotted the one he had shot at now tangled high overhead in a dogfight with Churchman. Where was the last one?

The answer came in a stream of bullets that impacted *Annie*'s portside wing and left a row of holes. David yanked the plane sharply right, then left and right again, trying to shake off his pursuer. A second burst of gunfire hit the Hurricane's engine. A thin stream of white vapor flowed back from the cowling and up over the glass of the canopy.

The third round of machine-gun fire from the 109 hit David's cockpit behind where he sat. Two bullets were stopped by the armor in back of the pilot seat, but another shattered the edge of the plating. A fragment hit the flier in the lower left arm. Just before it went numb, David felt a searing thrust from his elbow to his fingertips. His hand fell limply away from the throttle knob, and he could not raise it.

Reversing his direction again, David urged the Hurricane to regain some height as he headed back toward Dunkirk. He expected at any moment for the German to return to finish him off. His head spun, and he felt close to passing out.

From the radio he heard Churchman's voice. "Number five accounted for, but I'm hit. Losing oil pressure."

"I see you, Tay," Jimmy's voice answered. "Need help?"

Where had the last German gone now? "Tay," David radioed, "you . . . reach England. Jimmy . . . go with him."

"What about you, Tinman?"

"Go! I'll be . . . later."

The flow of glycol fumes was increasing, and David's cockpit was filling with smoke. He crossed the coastline, still reaching for the height he needed in order to bail out safely. Awkwardly he slid back the canopy, every movement of his useless left arm racking him with agony. Unbuckling his radio cable and the oxygen tube with difficulty, he readied himself to dive over the side. Three thousand feet of height now separated him from the Belgian countryside. He did not want to travel any farther inland, for fear of falling into German hands.

Plunging over the side, David kicked himself away from the airframe. His dangling arm struck the edge of the cockpit as he pushed off, and he vomited into his oxygen mask and passed out. . . .

When he came to he was floating at a thousand feet, not even able to remember how he had pulled the ripcord. Through vision that was all yellow and black spots, he saw *Annie*. The plane now spouted a trail of black smoke as it continued on toward the German lines. Vaguely he hoped that she would explode gloriously, right on top of some Nazi general.

At five hundred feet David he saw the last ME-109 return. It chased *Annie* at first, then apparently noticed the white disk of the parachute and dove after him. A hailstorm of bullets tore through the silky canopy on the Messerschmitt's first pass. The ground was coming up, and David tried to ready himself for the impact.

He cradled his left arm against his body, but even holding it made him feel close to blacking out again. The fingers of his right hand brushed against an odd jagged lump that protruded near his elbow. The pain reached his senses at the same moment as comprehension. Touching the exposed end of a jagged shrapnel splinter that was under the length of his forearm, the flier vomited once more.

The impact with the ground jarred him so badly that David did in fact pass out again. . . .

When he opened his eyes, he was staring stupidly at a diving ME-109 lined up to strafe him as he lay on the ground.

Some unknown instinct urged David to move—roll, crawl, but do something. His clumsy spin to the right dropped him into a ditch. He landed with his injured arm pinned under his weight, but this time the intense pain woke him up to his danger.

A line of machine-gun bullets tore up the ground where his parachute lay. David crawled into a muddy culvert and lay there as the 109 came back one more time. The incendiaries in the last burst set fire to his parachute.

Then the German left.

A few minutes later, a platoon of British infantry emerged from the roadside ditch where they had taken refuge. Later they told David that they had assumed the Messerschmitt had been after them. When they saw the smoldering silk of David's chute, they located him and pulled him out of the culvert.

☾꙲☽

The barrage that arrived at Cassel on May 26, the morning after the leaf-lets were dropped, did not consist of harmless sheets of paper. Just after dawn, German artillery opened up on the town, and the battle for the road to the Channel began in earnest.

The Gloucester mortarmen were busy lobbing shells onto the Wehrmacht positions below. Mac filmed the crew in action, loading and firing their weapon. He listened to the hollow ringing it made as it tossed the three-inch rounds into the valley. The shells exploded with much greater force than the puny tube seemed to offer.

Running from slit trench to slit trench and hugging the ground when a new barrage whistled overhead, Mac made his way toward the edge of the hill. One jump put him into the same hold he had shared with Cor-poral Castle the night before. The corporal was there again, too.

"Hey, Castle," Mac called. "You've got dirt all over you. You're almost buried in it. Why don't you brush—"

Mac stopped abruptly when he realized that Castle was dead. One of the first bursts had caught him above the level of the ground, and he was pierced with shrapnel. Mac knew that the trench would probably be-come Corporal Castle's grave.

When Mac reached the position of the forward artillery observer, he could see the progress of the German attack. A half-dozen panzer tanks milled about in the hollow below Cassel. As Mac watched, one of the British shells struck the rear of the lead machine, and black smoke poured out. The tank ground to a halt, and the hatches popped open as the German crew hastily abandoned their burning vehicle. Bullets from a Bren gun concealed in a barn mowed them down—all except the last man, who dove headfirst into a ditch.

"Bloody Hun. I hope he broke his neck," the artillery spotter observed.

The return fire from the Germans arched above the spot where Mac peered down from the brow of the knoll. A shell struck the farm build-ing that contained the Bren emplacement and set the barn's roof on fire. The men operating the machine gun continued to fire their weapon, but a trio of young pigs scampered out and ran down the hill.

Moments later, with the barn fully engulfed in flames, the British troops bailed out also. The two-man crew was uninjured, but not all the pigs were so lucky. The smell of cooking pork drifted to Mac on the morning breeze.

Another shell from the German artillery landed behind Mac's posi-tion, and the British mortar fell silent. It was possible that the fight had just gotten too intense in that spot and the mortarmen had moved to another. When some time passed without a resumption of the firing, Mac knew they had taken a hit. But the British resistance had done its work: The German tanks retreated back into the cover of the trees.

The artillery barrage continued pounding Cassel, leveling the baker's house. It seemed ironic to think that the Frenchwoman had fretted about a hole in her wall, when now not even one wall was left standing.

The bursts of German explosives struck the face of the hill just below where Mac and the spotter lay. The next blow was higher and the next almost to the top, as if the shells were climbing the mound to the city.

"Time to go," urged the soldier. "We aren't doing any good here anymore."

Mac allowed the rest of the film to grind through his camera. He automatically reached into the pouch at his side to grab another fresh reel. He was already in motion away from the artillery fire and hoping that he could find an intact cellar to duck into to change the film.

His fingers fumbled among the canisters, seeking the sealed edge that would identify the new roll. He found none. He had used every inch of film he had; until he got more, his role as a newsreel cameraman was at an end.

"Looks like I'm headed out," he told the lieutenant, whose command post was in what remained of the town's police station. "Hope I can catch a ride at the coast."

"Make for Dunkirk," the lieutenant said breezily. "Someone will accommodate you."

"I'll be back," Mac vowed.

"Yes, well, good luck to you." There was a forced cheerfulness in the officer's tone.

"When will you disengage?" Mac asked.

"Really can't say. We have received no other orders than to continue holding here, which we will for as long as we can."

"And then?"

"I suppose we'll be trying for Dunkirk, too."

"If you wait too long, this hill will be surrounded," Mac warned.

"I don't fancy German food all that much," the lieutenant said.

~ ೧◎ ~

The whole countryside around David's route of escape was in flames. Bridges, houses, and army vehicles added to the conflagration as the German barrage smashed down. The unending concussions of the shells drowned out the cries of the wounded and dying. David traveled through the wreckage with a group of six British BEF soldiers on their way to the coast. The name of Dunkirk was on the lips of every man.

At sundown, clutching his wounded arm, David Meyer staggered onto the grounds of the Ecole de Cavalerie. He and the BEF soldiers were stopped and questioned by two youthful sentries on the edge of the wood. Then they followed a troop lorry that had been converted into an ambulance to the British Casualty Clearing Station.

The CCS, which had been moved from the bomb-damaged right wing of the school to the church, now held over two thousand casualties. No matter how swiftly the surgeons worked, long lines of stretchers carrying French, English, and Belgian soldiers continued to grow longer. Lorries filled with the wounded streamed in.

David's companions asked an orderly the way to Dunkirk. Without good-byes, they left David on the front steps of the church and hurried on toward the smoking highway that led to the coast. It occurred to David as he watched their retreating backs that he had never asked their names, nor would he recognize their faces. And yet they had probably saved his life.

He tried to hail a harried, blood-spattered nurse in a tin hat, who rushed by him with a box of medical supplies. "My arm is hurt. Badly, I think. Shrapnel. Can I get it seen to here?"

She did not hesitate or offer even a word of sympathy. "Injured arm, boy? Look in there," she snapped, jerking her thumb toward the entrance of the church.

The floor of the sanctuary was covered with stretchers—not an inch of space between them. Light streamed through the remaining stained-glass windows to cover the wounded in a giant patchwork quilt of shifting colors: blue and red on the face of the pale, freckled boy with the missing leg and the row of amputees . . . green and yellow over the contorted face of the man who shouted for a nurse to administer some morphine. First it was bright and then dark as smoke momentarily blocked the sun. Once again the shadows broke and patterns grew vivid and distinct on bloody bandages and ghastly complexions. The great, cavernous room hummed with an unending moan. It was a nightmare of collective agony.

Hopeless and angry, the nurse glared at her charges as if she was infuriated at them. "There are only fourteen nurses here. These men won't escape unless they can walk." She snorted bitterly. "Injured arm? *You* can walk, can't you? The coast is that way."

David could not go on. "I've got to sleep. Can I sleep somewhere?" The world had taken on a sickly yellow pall again. He thought he might throw up if he could not lie down.

"If you can find a spot." She walked past him. "Steer clear of the area behind the altar. That's the only place we have to put the dying men." She scurried into the auditorium, leaving David to find his own refuge. It was obvious that the surgeons did not have the time or inclination to cut out a sliver of shrapnel while other men were bleeding to death before their very eyes.

Settling in beneath a heavy table in the foyer, David lay between the support and the cool stone wall. His arm rested on his stomach. Every breath meant a painful movement of the metal that seemed to grate against his bones.

He closed his eyes and listened to the distant shelling as it came nearer. He recognized the drone of aircraft engines: Heinkel, Stuka, Dornier, Messerschmitt. But for David, it was over. Suddenly and terribly over. David gasped as an intense pain shot through his shoulder. The urge to vomit swept over him again. Swallowing hard, he attempted to stay the violent reaction. He could not. Rolling to the side, he heaved bile onto the stone pavement. Then he passed out.

23

A Fascinating Jumble

It occurred to Nicholi Federov, the White Russian, that when the pieces of a puzzle finally fall into place, it is amazing how the completed picture leaps out.

The Gestapo spy was certain now that he knew Richard Lewinski's whereabouts. Putting Professor Argo's casual remark together with the reports from Oxford and Princeton had led Federov straight to the library of the Sorbonne and a stack of yearbooks. He had no difficulty locating photos of Lewinskis senior and junior. But it wasn't until he examined a staff grouping of stiffly posed academic figures that the information he sought was there, right under his nose.

In the back row of the professorial colleagues for the year 1910 was the face of Lewinski's father. Next to him, according to the caption, was Louis Chardon. Flipping to the student pictures again confirmed it: Andre Chardon had been a classmate of Lewinski's, and their families were connected as well. And Andre Chardon held some position in French Military Intelligence.

All that remained was a little snooping, which was what brought Federov to the Buci Market on this lovely day. From the house on Quai d'Anjou, he had followed Chardon's cook, Jeanette, with a rising sense of excitement that his goal was near.

Federov positioned himself a few feet from the cook and picked up a succession of melons, groaning aloud as he inspected each and replaced it on the pile. His handsome face was downcast and worried when Jeanette caught the sound of another heavy sigh.

"Excuse me, Monsieur," she said kindly. "May I be of some assistance?"

"Would you?" he asked with a pleading note. "My wife has taken the children and gone south. My cook has chosen this week to become ill, and I have unexpected guests who have arrived from Belgium . . . you understand?"

"But of course," Jeanette said sympathetically.

"I have hired a temporary cook, but I must do the shopping myself—something for which I am singularly ill equipped."

"But that is the easy part," avowed Jeanette. "I can help you."

Federov flashed his most charming smile. "You are so very kind. This melon—is it ripe?"

The cook sniffed the indicated fruit, then set it aside and selected another. "This one is better. What else will you be serving?"

"It may depend on the expense, because of the number who are arriving, you see. How does one know how much to purchase? In your household, for instance, how many do you feed and how many melons would you buy?"

"Ours is but a small ensemble. Right now there are only two adults, and one of them . . . la!" she exclaimed. "He eats like a stray cat. I put out a saucer of food for him, and he dines at midnight when he emerges from his basement lair!"

Federov's pulse was racing, but once Jeanette got started, she provided even more information than he could have hoped.

"Alas," she said, "my poor monsieur will have to cope with the strange one all by himself. I am also leaving for the south."

"Oh?" said Federov, pricking up his ears.

"My son lives in Nice," Jeanette volunteered, "and I am departing soon to join him there."

"Most interesting," Federov assured her. "Now tell me, how many melons this size would be needed to feed a group of ten?"

◯◯◯

Madame Rose was not at the train station today, Josie knew. There were important matters to attend to at the orphanage.

As Josie, Juliette, and Yacov stood outside the house on la Huchette, everything on the street looked much the same, except that there were many shuttered windows now. People had closed their homes and fled south.

But the big black coach gate and the bell rope remained as before. An echo of laughter drifted up from behind the wall. The gate swung open, and Josie, with Yacov and Juliette, entered the sanctuary of the courtyard.

What had changed? Long lines of laundry still waved overhead. The sun was still shining. The faces of the children were still light and happy and alive. Juliette was drawn into a game of hopscotch. It had been a long time since Josie had seen such happy expressions.

Now, however, there were twice as many faces as before.

"One hundred and fifty, give or take," Madame Rose explained. "You must be at the station by noon. An entire car is to be reserved for us on the two o'clock train."

∽

Rue de la Huchette had never seen such an army since the days of the French Revolution and the Reign of Terror. What a commotion!

Every child wore a two-cornered paper hat made of newsprint. This was because Madame Rose said it would be very hot in the sun at Gare d'Orsay, and she did not want any boiled brains or sunstroke or sunburn to contend with.

Jerome felt foolish at first, but he got into the spirit of the thing when the five Jewish Austrian brothers made trumpeting sounds and began to duel with sticks. Jerome stuck his hand between the buttons of his shirt and jumped onto an upturned laundry tub. Striking a pose, he declared that he was Napoleon Bonaparte and that Hitler was slime from the nose of a pig and that all Nazis were about to become cannon fodder.

He was cheered by everyone in the courtyard. He doffed his two-cornered hat in a gallant bow and led the cheer for France. Very stirring.

"You are a born orator, Jerome," Madame Rose said.

The hats were quite acceptable after that.

So. The time had come to leave No. 5. One hundred and fifty children were lined up ten across and fifteen deep for the march to Gare d'Orsay.

Like the French tour guides known as Universal Aunts, Madame Rose and her sister, Madame Betsy, held black umbrellas high above their heads. At the end of each row, the women students from the Sorbonne also held umbrellas. Five boys in wheelchairs each carried paper banners of the French tricolor, which had been made at the same time as the hats. The other two children who were lame held the tiny babies and the toddlers and were pulled in handcarts and wagons. Madame Rose declared that these were the captains of the artillery. Jerome pushed his friend Henri's wheelchair.

Papillon was in a high state of rat excitement. He perched on Henri's head, then skittered down his arm and back up again. He twitched his nose with great interest at the four oldest Austrian brothers who pushed the other wheelchairs. The youngest Austrian brother pulled a wagon.

Everyone carried paper-wrapped packages. These bundles contained two pairs of clean underthings, two pairs of socks, and one change of clothing.

It was too hot to wear sweaters, but Madame Betsy would not have them left behind. "It may be sweltering today," she croaked in her reedy voice when the boys complained, "but you will be sorry if you do not have something warm to wear in the fall!"

Madame Betsy was always thinking ahead and using interesting words.

Madame Rose agreed with her. "Remember, it will be cold again someday."

It was hopeless to disagree with both of the sisters at the same time.

So one heavy article of clothing, either a coat or a sweater, was tied around the waist of each child. In addition to this, there was lunch. Also dinner, breakfast, lunch, and dinner again. The food was all the same, but there was enough to live on for the journey: Cheese sandwiches wrapped in waxed paper, two oranges, and two apples were packed into the pillowcases of each traveler. This was then tied to the belt so it could not be lost.

"If you must abandon anything, leave only your extra clothes behind! But do not lose your food parcels," Madame Rose instructed. "One may run through the Tuileries as stark naked as the day he was born and still survive. Especially in this weather. But one must have food to survive!"

"And paper hats to keep one's brains from boiling," remarked Georg to Jerome under his breath.

Jerome pictured everyone naked except for the two-cornered hats and the umbrellas.

After that there was the very strictest command from Madame Rose that one could eat only when permission was granted and that any soldier who went through his provisions without waiting would just have to go hungry.

Jerome had seen the hungry people at Gare du Nord, so he resisted dipping into his supplies.

Madame Rose, umbrella elevated, tin whistle between her lips, took her place at the head of the procession. Madame Betsy brought up the rear.

Madame Rose puffed out her cheeks and let loose with an ear-splitting *FWEEEEEEEEET!* on the whistle.

There was no missing her intention. Papillon leaped up in terror onto Jerome's food sack and then scampered to the top of his paper hat.

"All right everyone! Stick together now! Artillery?" Madame Rose glowered down at Jerome and Henri and Papillon. "Are you all ready?" She addressed the rat. *"Marche!"*

ᴄᴏᴅ

Colonel Gustave Bertrand had still not arrived to pick up Richard Lewinski. His tardiness had made Josie late for the rendezvous at Gare d'Orsay. Madame Rose had specified in no uncertain terms that in order to be assured of a place on the train, everyone traveling with the orphanage would have to be at the terminal at least two hours before departure. That mark had passed twenty minutes ago.

The children played upstairs as Josie packed a small bag with food for their journey and placed it in the tiled foyer in preparation for leaving. Where was Bertrand?

She dialed Bertrand's private number. The phone at Vignolles rang a dozen times before it was finally answered by a feeble, croaking voice.

"Colonel Bertrand please?"

"The colonel? He is gone away long ago. Last night."

"Gone where?" How could Bertrand have forgotten Richard Lewinski?

"I do not know, Madame. They have simply loaded the trucks. Very many trucks, Madame. And they have all gone away. South, I think. Like the birds."

There was a knock at the door as she replaced the handset. Josie was pleased. She was sure that it would be Colonel Bertrand. He had come to retrieve Lewinski, and he was also apparently running late. Now Josie could leave with her conscience clear, her last duty discharged.

Poking her head through the doorway of the stairs to the basement, she called out, "Good-bye, Richard. We are leaving now." She thought she heard a grunt of acknowledgment, but in Lewinski's case it was hard to tell whether it had been directed at her or was part of some private reverie.

She flung open the front door. "Come in, Colonel," she offered, then stopped awkwardly. The short, dapper man who bowed on the front stoop was not Bertrand. Had he been sent in the colonel's place to retrieve Richard? Josie glanced past him, expecting to see a lorry. There was none. Instead, across the Seine, she glimpsed hordes of people carrying luggage and children and belongings on their way to Gare d'Orsay to catch the train south.

"I was told Colonel Bertrand would call personally," she began. "You are not who I was expecting."

"And you are not Colonel Andre Chardon, but you are a most charming substitute!"

"I am sorry; Colonel Chardon is not at home," Josie said, impatient at this latest interruption. So this fellow was not from Bertrand. Where was Bertrand? "I do not know when Colonel Chardon will return, Monsieur . . ."

"Federov. How unfortunate that I missed him. I am also a wine merchant, you see, and a friend of Colonel Chardon." He glanced at the bag of food in the foyer. "I am leaving Paris for Switzerland and only wanted to stop and wish him well. Who knows when we will all return? And when we do, Paris may be filled with strangers."

This was an ominous and unpleasant thing to say, Josie thought. But probably true. All the familiar faces were on their way to the train stations.

"When I see him, I will tell him." She began to close the door.

He put up his hand and held it open, then stepped in past her. "But of course!" he remarked. He glanced around nervously. "But you are Madame Marlow. We met at the Friends of Poland reception."

Josie vaguely remembered him. Had he provided the buckets of champagne? She gestured toward the bag to show that she was in a hurry. "You will have to excuse me, but we have a train to catch."

"A pity. I would have liked to renew our acquaintance. Perhaps I could just write Andre a note? It will only take a moment. I have a pen," he said, withdrawing one from his jacket pocket. "Could you locate a scrap of paper for me?"

Josie decided it would be quicker to accommodate this request than to try to refuse it. There was stationery in the Louis XIV desk against the wall of the foyer. Turning to fetch the paper, she was stopped by the barrel of an automatic pistol pressed into her ribs.

"Say nothing except what I tell you." Federov's voice was low and menacing. "Where is Lewinski?"

"You are making a mistake. A number of soldiers . . . Colonel Bertrand . . . will be here any minute."

"You are wrong, Madame. The colonel has been notified by Quai d'Orsay that Richard Lewinski left by plane for England some hours ago. Lewinski has connections at Oxford, we have heard. Bertrand believes the little Jew has flown the coop. No one is coming."

Josie blurted, "The cook and the housekeeper and the chauffeur are—"

"Gone." Federov jabbed the Czech-made automatic into her side. "There is no time for lies. The servants are all away, and we have already established that Colonel Chardon is out. I will ask only once more: Where is Lewinski?"

At that instant a roaring sneeze resounded from the basement, identifying the location of Federov's quarry.

"Very good," Federov said. "Then it is to the basement we must go. You will precede me down the stairs without making any sound."

Three steps from the bottom, the tread creaked and Lewinski looked up from the notes on his worktable. "Who is this?"

Federov shoved Josie down. She caught her heel and fell to the stone floor. "Richard Lewinski," Federov said, "I bring greetings from your former employer . . . Reinhard Heydrich."

Lewinski glanced toward a wrench lying on the table beside his Enigma machine. His fingers twitched.

"I would not if I were you," Federov cautioned. "This can either be quick, or it can be painful. It makes no difference to me, but it may be important to you."

Lewinski raised his hands slowly and backed away from the table as Josie got to her feet.

Motioning Josie over toward the wall, Federov advanced to stand next to Lewinski's notebook. He thumbed through the pages. "I see that my assignment was not a waste," he observed. "You are working on an Enigma machine. It does not look like you are successful, but one never knows."

"I beg your pardon," Lewinski said with wounded pride. "It most certainly does work!"

"Really?" Federov retorted as he peered into the cabinet of the decoding device.

"Do not touch it!" Lewinski barked in indignation.

Federov was enjoying the game. He touched the wheels and smiled smugly at Lewinski, as if to demonstrate who was in control. "A fascinating jumble. We will leave it here until the chief of security arrives in Paris with the Führer to examine your work." He inclined his head curiously at the two banks of dials and switches on the console. He flicked the top two switches. Nothing happened.

"Do not touch it!" Lewinski roared again. "It will—"

With an impish grin, Federov flipped the toggle.

His body stiffened in a rictus of electric shock as the voltage coursed through him, pulling him up on tiptoe. An involuntary exclamation of "Ahhhh" started on a low note and ascended the scale to become a shrieking, high-pitched cry. An electric spark arced from the barrel of the gun to the metal fittings inside the cabinet, and the basement lights dimmed to a pale orange glow.

The nauseating smell of burning hair filled the cellar, and Josie ducked her head toward the wall. The lights resumed their normal brightness. When she looked up again, she saw that Lewinski had separated two electric cords on the floor behind the cabinet.

The gun barrel was welded to the steel of the frame, and Federov was held upright by his grasp on the handle. When the power was shut off and his grip relaxed, he crumpled to the stones.

"I told him," Lewinski said.

Josie reeled back to sit down hard on the stairs.

Lewinski stepped over Federov to examine his machine.

Unable to remain, Josie half ran, half crawled up the stairs. She flung the door wide and gulped the air. She was glad the children were still upstairs. Across the Seine the crowds had swelled to fill the road from side to side.

Carrying his notes, Lewinski plodded up after her and kicked shut the door to the basement. "What a mess," he said glumly.

"Horrible." Josie leaned heavily against the door.

"Worse than that. All the circuits are melted. The machine is ruined."

"You will have to go with us, Richard." Her voice was barely audible. "This man was Gestapo. They know where you are."

"I suppose. And Andre will not be happy to have a dead man in his basement. The whole house will smell." At that, he put on his gas mask. "I told him not to touch it. You are my witness. I warned him."

Right, Josie thought, looking at Lewinski's smiling eyes through the goggles of the buglike mask. *Just like B'rer Rabbit told B'rer Fox to do anything but throw him in the briar patch!*

Perhaps Richard Lewinski was more practical than she imagined.

"Why build in such a dangerous switch?" Josie asked.

His voice was muffled. "I thought they might come. I thought they might want to play with it a bit before they killed me. It is such a lovely whirligig of a thing. Anyone would want to play with it; do not you think?"

24

In This Needful Hour

Gare d'Orsay, with its rococo ceilings and high, arched windows, looked more like a beautiful cathedral than a train station. Yesterday, Notre Dame had overflowed into the square with hopeful Parisians beseeching God to save France. This afternoon, all hope was redirected from the high altar of the church to Gare d'Orsay and the southbound trains. The terminal was packed with the desperately frightened population, who prayed to hear the shrill benediction of a train whistle that could save them from encroaching hell.

From the arched porticos to the gilded iron gates, the crowds spilled out to overrun the sidewalks and the curbs and the broad Quai Anatole France. From both directions along the walled banks of the Seine the people kept coming. They arrived much faster than the trains came and went. Little children and belongings in tow, citizens were packed so tightly in the hot sun that when one fainted, the press of the others held the body upright.

Into this throng marched the little army of paper hats and umbrellas. The wheelchairs. The little wagons. The pygmy columns fifteen deep and ten across. Towering at the head was Madame Rose. Tweeting her whistle and trumpeting like the lead elephant of Hannibal's troop, she began to pass through what seemed to be the impassable.

"Pardon! PARDON! We are the orphanage of la Huchette. We have a train car reserved. Pardon! You will step aside, Monsieur! Madame, you must move your heap of baggage. We have children in wheelchairs coming along."

For one moment only she paused and glanced back. "Oh,

Josephine," Jerome heard Madame Rose murmur. "Where are you, my dear?"

No time to wait; she forged on.

Hostile eyes stared at the raised umbrellas. Lips curled in disdain at the sight of cripples given the places of healthy French children. Comments were muttered at the sight of the lederhosen and kneesocks of the five Austrian brothers. Were these trains not saved for French children? Were the children of foreigners and refugees to be given priority over good, patriotic citizens of the Republic of France?

It was an outrage!

Progress stopped at the closed and locked gates of the Gare. Jerome could hear the angry comments of the people at the front who said they had been waiting too long to give up their places to the orphans of la Huchette. He heard the indignant bellows of those who pushed in at the sides and jostled behind. What right had these children to crowd ahead?

Madame Rose, stoic and self-assured, passed her papers through the bars of the gate to one of the three gendarmes who stood guard, lest anyone attempt to push the gate down or climb over.

"As you see, Officer, we have a car reserved by special order of the minister of transportation. It is all there. Very clearly."

Behind her the murmur grew more menacing, the words more harsh. The gendarme turned pale and nervous. The crowds were near to rioting anyway. Did he dare let these pass? Did he dare open the gate?

"One moment please, Madame," he said, taking the documents away with him.

Now there was a rough shove from a big, brassy woman with an enormous bosom and her sleeves rolled up like a stevedore. One of the students from the Sorbonne fell down. There was a small scream from Marie. Jerome recognized it. He had heard Marie scream many times.

He peered back to see his sister helping the Sorbonne volunteer struggle to stand. The student's black umbrella swayed back and forth and then slowly rose into its place on the perimeter of the band. Marie looked very angry behind the thick lenses of her glasses.

Jerome stuffed Papillon beneath his paper hat in case there was a riot. He checked around for some way of escape. Jump on the iron bars of the gate perhaps? Then he looked at Henri, stuck in the wicker wheelchair. Jerome decided that even if things got rough he would stick with Henri. They would ride out the battle together or not at all!

Even Madame Rose betrayed some nervousness, the first Jerome had ever seen. Her square hands fidgeted.

"Will they let us on the train?" Jerome whispered.

"Pray, my dear boy," she replied, scanning the mob inside the gate who were standing belly to back all the way against the chuffing train.

Josie knew they were too late to make the train even before they reached the edge of the ever-widening pool of humans and baggage.

The doll in her lap, Juliette sat on one of Lewinski's shoulders. Her legs were crossed daintily at the ankles; her fingers were entwined in his wiry red hair. Josie also held Yacov on her shoulder—a protection against the ever-increasing pressure building behind them.

Across the thousands of hats and heads between them and the gate, Josie spotted the unbroken square of the umbrellas. The children were not moving forward, but at least they were at the front of the throng.

"Pardon," Josie ventured. "We are meeting someone . . . that group at the front with the umbrellas."

A fierce, dark-eyed woman with bad teeth turned and snarled. "You say you are with them? That group of cripples and foreigners? They have taken our places in line when we have been waiting all day long! *Pardon you?* I will tell you what will happen if you do not get out of here now. . . ."

Josie backed away, letting a large group behind them inch forward. It was easier to move to the outer edge of the mob than to move even one inch nearer Madame Rose. It was hopeless.

They emerged a block away where the bridge known as Pont Royal led across the river to the Louvre. The umbrellas of Madame Rose and her little company were still in plain sight, moving and bobbing now before the entrance of the station. What was happening? Josie thrust Yacov into Lewinski's arms and climbed up on the thick retaining wall at the corner of Pont Royal to see.

"Room for one hundred and forty-seven passengers only, Madame." The grim transportation officer spoke to Madame Rose through the gate. "And you have one hundred and fifty plus adult volunteers."

"Our family has grown since the documents were issued last week, Monsieur le Chief." Madame Rose called him Chief, even though he was only a second-class official with no gold braid on the sleeve of his blue uniform.

"No matter. We take only what the papers say. There may be a riot all the same, Madame, when we open the gates! So I will tell you the decision that has come through this morning: No Jews or children of foreign extraction are to be put before French children."

These words were overheard by people beyond the perimeter of umbrellas and passed back with satisfaction. The news that justice had been served rippled outward as if a boulder had been dropped into a still pond.

"What about the cripples?" a husky female voice shouted.

The official agreed loudly with the opinion that only healthy and whole children would be transported on the train. A wheelchair would take up too much space. A cripple would require too much care. There were entire trainloads of ill persons that had already been transported. Why were these youngsters not in their places? Why had they not gone when they were supposed to go? Now they were here to take the places of healthy children, and they were obviously out of turn.

He was a cruel little man to say such things in front of Henri and the others who could not walk. Jerome did not feel so much pity for the five Austrian brothers. Even though they were Jews, they were not hurt by the remarks. They were only angry, and the brothers were usually angry about something. Boys like Georg and his brothers were perfectly capable of stealing bicycles from the mountains stacked at Gare du Nord and pedaling all the way to Spain if they had to. But what about these boys who had useless legs? They could not walk across Pont Royal without help. How could they pedal anywhere? Jerome was angry. Madame Rose was angry. But if anything else was done, the crowd would riot and people would be crushed and killed.

"They have all been out in the sun too long," Georg said loudly.

"They should have worn paper hats," Henri said from his chair. He laughed a bit, even though tears were hanging in his eyes.

"Their brains are boiled," Jerome agreed.

Georg eyed Jerome with a bit of resentment. "You are French. You have legs. You can go."

"I am not going," Jerome said, squinting up at Madame Rose. "I will not go, Madame Rose."

The anger in her eyes softened. She nodded, approving of his decision, even though he was a small boy and the Germans would soon drop bombs. Jerome knew she would not make him be a coward and go away while his dear friends were made to stay behind. And he loved Madame Rose for letting him be brave.

Marie read his decision in his eyes. "I will stay with you, Jerome!" she cried.

Could he deny her request when Madame Rose had been so kind to grant him his? Yes. "You are going, Marie!"

From her place she wailed and moaned. "Let me stay with you! I will not go. I will not!"

It made the crowd restless.

Someone shouted. *"Mon dieu!* Let her stay!"

"All right," Jerome agreed but shook his fist at her. "Now shut up!"

Having won, she obeyed.

Now Madame Betsy worked her way up from behind. It was decided what must be done. The sisters spoke in English because they did not want the nasty little official to know what they were saying.

"You must take the others south, Betsy. He will not allow any more than the number on the travel document to board the train."

Betsy smiled and nodded, but her eyes were hard. "He is an evil little creature." Still smiling, she nodded to him. "Look at him, Sister. Beady eyes and tiny Hitler mustache. No doubt he will cuddle up with the Nazis when they arrive. Just the type."

"Perhaps the first bomb will land on his head, and then we will not have to wonder about it. In the meantime, you and the volunteers get on the train. Take the little ones. I will stay with our special children and the sons of Abraham. I have an ace or two up my sleeve, Sister. I'll call Dupont's secretary at the Ritz. He's American. . . ."

"He's long gone," Betsy said.

"Whatever. I'll get a car," Rose insisted.

"It will take more than a car."

"You need to get on the train, Sister, and pray. God will answer. He always does. I will make it. And if I don't?" Rose enfolded her sister in her big arms. "Well then, remember . . . *There is a river, the streams whereof shall made glad the city of God.* . . . I promise you; we shall meet beside the river, Betsy dear."

And that was that. The gate parted just enough to let Betsy through. Bayonets at the ready, the gendarmes then escorted the well children, the French children, inside the terminal.

There was no way to get them through that crowd without the danger of them being crushed. An announcement was made on the loudspeaker that the orphans of the French patriots needed to get on the train. The crowd cheered them. One by one, the little children of la Huchette were lifted up and passed above the heads of the people. Hand to hand they floated from the gilded gates of Gare d'Orsay toward the train carriage that had been reserved for them in this needful hour. Likewise, Madame Betsy and the volunteers drifted over the human sea to take their places on the train out of Paris.

PART III

Now storming fury rose,
And clamor such as heard in Heav'n till now
Was never, arms on armor clashing bray'd
Horrible discord, and the madding wheels
Of brazen chariots rag'd: dire was the noise
Of conflict; overhead the dismal hiss
Of fiery darts in flaming vollies flew
And flying vaulted either host with fire.

John Milton,
Paradise Lost

25

A Wrong Turn

The halt order rescinded at last.

The panzers were soon knocking on the gates of Dunkirk, even as the Luftwaffe was battering it from above. Andre was ordered by Lord Gort to make contact with the French forces holding the eastern perimeter and report back. Gort even loaned Andre his personal car and driver.

Lille was the farthest outpost of the Allied withdrawal. Located fifty miles inland from the Channel, Lille was the toe of the sock into which all the remaining British and French forces had been squeezed.

Andre was to confer with General Prioux, head of the French First Army, and Third Corps Commander Laurencie. The meeting was held in the massive seventeenth-century brick citadel standing high at the west end of the Boulevard de la Liberté. Even as Andre entered the fortress, a German bombing raid had just ended and another artillery barrage pounded the east end of the city.

The council was another example of how massively convoluted and inept the Allied communications were. General Prioux believed that Dunkirk was to be used as a resupply base to maintain a foothold on the coast. He had not even been informed that the evacuation was under way. Swearing violently, Prioux ordered Laurencie to hold Lille while he went off to find Gort.

It was near the Belgian border on Andre's return trip that he ran headlong into a Waffen-SS reconnaissance unit. Gort's driver had taken a wrong turn and gotten lost on a deserted country lane. While trying to relocate the correct highway, they blundered into the German patrol.

Machine guns opened up on the unarmed Humber staff car, which crashed into a ditch after bullets from the MG-34s smashed the windshield. The driver was killed.

The Germans roared forward on their motorcycles. Andre dropped out of the low side of the upturned car and sprinted rapidly along the trench. Hunching over as he ran, he ducked into a culvert that went under the road as the lead cycle pulled up next to the Humber.

He could hear their shouts as they examined the car. Andre knew they would find his briefcase in the backseat. Fortunately, it contained nothing of a sensitive nature, but it would tell the soldiers that another occupant of the car had escaped.

Sure enough, a flurry of orders in German sent a motorcycle to either end of a quarter-mile stretch of road, while the rest of the group dismounted to follow their quarry on foot. Andre crawled through the drainage pipe to the far side of the lane and plunged into the densest mass of thorns and brush he could find.

He reasoned that a patrol of limited strength, operating on the edge of hostile territory, would not stay in one place for long. He would wait them out until they gave up the search. Why would they expend great effort for one unknown man?

Suddenly Andre realized that in the minds of the SS troops, his identity was not unknown. The thought was chilling: The Humber was clearly marked as General Gort's personal auto. If the prize was the highest-ranking British officer on the Continent, they would not give up easily. They might even call for additional troops for the search.

There was not enough distance between Andre and the road. He broke out of the thorn patch on the far side and starting running again.

The plot of timber and scrub was only a couple acres in size, and the clearing into which Andre emerged was occupied by a barn and a haystack. He ran across the open space, zigzagging as he went with the expectation of a shot being fired. The open ground was too broad to cross at once, so Andre ducked into the barn. He intended to go through and out the other side, using it as cover to regain the woods beyond.

He was met in the cool, dusty darkness with a bayonet presented at his throat. A voice from the shadows demanded in French that he raise his hands. Andre complied, and as his eyes grew accustomed to the dim light, he saw the nature of his captors. They were a ragtag band of ten or twelve men, mostly French army deserters with a couple of Belgian soldiers as well.

The leader demanded to know if Andre had come to arrest them. "By myself? Don't be an idiot," Andre replied. "There is a German patrol after me. If you know what is good for you, you will get out of here fast!"

The chief of the deserters laughed at the comment. "There are no Germans within twenty miles of here," he scoffed.

"Suit yourself," Andre said coolly, "but at least let me go then."

"Maybe he is telling the truth," one of the Belgians observed. "Look at the mud and the thorns on his uniform."

The leader grudgingly admitted that it was unlikely for a colonel to cover himself with dirt just to make a convincing story.

"If you are going to force me to stay here, give me a gun to fight with!" Andre demanded.

More scornful laughter was interrupted by a call from the lookout in the hayloft. "Some more men emerging from the woods, and they are wearing black uniforms."

The deserters rushed to every crack in the rough boards of the front wall. Unseen by any of them, Andre pushed out a loose plank at the back of the barn. He crouched beside the wall, examining the distance to the cover of the trees. It was too far and the Germans were already too close. The only shelter possible was the haystack. Andre flung himself across the intervening space, hoping that his rush had not been seen. He burrowed into the mound of moldy straw.

A shot was fired by the sniper upstairs in the barn. A German soldier fell, and replying machine-gun fire raked the front of the barn. The men inside fired back—a sporadic popping noise compared to the chatter of the MG-34s.

Andre steadily wormed his way deeper and deeper into the pile of hay. Even so, he could hear the shouts of the Germans as they encircled the barn. A fusillade of bullets soon poured into the farm building from three sides. The thin, flimsy panels were no protection for the deserters inside. Andre heard the cries as men were wounded. The feeble rifle bursts coming from the barn were reduced to fewer and fewer returns of the German fire. Finally they stopped altogether.

Andre could hear the poilus shouting for the Germans to stop shooting and they would surrender. The deserters were ordered to come outside and line up along the front wall.

The German officer in charge was obviously disappointed by their catch. He brusquely demanded to know if anyone remained in the barn. Only three dead men and two more too badly wounded to walk out, he was told. The structure was searched and the truth of the statement verified.

The SS commander ordered the prisoners to return to the barn. "You will be kept here until arrangements have been made to transport you."

As the last French soldier was herded back into the barn, he turned to ask how soon assistance would be brought for a wounded friend.

"Here is all the assistance you need," yelled the officer.

A French voice screamed, "Grenade!" and blasts of German machine guns began again. The grenade exploded with a roar, and new screams erupted from the barn. Andre heard a window crash as someone tried to escape, and he heard the shriek as the attempt was met by a rifle bullet in the face. The SS troops surrounding the barn took turns tossing in grenades. They laughed at the frantic efforts of the men trapped inside.

As the explosions died away at last, Andre heard the SS officer say, "Burn it!" There was a terrifying rush of footsteps as the Germans scooped up armloads of straw to dump inside the barn.

The amount of cover on top of Andre decreased. He was afraid to move, fearing that the least squirm would be visible. A fragment of hay slid down from his head, and Andre could see out! The toe of one of his boots protruded from the pile. Surely one of the Germans would see it!

A black-uniformed figure bent over the straw to gather another sheaf. "That is enough," Andre heard the officer say. "Light it and let's get out of here."

For a reason Andre was never able to decipher, the SS troops did not set fire to the haystack, too. Perhaps their only thought was to cover up the evidence of their actions. He waited until the barn was a roaring mass of flames, then emerged on the far side of his hiding place. Andre ran into the woods, completely unharmed.

❧

Sometime after midnight there was a lull in the shelling around the BEF Casualty Clearing Station at the Ecole de Cavalerie. It was the absence of explosions that awakened David Meyer from a shallow and troubled sleep beneath the table in the foyer of the church. Now the stillness of the night exposed the agonized pleas of the wounded.

Above him came the urgent voices of a man and woman. "Sister Mitchell, the Belgian king, Leopold, capitulated to the Nazis an hour ago. It is only a matter of time before they move to encircle us here."

"We can't leave our patients!"

"You must, Sister Mitchell! There is still time for you to pull your nurses back . . . the coast . . ."

"What about our wounded?" Her voice trembled with the horror of leaving over a thousand wounded soldiers to the Germans.

"We will take all we can! The rest we must leave to German mercy."

"There is no mercy in the Germans, Major!" Her voice choked.

"Then we must leave them to the mercy of God!" the man insisted.

"I can't desert them. . . ."

With a groan of agony, David slid out from under the table at the feet of the nurse and the BEF officer. "I've gotta get out of here," he gasped.

The nurse blinked dumbly at him. "An American? What are you doing under there?" Her eyes flitted to his swollen arm and rigid, purple fingers.

"I stopped to get this splinter out of my arm," David grimaced. "No time for that now."

Sister Mitchell reached down to help him to his feet. "At least you can walk."

The foyer, the nurse, and the officer swam before his eyes. He felt his knees buckle as the dull complaint in his arm changed to a scream.

"You won't get a mile unless we see to that thing." She clucked her tongue. "Nasty." She touched his index finger, and he choked off a cry. "Your fingers look like cow teats with a bad case of mastitis."

This was the boss lady, David guessed. He nodded in a jerky motion as nausea knotted his gut again. "Cow . . . yeah. Swell."

"Swollen all right. Quite."

Ten minutes later, the sleeve of his uniform cut away, David lay on a table in a side chapel of the sanctuary. The walls were lined with memorial tablets to honor the dead of the last war who had been trained here at Ecole de Cavalerie. The floor was littered with the wounded of the new generation of an old battle. What would their fate be with the Luftwaffe sinking British hospital ships at Dunkirk? David gazed at the carpet of wounded as though they already lay beneath a garden of white crosses. Young men, like him, who had fought, been wounded, received care, and now what did any of that mean to them? They were as dead as if they had been left to bleed to death on the field of battle. Dead men. Boys, who had not even begun to live.

Back home their mothers watched for ships streaming back to England and prayed their sons were on those ships. Young women like his Annie waited for word and hoped that the names of the men they loved would not be on the lists of dead, wounded, or missing. And what about the troops assembled on the beaches of Dunkirk? They looked over their shoulders and wondered about the comrades they had left behind. They looked ahead at the glassy sea and wondered if they would reach the shores of home again. They looked up through the smoke over Dunkirk as the Messerschmitts strafed them on the sand and in the water. . . . But at least they had hope.

There was no hope for the men left behind in No. 10 CCS at Ecole de Cavalerie on the River Lys. Located between Dunkirk and the German panzers, the school would be overrun and the river crossed in the German drive to the coast.

Sister Mitchell was still clucking at the enormity of the sliver of shrapnel. "Not too deep though. You're lucky. This will hurt a bit." Chatting cheerfully in an attempt to keep his mind off the pain, she grasped the exposed end of the six-inch metal splinter and pulled. It seemed to grind against his bones as she jerked it loose.

The room swam around David.

She happily held up the splinter, then tossed it into a metal bowl.

David groped for the bowl and threw up for what he hoped was the last time. "It didn't hurt that bad going in," he gasped.

With a touch of her finger she pushed him back on the table and poured iodine onto the wound. "An American RAF pilot. My heavens. Thank God we have you. Well, you've done your best. Most important thing now is that you get yourself back across the Channel. Back to Britain. Fly against the Hun again. You'll need to have this x-rayed when you get back. Make sure we haven't left anything in there. Our chaps will fix this properly for you when you get across. Eighty percent of all the wounds we treat are from shrapnel. Yours is no worse than most. This will do for now. The pain would have knocked you out if we hadn't removed it. What's your name?"

"David Meyer . . . Tinman, they call me," he replied through clenched teeth as she wrapped the arm in gauze.

"Tinman, is it? Lots of our lads stopping in here every hour asking the way to the coast. You can hook up with one of the lot and off you go! To Dunkirk!"

Then from a shadow beneath a Gothic stone pillar came a muffled cry. "Tinman! Is that you, Tinman?"

A figure with hands, arms, and head swathed in bandages sat bolt upright on a canvas cot. He resembled a mummy sprung to life. "Tinman. Is it you? It's me! It's your old friend, Badger Cross. Am I ever glad you've come along!"

Then the explosive joy of Badger crumbled into desperation. He stretched his gauze-mittened arms out in the general direction of David and Sister Mitchell. "Take me with you, Tinman! Get me out of this stinking hell! Please, old chap! I can't see . . . but I can walk. Walk me back across the Channel, will you? Point the way; I'll walk on the water, like Saint Peter! No hard feelings, Yank. Just don't leave me here to the Nazis!"

⸎

After spending all night in the woods and catching a fitful hour's sleep in the trunk of a hollow tree, Andre emerged into the morning light of the twenty-eighth of May. A village lay in a fold of the hills just ahead. The smoke from the chimneys curled lazily into the sky. There was no activity in the town and no guards patrolled the streets, but he crept cautiously along a line of hedge between a dairy and a blacksmith shop anyway. Since he had been lost before the encounter with the SS, and his evasive maneuvers had taken him several different directions, he now had no idea which side of the front line he was on.

A road sign near the edge of town gave directions in two languages. *Ypres* it said, and below that, *Yperen*. That the city was identified in two languages meant that he was in Belgium. The distance given to what was still an Allied-held strongpoint seemed to suggest that it was safe to show himself.

Andre went to the door of the house in front of the dairy. He had only a few coins in his pocket, but perhaps it would be enough to buy some milk. He had eaten nothing since noon the day before, and he was famished.

After he knocked twice on the door, there was a long delay before anyone answered. The woman who finally came saw his stubbled, dirty face and his torn and stained uniform and screamed.

There was a commotion in the back of the house and a man emerged, holding an antique fowling piece. He presented it in Andre's face and demanded that he clear off at once. "We want none of your kind around here."

"My kind?" Andre repeated blankly. Then, remembering the way he looked, he explained. "I am not a deserter. I had a brush with the Boche and escaped. Where is the local commander? He needs to know—"

"Get off with you, I said, before I shoot!"

Andre could not believe his ears. "I just want to buy some milk."

"I said *go!*" the man announced with finality. He cocked the shotgun with a serious air.

Andre raised his hands in submission and walked backward away from the house. He thought that the man must be crazy. Perhaps the town had been vandalized by deserters and Andre's appearance was too suspicious.

As he reached the main street of the village, the church bell began to ring. It pealed over and over again in a joyous, swelling sound. The doors of the houses flung open, and people suddenly appeared where none had been before. They were all smiling and talking in excited tones.

A group of Belgian soldiers appeared on the corner just ahead. They had no helmets or weapons, and their tunics were undone. They were laughing as they talked and smoked.

As Andre approached, they regarded him curiously. "What is happening?" he asked.

"Have you not heard?" a young, almost beardless private said. "The war is over! It was on the radio. The war is over!"

"The war is . . . ?" Andre was incredulous. Had he somehow slept more than one night, like a figure in a fairy tale? Or was he not awake and this was a dream now? "The war is over?" he said again.

"Yes, man," repeated the private, laughing. "King Leopold was just on the radio. You can believe it. The war is over."

"But how? Why?"

A flicker of movement caught Andre's eye from the second story of the house on the corner. A heavyset woman was vigorously waving a white sheet as if airing the bed linen. But then she hung it over the railing and pinned it in place.

Suddenly Andre understood. "Belgium has surrendered." He groaned.

"Sure," the private agreed, staring at Andre as if he were an escapee from a mental hospital. "That is what we said: The war is over."

"Not for me," Andre said wearily. "Not for me."

26

The Evacuation Corridor

The sudden and unexpected capitulation of the Belgians created a massive immediate problem for the French and British soldiers in the evacuation corridor. Twenty miles of front from Ypres to the sea, supposedly guarded by the Belgian forces, were now unprotected. It was a gap through which all of Wehrmacht Army Group B could have swept unopposed. If it were not for Lord Gort's willful disobedience—if he had not sent British troops north, in direct contradiction of his instructions—the evacuation would have been crushed.

As it was, General Bernard Montgomery's Third Division stepped smartly into the hole left by the Belgians and took over the guard duties. They made the remarkable maneuver in one night, before the Wehrmacht had time to exploit the opening.

When Andre arrived at Ypres, he found out that General Gort had moved his headquarters from Premesques to Houtkerque. The new command post was out of Belgium and back in French territory. Significantly, it was only a dozen miles from the Channel.

Andre caught a ride with some British artillery forces being withdrawn toward Dunkirk. When he came upon them, they were completing a sad but very necessary project: destroying their equipment. Cannons were packed with explosives and their barrels destroyed. Papers, money, uniforms, and supplies were heaped up, doused with gasoline, and set ablaze.

The trucks needed for the withdrawal were loaded with men and lined up for the move. All the other vehicles, like those that had towed the heavy artillery, were drained of oil and water and then left running.

It was a strange, weirdly pathetic scene. The great machines shuddered and shook, like the dying convulsions of faithful elephants.

Halfway between Ypres and Noordschote, the column ran into a German tank that emerged without warning from a side road. It struck the center of the convoy, blasting a lorry loaded with men into a flaming heap of rubble.

The front half of the column roared away, leaving the following line of vehicles trapped by the burning debris on a road too narrow to quickly turn around. The soldiers jumped out of the canvas-covered transports and took cover in the ditches as machine-gun fire sprayed the bushes.

Once again Andre found himself burying his face in a muddy drainage ditch. The British Tommies had almost nothing with which to fight back. The rifle fire they used to defend themselves did nothing but bounce off the PzKw-II. It rolled forward, shoving the burning hulk of the truck out of its way, then pivoted sharply and moved again toward the line of men cowering in the ditch.

Every time its main gun fired, a 20 mm shell spelled the end of another truck or troop lorry. Soldiers near Andre, seeing no escape from being crushed by the oncoming tank, jumped up and tried to run into the woods. Every time they did so, the probing fire of the machine gun sought them out and cut them down.

On the other side of the road from Andre, a soldier had somehow located a Boyes antitank rifle. This shoulder-fired weapon propelled a shell supposedly capable of penetrating tank armor. As the machine gun mowed down those in front of it, the Tommy with the Boyes rifle popped out. He threw the weapon up and loosed three rounds in quick succession. The impact of the recoil knocked the soldier down, and he lay against the trunk of a tree, groaning with the pain of a dislocated shoulder.

But at least one bullet had penetrated a thinner part of the armor. It must have killed or wounded the driver, because the tank's engine gave a bellow like an outraged bull, and the tank slewed sideways in the roadway.

Next to Andre another panicked soldier jumped to his feet and attempted to run. Even though the PzKw-II was temporarily incapacitated, its machine gun was still active. The man had only taken two steps when his body toppled across Andre's legs.

Pushing the weight of the dead man off his knees, Andre's hand came in contact with a heavy pouch that had fallen from the Tommy's shoulder. It was a sack full of grenades.

The tank sat idle in the middle of the road, its engine rumbling. No one moved in the ditches anymore, and the German machine seemed to be searching for its next victim.

Mistaking the inactivity for opportunity, fifty yards down the road a British truck roared backward out of the ditch. The driver frantically whipped it back and forth across the pavement, attempting to turn around and escape.

The slumbering tank snorted and lumbered forward, its snout pivoting to bring the guns to bear. Lying absolutely still as the tank passed, Andre hugged the sack and steeled himself for what he had to do next. At the moment he was even with its treads, he ripped open the pouch of grenades and began pulling the pins. Two at a time, he yanked the safety rings free until eight live explosives hissed in the bag.

Andre sprinted across the road behind the tank. He threw the pouch as hard as he could underneath the center of the PzKw-II, between its treads. Flinging himself over the shoulder of the road, Andre rolled into the ditch. All the time, as the seconds were ticking past, he wondered if the tank would be clear of the pouch before it exploded.

Someone inside the PzKw-II must have spotted Andre's dash. The tank turned abruptly, its left tread stopping as the right side clanked ahead.

It was in this position when the grenades exploded. There was a muffled roar that seemed to swell in volume—like a peal of thunder, heard at first far away, that grows as it rolls over the land. Even in its death, the German tank was a lethal weapon. Steel shards, fragments of its corpse, whizzed off into the woods. Several more British soldiers, who were unwary enough to watch the explosion tear the machine to pieces, were impaled with fragments of its armor. Andre lay curled into as tiny a space as he could manage until after the last chunk of metal and detonating shell had whined by.

൭

The glorious heroes of France stared down from their portraits at the last gathering of the students of the Ecole de Cavalerie. Even though Paul had not mentioned his purpose in calling the meeting, it was widely known that the subject would be the evacuation of the school.

The hall was occupied by the remaining five hundred cadets ages sixteen and seventeen. Each was dressed in his finest dress uniform, as though going to a contest for the pride of the institution.

"Cadet officers," Paul began, "I congratulate you. You have acquitted yourselves with honor as befits the inheritors of the finest traditions of the school and *la belle Français*. You have done all that was asked of you and more. The defense of Lys is in hand, ready to be turned over to your successors. The trucks for the evac—"

Paul had not expected to be interrupted, and the figure of Sepp, rising politely to stand at attention, caught him by surprise.

Sepp took advantage of the silence to ask a question. "Your pardon, Captain, but how many troops are coming to occupy the position?"

"I have been informed that elements of the First and Third Cavalry, as well as a contingent of British—"

"Excuse me again, Captain, but will the number reach the fifteen thousand that you yourself indicated are required for adequately meeting the German advance?"

Paul knew that he had been set up. The cadets had planned to use his own words against him, and now they had sprung the trap. "If you are ordered to leave, you must obey," he said.

Raymond rose to stand beside his friend. "If so ordered, we will obey. But if thereafter we choose to return and fight beside the others for the preservation of the school, the wounded, and our dignity, is that not our right as free Frenchmen?"

Gaston stood to speak. Less sure of himself than the others in front of a large crowd, he nevertheless had practiced his speech beforehand and delivered it boldly. "May I remind the captain of the example of the cadets of St. Cyr in the Great War. When one of them said to his commander, 'You are sending me out to die,' the reply was, 'I do you that honor, sir.' Captain, how have we offended you that you would deny us that honor?"

A tear started in the corner of Paul's eye, and his throat constricted. "It must be understood that no one is compelled to stay, and no shame attaches to leaving."

The cadets all stood as one and faced him.

Paul's voice choked off and he could say no more.

"Captain," Sepp concluded for him, "what can be better for a soldier of France than to live honorably, die gloriously, and to be remembered as faithful to the end?"

Paul could do no more than nod. Twin rows of tears stained his cheeks. But that motion of acquiescence was enough to set off thunderous applause and shouts of triumph.

Gaston turned toward his friends, straightening his collar and tugging at his spotlessly white gloves. "*Mon dieu*. What a handsome corpse I will make, *mes amis*."

◎

"It has always been understood that British forces would be evacuated by British ships and French troops by French ships," Lord Gort pointed out at his early morning meeting with Andre. The general was snipping the ribbons and medals from his spare uniform.

"That may have been the understanding, sir," Andre replied, "but it is not working. Most of the French navy is in the Mediterranean. The trawlers available are wholly inadequate to the task. How else do you account for the fact that close to fifty thousand British soldiers have been evacuated so far and only five hundred French?"

"Six hundred fifty," replied Gort peevishly. "Why bother *me* with this anyway, Chardon? You should take the matter up with Captain Tennant in Naval Operations, or with my replacement, General Alexander." Gort continued removing any marks of distinction to keep some German soldier from claiming them as souvenirs.

"Sir," Andre said slowly, trying to keep his rising anger from coming through in his voice, "to them I am no more than another French soldier and none of their concern. If you, however, could raise the issue with your Admiralty . . ."

"All right, yes." Gort waved his hand in dismissal. "But my primary remaining task is to see to the defense of the perimeter. If the rear guard is not effective, none of us will be getting off." It was clear from Gort's tone that the discussion was at an end.

"In that case, sir, I request that I be allowed to pursue the matter as your personal representative, beginning with my study of the activities at the harbor."

Gort nodded curtly, anxious to put the matter behind him. "But, Chardon, whatever you do, you must be ready to leave by midnight the day after tomorrow if you expect to evacuate with my staff."

"General," Andre replied quietly, "if my countrymen are not provided for by then, I will not be going with you."

ᖆ

"What day is it, Tinman?" Badger Cross walked with his head thrown back, like a child trying to see through a blindfold in a game of blindman's bluff. He grasped David's good arm with one hand. His other hand extended in front of him.

"It's May twenty-ninth, I think," David replied, attempting to reconstruct the events of the last twenty-four hours. By now what was left of his squadron would be back in England. His mind leaped to Annie Galway. He wanted to see her again.

Badger muttered, "If it's the twenty-ninth . . . it's almost my birthday. I would have been twenty-one, if it was my birthday."

"You'll still be twenty-one, Badger."

"Where are we now, Tinman?"

"Same place we were last time you asked. On the road to Dunkirk with about a million other guys," David replied. "Don't worry about it."

"You know, every year on my birthday . . . at home I mean . . . since I was a kid, my mother always fixed me strawberries and cream with tea. Sort of a tradition. Lovely, it was."

"You never seemed the strawberries-and-cream type of guy, Badger," David retorted.

But with every mile Badger had become more and more strawberries and cream. Nostalgia for the simple luxuries of everyday life occupied his conversation in unending monotony. The long column of retreating men had already been strafed twice in four hours. Badger talked as though everything in his life was past tense, already over. It seemed like such melancholy drivel for somebody as tough and mean as Badger Cross, David thought.

At the sound of an airplane, Cross craned his bandaged head back. "What's that?" he demanded. "Ours or theirs?"

This question was important. David searched the sky for the source of the noise. When he spotted the lone black dot high overhead, the answer was clear. "Dive-bomber!" he yelled. "Clear the road!"

Even though the open ditches that lined both sides of the highway offered no real protection, a thousand men forced their way into the shallow depressions. Those who arrived first were either shoved out of the way or buried under a pile of bodies seeking to fill the same tiny space. Latecomers burrowed inside the heap or were roughly pushed away to become tangled in the thorny hedges that bordered the road.

With both hands clamped on David's good arm, Cross stumbled toward the grassy verge. The Stuka was already beginning its run.

"Make room!" David shouted. "Blind man! Make way!" His wounded arm was painfully jostled. He made no progress trying to protect it and force a path while Badger clung to his other arm.

As if sensing the difficulty, Badger lunged past David. Elbows swinging wildly, Cross collided with two soldiers of the Royal West Kent Regiment, splitting them like an unstoppable rugby player en route to a goal. "Here, Tinman," he bellowed. "This is our space!"

At the Stuka's scream, terrified men buried faces in the dirt and clamped steel helmets down over their ears. A few raised .303 rifles and fired at the swooping form, as much in defiance as with any real hope of damaging it. At two thousand feet, five objects detached from its undercarriage and the warplane pulled out of its dive.

Bombs—a thin, high-pitched replacement for the Stuka's siren— whistled downward. In rapid succession, explosions shook the roadway, blowing large craters in the pavement and spinning out lethal shrapnel fragments. Those nearest the blasts were tossed around like leaves in a windstorm. Hastily abandoned gear flew skyward; packs and canteens sailed into the air. A soldier next to David was struck by a mess kit. He screamed, "I'm hit! I'm hit!"

The plane retreated. Ten men lay dead. A dozen were maimed from two bombs that had landed on the road. Two of the dead stood frozen in upright poses in the thornbushes. Six of the wounded bled from jagged wounds. Two had lost limbs. These were as good as dead, David knew.

For the rest, most of the injuries were slight. The soldier hit by the tin pan was heartily insulted for his mistake. There was an outpouring of abuse borne out of helpless terror. It was as though by making that one man the target of scorn and ridicule, the others could somehow remove the stink of fear from themselves.

Gradually, in jerky movements, as if the column were a single animal stretching and testing itself for injury, the soldiers got up from the ditch. David stood, helped Badger to his feet, and pointed him back toward the highway.

An infantryman pointed to the RAF insignia with disdain. "Air Force?" he sneered. "What good are you, lousy flyboys? Why do you let that happen?" He pointed to a chaplain administering last rites to a man whose life was pumping out of a ragged hole in his neck.

"Nothing but Nazi planes for days," another chimed in. "Get on, be off with you, worthless—"

Badger swung a clumsy right in the direction of the speaker. His gauzed fist connected only with air, and he sprawled awkwardly.

"Leave it," David said to Cross. "Come on, we can get moving again."

"Stinkin' RAF," the call came after them. "A blind man and a busted wing. Good riddance!"

⚘

The knife blade of *Intrepid*'s bow sliced through the waves toward Dunkirk in Northern France. She was on her third crossing of the Channel on the twenty-ninth of May. Each load of weary soldiers picked off the eastern mole in France filled her to capacity with eight hundred members of the BEF spared from the crushing embrace of the Wehrmacht. *Intrepid* was so good at her job that she could unload in Dover, England, in half an hour.

The morning had been cloudy and the sky sheltering from Luftwaffe attacks. But now, after noon, the overcast was burning off and bright blue peeped through.

Trevor Galway was on the bridge beside Captain Vian. Officially second in command, Trevor was actually functioning as an extra lookout.

His binoculars scanned the sea for submarines and mines and, increasingly now, had to inspect the sky for planes as well.

Picking out a black dot dancing on the waves, Trevor inspected it, then pointed it out to Vian. "Small boat about a mile distant, sir," he reported. "It appears that it is being rowed."

Intrepid altered course slightly to intercept the route of the sighted craft. Trevor went down to the rail to oversee the loading. Once alongside, twelve soldiers of the Devon Heavy Regiment, paddling a lifeboat with the butts of their rifles, were plucked from the water.

Their sergeant, a portly man named Clifford, protested when he was informed that the rescue vessel was headed to Dunkirk to embark another load before returning to England. "Why didn't you just pick us up goin' the other way?" he asked. "We don't want to go back; it's 'orrible there!"

"Orders," Trevor explained. "When we are loaded, we don't halt to take anybody else, in case we get attacked while we're stopped."

"In that case," Sergeant Clifford blustered, "put us off again! We'll just keep rowing ourselves. We was makin' it all right!"

"I don't think you want us to do that," Trevor said.

"And why not?"

"Because you were rowing toward Calais when we found you, and it's already in German hands."

27

Waiting Ships

The port of Dunkirk was a mass of ruins: sunken ships, burning warehouses, and the eerie remnants of cargo cranes. The twisted frames of the lifting scaffolds leaned over the waterways like ancient, tired gallows. In short, the inner harbor was unusable for the evacuation. Ships entering were likely to run afoul of submerged wreckage, if they were not themselves trapped in its winding leads and bombed.

As early as the twenty-seventh of May, Senior Naval Officer William Tennant had concluded that the inner port was not serviceable. He also knew that the operation from the beaches east of Dunkirk was too slow. The good news was what he discovered about the two breakwaters that formed the entrance to Dunkirk Harbor: Two ranks of concrete pilings jutted over a thousand yards out into the Channel and were virtually untouched. Commander J.C. Clouston, pier master of Dunkirk Harbor, was assigned to make the most of the opportunity provided by the jetties.

When Andre joined Clouston at the eastern mole on the morning of May 30, the evacuation was proceeding better than anyone had hoped. As Andre watched, soldiers marched four abreast along the wooden walkway that topped the breakwater. With the tide in, climbing onto the destroyer *Sabre* that was moored to wooden posts alongside the jetty was a speedy proposition. The heavy overcast of the day provided relief from Luftwaffe attacks, and the Tommies embarked as cheerfully as if they were taking a holiday ferry to the Isle of Wight.

In less than an hour's time, *Sabre* loaded five hundred men and pulled smartly away from the mole, bound for Dover. A minesweeper slipped in to take its place, and the smooth operation continued.

But the problem continued to gnaw at Andre: Few of the departing troops were French. "Why aren't more French queued up to leave?" he demanded.

"A lot of reasons," Clouston replied. "Language problem, mostly. The poilus don't understand when told to leave their kit behind, and they don't like it when we break up their units."

It sounded to Andre like an excuse. "Don't you have anyone to interpret for you?"

"Lieutenant Solomon speaks excellent French, but he can't be everywhere at once."

It was another excuse, but this one could be dealt with.

"Will you let me help?" Andre asked.

"Certainly."

Most of the English officers handling the embarkation had only a limited knowledge of French. Shouting *"Allez, allez!"* at the poilus produced only contemptuous sneers. But while Andre was able to assist a few of his fellow soldiers, his sense of frustration grew even greater. The real reason no French were being embarked was that there were none in line. The queue that stretched down the length of the breakwater and back into the smoke-filled streets was packed with English soldiers. If French troops joined the end of the line, they were roughly pushed aside or told to leave the harbor and go to the beaches. Clearly there was nothing Andre could do as one lone voice in the face of this "English ships for Englishmen" attitude.

From where the unending line of British soldiers tramped down the plank walkway and onto the waiting boats, Andre could look across the mouth of the harbor entrance. There, no more than a quarter mile away, was the similar but unoccupied western mole.

Andre studied the ships tied up at the breakwater. There were three destroyers, two ferryboats, and a dozen smaller craft all loading at once. But for all the activity, another six boats waited off the jetty for their turn.

Andre approached Clouston with his idea. "Why can't we use the western mole as well and send the French troops over there?"

"No reason at all, except that all the waiting ships think they are to come here."

"Can I use your authority to make them change destinations?"

Clouston laughed. "My authority? You can try. Here, take my pistol . . . it may carry more weight. But Chardon," he added in a more serious tone, "don't tell anyone I said that, all right?"

Andre located a colonel of the French First Army and told him about the new plan. The officer agreed to round up as many poilus as he could and direct them to the western mole.

Now to find a boat. Andre caught a ride with a motor launch out to the *Bristol Belle*, a hundred-foot-long steamer lying offshore. The ship was practically an antique—a twenty-year-old side-wheeler with a shallow draft and a single stack amidships. She was a jumble of odd angles and curious projections: a jutting prow whose sleek line disintegrated where the great round bulges of the paddle-wheel guards stuck out. A canvas-covered flybridge was suspended above her foredeck.

Andre jumped from the motor launch to a narrow walk that encircled the girth of the starboard wheel. There was no ladder, but by putting one foot on a window ledge he boosted himself up to the rail on the open top deck and clambered over. The *Belle* idled slowly, waiting her turn at the mole. The twin lines that swept up to a single mast on her foredeck were still hung with pennants and signal flags from her last duty before Dunkirk: pleasure excursions on the Thames.

Andre found the captain, an anxious-looking man named Pert, nervously pacing the flybridge.

"Absolutely not!" Pert insisted when Andre explained what he needed. "It's bad enough waiting here. We could be bombed any second. The *Belle* was never made for work like this. Besides, the western approach is in range of those German guns between Dunkirk and Gravelines. I won't chance it, no matter who you say authorized it."

Andre considered taking a launch to another of the transport ships in the hopes of finding a more receptive welcome, but his anger flared at the waste of time. Whipping out the pistol, he snarled, "All right, here is your choice: Either take this ship to the western jetty and risk the guns of the Germans, or be on the receiving end of one Frenchman's gun right now!"

"You can't mean it!" Pert backed up against a bulkhead.

"Try me!" Andre growled.

"What's this, Cap'n?" called the *Belle*'s mate. "What's up then?"

"Do whatever he says!" ordered Pert in a squeaky voice. "He's a crazy man!"

The *Bristol Belle* reversed course, heading out to sea and rounding the harbor entrance to the west. Captain Pert's fearful glances alternated between his navigation, the western horizon where the German artillery lay, and the .38-caliber Webley revolver in Andre's hand.

By the time the *Belle* had steamed around to the other breakwater, a line of men from Blanchard's First Army stretched down its length. They made the *Belle* fast to the pilings and began an orderly filling of all the available space. Andre noticed with satisfaction that when given the opportunity—and orders in their own language—the poilus were as manageable as the Tommies.

Many of the embarking troops paused beside Captain Pert as they passed down the gangplank. Snatching off their helmets, they shook Pert's hand and fervently proclaimed, *"Merci, merci! Que le bon Dieu vous benisse!"*

Even the heart of the apprehensive captain was touched. Five hundred men crammed aboard the upper and lower decks, and the iron railings were crowded with poilus perched on them. Pert stared at the bleak faces of the men left standing on the quai and muttered, "Tell 'em we'll be back, soon as we can."

When Andre had repeated this assurance, Pert ordered the hands to cast off, and the steamer put about for Dover. "S'pose you'll make the crossing with this lot," the captain said.

Andre shook his head. "Take me alongside her." He pointed to the low form of the open-decked river steamer *Princess Louise*, steaming in lazy circles off the tip of the estuary.

"Make sure you keep your pistol handy," whispered Pert as Andre prepared to leap to the *Princess*. "I know her master. He's a mean 'un."

❧

Mac climbed the flight of concrete stairs that led up from the Embankment to the Savoy Hotel in London. At the corner, where the steep alleyway met the Strand, was the public house called the Coal Hole.

It was a two-story establishment. Upstairs, in a room full of round tables, the office workers and clerks gathered in their starched shirts and ties. Downstairs—a dark, snug chamber of exposed beams and wooden stools—was the retreat of the men with blue sleeves rolled up above mammoth forearms. It was to the lower compact space that Mac directed his steps.

John Galway was standing under the grimy bowl of a wall lamp. He had a pint of Guinness in one fist and was driving home a point with the other. "I tell ye, the Italians are just waiting to stab France in the back. Mark me words." He sloshed dark brown fluid over his listener as he gestured with the wrong hand. "If they think they can do it without risk, those *Fascisti* and their goggle-eyed, lantern-jawed toad of a leader will be over the Brenner Pass quick as you can say Musselleeeni."

Mac grinned. "Il Duce says 'Italian honor is not for sale . . . ask me about a lease!' Talking politics again, Mr. Galway? I thought Annie said it was bad for your blood pressure."

"Ah, McGrath. Right you are, but a pint is a sovereign remedy to keep things level," Galway observed. "Join me?"

Mac and John Galway were soon in a corner of the Coal Hole, each with a fresh pint in hand. "What do you hear from Trevor?" Mac asked.

"Not much. *Intrepid* has been on convoy duty. I did get a curious call from him last evenin' from Portsmouth."

"Curious how?"

"Couldn't say much on it, but he told me, 'Da, somethin' is brewin'. Don't be surprised if you don't hear from me for a while.' Then he rang off."

Mac pondered Trevor's words for a time. "What do you think it means?"

Galway leaned close to Mac, though there were no nearby drinkers. "I think it ties up with a uniformed bloke who came around my boat, *Wairakei*, this mornin'. Said he was from the Small Vessel Authority, or some such."

"What did he want?"

"*Wairakei* is requisitioned. Wouldn't say what for, with everyone bein' so tight-gobbed these days, but he said to get her down to Ramsgate by tonight. Fact is, I'm here fortifyin' myself for the voyage just before shovin' off. Care to join us?"

"Us? Is Annie going, too?"

"Aye, and Trevor's great duff beast of a Saint Bernard as well. Goin' up agin Annie when her mind is set . . ." Galway pretended to shudder. "I'd druther swim the Channel with both hands tied behind me back!"

Mac thought quickly. "Do I have time to run for my camera?"

"Finish your drink first," Galway said. "Then welcome aboard."

Less than an hour later Mac canned the clutter of his boardinghouse room, then scooped up his camera bag, a rain slicker, and a photograph of Eva grinning in the midst of her refugee students at the school in Bettws-y-Coed, Wales.

He had intended to take the train to Wales in the morning. He meant to surprise her, sweep her off her feet, and marry her all in the same day.

Life together would have to wait a bit longer.

"*Just live, Mac,*" she had told him the day he had asked her to marry him. It now seemed so long ago.

Mac glanced at his reflection in the mirror and shuddered as a thought flashed through his mind. What if he did not survive the journey? What if he didn't come back to sweep her off her feet and carry her off into the sunset?

He wanted to speak to her. Tell her how he felt. Just in case . . . just in case.

There were only three telephones in the Welsh village of Bettws-y-Coed . . . no way to contact her.

He dashed down the stairs and rang the London TENS office, hoping John Murphy was there to answer the call. Mac could trust Murphy to tell

Eva. Murphy was a man of fine words. He would know how to put it so Eva would know how much Mac loved her . . . if Mac never came back.

One ring, two, three.

A female voice answered in slightly accented English, "TENS London. How may I help you?"

Was it Eva on the other end of the line?

Mac stammered, "M-Murphy. I need to talk to John Murphy. This is—" he paused—"Eva?"

"Yes. This is . . . Eva. Mac?"

His eyes widened in surprise. "Are you in London?"

"Mac? Darling?"

"Are you here?" he asked again.

"We heard you were coming back from France. Murphy sent a wire. I came here. I was going to surprise you! Oh, Mac! Where are you? Where?"

"Eva! I can't talk. Can't stay. I called Murphy so he could tell you. I didn't think I could reach you in Wales. I'm going out on a rescue ship. Crossing the Channel. Back to France."

"When?"

"Now. On a little ship called *Wairakei* with Trevor Galway's father. You remember Trevor?"

"Yes. Yes. But why? Oh, Mac!"

"I was coming to Wales in the morning to marry you. But then this . . . this . . . so I wanted to tell Murphy to tell you . . . that if . . . I mean when I get back . . . when I'm back here . . . let's not wait another day."

Eva was crying. He knew it though she wasn't some noisy sobbing dame. He just knew she was crying—not because he was here, not because he was leaving without seeing her, but because she loved him.

Her voice was soft, almost a whisper. "Mac. I would ask you not to do anything too courageous if you love me . . . but it would be against your nature to heed such a request. And so . . . my darling Mac . . . please . . . live . . . come home to me. Please."

28

Surprising Modes of Conveyance

The air of the meeting at French Admiral Abrial's headquarters was less than cordial, even icy. The atmosphere was not helped by the surroundings: Bastion 32 was a windowless concrete bunker. Its chilled walls dripped with condensed moisture. About half the time the power supply failed, leaving a candlelit interior that could have been a dungeon.

Acrimony was the order of the day. Despite Andre's efforts at commandeering ships to rescue French soldiers, it was still not close to adequate. And if the discrimination in the rescue effort was not bad enough, General Alexander, who was replacing Gort in command of British forces, indicated that the evacuation would end in the early morning of June 2, less than seventy-two hours away.

The French officers, Admiral Abrial and General Fagalde, were aghast.

"It will mean thousands of French soldiers abandoned to the Germans," Fagalde protested.

Alexander shrugged as if it were no concern of his. "There are French destroyers lifting French soldiers; are there not?"

Abrial looked to a bone-weary Andre to answer the question.

"The *Siroco* is still operating," Andre admitted. "But the *Bourrasque* hit a mine on her way to Dover. She's gone."

Alexander still looked as if the matter were no further concern of his.

Abrial and Fagalde exchanged glances, each evidently hoping that the other would have some persuasive argument to be used with the British.

Andre thought about his day's piracy and how effective his use of the pistol had been, though he had never been forced to fire it. Perhaps it was time for coercion on a grander scale. "Is it not true that all the defenses of Dunkirk are now manned by French troops?"

Fagalde, whose men had defended the line of the Aa canal, nodded. "It will be so after tonight, when General Laurencie's 32nd Infantry and the 68th Division are all in place."

"And if they were to surrender to avoid needless bloodshed, what would that do to the remaining evacuation?"

Alexander sat bolt upright in his chair. "Extortion!" he shouted.

Abrial grinned at Andre and then coolly remarked to the British contingent, "Call it what you will, gentlemen. The fact remains that if, from this moment forward, French troops are not evacuated in equal number with English and the evacuation extended as much as possible, we will be forced to seek the best terms we can from the Germans."

"All right," Alexander grudgingly acknowledged. "You have us over a barrel. We will allot future transportation fifty-fifty, to continue as long as possible. Provided," he verbally underlined, "provided the French perform the rearguard duty as planned."

⊙⊙

Andre worked into the afternoon at his improvised evacuation station on the western mole. The official change in British policy was not yet widely known, but even so, more ships were making their way to the line of French troops.

There were setbacks, of course. *Siroco*, a French destroyer, was packed with men and on course for Dover when she was torpedoed. She might have still survived to deliver her cargo of frightened men, but a passing German bomber finished her off.

It was nothing Andre could even think about. He steadied the stream moving down the plank walkway and waved the new steamers, ferries, trawlers, and passenger launches into position as each ship filled and moved away.

⊙⊙

At three in the afternoon the torrent of refugees pouring across the bridges into Lys slowed to a trickle. Gaston had been busy all morning directing traffic and gathering what information he could. He was told that the Germans were no more than ten miles away. They would reach the valley of the Lys by tonight.

At one point an open-topped car loaded with men in French uniforms arrived at this checkpoint. Gaston demanded to see their papers. "Get out of our way, puppet," the fat, swarthy driver sneered. "Stay and play toy soldier if you want, but leave us alone!" The deserter revved up the engine as if to run Gaston down.

Gaston snapped his fingers. From behind the shelter of a pile of sandbags, the snout of an antitank gun rolled forward to poke through a gap in the barricade. It pointed straight at the grill of the car. "Come ahead," Gaston said calmly.

The driver and the eight men stuffed in the seats lifted their hands into view.

"I thought so." Gaston yanked open the door. He dragged the driver out on the pavement by the scruff of his neck. "We shoot traitors here. Or perhaps you would like to volunteer to aid with the defenses?"

The men hastily nodded their willingness to be of service. "Excellent!" Gaston said. "Lieutenant Beaufort, escort these new recruits to Captain Chardon. He has a number of empty sacks that need to be turned into sandbags!"

৩৩

It was quiet at No. 5 Rue de la Huchette tonight. Too quiet. The tiny remnant had taken refuge behind the gate and slid the iron bolt in place. Yet still, Josie felt the approach of Evil.

How to get out of Paris?

Rose believed in lists.

> *Seven special children:*
> *Five in wheelchairs, two on crutches*
> *Five Austrian brothers*
> *Jerome and Marie Jardin*
> *Josephine, Lewinski, Juliette, and Yacov*

"And a partridge in a pear tree," Madame Rose said as she added her name to the column. She glanced up at Josie, who sat in the dim glow of a single candle. "That makes nineteen of us altogether. Even two automobiles will not be enough. I can't drive anyway."

"Neither can Lewinski." Josie ran a hand over her aching head. Even if there were three vehicles, she was the only driver. A truck perhaps? An unused troop lorry? Why not ask for the Pan Am clipper or a zeppelin?

"What we need is a transportation prayer." Rose scratched possible modes of conveyance on the list to submit to God. She included everything from a troop lorry to an airplane. "The Lord approves of common sense. And when common sense fails, then there is some other course we are meant to sail."

Hours on the telephone over the last several days had brought no answers. Everyone was leaving or already gone. If some acquaintance had a vehicle, it was already packed or there was no petrol to be had. Madame Rose prayed with the same fervent faith with which Sister Angeline had prayed in the cellar of the Cathedral of St. John in Warsaw that last night. Josie hoped the two women wouldn't have the same end.

"We need a true miracle, Josephine." Madame Rose's words were not fearful but simply a statement of fact. "You know what will happen to the special children if the Nazis lay hold of them. Their fate will be the same as that of the Austrians, my little sons of Abraham. And your little ones as well. It is a fearful thing, this total war of Hitler's—what it does to children." She shook her head sadly. "They've made war on the apple of God's eye, my dear girl. Pity the German nation. They have made war on heaven, and heaven will not be silent forever."

But heaven was silent tonight, Josie thought glumly as she stood out beneath the star-flecked sky over the courtyard.

The children were asleep now in the corner room of the ground floor where beams and joists and supports were the strongest.

"Just in case," Rose said.

The windows were open. The scent of flowers was on the air. Crickets chirped and the cicadas hummed. But there was no word from heaven.

∽ᐰᐁ∽

Gaston's lieutenant was out of breath when he arrived across the bridge to deliver his message. "Captain Gaston," he said, panting, "tanks approaching the far side of the river!" It was dark, and no further refugees had crossed the bridge in several hours.

Gaston and Sepp, who had been arguing over who owned the right to place the last of the school's machine guns, stared at each other and then ran over to the island.

Crouching behind the sandbag barricade, Gaston squinted through a gap. Sure enough, two armored vehicles were driving along the riverbank, nearly to the junction with the road to Lys.

"Prepare to fire," Gaston said to the gun crew, even though he could see that the piece was already loaded and aimed at the center of the span. "Wait for my signal," he added.

The first of the machines hesitated at the crossing, as if the driver suspected something amiss. The two vehicles circled the end of the structure like a pair of dogs sniffing out a scent. Then the lead machine turned onto the road and started across.

"Steady," Gaston cautioned, even though his own voice cracked as it had done when he was four years younger. "Wait till he gets halfway over."

"Gaston!" Paul Chardon's voice said sharply.

"Captain!" Sepp answered for his intense friend. "You are just in time to see us fire the first shot for the honor of the school!"

"Just in time to save you from a bad mistake," Paul clarified. "Did neither of you notice that the vehicle you are about to destroy is a Hotchkiss tank and is one of ours?"

Paul seized a tricolor flag and waved it over the barricade. A moment later, the hatch of the lead tank popped open. The tank commander waved back; then the two machines rumbled forward across the bridge.

ೲ

Josie sat alone for a long time listening, hoping. Rose came out into the courtyard sometime after midnight and sat beside her. They gazed up through the patterns of empty clotheslines without speaking.

And then, from the open window of the corner room, a small voice piped, "*Mon dieu!* It is the Anteater!"

"Jerome." Rose shrugged. "Another nightmare." She got up to see him.

Jerome croaked distinctly. "Hey, Henri! The Anteater. The siren. The *Garlic*. The *Garlic*! Henri, we have to tell Madame Rose!"

Josie smiled at the muddled nonsense of Jerome's dream. Other children moaned with irritation at being awakened.

Rose slipped inside quietly. Her whisper drifted out through the open window. "Jerome, *mon petit pêche*, you are dreaming again. . . ."

The boy's reply boomed as if he were shouting across a wide field. "Not a dream! I heard a Voice in the siren, Madame Rose."

"There is no siren, Jerome. Very quiet tonight. Peaceful. You see?"

"Wake everyone up!" he insisted. "We have to be ready! The siren will go, and then we will leave!"

"No, no, Jerome. Only a dream, little one. You must go back to sleep. Shall I sing—?"

"*Listen to me!* Madame Hilaire—the Anteater! She sucked us out the window of the *Garlic*, but . . . she is afraid of the siren!"

"*Je comprends*, Jerome, But now—"

"Listen!" Jerome interrupted again. "When the siren goes, it is the only sound Madame Hilaire can hear. She is frightened of it. She and the Thief run away to the shelter, because they are afraid of the bombs from the Boche that might drop on the *Garlic*. But there they stay all night, and we all get on the *Garlic* and . . ."

"The boat. You mean . . . the boat? Who told you this?" The response of Rose was no longer patronizing, no longer soothing.

"*Oui*, Madame Rose. The Voice! I have heard it! We must get up now and be ready for the air-raid siren!"

⌒☉⌒

Rose Smith was a sailor and the daughter of a sailor. How many times as a girl had she shoved off from the California coast to sail to Pelican Cove for a picnic on Santa Cruz Island?

What was the wide and gentle River Seine compared to Pacific winds and Channel currents and dolphins jumping in a bow wave?

It all made perfect sense, Rose said to Josie.

Of course God did not answer their transportation prayer with automobiles, because there was only one driver. God did not send a zeppelin or the Pan Am clipper, because no one knew how to fly.

But Rose could handle a boat. It was a perfectly logical miracle—a miracle even though it was logical.

They were all ready when the air-raid siren wailed into the blackness of the Paris night. The doors of the carriage gates swung back. Guided by the five brothers, Jerome, and a very intense little rat, the wheels of the chairs clattered over the cobblestones. A baby, bundles, little girls, and little boys hurried across the deserted Place St. Michel as the shrieking alert warned anyone left in Paris to take cover.

Then the high, long whine stopped. There was a sudden and eerie silence as the nineteen souls in need of a miracle turned onto Quai des Grand Augustins. Footsteps and panting breaths were loud in their ears as they rushed past the locked boxes of the booksellers' stalls. Only the stars illuminated the dark surface of the Seine. Paris seemed like a ghost town.

And then in the distance came the deep bass drone of the Dornier engines approaching from the east. Far beyond the heart of Par is searchlights popped on, throwing wide and beautiful beams of light skyward. Then the staccato cracking of antiaircraft fire was added to this terrible and wonderful concerto. The whistle of bombs followed, then the drumroll of explosions as the Renault factory exploded to create a false dawn on the far horizon.

"Do not look back," Rose warned the troop. Heads snapped forward as if by looking they would turn to salt like the wife of Lot fleeing the destruction of Sodom.

The statue of King Henri on Pont Neuf glowed a hellish orange in the reflected light. The surface of the Seine seemed to be on fire. The crack of antiaircraft guns rolled toward them. Great pillars of light swept above their heads, and the crescendo of battle increased all around.

Steep stone steps led down to Quai de Conti, where the *Garlic* was moored. With the help of the five brothers, Rose, Josie, and Lewinski carried the wheelchairs down one at a time as the air trembled and the sound of battle rolled over them like thunder. Marie guided Juliette down the hatch. Jerome carried baby Yacov into the hold and deposited him inside a coil of thick rope. Yacov wailed a protest, but he was safe unless the boat took a hit.

The Dorniers were directly overhead! Across the river a building on the Right Bank exploded in a geyser of flame and debris. Eardrums compressed painfully.

Jerome clambered belowdecks and cranked the engine. A true miracle! It started willingly.

Taking the helm, Rose called for the lines to be cast off.

They had recaptured the *Garlic*!

Jerome, Papillon on his shoulder, struck a Napoleonic pose at the bow as the péniche shuddered, coughed, and slipped away from the quai to glide away from the ancient stones of Pont Neuf.

29

A Radical Twist

At dawn the following morning Andre noted with satisfaction that another day of cloud cover would keep the Luftwaffe at bay. The tide was out, and at Dunkirk Harbor that meant a drop of fifteen feet. There were not enough ladders to accommodate the queue and keep the embarkation moving, so Andre walked halfway down the column and singled out a group of French infantrymen.

"Take those axes," he said, pointing out a bin of firefighting equipment on the quai. "I want you to chop down every telegraph pole you can find in thirty minutes and bring them back here. Bring the wire too."

"What's in it for us?" a poilu grumbled.

"You will go to the head of the line," Andre promised.

Soon the west end of Dunkirk Harbor rang with the sound of axes, as if it were a lumber camp. As each pair of men returned with a pole, one end was placed on the deck of a waiting ship. The top was secured to the pilings of the jetty with a loop of wire.

Beginning with the ax wielders, the row of evacuees moved twice as fast. The poilus slid down to the decks below, each taking a turn at the bottom steadying the device for the next man.

Andre heard a whistling noise, and a fountain of water geysered up. There were still no planes overhead in the dark cloud mass. No Stukas screamed toward the docks, no Heinkels clustered to drop their payloads. What had caused the explosion?

It took a second blast that turned a wooden-hulled trawler into matchsticks before Andre figured it out: These were the incoming shells of the German artillery just west of the city. The Wehrmacht advance had indeed crept close enough to bombard the harbor. The respite from attack was over.

"Hurry!" Andre demanded. "Move, move!"

Another shell hit the center of the causeway. A dozen men were flung into the water. A gap in the mole ten feet wide now opened above the swirling water.

Once again Andre organized a working party. "Bring back all the planks you can find. Drag them out of the rubble or chop them loose from buildings if you have to. Collect any doors you find also . . . anything to bridge the gap!"

Through the shelling the line kept inching forward. All the men realized that no safety would be found by turning back. The only hope lay in escaping from the punished ruins of Dunkirk altogether.

When the artillery barrage stopped after an hour, Andre found that he could continue directing traffic and still think about other things. It wasn't that good a discovery. He began to worry about Juliette and Josie. And through the day, something else nagged at the back of his mind.

In the afternoon, he was relieved by the First Army colonel who had helped organize the withdrawal. "You have done a magnificent job, Chardon. Why the Boche gave us this chance, we may never know. Heaven help those on the receiving end of the panzers now. I would rather be here than face what they are facing."

"What do you mean?"

"Have you not heard? Some of the panzers have turned around after hammering Lille. They are now facing south, ready to invade the rest of France."

There it was, out in the open at last. Escaping from Dunkirk was not the final answer; the war still continued. Even if Andre lived to flee to England, his war was not done. The secret of Enigma was still vital; Lewinski had to be rescued before Paris was surrounded.

Andre would have to leave with General Gort, if only to return at once to Paris for a different sort of evacuation. The future of France might depend on it.

⟨இ⟩

It took three tries for David Meyer and Badger Cross to actually enter the fortifications of Dunkirk after they reached the city. The first two approaches had been heavily damaged by German bombs, and the bridges over which the roads passed had been knocked out. The highways were blocked with burning vehicles and the wreckage of earlier attacks.

In contrast to the unorganized, moblike nature of the retreat toward the coast, the aspect of the third entry was businesslike. Despite the brown haze and the spreading black cloud from the burning oil tanks, the entrance had an orderly, confident appearance. The perimeter was strung with miles of barbed wire, and the gate was flanked by a pair of sandbagged machine-gun nests.

But giving the lie to this stalwart bearing was a steady stream of civilians who were leaving the city against the flow of British soldiers. To David, the whole scene had an air of unreality, like the fragments of a symbolic but confusing dream. A military policeman stopped all incoming groups and directed the senior officer of each footsore band to the building housing the embarkation officer.

When David and Badger reached the roadblock, the police sergeant looked them over and hummed to himself. "We have no regular RAF organization here. My advice to you is to ask embarkation if you can hook on to another regiment. Straight ahead, second left. Big brick building with a queue of men straight out the door, I should imagine. Good luck."

The line waiting for the officer in charge of the evacuation not only ran out the door but halfway down the block. There was much shuffling in place and speculation about what was happening, but no real forward progress. It was like being back in school and being told to line up without being told why.

After standing for two hours, David saw a major come out and walk down the row of men. Every dozen paces he stopped and repeated the same message, like a schoolmaster instructing new pupils in the rules of behavior. "The embarkation officer cannot possibly get to you in the next four or five hours. I suggest that you stay close about this area but come back this afternoon."

"What about rations? medical care?" David asked.

The major shrugged. "Catch as catch can, I suppose. Off you go. Jerry has been pounding us pretty regular, so you don't want to be caught out in the street."

"Flaming army," Cross muttered as David led him away toward a hotel at the end of the block. "Exactly why I joined the air force!"

A portly Belgian man with a ring of keys that appeared to weigh five pounds stood outside an inn named the Pelican. Having located the one key he sought, he locked the front door and turned to leave.

David stopped him. "Is it possible to get a meal, or a room, or both?"

The man shook his head with a chuckle, jingling the cluster of keys like sleigh bells. Then he paused and, as if the absurdity of the request was too great to stand, guffawed. He laughed until tears came, then pulled a handkerchief out of his pocket to wipe his eyes. "There is no one left. The cook, the maids, the desk clerk. All have gone. And now I am leaving, too."

"Can't we at least buy some food from you?"

The Pelican's proprietor gave a negative reply, then stopped and stared at the increasing number of soldiers wandering up and down the street. He turned, studied the glass panels of the door, and laughed again. "What am I thinking?" he said, striking his forehead with his palm. "Go in, gentlemen, and thank you for your courtesy. Make free with what you find . . . better you than the Boche. *Bonne chance*. Good luck!" With that he unlocked the door again and rode off on a bicycle toward the highway.

⊗

The men boarding *Intrepid* along Dunkirk jetty double-timed over the plank walkway and swung smartly aboard the destroyer. Trevor smiled as he supervised the loading; it was going so well that they might shave another thirty minutes from the next round-trip.

It was almost time to cast off. Eight rows of men were crammed into the deck space between the rail and the ship's superstructure. Stained and bestubbled, they all still wore their helmets and sported smiles of relief.

Trevor signaled the bridge to get under way, and the drum of *Intrepid*'s engines increased in pitch. The lines were dropped, and the destroyer swung away from the mole.

Glancing around the deck, Trevor noted an exchange between the lookout from his perch on the funnel and the sailor manning the multibarreled Bofors gun just below. The lookout was pointing upward. A single twin-engined shape cruised slowly past, not attacking or hurrying, but loafing along as if on a tour of inspection. A reconnaissance mission, without a doubt. Trevor knew exactly what would get reported:

> *Weather clearing. Many men and ships concentrated along jetties. No enemy fighter opposition. Very little antiaircraft fire.*

Silently Trevor urged his ship to greater speed—to get clear of the mass of boats moving around the evacuation area, to get out where there was room to maneuver. But it was already too late. Winging in from half the points of the compass was wave after wave of German bombers—Dorniers and Stukas, even some Trevor did not recognize.

The alarm gong pealed, and the smiles froze on the faces of the evacuees. The Bofors gunner tilted his weapon skyward, and its rhythmic pounding tore away the last sense of the day's haven from attack.

Clear of the harbor mouth, *Intrepid* began a series of high-speed turns, designed to make her harder to hit. Not so lucky were the vessels still berthed at the mole. The *Grenade* took a hit aft, and another bomb struck a fuel tank. The ship burst into flames. The *Calvi*, a trawler, received a bomb amidships and sank right beside the other two boats to which she was still tied.

Intrepid's antiaircraft fire was weaving a curtain of black puffs of explosions in the sky over her. A plunging Stuka released its load of destruction, missing the prow of the destroyer by a scant hundred yards. The dive-bomber pilot then returned to his chosen prey, machine guns blazing.

As if sensing what would happen, Trevor was already moving forward toward the antiaircraft position. He was close enough to be spattered with blood when the Bofors gunner was ripped up by slugs from the strafing run. Trevor grabbed the curved handles of the weapon as the dead man slid out of the harness.

Intrepid made a tight turn away from the dive of the Stuka, which rolled and pulled up after its run. Trevor's aim led the German plane as it climbed, painting a ladder of black smudges of flak directly in its path.

No more than five seconds of this duel took place before the dive-bomber and the shell bursts tried to occupy the same space. The tail of the plane shattered, and it flipped over in the air and fell that way. The fractured canopy of the cockpit led the plunge into the sea.

Captain Vian subscribed to the theory that lightning never struck twice in the same spot. As bomber after bomber unloaded sticks of explosives, Vian ordered the destroyer steered toward each towering fountain of water that erupted.

A bomb burst directly alongside *Intrepid* as she made yet another radical twist. It was a miss, but shrapnel from the casing showered the deck with steel splinters. Forty men in the tightly packed front rank were wounded or killed, unknowingly protecting those behind them.

⚭

There were no provisions remaining in the kitchen of the Hotel Pelican. Unwashed dishes were stacked in the sink. A half-full bottle of wine sat on the counter beside the enormous old-fashioned gas stove.

David took a whiff of the bottle, sipped the contents gingerly, then passed it to Badger. "Go easy. That may be all we get for a while."

Badger tasted the sour stuff and shuddered. "Why is it the Frogs can't brew a decent ale? What I'd give for a pint of Newcastle Brown and a ploughman's lunch."

Badger had been conjuring visions of food for days. Strawberries and cream for his birthday. Steak-and-kidney pie at The Green Man pub. A pint of beer. Scones. Marmalade. He spoke of common fare with the nostalgia of a condemned man thinking of his last meal before being hanged. Badger had stopped believing that he would ever touch the shores of England again. The lifelong tradition of strawberries on his birthday was sure to be broken. Badger was convinced that this was the omen of his impending death. So strong was this morbid conviction that David began to believe it as well.

Strawberries likewise had become an obsession for David. As Badger downed the wine and spoke wistfully of home, David tore through the cupboards, praying that even a spoonful of strawberries remained in the bottom of a pot of jam somewhere. No luck.

David stared dejectedly at an empty hutch. On the top shelf behind a pewter teapot he spotted what appeared to be the molding of a door. "Hold on, Badger." David repositioned him beside the stove. "I think I've found something."

At that, he tipped the hutch forward, sending it crashing down across the flagstones. Bits of pottery shattered and sprayed the room like shrapnel.

Badger jumped and shouted, thinking that a bomb had fallen.

Instead there was a door opening to a flight of steps that led down to the cellar. After a moment's exploration, David returned and led Badger into the basement pantry.

A round of cheese was soon divided by David's jackknife, and this was washed down with the remains of the red wine. Cross sat on a sack of onions. Though awkward with his gauze-wrapped hands, he ate and drank while David continued examining the cupboards and wine racks. Champagne. White wines with German labels. Napoleon brandies. Red Bordeaux of fantastic vintages. But all of this seemed of small consequence compared to the absence of strawberries.

There was, however, one crate containing tins of sardines. David stuffed his pockets full and snatched two bottles of brandy off the shelf. His arm was throbbing. This seemed the most logical medication for his pain.

"No strawberries, Badger. But guess what I found—"

Badger's guess was interrupted by the arrival of twenty dusty soldiers who gratefully tramped into the cellar as if they had located the Promised Land. David shoved his discovery into his tunic.

"'Scuse us for barging in, mates," said a corporal, "but the Hun is fixing to paste Dunkirk right good and proper. We was hunting a good place to go to ground, and it looks like we got it. Care to share your provisions?"

The first bombs rained down on the city before the corporal and his men had settled themselves. But with an elaborate air of unconcern, the noncom knocked the tops off of twenty-one champagne bottles. As the earth rolled, the beams creaked, and dirt filtered down from the floor above, the corporal proposed a toast. "Your very good health."

That the Germans did not share this sentiment was proven by a sudden explosion that seemed to lift the floor under the cellar. The walls of the Hotel Pelican shivered, and brick dust filled the air.

"Hey, Corp," one of the soldiers called. "Are we safe here?"

"Safe as houses. This building is three stories tall. Even if Jerry landed one smack on the button, it'd not come clear to us before blowing up, now would it?" The private did not look convinced, but the corporal only said, "Here, have a fig," and he passed around a box of dried fruit.

David thought about the giant gas stove that was directly above their heads. One well-placed incendiary and they would all be cooked like holiday geese.

The raid seemed to last for hours, and when it was finally over, David and Cross went back upstairs for fresh air. All the windows in the lobby had been blown out. Shattered plaster, overturned tables, and fallen chandeliers littered the carpet.

Outside the Pelican, the street was almost unrecognizable. A brick structure across the street had taken a direct hit and collapsed its upper two floors into the basement.

"Give us a hand!" called a captain urgently. "There are fifty men trapped below-stairs."

The unmistakable hiss of gas was clearly heard. One lick of flame and the whole heap would explode, taking rescuers up with the fifty men beneath the rubble.

Noticing David's upper arm and Badger's bandaged face and hands, the captain waved them away. "Get back inside then. The Luftwaffe is not through yet."

A second and a third bombing attack were endured in the confines of the cellar. As Badger placidly waited for his death, a section of wall collapsed on two soldiers, who were dead before they could be dug out. The atmosphere grew more and more foul in both senses of the word. Most of the soldiers were sleeping, but a few took on an edge of belligerence with the champagne.

"Where is the bloody RAF, anyway?" the corporal slurred. "Glad you two are here . . . get a taste of the real war . . . instead of your la-ti-da fairy planes." He hiccupped loudly. A bleary chorus of agreement came from the few who remained conscious.

Badger rose and turned his bulk toward the speaker's voice, but David stopped him. "Too many," he said quietly. "Besides, let's go check on our ride."

When they emerged again into the murky sunlight of the Dunkirk afternoon, they ran immediately into the same major David had seen out-side the embarkation office. "Don't bother going back there," the major said. "The Germans have been bombing every ship that tried to put in at the harbor. Even if—when," he corrected himself, "when some arrive to-night, there are thousands ahead of you. Best make your way over to the beach and wait there. The Royal Navy will be along. You can count on it."

⊗

"Ahoy, *Wairakei*!" called a tone of authority over a handheld mega-phone. "Can you hear me?"

Annie waved a hand to signal her agreement. Mac doubted that her voice could have been heard over the bubble, drum, and purr of the other engines.

From his perch on top of the aft cabin of *Wairakei*, Mac could count fifty vessels of all shapes and sizes. Smelly fishing trawlers followed in the wakes of gleaming white yachts, and barges with rust-colored sails and black hulls idled next to polished mahogany speedboats.

"Form up on the *Triton*." The voice carried over the water. "She's your guide for this trip. Good luck to you."

All afternoon and evening, since *Wairakei* had arrived off Ramsgate breakwater after her daylong journey down the Thames, more and more watercraft had been joining the strange flotilla. Now, at ten at night, she and her flock mates were setting off on the first leg of the great adventure.

Annie's father was belowdecks, checking the engines. The top of his shining head appeared, framed in the hatchway. "Annie, girl," he bel-lowed, in a voice that was no doubt heard three boats away, even with-out a megaphone. "Annie, mind the rev's on number one. She idles a little fast."

"We're shovin' off, Da!" Annie shouted back.

"High time it is, too! Mr. McGrath!"

Mac jumped and almost tripped over the mainsheet.

"Make yourself useful! Haul in those fenders. We want to look ship-shape. Lively now!"

Mac was not sorry when the bald dome of John Galway returned be-low. After hauling in the fenders as ordered, he asked Annie why she was steering instead of her father.

"Oh, Da knows every vibration and sound. He says he can hear one grain of sand in a fuel line. For this stretch of water there's no pilotin' to be done, just follow the leader. He's happier stayin' below watchin' after the engines."

The small armada moved out. Already gaps were appearing in the line as some of the bigger vessels could barely throttle down to match the struggle of the smaller boats to keep up. "How long will the crossing take?"

"Depends on the wind and the currents," Annie answered. "It's not but forty miles, and we could do it in four hours if we went straight across."

"What do you mean, *if*?"

"Oh, we can't steer direct over. There's sandbanks and mines between here and there."

"Swell." Mac was beginning to wonder about the wisdom of his decision to join this enterprise. He looked around as the darker hulls of the rest of the fleet faded into the backdrop of night. "Say, I suppose we're all blacked out because of air attacks?"

"Only partly . . . there're the U-boats to consider, too."

Mac walked forward to *Wairakei*'s rounded prow, then continued his circuit of the deck to the stern. When his inspection did not answer his question, he again entered the wheelhouse. Duffy raised his massive head from where he sprawled on the wood floor, then lay it back down. "So, where's our arms?"

"Goodness, Mr. McGrath, we don't have any."

"No machine gun? Not even a rifle? What do we defend ourselves with?"

Annie laughed. "Da keeps a pair of cutlasses hanging on the wall of the cabin. I think they're used to repel boarders."

"Sure," Mac agreed. "By Nelson at Trafalgar."

30

An Endlessly Long Night

The heavy overcast had become a soupy fog that clung to Mac's raincoat and dripped from the matted ends of his hair. His eyes were strained from trying to make out shapes in the lightless crossing of the Channel. The night seemed endlessly long, and the need to keep everything blacked out added to the gloom and apprehension.

The barest gleam from the stern of the ship ahead was all that could be glimpsed of her, and sometimes that, too, disappeared. How could Mac watch for enemy ships or submarines when he could not even see two boat lengths ahead?

Moving from the roof of the pilothouse, Mac went to the prow of the ketch. Leaning over and peering at the waves just ahead of *Wairakei* conjured up a whole new element of evil. Even the smallest swells seemed to rush down on the little ship, and each carried a sinister, unexplained dark shadow, in which it was easy to imagine a floating mine. Mac's mood alternated between gritting his teeth at the expectation of an explosion and a moment's sigh of relief when the wave rushed past.

Mac tried to imitate John Galway's attention to noises. If sight was impossible, perhaps he could use sound. The Channel was anything but quiet, and that was part of the terror. The drumming engines of unseen ships, muffled by the layer of mist, came from everywhere and nowhere, all at once. More than once the sound of another ship dramatically increased in volume, as if it were on a collision course with *Wairakei*.

Mac's senses were on edge. His whole body tuned for danger. When a looming black bow appeared unexpectedly out of the fog less than twenty yards away, Mac shouted a warning before the hazard had even fully registered. Annie spun the wheel, more by instinct than planning, and the enormous shape of a freight barge slid past, close enough to touch. An instant later, bellowing foghorns came too late to prevent the screech of rending metal and panicked screams. Mac shuddered at the thought of the victims claimed by the dark water, even without the Nazi killing machines. The blackness and the confusion were enemies enough. He redoubled his efforts to pierce the fog with both eye and ear, still without much success.

Annie steered *Wairakei* through course changes while her father continued to tinker with the engines. During one of these swings, Mac turned around to watch one of the few things actually visible in the night: the wake streaming away from the stern. He was trying to make sense of their new heading and had taken his eyes off the ship ahead when something bumped against the hull directly beneath him. Certain it was a mine, Mac flung himself to the far side of the ship as if he were a child again and the floating bomb were an angry dog that could be escaped by running. It was already too late to call out a warning.

No explosion came. *Wairakei* continued on without interruption. Mac wondered if her wooden hull had somehow protected her against a weapon designed for metal ships. Racing for the stern, he peered over in time to see a large piece of driftwood spin away on the wake.

Eventually the fog raised into a gray layer that hung overhead like a theatre curtain drawn halfway. The change allowed Mac to make out the dim shapes of other vessels that he had not known were anywhere nearby. He checked on the ship just ahead and on a fishing trawler to port and astern. Ahead and to starboard, a couple hundred yards distant, was the white, sleek outline of someone's private yacht.

As Mac watched the expensive plaything knife through the waves, he saw a vertical dark stripe silhouetted against the momentary brightness of the hull. Something was really there: a solid black pole upright from the surface of the water. It could only be a submarine. "Periscope!" Mac yelled. "U-boat over starboard! U-boat!"

"Are you sure?" Annie questioned.

"Absolutely! How do we warn the others? Where's your radio?"

"Never had one. Flare pistol? In the locker behind me."

"Quick . . . there'll be a torpedo in the water any minute now." Mac tore open the locker, throwing out rain slickers and life vests to land all over Duffy. The dog sat up with an enormous *woof* and shook himself free of the pile.

Emerging from the heap, Mac snapped open the Very pistol and checked to see that it was loaded. The gun was already raised and his arm outside the cabin when John Galway emerged from the engine room.

"What's all the noise, then? What are you about there, Mr. McGrath?"

"Submarine! A U-boat, Mr. Galway! We need to warn—"

"Hold on! Where did you see this craft?"

"Not the whole thing, just the periscope! Right over there," Mac said, pointing.

Galway took the flare gun from Mac's hand but made no move to fire it. Snapping on a tiny chart light, he consulted a map. Annie's father muttered to himself, "Naw but six fathoms hereabouts . . . not enough water to hide a sub . . . sandbank," he concluded.

"What?"

"What you saw was the mast on top of a sunken freighter. You remember that last turn we made? That was to steer us around the sandbank and the wreck. A good job you didn't fire this thing, Mr. McGrath! Might have brought down the whole of Germany right on our heads!"

Badger and David and thousands of other soldiers waited all night for ships that did not come. Sometime after three in the morning, the bombing raids stopped and David fell into an uneasy sleep. He dreamed of Annie fleeing down a country road, pursued by a Messerschmitt. In his vision, he tried to scream at her to get off the road. But no sound came from his mouth, nor could he run toward her to push her out of the way. She was only an arm's length distant when the tracers from the ME-109 caught up with her. . . .

"Keep a sharp eye out!" John Galway yelled at Mac. The camerman stood on the canvas-wrapped boom, clinging to the foremast, as he strained for the first glimpse of the Dunkirk shore. It was just past four in the morning and starting to get light.

"Wait!" Mac called back. "I think I see something!"

"Where away?"

Mac did not know the correct ship terminology, but he indicated with his hand the direction toward a white object dimly seen against the gray horizon.

"I hear breakers, Da!" Annie said. Duffy sat up and whined, as if he, too, had heard or sensed some change.

"Can you make out the shoreline?" Annie's father shouted.

"It's just . . . yes! I can see it now!"

The same heavy gray overcast that had protected the little ships from the unwelcome attention of the Luftwaffe had also brought the boats to grief on the shoaling sands of the French shore. A thin horizontal line appeared suddenly on the horizon, separating ashen sky from leaden sea.

John Galway spun the wheel in his hands, and the boat swung about to parallel the coast. The fog parted just enough for all three to get their first glimpse of their destination.

A ghostly form welcomed them to France. Mac saw the stern of a white sloop directly ahead of them on the beach. It lay high and dry, marooned on the gravel above the falling tide. Mac searched the wreckage for its crew, only to discover the truth: He saw the stern because that was all of the craft that remained. The front two-thirds of the ship had been torn away and destroyed. It was not an auspicious omen to accompany their arrival.

And if the first view was a portent of tragedy, the next vision stunned Mac. *Overwhelmed* was not too strong a word, since it took him some time to remember to begin shooting film. The shore was covered with sleeping men. There were thousands and thousands of them—too many to count. Mac stopped filming long enough to examine the lens with suspicion and then look with his naked eye. The reality just did not seem credible to either man or camera.

"Right," Galway observed tersely. "We've got our job cut out for us then. Mr. McGrath, let Annie take over as lookout. You're the leadsman. *Wairakei* draws five feet, so keep us in fathom to be on the safe side. We'll load up and ferry the lads to yon great destroyer there."

Mac spun about, still filming as he gyrated. Into focus leaped a warship that had materialized unexpectedly out of the fog behind them. He forced himself to slow down. That piece of film would never be usable; it would make audiences seasick.

"Put away your pretty toy! There's work to be done!" John Galway barked.

~ ❧ ~

David awoke with a start to find his shirt soaked in sweat and dawn creeping over the beach. Somehow during the night, the number of men had doubled or even tripled. It looked like the seashore had been thickly planted with low bushes that rustled and moaned despite the absence of a breeze.

"There's a boat!" the artillery captain called. Suddenly the bushes came to life and pursued the retreating tide. The bobbing white object was a motor launch with a crew of four sailors. As they swept onto the sand, twenty times as many men as the little boat could possibly hold crowded around.

"Where is it, Meyer? Help me to it," Badger pleaded.

"Not this time, Badger," David replied, his heart sinking with the words. "It's not our turn."

"No more, no more! You'll swamp us," cried the naval officer, jumping into the shallow sea and wading ashore. "Listen, men, we're from the destroyer *Jaguar*. Chin up! We're here to get you off."

If the officer had expected a rousing cheer of welcome, he was disappointed. The wave of humans who had rushed into waist-deep water glared with envy and hatred at the fifty men who received places in the launch. Then, stoically, they turned about and returned to the sand.

The lieutenant commander stayed ashore. He went from group to group, locating the unit officers and giving them instructions. "Form into proper queues," David heard him say. The artillery regiment brightened at this. Even though the prospect of a speedy rescue was not at hand, the soldiers preferred to be given clear orders. Even when the order had no immediate benefit, just the sense that someone was actually in charge improved the outlook for many. It was the first sign of organization they had seen in days.

Within minutes, serpentine formations of men snaked their way from the dunes down to the water's edge. There was no reason for the lines to curl and loop, except for a very human wish to feel nearer to the front than the actual number of places suggested.

It took the first boat half an hour to return, but with it came two more small launches. The line inched toward rescue in an agonizingly slow process. David kept his good hand on Badger's shoulder as the two moved up, trying to act and sound reassuring. "There's the next boat coming already. The system is figured out now."

Badger nodded without speaking, but David knew that his words were not convincing. A painfully unwelcome but impossible to prevent mental calculation hit: The three small boats were removing only three hundred men an hour from the beach. In the line with David and Badger were five hundred others, and there were queues coiled along the beach every two or three hundred yards.

Some of those waiting exhibited a mechanical quality, as if their human consciousness was submerged because of fear. The private in front of David dug a hole in the sand and crouched in it. When the launch returned and the men shuffled forward, the soldier abandoned his shelter, moved up a few feet, and began digging again.

A lone Messerschmitt sized up the beach and found the pickings too good to resist. The fighter plane circled the crowded shore like a fox sizing up a flock of chickens for the fat and the slow.

The artillery captain abandoned the line and ran toward the cover of the sand dunes. Up and down the coast, others also panicked and turned to flee.

"Don't run!" yelled a burly regimental sergeant major. "Stand fast!" The man's courage was meant to be infectious.

But even more convincing in David's mind was the shout raised by the lieutenant commander: "You'll lose your place!"

The ME-109 flashed overhead. A row of tracers glinted, and little bursts of sand flew up on both sides of David as the bullets impacted only a few feet away.

With ample other targets to select, the machine-gun fire ceased. Mystified, the soldiers watched the plane waggle its wings, then take off east.

"Respect for our bravery?" Cross asked David.

"Guns jammed," David replied.

There's ten feet . . . nine . . . eight . . . hold it." Mac's voice called out the depth of water as *Wairakei* slipped onto Bray Dunes beach, east of Dunkirk. The line of men that stretched back from chest deep in the sea numbered five hundred or more. Up and down the beach were similar waiting columns, every couple hundred yards.

John Galway locked down the anchor winch, and the ship hung, stern toward shore, at the end of the cable. The ketch had already made more trips between the shore and the waiting destroyer than Mac could remember. He had long since given up any thought of filming the operation, because he needed both hands free to haul waterlogged soldiers over the rail.

As Mac watched, another lifeboat approached the shore. Some of the rescue vessels drew too much water to get close enough for the men to board directly, so lifeboats and dinghies and the captain's launch from the destroyer were working the surf. It was not without hazard. The boat nearing Bray Dunes was now rushed by three times as many men as could really fit it at one time. When the Royal Navy sublieutenant in charge of the boat warned them to clear off and wait their turn, he was ignored. The already overloaded craft shipped water over the rail, spun broadside to the waves, then flipped over, scattering the Tommies and drowning the lieutenant.

Early on, the same fate seemed destined to overtake *Wairakei*. Wanting to ease the loading process, John Galway had allowed the ketch to almost drag her keel on the sand. Immediately she was surrounded by two hundred soldiers trying to climb on board from all directions at once.

Even the sturdy twenty-ton craft seemed likely to either capsize or run aground.

Then Mac remembered something Annie had said in jest the night before. Dashing into the main cabin, he pulled an antique cutlass from the pair on the wall. Waving the sword, he raced around the deck like an actor in a pirate movie. When the sight and sound of a giant, barking, slavering dog was added to the mix, the men backed off and agreed to wait their turn.

But in order to take no unnecessary chances, after that episode John Galway purposely kept *Wairakei* deeper than before. He forced the men to swim the last few feet, giving them no opportunity to mob the boat.

Some of the soldiers were so dead tired that they could do nothing to help themselves. In those cases it took both Mac and Annie's father to hoist them aboard. "One, two, three, heave!" John Galway called, and another inert body sprawled onto the deck.

Galway kept up a running patter of encouragement. "Don't I know you?" he asked. "Song-and-dance man? No? Picture shows, then?" To others lost in despair or grieving the death of a friend he would say, "Buck up. Never mind this little setback! We'll pay off that Hitler fellow; you'll see."

Mac marveled at the way John Galway not only plucked them from danger but lifted their spirits. Mac himself got a boost from listening—a renewed belief that everything would work out after all.

Fully loaded with another seventy-five evacuees, *Wairakei* prepared to run up her own anchor line and steam out to the waiting destroyer. "Propeller's fouled," Galway called when the ship failed to respond to the throttle. "McGrath, take the boat hook and free it. Must be a bit of line wrapped around the shaft."

Picking his way through the clutter of exhausted forms stretched over every possible inch of space, Mac took the gaff and leaned over the rail. There was something down there, near the props. Mac poked it with the boat hook. It resisted at first; then he got a grasp on it and the object floated free, surfacing under his face. It was the body of the drowned lieutenant.

◦◯◦

As the tide retreated down the shelf of the Dunkirk coast, the columns of waiting men merely stretched farther back before disappearing among the dunes. To Mac's eye, this had the curious effect of making it seem that the number awaiting evacuation grew larger instead of smaller with every boatload ferried out to the destroyer.

A mysterious dark column jutted out toward the sea. It had not been there on any of the earlier trips, but it looked like a dock where none had been before. As the ketch got closer to the beach, a swarm of men could be seen crawling around the structure. Soon the nature of the object became clear. As the tide withdrew, a lorry was driven over the hard-packed sand to the front of a line of similar trucks. The soldiers climbing around the vehicles were lashing them together with cables, building an unorthodox but useful pier.

By the time *Wairakei* had completed a few more round-trips, the improvised jetty extended several hundred yards seaward. The tires of the trucks had been shot out to settle the machines into position in the sand. An impromptu walkway made from salvaged lumber was secured to the tops of the trucks.

The idea took hold and spread. Several more of the ingenious "lorry jetties" were begun to speed the evacuation of the waiting thousands.

"The sky is clearin' a bit," John Galway observed as the ketch drew alongside the lorry jetty.

The inventive wharf was working well. Both deeper draft ships and shallower ones like lifeboats took advantage of the chance to pick up soldiers without going too close to the shore. There was something more orderly, more military about the process, too. Marching down the walkway to climb aboard instead of swimming and seeing the regular trips made by the little ships took the edge of panic off the men. There was less of the overcrowding that had happened earlier in the day.

Annie's father still kept a watchful eye on the depth under the *Wairakei*'s keel. He did not want them to run aground. With Mac assisting, John Galway waved for Annie to let the boat creep forward a little farther.

Behind them a trawler was also coming to the pier. Needing even more depth to operate than the ketch, the fishing boat docked just astern of *Wairakei*.

After an entire day of almost no challenges by the Germans, the sound of planes overhead was momentarily ignored. Then the skipper of the trawler looked up and saw the flight of Heinkels sweeping in from the north to line up for a bombing run.

In his panic, the skipper of the trawler shoved the gear into forward instead of reverse and gunned the engine. The collision at *Wairakei*'s stern whacked Annie's head against a spoke of the helm and knocked Mac overboard.

Flying over the rail, Mac had an instant to be glad that his camera was in the cabin and not slung over his shoulder. Then he hit the water and came up sputtering.

The Heinkels unloaded their bombs farther up the beach. One of the improvised jetties took a direct hit, and the bodies of men and the wreckage of trucks were blown skyward in company with a Thames River passenger launch. Duffy ran around the deck, barking wildly and knocking more men over the side.

Mac saw John Galway scoop Annie up and fling her over his shoulder. He shouted, "Get by, you daft dog!" making Duffy slink back into the cabin. Then, since the trawler was already steaming full speed astern and the way was clear, he put *Wairakei* into reverse as well.

The little ship shuddered all along her forty-foot length, and green water churned into foam under her props, but she did not move. "We're stuck fast," Galway yelled. "You men, give us a hand to float her, or she's a sittin' duck!"

The German bombers were returning from the last pass and lining up for another run. "Over the side," ordered Galway, "all of ye. We've got to lighten ship and push her free!"

The men already on board obliged. They jumped into the four feet of water and struggled to help the ketch escape from the sandbank that held her prisoner.

As Mac was already in the water, he stayed there and helped push the boat. "Heave!" he yelled. "Again!"

The engines roared, but still *Wairakei* was stuck fast. "Rock her!" Galway called.

A line of three Heinkels, having already dropped their bombs, opened up on the beach with machine guns. The orderly queues waiting their turn to board were shattered and torn apart, and then the planes directed their line of fire toward the ship.

Some of the men nearest Mac turned to flee. "It's not any safer out there!" he bellowed. "Stay and help!"

Rows of tracers shot up the jetty, flinging men right and left off its length and into the sea. The bullets clanged into the metal roofs and hoods of the trucks, drowning out the screams.

"Again!" Mac implored. "Rock her again!"

With the engines at full throttle, when *Wairakei* did break free, she shot backward away from the jetty into deeper water. John spun the wheel, pivoting the ketch away from the dock. The line of tracers plowed into the water exactly where *Wairakei* had been, throwing up a row of splashes. The bomber flashed past overhead, almost close enough to touch.

The ketch headed out to sea, zigzagging as she went. Back near shore,

Mac stayed in the water until the last Heinkel had departed. Then he pulled himself out on the jetty just in time to watch *Wairakei*'s stern shrink smaller and smaller out into the Channel.

It was almost midnight when the British Expeditionary Force ambulance screeched to a halt in front of Paul's headquarters at the Ecole de Cavalerie.

A middle-aged British major of the Grenadier Guards dashed into the bomb-damaged school. The man was filthy and splattered with blood. *Someone else's blood,* Paul thought, as the man faced him in the lantern light.

"The Germans are just beyond the river, Captain," the major exclaimed. "I have been sent . . . that is . . . HQ has heard that there are still English nurses here at the CCS. An oversight. They should have been pulled back days ago."

The man's face was pale. Both he and Paul understood fully what the order meant. The nurses were to be evacuated and as many more of the wounded as the time left allowed.

The remainder of the wounded would be abandoned to await the arrival of the German panzers. French. English. Belgian. Perhaps the Belgians would be spared because of the capitulation of King Leopold. It was no secret what the Germans would do to the others. Only a fierce rearguard action could save them now.

Cautiously, guided only by starlight, Paul led the major toward the chapel. Abigail Mitchell had just come out of the operating room. Her feet were covered with blood to the ankles. In the dim light it looked as if she were wearing high red shoes. Her strong features reflected her exhaustion.

"Sister Abigail Mitchell," the major saluted. "Orders from HQ. You have twenty minutes to gather your nursing staff and to prepare to fall back."

Abigail Mitchell argued against the withdrawal, but her reasoning was foolish and she knew it.

Twenty minutes passed, and she stood at the open back of the ambulance as her staff climbed aboard. She extended her hand to Paul. "What can I say, Captain Chardon?"

"Say you will have dinner with me when this is finished."

At his cheerful remark the cold Sister Mitchell melted and dissolved into tears. He put his arms around her in a gesture of awkward tenderness. "If the thought of dinner with me upsets you, *ma chèrie* . . ."

"Oh stop it, Paul. Please. Not now. How can I leave you?"

He cupped her face in his hands and kissed her. "Because you are very beautiful. And strong. And you have given everything here that you can give. Now we must give what we can for the sake of honor."

"I don't know what to say."

"Then say that you will pray for us. Promise you will remember."

She nodded. The major barked an impatient order that they must get to Dunkirk before the Germans. He pointed out that there was nothing between Dunkirk and the Germans but the Ecole de Cavalerie.

"We're already ten minutes late! If you don't mind, Sister Mitchell. I'd like to get home in one piece." Then to Paul, "If I were you, Captain, I'd pull my men back. You might be able to get on a boat before the German army overruns Dunkirk."

"How long will that be, Major?"

"They'll cross the river right here at Lys tomorrow and then . . . whoever is left at Dunkirk is a goner, as the Americans say."

"How much time do you need to clear the beaches?"

"They just keep coming. At least two days for the chaps there now."

Paul nodded gravely. "Then we shall stay. Defend the hospital and . . . we will do what we can to buy you time at Dunkirk."

The major glowered at him as if he were crazy. "You're going to stay and fight? Has it occurred to you that you'll all be killed?"

"Indeed. Perhaps we few may have the honor to die for France."

"You think you can do what the entire Allied army couldn't do? Hold the panzers here? On the other side of the Lys?"

"We will."

"At least send the boys out. Let the seasoned troops bear the brunt of it."

"These boys, as you call them, *are* my seasoned troops, Major."

After a minute the words penetrated. The major drew himself up in a crisp salute. He could not speak.

"Hurry now," Paul urged. With one last glance of farewell at Abigail Mitchell, he closed the doors of the ambulance and turned back to his task.

∽⊙∾

When the launch pulled alongside the destroyer *Keith* Andre felt unspeakable relief and surprise. To be free of the tiny scrap of coastline was to be released from the iron jaws of a trap. The smell of ocean breeze, though tainted with oil and diesel fuel, seemed clean and sweet compared to the pervasive stench that hung over the beaches.

But if the flow of cleaner air carried an aroma of release, his personal safety was still difficult to comprehend. Even while working for the evacuation of others, part of Andre's mind had told him that he would never be rescued. Now the thought of being free to return to the battle became real to him. On the other side of Dunkirk, did lines of French soldiers still hold out against the Germans? Would it be possible for those rescued from the beaches to regroup and enter France from the south to fight for Paris?

He gripped the cold, damp steel of the railing. The seawater and the sand that scrunched in his boots reminded him of what he had left behind. Andre rubbed his hand over his salt-encrusted, bearded face.

A voice at his elbow said something. Andre roused himself from contemplating his escape and turned to find a white-clad steward offering a mug and a silver teapot.

"I said, would you care for some tea, sir?"

"Yes," Andre agreed, "but be careful."

"Sir?"

"I just convinced myself that I'm really here; I don't want to start doubting all over again!"

Here and there fires still burned on the dunes from the targets of successful Luftwaffe attacks. In the direction of Dunkirk, an ominous red glow hovered in the sky.

Out on the water, everything was pitch-black. The rescue ships went about their duties without lights, to avoid more aerial assaults and to hide from prowling German U-boats and S-boats. Unless a small craft passed close by, the only sign that betrayed the presence of the armada of rescue vessels was the swirl of phosphorescence in their wakes.

On the far horizon, directly in front of the deep crimson bowl that surrounded Dunkirk Harbor, a white flare lit the night. A dark outline of a ship, tilted at a crazy angle, was momentarily silhouetted against the brilliance. In a few seconds, Andre saw the shape slide downward, extinguishing the light as if the cover of a giant lantern had been shut over its beam. "What was that?" he asked the steward.

"Can't say for certain, sir. From the size I'd say another destroyer— probably a torpedo got her."

It was a short while before midnight. Andre stood at the railing of the *Keith* and marveled at the course of the last few days. Since reaching the Dunkirk Perimeter three days before, he had not slept more than fifteen minutes at a time.

The physical letdown that accompanied release from duty was profound. Andre leaned heavily on the rail, discovering for the first time that he was exhausted.

Too tired to even worry about U-boat attacks, Andre stumbled below and stretched out on the floor in a corner of the wardroom. He was asleep almost immediately.

32

A Pillar of Cloud by Day

S moke from the bombed-out docks of Rouen darkened the sky as the *Garlic* navigated the waters of the Seine.

Just ahead Josie could plainly see that the Luftwaffe had been at work on the river port. It had been an important embarkation point for British and American reinforcements in the last war, and the German High Command was taking no chances.

A thick plume of oily fumes obscured for a moment the castle where St. Jeanne d'Arc had been imprisoned in the struggle against the English in 1430. The black smudge in the predawn canopy over Rouen was only one more reminder that, like the martyred St. Jeanne, the soul of France burned on the pyre of war once again. The old walls of the town that had defied Henry V in 1415 had been broadened to boulevards and planted with trees. The ancient vigilance of Rouen had been forgotten, and now the beautiful Gothic city was in flames for a mile and a half along the quais. On the left bank of the river, the two train stations of Gare d'Orleans and Gare de la Rive Gauche were wrecks of twisted metal and charred girders.

"On your toes!" Rose shouted forward to Josie as they rounded the bend and spotted the narrow finger of Ile Brouilly in the center of the river. Just beyond the little island was the larger island of Lacroix and then the bridge across the point where the river narrowed. Was the span still intact? Or had passage down the Seine been blocked by rubble from last night's bombing raid?

"I can't see to the bridge," Josie replied, peering down the right fork of the stream.

"What is ahead?" Rose hailed Lewinski who, with Jerome beside him at the rail, peered through his gas mask from port while Josie and Georg, one of the five Goldblatt brothers, checked to starboard.

"The Pont Corneille still stands!" Lewinski shouted back.

Then Jerome added the warning, "There is a small vessel sunk beside the piling. It will be a difficult passage, Madame Rose!"

Rose chose to navigate down the left branch, past the sunken boat that lay, bow up, against the arched piling of the low bridge. Close enough to touch the shattered hulk of the unfortunate ship, the new coat of paint on the hull of the *Garlic* scraped against the iron mooring rings set in the stone beneath the ancient structure.

The river was up. Josie held her breath and ducked instinctively as they slipped under what seemed more a tunnel than a bridge.

Beyond the two islands the Seine straightened, and in spite of the fact that the wreckage of a dozen larger ships lay half submerged, navigation became easier. The Gothic towers and chalk hills of the town slid away before the children sleeping belowdecks awakened.

Even after the sun came up, however, the smoke above Rouen still obscured the sky behind them. Josie was certain that the same planes that had destroyed the ships and quais of Rouen would soon be skimming like hawks over the river in search of new prey.

CSD

When Andre awoke on June 2, dawn was breaking. The destroyer was still on station off the beach, but Lord Gort had departed for England. Sometime in the middle of the night, the former commander of the now-defunct British Expeditionary Force had left by speedboat for Dover. The general would be facing an inquiry into how the disaster in France had happened.

But also during the night, hundreds of battered and weary soldiers had boarded the *Keith*—men who would now be in a German prisoner-of-war camp if it were not for Gort's leadership during the withdrawal and the French rear guard. In every compartment and companionway, Andre stepped over soggy uniforms that contained worn-out British troops.

The same steward, his white uniform still neatly pressed, offered Andre another steaming cup of tea and a hard biscuit. The servant apologized for the poor fare, but to Andre it was a feast. Sunday brunch at the Ritz could not have been more appreciated.

Feeling refreshed, Andre went back on deck to help aboard men who could hardly stagger and to translate the worried questions of his non-English-speaking countrymen.

The destroyer wallowed in seas that were much rougher than the night before. The rising wind increased the height of the waves. When Andre regained the rail he could see the whalers and lifeboats being tossed around as they made their interminable journeys back and forth between the beach and the destroyers. The increasing roughness of the sea and the extra effort required to pull against the wind made the job even tougher for those just now arriving alongside the *Keith*.

As the pale wrap of early morning light replaced the cloak of the night, Andre was startled by the huge number of ships around him. From his vantage point at the stern of the *Keith*, he could see destroyers, minesweepers, and tugboats. Each of these larger vessels was surrounded by a flotilla of smaller craft, coming and going, unloading men and leaving again for the shore. It was like watching multiple hives of bees, each with a queen served by hundreds of drones. The activity was astounding.

By eight o'clock, the *Keith* was packed full and ready to steam for Dover Harbor. Andre helped the last of a platoon of Royal Irish Fusiliers over the side. The small boats headed back for shore, to continue the evacuation by ferrying soldiers to the nearby destroyer *Basilisk*.

As the *Keith* got under way, Andre's view was toward the southwest. A pall of black smoke had replaced the reddish glow that identified Dunkirk. Andre was reminded of the biblical account of the Exodus—*the pillar of cloud by day . . . the pillar of fire by night*. Still, he was pleased to be going away from and not toward that menacing gloom.

A smaller shadow detached itself from the cloud and rose into the sky. As Andre watched, it resolved itself into half a hundred tiny specks. The swarm aimed directly for the *Keith* and the ships around her.

Three Stukas peeled off from the formation and dove for the destroyer. Andre watched their plunge in fascinated horror, knowing that nothing he did could possibly make any difference.

A pair of antiaircraft guns began their rhythmic pounding, and black bursts of smoke appeared in front of the swooping warplanes. Andre saw the release of the bombs and shuddered in anticipation of what was coming.

Two bombs plunged into the water near the *Keith*'s bow, raising geysers of water that fountained over the deck. Five sailors were washed overboard, just before the third bomb went down the destroyer's smokestack.

There was a tremendous crash, as if the ship had run into a stone wall at full speed. Andre bounced off the armor around a gun housing and was thrown to the deck. He felt the deck plates lift under his feet, as if a geyser were trying to erupt there, too.

The *Keith* gave an agonized groan of twisting steel and failing seams. From his prone position on the shuddering metal, Andre watched a burst of flames, smoke, and steam shoot skyward. The destroyer leaned to port and kept heeling, tumbling Andre against the gunwale.

As the ship settled lower in the water, the shriek of whistles, the bellow of Klaxon horns, and the clang of gongs all mingled to scream its death knell. More Stukas dove on nearby rescue vessels, attacking a pair of minesweepers and another destroyer.

"Abandon ship!" came the cry. It was picked up and carried forward and aft and down into the ravaged insides of the dying ship. Those not killed or wounded in the blast swarmed on deck. Some did not wait but dove over the side, whether they had life jackets or not.

A heap of life preservers on the aft deck was blown apart and scattered by one of the bombs. As the ship listed, several of the jackets slid across the deck. Recently rescued soldiers chased them across the tilted surface like children after runaway pets.

One scooted straight into Andre's hands. He slipped it on, tightening the straps with a savage tug since his safety depended on the grasp of the device. As he balanced on the rail before jumping over the side, another dive-bomber targeted the nearby minesweeper *Skipjack*. It took two direct hits and exploded with a roar.

The concussion rolled across the water, breaking Andre's grip on the rail and pitching him headfirst into the sea. His head struck a floating piece of debris, but he managed to stay conscious and fling an arm over the beam. Choking and sputtering, Andre paddled away from the rapidly sinking destroyer as waves continued to roll over him.

⟨෴⟩

Horst von Bockman stood up in the turret of his PzKw-III. Through his field glasses, he studied the outlines of the town of Lys beyond the intervening screen of trees. The orders Horst had received were simple. They told him that this area was held lightly by a cobbled-together force, including some military school students. He was to punch right through their undoubtedly feeble resistance and drive on to the Channel. Time was of the utmost importance. The Führer, while not admitting that his halt order had been a mistake, was now screaming at the German High Command not to let any more Allied troops escape.

Horst directed his armored reconnaissance patrol forward to scout the bridge and the main road. He moved his tanks to the edge of the river, flanking the highway on both sides.

The lead armored car approached the trestle. Like a chase scene from a motion picture, three Kfz 231s in succession turned the corner at high speed. Each tipped up slightly as they rounded the curve.

Almost at once they were hit by converging streams of machine-gun fire. From both sides of the town and from the island in the center of the river, bullets ripped into the scouts.

The first driver immediately lost control of his vehicle, bouncing it off a low stone wall. Then as the driver overcorrected, the car turned in the opposite direction and smashed headlong into the wall on the other side.

The second car plowed into the first, knocking the already damaged unit onto its side. Metal shrieked as the force of the impact scrubbed the side of the armored vehicle along the pavement of the bridge.

Machine-gun fire continued to pour into the span, and to this was added the sharp crack of a small but well-aimed antitank weapon. The first round punched through the roof of the overturned scout car, passed completely through it, and exploded on the front armor of the second. There was no further motion from either vehicle, both of which now burned furiously in the center of the bridge.

The remaining armored machine did not even turn around. It drove in reverse at high speed back to the safe end of the bridge. But even here, no protection was guaranteed. A round from another antitank weapon, located somewhere on the far bank, reached out and tagged the scout car and spun it around.

"Covering fire," Horst ordered, and the guns of his tanks opened up on the town's defenders. A building on the island was crumpled by the first blast, and a shot fired by Horst's own tank crashed near the location of the first antitank weapon.

More antitank rounds came toward his position from a slightly different angle. It was clear that the defenders knew well the lesson of how to use mobile weapons: fire and move, fire and move. Horst had only just buttoned up the hatch when a shell splattered against the front plating of the panzer.

"We will have to withdraw," he said, "and bring up the artillery."

33

That Could Have Been Me

Andre's inflated life vest and the death grip he had on the wooden plank kept his head out of the waves part of the time. But the swells that did roll over him covered him with oil and diesel fuel. Opening his mouth to gasp for air at an inopportune moment filled Andre's throat with the guck. He gagged and vomited.

His eyes were sticky with oil and burning until they swelled almost shut. He paddled with his free arm, peering through blurred vision and hoping that someone would pick him up before his strength gave out.

A tugboat picked its way among the wreckage. It twisted and turned to avoid running over survivors and dodged Stuka attacks as it gathered in men who called for help. Andre could barely see its shape looming ahead, but he tried to swim and push his bobbing makeshift float toward it. Once he attempted to wave, but the motion pushed him under the breakers and set off another seizure of coughing and retching.

The plank bumped into someone else drifting in the sea. "Grab on," Andre called in English. "Help me! We'll try for the tug." There was no reply. He nudged the silent form. "I said, grab on," Andre tried in French.

When the body was rolled over by another wave, a drifting corpse reproached Andre with sightless eyes. Andre pushed so hard away from the apparition that he dunked himself again. This time he lost his grip on the plank. Flailing wildly, Andre shouted, choked, and sputtered. He called for help in every language he could think of and called on God to save him.

The knotted end of a rope bounced off his head, and the cable fell across his outstretched arms. "Hold on, chum," a cheerful voice called. "You'll be all right!"

The rope slipped through Andre's numb and oily fingers, and he cried out that he was not going to make it. At the very end of the cord, his hands closed around the knot, and he was dragged through the water by the motion of the ship. At any second the pressure of the wave would break his hold and he would spin off astern of the rescue boat.

Andre felt the rope being pulled toward the ship, felt himself being drawn close to the hull he could only dimly make out. Two pairs of strong hands reached down and grabbed him under the arms. He was hoisted aboard the tug *St. Abbs* and laid on the deck. Soaked, oil-covered, puking, and half drowned, he attempted to thank the crew. But they simply nodded and went about their business of rescuing others.

When Andre had recovered some from his own near drowning, he watched the proceedings as the tug's crew methodically loaded and stacked men who were without any ability to help themselves.

Captain Berthon of the *Keith* had been picked up by the tug also. A major of the Grenadier Guards and some of his men rowed to the larger vessel in a lifeboat. When they climbed over the side, the rowboat was made fast and towed behind for use in other rescues. Over a hundred men snatched from the embrace of the sea were sprawled on the decks of the tug.

The man propped next to Andre was dying, punctured by multiple shrapnel holes. A chaplain bent low over him, murmuring words into his ear. The man's hand gripped the parson's, seeming to cling to the world by that touch alone.

A Stuka appeared overhead. Its siren screaming, the dive-bomber plunged toward the tug. There was no way to fight back. Even those who still carried weapons were too tired to raise them.

In the pilothouse, the helmsman spun the wheel. The tug slithered over the surface of the sea like a mouse avoiding the rush of a hawk. It was all guesswork, really. No way to predict which move would equal safety and which might carry the boat under the falling explosives.

What impressed Andre the most was the way people carried on their tasks. As bombs exploded on both sides and then in front of the tug, a brace of burly seamen went on throwing lines to men in the water, lifting them up, and shouting words of encouragement. A medic moved among the injured, wrapping wounds with gauze and dispensing what comfort he could.

An explosion close astern lifted the aft portion of *St. Abbs* clear of the water and slammed it down again. Several men near Andre panicked, thinking the tug had been hit and was sinking. The chaplain, now hugging the dying man to his chest, ignored the blast and continued to repeat, "*I am the resurrection and the life. . . .*"

The medic asked Andre if he was injured and gave him a bit of rough sacking to scrub the worst of the oil from his face. A canteen of fresh-water was passed for Andre to bathe his face. The cool fluid was amazing relief to his inflamed and swollen eyes. It was an oddly commonplace action that Andre felt the irony of: washing your face while there was an immediate likelihood of being blown to bits.

Twice more the Stukas attacked the tug, which seemed to bear a charmed life. The old coal-burning firebox belched black smoke and cinders from the stack. The wind over the Channel blew the smoke into long streamers, marking the tug's path as it twisted and turned in the fountains of water thrown up by the bomb blasts. Andre heard the terror in many voices as men in the water cried for rescue and men already on the tug cried out in fear of the Stukas.

Like a chronicler of every tragedy, *St. Abbs* was present as ship after ship was struck and sank. The wreckage of the *Keith* slipped below the waves. *Basilisk* went down. And the minesweeper Andre had seen bombed rolled over and floated belly-up. Andre shuddered with relief when he remembered that he could have been belowdecks instead of topside and blown clear. Though still in danger themselves, the men on the tug observed with fascinated horror and despair as the minesweeper went to the bottom. Hundreds of men were still trapped inside. The face of every soldier expressed the same thought: *That could have been me.*

The Stukas swooped away to the east. For a time the only sounds Andre heard were the steady thrumming of the tug's engine and the cries for help that still came from every side.

Then a new sound was added to the rest. Faint at first, a buzzing reached Andre's ears that was not the high whine of the Stuka engines but a lower-pitched hum.

A single dot detached itself from the shoreline and rose overhead, as if following the plume of the tug's smoke. A lone Heinkel bomber floated lazily into view. There were no fighters to harass it and no anti-aircraft fire to annoy it, so it came forward with no evasive maneuvering at all. Like a sightseer out to view the carnage, it flew straight and level at no more than a thousand feet off the water.

Whether it had really tracked the ship's exhaust or if *St. Abbs* was the only object still moving on its own through the floating wreckage, the bomber was definitely attacking. All those who were able to watch the warplane did so, willing it to pass by. Andre's mind was screaming to be left alone. Hadn't they been through enough already?

Andre held his breath as the Heinkel passed overhead. No bombs fell; no machine guns opened fire. In concert with a hundred others, Andre breathed a sigh of relief. Perhaps the bomber was only on an observation mission, to report on the success of the Stukas.

Just past the bow of the tug, dark objects began dropping from the belly of the plane. They hit the water in the path of the ship, but all failed to explode. A soldier near Andre laughed. "Good luck for us at last! A poor pilot and a rack of duds!"

But the skipper of the tug knew better. He threw the helm hard over to avoid the delayed-action explosives, but they were too near and the tug too sluggish. The prow swung to starboard, and the hull of the ship drifted broadside toward the floating bombs.

The first explosion blew up the low freeboard of the ship. A hole was torn below the waterline and the plates buckled upward. Shards of the hull pierced men lying on the deck, and others were dead from the concussion before being flung into the water.

The ship corkscrewed from the force of the first blast, exposing its keel to the full impact of the second. *St. Abbs* broke in two and rolled over as she sank into the Channel. In her dying convulsion, she carried most of her passengers with her to the bottom, leaving in thirty seconds no more trace of her existence than a handful of floundering men.

Tossed into the air, Andre was surrounded by a jet of steam that was the tug's last breath. He landed in the water again, while all around him rained chunks of coal and flaming embers from the firebox. For the second time in an hour, he was near to drowning, sucked under by the demise of the tug.

Sinking until he thought his feet would touch the bottom, Andre's lungs were flaming for want of air. He struggled to get back to the surface, endlessly far above. Andre's thoughts ran down sluggishly, like a clock about to stop. Perhaps it was time to open his throat to the sea and get this over with. What was the point of further struggle?

With his last despairing lunge, he strained for the surface but thumped into something floating on the water. His hands scrabbled over a rough exterior and found a trailing cord. Pulling himself upward on the rope as if climbing out of the depths, Andre emerged near the one thing anywhere nearby that was still intact: The lifeboat being towed astern of the tug had been blown free of its cable.

It took fifteen minutes of simply hanging on the line before Andre had strength enough to even attempt to pull himself into the boat. Even then, it took three tries before he slumped into the bottom.

The tide and the currents running through the Channel played games with the lifeboat and its barely conscious occupant. After having been blown up twice and sunk twice, Andre and his unmanaged craft drifted east toward the German-held shore.

☙

"Commander Galway!" called the spotter on *Intrepid*'s bridge, "Take a look at this! I think I'm seein' things!"

"After thirty-six hours nonstop, what would make you think that, Collins? What is it that you think you see?" Trevor pivoted in the direction indicated and raised his binoculars as he asked the question.

"Over there, sir," the lookout replied. "A mile on the port quarter. It . . . I think it's a dog!"

Peering through the glasses, Trevor confirmed that a large rust-colored canine was poised like a figurehead on the bow of a half-submerged ship. "All ahead full," he ordered, trying to keep the panic out of his voice. "Good eye, Mr. Collins. That not only is a dog . . . that's my dog and my dad's ship!"

Wairakei had sunk to her rails. The deck aft of the wheelhouse was awash, and the triangular bow jutted skyward like a tiny wooden island. Shattered windows and riddled hull made it seem as if the Luftwaffe had been using her for target practice. As *Intrepid* idled up alongside, Duffy gave a mournful howl, announcing his readiness to leave his perch as soon as possible.

Trevor anxiously scanned the deck and the water around the ketch for the figure of his father. He was on the point of jumping across to *Wairakei* when John Galway stood up inside the battered remains of the cabin and climbed the slanted deck. "Shut up, daft dog," he bellowed. "So," he said to Trevor, "it's yourself come at last?"

"Da! Are you all right?"

"No, I'm not all right! Look what those bloody Huns have done. Had to stay out of sight to keep them from strafing again, but yon demented beast would not keep quiet!"

Trevor sighed with relief. His father's temper left no doubt that he was in fact unhurt. "Come aboard then."

"Send someone across to help me with Annie."

"Annie? Is she—"

"I'm all right, too!" Annie Galway likewise emerged from the devastated pilothouse. A bandage was clumsily wound around her head, but the smile she flashed Trevor convinced him of the truth of her words. "Be quiet, Duffy," she scolded. "Look, Trevor is here to take us home."

☙

The first shells whistled into Lys a little after nine at night. Sepp was at his post in the bell tower of the church. There was a rushing sound overhead, and then the night exploded as a house one block behind St. Sebastian took a direct hit. The fragments of roof slates that flew through the air were as deadly as the metal slivers from the artillery round.

A second shell dropped into the square in front of the church. It crashed against the fountain, showering the plaza with bits of stone and a geyser of water.

The third detonated on a car parked outside the church. The hood of the auto spun into the air, a glowing, red-hot evil spirit that swooped down the street as if alive, and killed two cadets.

These visions created an instantaneous new thought for Sepp: *The arms of war turn even commonplace things into weapons of destruction.*

"Down!" Sepp yelled at his fellow lookouts. They lunged for the ladder, groping in the darkness for the skinny uprights. "Hurry, hurry!" Sepp urged in a rhythmic monotone. He waited until all the others had preceded him, then swung his leg onto the rungs.

Another 155 mm round arrived. This explosion hit the church tower about halfway up. In a thunder of shattering bricks and mortar, the top of the column collapsed. Sepp was knocked off the ladder and hurled to the level below.

Almost by accident, he reached out and grasped the bell rope swinging nearby. The wildly oscillating cord wrapped itself around him as much as he succeeded in grasping it. He slid and fell through a newly created gap in the floor, down to the center of the sanctuary.

An hour later, Sepp was at his post by the river. Despite the pain from his cracked ribs, he had time to wonder why the Germans had not attempted to cross the bridge again. The shelling went on and on, without letup, but no assault came.

He drew a careful breath, since an unguarded one hurt. He thought the Germans must not know the true strength and disposition of the troops guarding Lys. Perhaps they believed there were more than actually held the town.

A shadow moved on the far bank. Instantly a dozen rifles and two machine-gun positions opened fire. The night was braided into woven strands of light and dark by the flashes and streams of tracers. When the German side of the river responded, the lines of bullets so crossed in midair that it seemed they must knock each other down and fall into the river. Then the crackle of arms tapered off, and both banks of the Lys were silent again.

"In the dark," Sepp remarked to Cadet Treville, "they cannot gauge our capacity. The fact that a lucky shot took out that first armored car makes them wary of the bridge."

"Will you tell Captain Gaston that it was a lucky hit?" Treville teased.

"Get back to your post," Sepp ordered, feeling the ache under the yards of sheet wrapped around his middle. "Dawn will change things, and we must be ready."

34

The Bridge at Lys

Horst was in the half-track he used as a command vehicle, receiving a reprimand from the newly arrived SS General Reuf.

"Why are you not across the river already, von Bockman? Here I am with a division of infantry, ready to move onto the beaches and capture fifty thousand Britishers, and I find the road blocked and our armor sitting idle on this side."

Horst tried to remain patient. "Resistance was stiffer than we anticipated."

"Why have you not called in the bombers? Level the entire town, especially that obvious command post up on the hill."

"That command post is a hospital and clearly marked," Horst said, his anger rising in spite of his effort to control it. "Would you bomb a hospital?"

"If it serves the Reich," said the SS officer with menace behind the words. "In fact, I have already asked for air support but was told that the Luftwaffe is completely engaged in attacking the shipping and the beaches. In any case, that is not our immediate concern. Why are your tanks not across that bridge?"

"The fact that the bridge is still intact worries me."

"Worries you!" exploded the general. "Seize the opportunity at once!"

"It should not be intact. It makes me wonder what sort of trap the French are trying to lure us into. I propose sending a flanking movement downstream to come in behind the town."

"Nonsense," the general exclaimed. "Major, you will clear the roads of your machines. I will bring up my own tanks, and we will get this advance moving again!"

⟨∽⟩

The main building of the Ecole de Cavalerie rapidly filled with additional wounded, for whom there was no more room in the damaged dormitory. Paul Chardon was in his office, meeting with the newly arrived commanders of the British Guardsmen contingent and the French cavalry detachments.

"With our five hundred men and those you gentlemen have brought up to the line," Paul said across his heavy oak desk, "our strength is in the neighborhood of two thousand. That should give us the ability to hold out here for at least a day, perhaps two."

"But your five hundred men, as you call them, are schoolboys," protested the senior French colonel. "They should be withdrawn at once."

"My 'schoolboys' have been preparing for this defense for months, Colonel. Your officers would do well to heed what my cadet officers have to say. How many more reinforcements may we expect?"

The Allied officers exchanged a look.

"There will be no more reinforcements," the French colonel said.

A cadet, crisply dressed in his uniform, presented himself at the door. "What is it, Denis?" Paul asked.

"Captain Gaston reports armored vehicles approaching the bridge, sir."

"Tell him to blow the span to the south shore at once," Paul ordered.

Denis saluted and had turned to leave when the whine of an artillery shell screamed down. The round came through the roof at the front of the building and burst in the corridor outside Paul's office.

The concussion knocked Cadet Denis across the room and into Paul. The body of the sixteen-year-old received the shrapnel and the stout oak desk absorbed the blast, saving Paul's life. The other Allied commanders were not so fortunate; they were exposed to the full force of the concussion and died instantly.

⟨∽⟩

Artillery fire raked the town all night long. Shells from the German 155 mm guns rained down on Lys. The Hotel de Pomme d'Or, once-favored haunt of the titled nobility in the nineteenth century, disappeared in a cloud of brick dust and shattered mortar. The tower of the church took several more hits until it was reduced to a heap of shattered stone.

Explosions also rocked the school, but because most of the barrage was directed at the heart of the city and the buildings on the island, the Ecole escaped serious damage.

The cadets and the other defenders wisely held their fire, knowing that a rifle shot aimed in the dark could scarcely damage the panzers but would certainly draw a twenty-pound bomb in return. Inside the crypt of the church and the cellar of the Hotel de la Cité, the cadets bided their time, waiting for the shelling to cease.

At daybreak on June 3, the shelling lifted. Gaston returned to his command post on the island and, under cover of the sandbagged parapets, repaired the damaged lines that ran to the demolition charges.

A pall of smoke hung over the town and floated over the river, an acrid curtain of biting fog. Gaston could not see across the river, but the sudden resumption of machine-gun fire ripping into the barricade and singing off the stonework into the town let him know what was coming.

The rumble of tanks approached the bridge. A 37 mm round shattered the cornice of the building just above him. The raining fragments killed Cadet Lieutenant Beaufort, and a chunk the size of a man's fist landed on Gaston's head. It knocked him to the paving stones and left a gash behind his ear.

When Gaston was struck down, his antitank crews began to fire without waiting. They loaded and launched cartridge after cartridge of the 25 mm shells, wasting much of their ammunition when it bounced off the front armor of the panzers.

More shells landed nearby, tearing apart the gun crew. Bullets from across the river and from the tank weapons poured in, keeping other cadets from being able to take their places.

The forward tank rolled to the midpoint of the bridge, blocked by the remains of the armored cars. It nosed against them, then pushed them aside. There was a momentary contest between the strength of the tank and the stone wall. Then the three-hundred-year-old rampart yielded. The tank pushed the carcass of first one and then the other Kfz 231 over the edge and into the river.

Gaston felt someone shaking him. He did not know where he was. In fact, he believed that he was home in bed and his mother was trying to awaken him. "I don't have to get up yet," he mumbled. "And I have a terrible headache."

"Captain!" Cadet Plachet urged. "Wake up! The tanks are on the bridge!"

Gaston awoke to the danger. Despite the throbbing in his head and the distraction of seeing everything double, he pulled himself over to the plunger of the detonator. The tanks opened up on the island with their machine guns and cannons, blasting chunks of stonework out of the walls and ripping into the sandbags.

The French soldiers and the cadets stationed on the island and on the

Lys shore fired their antitank weapons, but this morning nothing seemed to be working.

Gaston waved his men back to cover behind the heaps of rubble that had been the buildings on the island. The third tank in the column that rumbled onto the bridge bore the personal pennant of an SS general.

There was not an instant to spare. Gaston twisted the plunger to unlock it then, pulling it up, jabbed it home. The force behind the blow on the handle made it seem that he was trying to knock the bridge down by the strength of his arm alone.

The lead tank gunner spotted Gaston at the same instant and swiveled the machine gun toward him. Flecks of rock spun into the air from the ricochets, blinding Gaston and lacing his face with fragments.

Then the bridge erupted with a roar. Beginning at the end nearest the island, the centuries-old arches heaved upward, as if living things were emerging from under the water. Each vaulted span shattered in turn, catapulting boulders into the air. The tanks reared on their treads like startled elephants, then dropped submissively into the river.

∽

The course of the Seine turned south again after Rouen. The farmlands of Normandy spread out in a peaceful carpet of vivid color. There was no war here.

"Up on deck!" Rose ordered when the first stirrings were heard below. She scouted the banks of the wide river and brought the *Garlic* into a lee where a stand of willows dipped their branches in the quiet waters. There the boat was moored. Lewinski, Jerome, and the five brothers went to work gathering branches to camouflage the dark hull of the péniche.

Personal needs were taken care of on shore. Boys walked or were carried by Lewinski to the bank on the left. Girls all traipsed to the right. Faces were washed. Clean underthings put on. Dirty clothes rinsed in the river. Only then did the children gather on deck for prayer and a breakfast of tinned biscuits and jam. A jug of apple juice was cautiously sniffed by Rose, then declared drinkable and shared all around.

Lewinski, looking oddly happy and at peace, held Yacov on his knee and watched over the congregation from a place in the sun. He did not wear the obligatory gas mask. His nervous hands were twirling a willow branch.

"I will carve whistles if you will bring me sticks," he told the boys and Juliette and Marie.

Then Josie said to Rose, "Even sailors and the daughters of sailors must sleep sometime."

It was noted by those who had lived at No. 5 Rue de la Huchette with Madame Rose that in all the time they had known her, no one had ever seen her sleep. They all assumed Madame Rose never needed sleep. She had always been up and dressed before they arose and never to bed before they were all tucked in.

Therefore, it was a matter of great interest when she growled at them now to all go away. She placed a blanket on a cotton sack in the bow, where the willow branches made a curtain, and promptly began to snore.

Madame Rose snoring? It was much more amazing than the sound of bombs.

⤫

"Send that SS engineer company here on the double," Horst ordered.

When the captain of engineers arrived, he looked around for the SS commander.

"Your general," Horst informed the man, "is at the bottom of the Lys. You are now under my authority." Whether true or not, the claim worked.

The bridging unit brought up pontoon sections to construct new spans for the river and inflatable boats. Horst ordered the SS infantry into the rubber rafts. "We will supply the covering fire. Your job is to get across the river and establish yourselves on the island."

The south shore of the Lys disappeared in the smoking roar of cannon and machine-gun fire. The defenders on the island and Sepp's troops in the city were reduced to shooting back blindly over the tops of their shelters.

35

Guessing Games

Throughout the morning Madame Rose rested while the children played or simply sat and watched from the shelter of the willows. A half-dozen times the moaning of aircraft passed overhead. They were too high to identify. French Moranes? British Spitfires? German ME-109s?

Josie did not want to know, but the boys played guessing games. If their conclusions were correct, then four formations out of the six had been Luftwaffe. They were headed in the direction of Le Havre. It was not a good sign.

Richard Lewinski had carved willow whistles for all passengers before the *Garlic* chugged away from the bank around noon. The Seine snaked south to La Bouille, then north to Duclair. One more long U brought the *Garlic* to Caudebec, and then the bends began to straighten. The wide mouth of the Seine River opened to the sea and the great port of Le Havre in the late afternoon. The Canal de Tancarville, fifteen miles long, connected the Seine directly with Le Havre, enabling ships to escape the tidal changes in the estuary.

Today Rose chose not to go to the port city by way of the canal. She guessed rightly that the planes that had swept over them had been heading for the Tancarville and the vessels in the locks. Tall plumes of smoke marked where those craft had been spotted and destroyed.

"Ducks in a barrel," Rose said grimly as the shallow-bottomed *Garlic* moved easily across the estuary at slack tide.

Entering the bay, it was plain to see that like Rouen, Le Havre had been hit hard. The gray film of dissipating smoke was visible from miles away. Its shipbuilding and sugar refineries were the envy of all Europe.

Eight miles of quais and 190 acres of water area made the port of Le Havre one of the most important harbors of France. The Bassin de l'Eure alone was seventy acres, and it was there that the great ocean liners of the Compagnie Géneralé Transatlantique were berthed.

"I had hoped to get fuel there." For the first time Madame Rose's voice registered concern, Josie thought. The masts of the péniche were still down, lashed to the decks. Fuel in the tank was alarmingly low. Perhaps not enough to reach England, Rose confided to Josephine and Lewinski.

But to chance being in the harbor of Le Havre could be fatal.

"We will sail north along the coast," the old woman decided as she inhaled the fresh salt aroma of La Manche. The color returned to her cheeks. "There is the little port of Fécamp. They might have fuel. And if Fécamp is being attacked, then Veulettes. Or Dieppe north of that. And farther . . ."

"Calais and Boulogne are fallen," Lewinski said. "This General Guderian captured Abbeville and then swept north to take the Channel ports. By now he may have turned south again, Madame. We must be very careful, whatever harbor we enter for fuel."

Madame Rose stuck her lower lip out. Her mouth turned down as she considered the warning. "We have no compass," she said flatly. "Give me a compass, and I can sail around the world in a bathtub. But I feel the lack of a compass. Beyond this estuary the Atlantic is a vast place. The Channel current could carry us away if we were to run out of fuel. . . . We must stay within sight of the coast, then cross the Pas de Calais."

Lewinski's cheek twitched nervously at this remark. The narrow strait between France and England was sure to be filled with battleships, mines, and who could say what else?

"Madame." He bowed his head in a gesture like a gawky schoolboy studying an insect. "As I have explained, the entire French shore along the Pas de Calais is in the hands of the Boche. It will be far too dangerous."

"Yes, very dangerous," she agreed.

For an instant Rose seemed undecided. Was that a flash of fear in her eyes? Josie wondered.

The shouts of Jerome and Henri and Georg pulled her attention as they emerged victoriously from the hold with a cane fishing pole in hand. Wearing his tall boots, Henri rode on the back of Georg, and the boys paraded to where the others sat together at the bow. The wind pulled hair back from newly freckled faces. Big ears stuck out. The boys were grinning—all of them.

And the girls? Surrounded by cables and sitting in a pen of canvas, Marie and Juliette shared imaginary tea with the baby. As if it were all simply a great adventure, like ladies on the deck of an ocean steamer, they must have their tea.

"Look how completely they trust," Rose remarked quietly. She flexed her fingers and wiped the perspiration off her sunburned forehead. The cry of seagulls sounded as they circled overhead and then spun off toward the north. Her eyes narrowed as if she was hearing another voice.

Some decision was made in that instant, Josie knew. Some thought, some vision, entered the old woman's mind. She brought the *Garlic* about as if to follow the course of the gulls to the north along the seacoast.

"The children may remain on deck. But secure them with lifelines," Rose instructed. "The sea can be rough in the Channel, and they will certainly all be sick," she added cheerfully.

❧

Mac pitched in to help with the building of still more of the improvised jetties. Since he was not a part of any unit on the beach, he figured that making himself useful would be remembered when it came time for getting out of here.

He and a party of men from Royal Army Ordnance were dispatched to La Panne to round up more discarded vehicles. There had been a Stuka attack a few minutes before their arrival, and the most promising lorries were bombed out and smoldering.

One truck had been overturned by the blast, but it appeared to be whole. If it could be righted, it would take its place as part of a pier.

"'Fore we go to heavin' on it," an ordnance corporal said, "what say we look to see it isn't full of bombs or some such?"

The rear doors resisted tugging but succumbed to the blows of a fire ax. "Blimey," the corporal exclaimed, staring. "This is a NAAFI lorry!"

NAAFI was the source of personal items for the servicemen. The truck was loaded with all kinds of food and other treasures. Soon men were loading their arms with cartons of cigarettes, bars of chocolate, and new pairs of shoes.

The corporal passed some jars to Mac. "Help yourself, mate. No use leavin' it for the Jerries."

Mac stuffed a handful of chocolate bars into his jacket and added a tin of something without even glancing at it. There would be no more work done on the jetty by this party; it was clear. Mac went off to look somewhere else for a ride.

❧

How long Andre drifted in the open boat, he could not say. It was the noise of the breakers crashing ahead that roused him, and he saw at once the danger he was in. The lifeboat contained only a single remaining oar. Struggling against his still-overwhelming weariness, Andre rigged the paddle as a primitive rudder and used it to aim the bow of the craft toward the land.

A swell rose under the keel of the boat, and for an instant it surfed along the crest, propelled toward the shore. Then the wave outran Andre's ability to keep in position, and he drifted again between the crests.

A vagrant surge turned the boat half around and left it in danger of broaching. Desperately sweeping the oar, Andre forced a correction to the lifeboat's course. It swung ponderously about, while Andre divided his attention between the shore ahead and the next wave racing up from astern.

This time the crest of the breaker caught the full weight of the vessel, pushing it beachward, as if it had been fired from a cannon. Andre worked with frantic haste, expecting at any moment to be turned sideways and capsized.

The instant the keel grated on the sand, Andre jumped out, leaving the lifeboat to the rough hands of the sea. He was safely back on shore, but where? He knew that the currents and the wind had driven him east toward Ostend, but how far east? From behind the spit of land on which Andre had grounded, he could not even see the smoke of the ruins of Dunkirk. All he could do was start toward the west and try to find another ship.

Hearing sounds approaching the beach, Andre hid himself in the brush behind the dunes. A German soldier appeared out of a draw and walked toward the water, passing within fifty feet of Andre's hiding place. The soldier was young and had his rifle slung across his back. As Andre watched, the rifleman took off his coal-scuttle helmet and wiped the sweat from his forehead.

"Fritz! *Wo bist du?*" the soldier called.

Another German within hailing distance? Andre worried. *What if there is a whole patrol?*

When the German had called twice more, a little white dog burst out of the shrubbery and ran to the soldier. "Fritz," he scolded. "You bad dog!"

The Wehrmacht trooper knelt down to scratch his pet's ears. His Gewehr service rifle was still loosely hanging across his back.

Andre rushed forward, striking the back of the German's neck with his forearm and knocking him face-first into the sand. Pulling up on the weapon tightened the strap where it crossed the man's throat and chest.

Andre pressed his foot against the soldier's neck and yanked upward on the rifle. The German's hands fluttered around his throat, and then he lay still while the dog bounced around on the sand, yapping and barking.

Andre removed the German's rifle, cartridge belt, canteen, and helmet and faded into the dunes, heading toward Dunkirk. When he looked back, the puppy was sitting on the sand beside the body, pawing his master's outflung arm and whining.

◔

One of Gaston's antitank guns had been knocked out. He took personal charge of the other, using it to blow the rubber rafts out of the water. The problem was, for every boat that he destroyed, two more seemed to take its place.

An SS sergeant stood on the stern of yet another inflated craft. With one hand he directed the boat toward the island with the tiller of the tiny outboard motor. With the other he fired his MG-34 from the hip. Gaston saw the man snarl as he snapped out orders to the two little rafts on either side. He was resourceful, that sergeant. The two flanking boats contained men with grenade launchers that lobbed explosives toward Gaston's position, even as the sergeant sprayed bullets to keep the defenders from firing back. It was a well-executed attack.

Gaston took particular pleasure in squaring the sights of the antitank gun on the sergeant's chest. The 25 mm round toppled the German into the water. The rubber boat, left without a helmsman, skittered crazily over the river, like a spooked horse, before being punctured by the hail of gunfire and sinking in midstream. The other two boats turned back.

Gaston called his runner to him. "I want you to carry a message to Captain Sepp. And when you have delivered it, stay with him. Tell him that the attack here is increasing. I do not know how long we can hold, so I am going to blow the bridge between the island and the town, lest the Germans get it intact."

"Yes, Captain Gaston. Anything else?"

Gaston looked off in the distance for a second. "Tell him to die gloriously."

36

Singled Out

Andre reached the outskirts of the Dunkirk Perimeter after dark. On the way he narrowly avoided two German patrols but eventually reached Nieuport Bains near the eastern end of the Allied-held territory. The beach was crawling with Germans preparing for a nighttime assault on the defenses.

Ducking back out to the road, Andre found it to be unguarded. He jogged along the verge, ready at any second to fling himself into the brush. When he had covered a half mile down the darkened highway without seeing or hearing another person, a shot flashed from the darkness ahead and a bullet whizzed past his ear.

"Halt!" a voice commanded in English.

Andre called back, "Don't shoot! I'm French."

"Come in slowly then," he was told, "with your hands in plain sight!"

Andre was escorted at bayonet point to the field hospital, which doubled as the headquarters of the sector's defense. "You are about to be attacked along the shore," he told the lieutenant who interrogated him.

"I have no doubt," said the weary officer, running a hand over his stubbled face and rubbing his bloodshot eyes. "We're trying to evacuate the nurses and the walking wounded."

A tall figure in a rumpled and bloodstained nurse's uniform passed the cubicle and looked in at Andre's oil-streaked face. The nurse turned back. "It is Colonel Chardon; is it not?"

"Ah, Sister Mitchell," Andre recalled. "So you are successfully withdrawn from the school. Do you know where I can find my brother? Has he already taken ship for England?"

"Do you not know?" she asked. "He has refused to leave. He and the students of the Ecole are fighting the rearguard action so the rest of us can get away!"

⨎

North by northeast the compass would have read if the *Garlic* had possessed a compass. Which it did not.

This might have been a disaster had it not been for the resourcefulness of Jerome. An old, water-stained maritime chart was dug out of a musty locker. There was a spot of green mold marking Le Havre, and a tear through the inset map of Dieppe. But every shoal and sandbar that had been in the Channel seventy-five years ago, when the chart was printed, was marked for Madame Rose to study.

It was after dark. Rose hugged the shoreline. By keeping the sound of the breakers always on her right, she stayed in touch with the coast. It was a trick she had learned in California, she said, to help navigate in fog.

Here and there a wink of light from the shore gleamed out. She steered the péniche far enough from the shoals to be safe but near enough to land that if the wheezing engine of the ancient barge died, there still might be some hope of making it to shore.

Thirty miles up the coast from Le Havre was the fishing village of Fécamp. It was here that Rose hoped to obtain fuel for the *Garlic*. She judged their progress as a tedious six knots. That meant five hours from Le Havre to Fécamp.

Five hours had passed, and still her scouts had not spotted the lighthouse or the warning buoys that had been plainly identified on the chart as marking the entrance of the tiny harbor.

Marie, blinking through the thick lenses of her spectacles, caught sight of a glimmer. She shouted cheerfully that the harbor for Madame Rose had been found. But it was merely the moving lights of some vehicle that, heedless of the blackout, had no covers on the headlamps.

The breakers roared against the beaches to their right. The wind grew cold. Josie took Juliette, Yacov, and Marie below and covered them with coarse woolen blankets. Marie asked if Madame Rose would come to tuck her in. Would Madame Rose come and sing her to sleep and help her say her prayers?

Explaining that Madame Rose was busy, Josie added that perhaps she would come later. She tried to stand in for the old woman's nighttime ritual, but Marie was not content.

"Madame Rose is steering the boat. The boat will rock you to sleep. Therefore, Madame Rose is rocking you to sleep."

This explanation satisfied Marie and she slept.

Six hours passed. No harbor of Fécamp. Then seven. The engine chuffed onward.

"We have missed Fécamp," Rose said. "They blacked out their entrance lights and we sailed past them."

Josie wondered about the fuel.

Lewinski taught Jerome, the five Austrian brothers, and the special children how to play a Polish tune on their whistles. They grew weary. Some went down to sleep out of the wind. Lewinski carried the boys who could not walk. He joked with them and asked Henri where he had gotten such fine boots.

Josie thought that Lewinski was a very human fellow when he was pried away from his machine. He came up and played with his whistle, making a piping noise like a bird in a thunderstorm.

The noise of the surf was more distant. Madame Rose corrected their course, bringing the vessel in parallel with the roar.

Unable to stay awake any longer, Josie fell asleep against the heap of canvas of the sails. . . .

When Josie awakened, it was still dark, and the shudder of the *Garlic* had stopped. The engine was silent. The vessel rocked gently on the swells. The crash of the breakers had shifted to the left side of the craft. Had they turned back? Had the engine failed?

"Out of fuel," Rose said to Lewinski when his mellow voice called from the nest he had made for himself beside the anchor.

"Will we be caught in the breakers?" His voice was calm.

"I think not. The current has us. We are somewhere between England and France, drifting very slowly toward America."

For hours the disabled *Garlic* floated in the current of the Channel. There seemed to be no help for it. Josie asked Madame Rose if they could put up the masts and pull up the sails.

"*Step* the masts and *hoist* the sails," Rose corrected. "No, dear, I'm afraid not. Even with everyone onboard, we are still not enough for a task like that. We will certainly fetch up somewhere. But don't lose hope," Rose told her. "Look how far we have come in this old tub of a ship."

The night itself gave no cause to feel frightened. The engineless boat was never completely quiet. The ancient hull creaked and groaned like a poor old soul with the miseries—definitely a complainer.

Josie found herself wondering how far the barge had traveled in its lifetime, how many ports it had visited, how many strange cargos it had carried. She would bet that it had never seen passengers like this assortment, no matter how exotic its past.

A low hum joined the squeak of the rigging. It grew in volume. The source of the noise was a puzzle. It seemed to come from all around, all at once.

"Rose?"

"I hear it, too," Rose said.

A gray hull loomed out of the darkness on the *Garlic's* port beam. Madame Rose clanged the signal bell, the only warning device the barge carried. The clamor loudly pierced the stillness.

A foghorn bellowed from the new ship—an angry sound. The prow of the vessel swung away from the *Garlic*, missing by fifty feet but still too close. Josie felt as if her heart would jump out of her chest.

Another horn blasted from the other beam of the barge, then another from astern. "It's a whole fleet!" Rose said. "Light the lantern, Josephine. Now it doesn't matter who they are. We don't want to be run down!"

In response to Josie's lantern, the first ship came alongside. Her bow said that she was the *Lotte*, and the square box of her pilothouse forward of the cargo boom said her home port was Harfleur.

"Fishing trawler," Madame Rose remarked.

The children, awakened by the noise, poured up on deck.

"What has happened?" Jerome asked. "Are we there yet?"

A spotlight beam from the *Lotte* played over the deck of the *Garlic*, making Josie and the children squint.

"*Mon dieu*," a voice said in French. "What is this? A floating nursery school?"

"A kind of Noah's ark," Rose called back. "We are out of fuel. Can you spare us some?"

"No, but we can give you a tow."

"Where are you bound?"

"Does not everyone know? We are the fishing fleet of Harfleur, bound for Dunkirk to rescue our boys from the Boche!"

⟨◎⟩

The dunes north of Dunkirk bore the imprint of thousands of tramping boots.

The tide was out, exposing a jetty made of lorries. A hundred yards up the beach two more piers had been constructed of freight barges that had been run aground and the bottoms knocked out. High and dry, they were now out of reach of the swarm of little ships, yet long lines of men stretched beyond them into the water.

From the hills down to the water, the sand was littered with clumps of newly arrived men. Fifty or a hundred in a group, they gathered around their unit's leader as if they were scouts on a campout.

David and Badger joined a group of half a hundred from an artillery

regiment. They were a sullen company, having retreated without ever firing a shot. The regiment had moved forward into Belgium on the first
day of Blitzkrieg. But because of the refugees clogging the roads, they
had stopped short of their preassigned position and withdrawn in the
face of the German onslaught.

They had been withdrawing ever since.

Now they had been forced to abandon their weapons as well. An
artilleryman who had been trained to fight from behind the breech of a
cannon has no purpose in life when he has no artillery to fire. These men
felt the shame of never having inflicted damage on the enemy. More
than any group David had met, this regiment had accepted the stigma of
running away.

David spoke with a captain and asked if he and Badger could join the
group in waiting for evacuation. "Can't think why you'd want to," the officer replied listlessly. "You and your friend have obviously seen action.
Someone should save a place for you at the head of the queue."

The captain returned to staring out at the line of breakers. Some of
his men were sleeping. Others were scooping out shallow pits for themselves. None seemed interested in talking. It was dusk, and each man
was alone with his gloomy thoughts.

A low, incessant drumming of many engines announced the return
of another flight of Heinkels to bomb Dunkirk. David counted the
heavy-bodied twin-engine planes until his tally reached ninety-nine;
then he gave up. His arm ached. He wondered if he had made a mistake
leading Badger out in the open and leaving the safety of the shelter.

The bombs whistled down on the docks and the warehouses and the
oil tanks of Dunkirk. But the heavy thump and rumble of high explosives were missing, and the objects falling from the German warplanes
resembled bundles of sticks.

"Incendiaries," David muttered to Cross.

Orange flames licked at the shattered rubble left from earlier explosions, and the fire soon engulfed the smashed businesses and hotels of
the city. Brown and gray columns of woodsmoke rose to join the black
fumes from the burning oil tanks.

"Poor sods," Badger murmured, "but it'll be us next."

David knew Badger was referring to the soldiers who huddled in the
cellars, believing they were safe there. But tons of debris, piled over their
hiding places, now became massive funeral pyres.

Badger had grown very fatalistic. To counter this despair, David became ever more obsessed with strawberries. He had come to think of
Badger's upcoming birthday as a symbol of their survival.

The men on the beach did not escape the attention of the Luftwaffe either. As the Heinkels unloaded their bombs, each made a lazy circuit of the town and the harbor, ignoring the intermittent fire of a French antiair-craft battery. The planes searched for targets of opportunity to machine gun, and many of their pilots spotted the clusters of men on the beach.

A Heinkel roared over the dunes, lines of tracers winking into the sand. The machine flashed overhead and was gone.

But that was only the beginning. For the next fifteen minutes, bomb-ers buzzed the beach from every conceivable angle. Some burst into view suddenly from out of the thick smoke over the town. More could be seen turning over the harbor, inexorably charging toward the mass of men.

When it was all over, fifty men were dead and thirty more wounded. As many were struck while running away as were hit sitting still.

"Glad that's done," breathed the artillery captain. "Now if the navy will just hurry up, we'll get off this bit of shingle before Jerry comes back at dawn."

The blazing town of Dunkirk continued to draw bombs. David watched the leaping tongues of flame that pinpointed the location for the Germans. He described for Badger the nature of each target by the color of the explosion. Dark red flames erupted over an inferno that had been someone's home or shop. Bright orange was an oil-storage tank. The bundles of incendiaries burst with glowing green light. It was an un-matched fireworks display accompanied by rolling thunderous drums.

A new brightness joined the exhibition. High over the beach came the hum of a single aircraft, barely to be distinguished from all the other noise. A brilliant purple light cracked the night sky over the sand. It was followed by another and another and another, until the air blazed with violet torches that swayed as they slowly descended.

"Flares!" came the cry.

It was a time to feel naked. The weird illumination made each man feel exposed, singled out. When even the cover of darkness is ripped away, what hiding place remains? The purple glow reflected on David's upper arm and Badger's bandaged face and hands, as if to especially mark their owners for destruction. It was possible to be in the middle of twenty thousand men and feel very alone.

There was a stirring in the dunes. The instinct to run was almost over-powering. But run where? As if reading the terror in every man's mind, a tall lieutenant in the uniform of the military police leaped to his feet and cried, "Steady on, lads! Don't move! It'll do you no good to panic!"

Unmoving, David held his breath as the shrill whistle of the first stick of bombs screamed from above the flares. Two hundred yards up the beach, geysers of sand erupted into the air, flinging men like rag dolls and a two-ton lorry like a child's toy.

The officer was right. There was nowhere to run, nothing to do but wait and pray that the next load did not fall on him. David sprawled flat in the sand and covered his head. Badger cringed lower with every blast. The concussions deafened them both, shutting out the screams of the dying.

When the bombers passed, David and Badger were still alive, but a group of twenty men who had waited one dune behind them lay in pieces.

Now not even darkness offered safety. The Germans, it seemed, were intent on preventing the evacuation of any more troops.

David could not help wondering about the wounded soldiers they had left behind in the hospital at the Ecole de Cavalerie. By now they were probably not any better off than those whose blood leached into the sands of Dunkirk. Had the River Lys finally been crossed by the Germans? How long did the men on the beaches have before the Panzer divisions were blasting them from behind while the Stukas worked them over from the air?

The defenders of the perimeter could not hold out more than hours longer, David figured, by the numbers who were staggering to the coast. And that meant only hours were left to escape the carnage of Dunkirk.

37

By Force of Will

Before daylight on the fourth of June, Andre crept out of the lines, under the noses of a British machine-gun crew. He hoped, for their sakes, that they were either more vigilant or already evacuated when the Germans came. Still, he reflected that no one in his right mind was traveling the direction he had chosen. No one except him was sneaking out of Dunkirk and deliberately heading toward the Germans.

Andre had explained the desperate situation of the cadets to as many officers as would listen, but in the final analysis, each had promised nothing. Everyone was done in; none saw the mission as anything other than suicide. "All the troops who can possibly disengage are here to be evacuated," he was told, "not going back into danger."

That was why Andre was so surprised when he heard the sounds of a jogging cadence being called out in French. Flat on his belly, peering from behind a clump of grass, Andre watched the swirling mist as a group of black soldiers trotted into view.

Like fragments of an odd dream, they emerged from the fog. The men were dressed in baggy white breeches, scarlet vests, and red, Turkish conical-style hats. There were about fifty of them. They ran in perfect rhythm, rifles slung, packs on back, and the blades of their bayonets drawn and carried upright against their shoulders. Shaking himself out of his confusion, Andre figured out that they were Senegalese troops. They had almost passed by when he called out to them.

Instantly they surrounded him. Their leader, a sergeant as dark as midnight with a saber scar that crossed both his lips, saluted. "Colonel," he said in pleasantly lilting French, "would you be pleased to lead us? We have lost all our officers, nor can we find Germans to fight either."

Andre explained that he was returning to the cavalry school for what would certainly be a grave struggle.

The sergeant made a sweeping bow. "Direct us, Colonel," he said. "We wish to be of service to France."

With Andre at their head, the contingent of Senegalese troops jogged toward Lys.

They heard the noise of an aircraft's sputtering engine. A Stuka, obviously already damaged from its low altitude and slow speed, wavered into view. The warplane nosed over and dropped into a nearby field. It landed mostly intact, and Andre saw the canopy of the plane slide open.

The Senegalese sergeant gave an order, and without breaking stride, ten of his men loped across the field to the Luftwaffe craft. They dragged the occupants from the plane, and Andre shuddered as he saw bayonets rise and fall in short, chopping motions.

"Already you have brought us good luck," the sergeant said. "Let us go find more Germans to kill."

෨

Far out on the water there was a brilliant flash against a leaden curtain. The weather had closed in around the beaches of Dunkirk, obscuring the view of the gleaming White Cliffs of Dover across the Channel. The soldiers waiting in the queues groaned when their view of home and safety was snatched away.

At least the lowering clouds prevented the Luftwaffe from renewing their attacks. A brief respite from the constant fear of being bombed or strafed was a welcome relief.

David studied the wall of gray that separated him from England. He stared as if he could pierce it by force of will and see Annie there, waiting for him. See her in his arms. A beam of light broke through the overcast. It danced on the surface of the Channel, highlighting the waves. The ray broadened to become a shimmering band of silver. Like something tangible, it moved across the face of the sea, directly toward David. Halfway to him, it broke in two, and the first patch of glowing light continued his way, while the other part retreated to the English shore.

Fascinated, almost hypnotized by the spectacle, David scarcely noticed that he and Badger were now at the forefront of the waiting column. Their feet were splashed by the waves that ran up on the French coast. A boat was returning again, making its way to shore.

Behind David and Badger, a man broke from the ranks and sprinted forward into the surf. "Take me," he begged, though he came from far back in the mob. "I can't stand it anymore!"

The lieutenant commander drew a pistol. "Get back in line," he ordered, "or I'll shoot!"

Sullenly the soldier returned to his place and melted back into the crowd. There was no outcry raised against him that David could hear, no demand that the man be punished.

The boat grated on the shoal, and this time an officer jumped out and ran to the beachmaster. They held a whispered conference, while David and the others at the head of the line secured the launch against the tide's pull.

The lieutenant commander's face turned grim as he addressed the crowd. Badger Cross leaned his head forward to listen, as if he had been deafened instead of blinded.

"*Wakeful* has been torpedoed," the officer said, "after the launch delivered the last lot on board. She went down on the spot. I'm sorry. I have been told that larger ships are not getting into the harbor. My advice to you is to go back to Dunkirk. Otherwise you'll have to remain here and hope another comes along."

Cross shook his head sadly. "I knew I'd never come away. I've seen my last birthday, Tinman."

❧

Cadet Raymond heard the firing from upstream, but no Germans came near his position. The sound of approaching engines on his side of the river came from the direction of the school. Captain Chardon, his arm in a sling, rolled up in a truck followed by two Hotchkiss tanks. Raymond reported that all was quiet and asked if the time had come to destroy the bridge.

"Not yet," Paul said. "I think we have a use for this crossing still." Swiftly he outlined his plan. "The Germans now know our true strength. And their artillery keeps us so pinned down that we cannot send Sepp or Gaston any reinforcements. At nightfall the Wehrmacht will cross in force. What we need is a diversionary assault. Perhaps even knock out their guns." He pointed his thumb at the tanks.

Raymond knew that their two lightweight and lightly armed vehicles were scarcely a match for the panzers. "We must go at once, before they mount an attack this direction. I propose sending a troop of our cavalry along as well." He could not believe that he said that. It had just popped out.

Paul smiled at his young protégé. "I thought you'd say that. Take your force across the bridge and set up a defensive perimeter on that side

to keep the road open. Your column of horses and the two tanks will circle toward the battery of German guns. Do what damage you can and
come back immediately. Remember," he admonished, "if you are too
slow, the bridge will have to be demolished and you will be stuck on the
other side."

The oddly mixed column of Raymond's twenty-five horsemen, one
hundred British Grenadier Guards, and two rumbling Hotchkiss units
spurted across the river on the swaying bridge. Lighter by almost ten
tons than any of the panzers, the French machines were able to cross the
creaking structure to launch the attack.

The guards unit was detailed off to protect the approach to the
bridge, having been given strict instructions by Paul that they were to fall
back to the north shore and blow the span at the first sight of a serious
German offensive.

The cavalry troop went south into the woods, their horses traveling
at a fast walk. The flanks of the line were defended by the tanks. There
was no opposition, even though Raymond could hear the shooting in
the direction of Lys continue.

It was a wide swing away from the river, but one designed to bring
them in behind the location of the batteries that were shelling the town.
Perhaps the German maps did not show the suspension bridge, so they
were unaware of another approach to Lys. Or perhaps they were so su-
premely confident of their overwhelming force that they felt no need for
anything other than a frontal assault. Whatever the reason, Raymond's
force met none of the enemy as they pivoted toward the sound of the
guns. The Germans were so unused to anyone attacking them since this
campaign began that they had not bothered to post any guards.

⌒⊙⌒

Gaston had been wounded again. Besides the wad of bandage taped behind his ear that looked and felt like a pack of cigarettes, he now had a
gash on his chest.

He thought what a close call it had been. The bullet had ricocheted
off the brim of his helmet and plunged into his collar. The steel hat
sported a hole just above his eyes, and there was an angry red tear that
ran along his breastbone.

The little band of defenders was shrinking rapidly. From over two
hundred with which Gaston had begun his defense of the island, only
forty remained alive and unharmed. Both antitank weapons had been
demolished, but then they were without any more ammunition for
them anyway.

Every hour the shells of the big guns and the mortars rained down on his position. After a twenty-minute bombardment, the shelling ceased, which was the signal that the waves of rubber rafts would again be crossing the Lys. If it were not so terrifying, it would be tedious.

"They are coming again," Gaston shouted as the firing stopped. The last shelling had taken a further toll on his forces.

"Captain," a voice called, "I am almost out of ammunition."

"I also," came the cry.

"And I."

Gaston eyed the sack of grenades and what remained of the box of machine-gun ammunition. "Grenades and bayonets then," he shouted back.

Gaston saw Cadet François stand to hurl a grenade, saw him shot down and fumble the explosive onto the ground. Burying his head in his hands, Gaston hid from the blast that erupted over the island. He called out the names of the last cadets he had seen alive . . . and got no response.

Ammunition exhausted, grenades gone, and reduced to his bayonet alone, Gaston thought about surrendering. He decided he could not give up. Not while Sepp and the others lived and continued to fight.

Racing to the edge of the island nearest the town, Gaston flung himself off the pilings that remained of the demolished bridge. As he did so, he saw that a handful of other defenders—French cavalry and cadets—were likewise swimming toward Lys. The island now belonged to the Germans, but the battle would be continued from the wreckage of the town.

Rifle shots cracked behind him, throwing up splashes of water. He heard each *snap* as the round was fired, the *zing* of the bullet and the *hiss* as it struck the water. But none found him. The small arms that replied to the Germans from Sepp's position spoiled their aim.

Gaston continued pulling strongly toward safety. As he swam, he realized that the lump of bandage behind his ear would make an excellent white target for a marksman.

As Gaston reached the shore, Sepp dashed down to the water's edge and helped drag him behind the sandbag barricade. Gaston heard his friend give a grunt of pain, and Sepp abruptly dropped his arm.

"Sepp!" Gaston cried out. "Where are you hit?"

Sepp's mouth worked, but no sound came. He gestured weakly toward his side.

Ripping apart his friend's tunic, Gaston's hand came away covered in blood. "Help!" Gaston cried. "Help me! Captain Sepp is wounded!" No one replied; no one moved to help. The few who remained alive on the shore fired at the Germans or nursed wounds of their own. For the rest, Gaston could see them fleeing away from the river. "Will no one help?" he pleaded.

Sepp seized Gaston's hand and squeezed it hard. He struggled to speak. "Gaston," he said weakly. "You . . . must go."

"Never!" Gaston swore, his eyes smarting with tears. "I will stay here and die beside you!"

"Listen to me!" Sepp whispered fiercely, urgently. "France . . . still needs you. Get away . . . *une battaille perdu . . . n'a pas la guerre.*" Sepp's voice sighed to a stop, the clock of his life run down.

Gaston took his friend's rifle and tore the badge of his rank from Sepp's collar. "*Au revoir.* A battle lost, but not the war." Then he ran away toward the north, dodging from a heap of stones to hide behind a burned-out vehicle.

✑

Horst von Bockman dispatched a column of armored cars along the shore of the Lys toward a downstream crossing. The inflated boats had been thrown back so many times that even though the assault continued in front of the town, something else needed to be tried.

The barrage stopped, and yet another wave of rafts attempted to cross the Lys. It was difficult to understand how the town continued to resist. Almost all the buildings had been leveled, the island was a heap of flaming ruins, and the air was so thick with smoke that breathing was difficult.

How much longer could the Allied soldiers continue to hold?

38

Save My Sons

With carbines unslung and resting across the saddlebows, bayonets ready like sabers of old, and most importantly, sacks of grenades, Raymond's column prepared to attack.

The assault was led by the Hotchkiss tanks, rattling along at their top speed of seventeen miles an hour. But close behind were the cadets of the Ecole de Cavalerie.

The artillerymen were between barrages. The officers smoked in the shade while the soldiers stacked shells in preparation for another bombardment.

The Germans looked up, startled, as the tanks rolled out of the forest. The armored machines fired their 37 mm guns, destroying one cannon and blowing the carriage out from under another. The Wehrmacht troops scattered. Some of the officers futilely fired their sidearms at the attackers but were cut down by machine guns.

Raymond heard one lieutenant yell angrily for his men to stand and form a line, then watched the officer turn with bewilderment to face the onrushing rank of horses. He raised his machine pistol, but Raymond shot him in the chest. The German's gun loosed a burst into the ground as he fell.

The charge tore apart the cannoneers. While the French tanks scuttled in a circle around the perimeter, picking off strays and keeping the Germans from reforming, the horsemen selected their targets.

Raymond chose the cannon farthest away and galloped his bay horse over to it. As he approached, a German soldier who had been hiding behind the gun carriage got up and leveled his rifle. Raymond put the horse into a jump. The front hooves of the bay smashed into the man's head.

With the horse prancing nervously, Raymond watched as his cadets spread themselves out to each of the gun emplacements. Each student took the sack of grenades and prepared for the destruction they had planned.

When all were ready, Raymond pulled the pin on a grenade, dropped it back into the pouch, and tossed the sack under the cannon. Then he set his mount racing back toward the woods.

When Raymond approached the next emplacement, that cadet did the same maneuver and so on down the line, retrieving the riders and re-forming the rank. By the time Raymond had reached the fourth artillery piece, the first explosion shattered the air. The cannon jumped off the ground; the gun bent in half. Then the weapon flipped over on its side and leaned against the ground, propped on its now-useless barrel.

҈

Horst's tank followed the column of armored cars hurrying toward the downstream crossing of the Lys. Sporadic rifle fire pinged against his ve-hicle's armor to let him know that the French on the far shore were track-ing his progress.

When the line of panzers had covered four of the five miles, Horst was amazed to see the suspension bridge still intact. The needless sacri-fice of his men in the continuing frontal assault on the town could cease and a sweeping flank attack substituted.

The next order of business was to secure the crossing and guard it against demolition. Horst knew that, for whatever reason the bridge had not already been destroyed, it would be as soon as the German interest in it became apparent.

That he had reached the correct conclusion too late was demon-strated when the lead armored car exploded in a gout of flame, struck by an antitank round fired from the south side of the river. Horst ordered his remaining machines to swing into line abreast, taking advantage of the cover of the brush to charge the position ahead. Whatever Allied re-sources had crossed the Lys, they could not be much compared to the armored unit.

Small-arms and machine-gun fire rattled off the German tank. His gunner responded by lobbing a high-explosive round into the clump of trees ahead. The shot was rewarded with the sight of several bodies in British uniforms flying through the air.

"Major," Horst's radio operator said, "I have picked up a garbled transmission from our battery . . . something about being attacked."

It had to be a mistake. The artillery park was well back away from the river, and the Allies had no force across the river unless . . .

"Pivot right ninety," Horst shouted to his driver. "All units, watch for flank attack!"

Another armored car responding to Horst's warning swung broadside to the British detachment at the same moment the tank destroyer launched another round. The Kfz 231 was bowled over from the force of the impact, smashing down a tree trunk and ending up on its roof, a smoking ruin.

Ahead was another tank, bearing down on Horst. It was about the right size and shape to be one of the smaller Czech-made Panzer units, but it was coming from the wrong direction. The Hotchkiss tank fired first, an armor-piercing shell that narrowly missed Horst's turret and flew across the river before splintering an elm.

"Armor-piercing . . . left thirty . . . fire!" Horst ordered.

The round penetrated the front armor of the French tank and divided the body of the vehicle as if an opener had been applied to a tin can. "Major," the machine gunner reported. "Another Hotchkiss at right ninety."

The gun of Horst's tank was already pivoting to track the new threat when the woods suddenly swarmed with horsemen. The machine gunner fired, knocking a rider out of the saddle and disemboweling a horse when the troop swept past, making for the bridge.

"After them! That is why the bridge is still intact!"

∽

Raymond could see the bridge ahead beyond the last screen of brush. Machine-gun bullets and high-explosive rounds were tearing up the cover on all sides. He urged his horse to redouble his efforts.

The German tanks and armored cars were racing along the shore to cut them off. The Guardsmen had abandoned their hopeless position and were retreating back across the span. At any second they might detonate the demolition charges.

Behind him the remaining Hotchkiss tank exploded, victim of another German tank. Now there was only a handful of riders jumping over logs and racing death to the remaining link with safety.

Some instinct told him to yank his mount to the side. The obedient horse spun sideways, leaping a ditch just as another shell exploded against a tree trunk where his former path would have carried him.

Raymond felt a searing pain in his leg. He looked down to see that a shrapnel splinter had gouged a furrow in his leg. But worse, it protruded like a spike from the body of his mount. He tried to pull it out, and the horse nickered in agony.

The bay faltered. It stumbled, recovered, stumbled again. "Not yet," Raymond urged. "Not now! Go! Go!"

The beast responded to this entreaty with a lunge forward, redoubling his efforts to escape the terrible pain.

⟡

"Left ninety," Horst ordered. "High explosive . . . fire!"

He aimed at the movement he saw on the north bank, knowing that the suspension bridge would soon be destroyed if he could not prevent it.

The guns of the German panzers reached across the River Lys. Below the fighting drifted the bodies of those who were already done with the battle. German and French together, floating in the amiable comradeship of death, while overhead the machine guns and cannons roared, arguing with each other over the right to claim the river, the crossing, and the fate of France.

⟡

Andre and his eager Senegalese arrived at the River Lys by the dirt track that led to the suspension bridge and found themselves suddenly immersed in a battle. They unslung their rifles and sprawled forward on their bellies, taking aim across the river.

Below him Andre could see his brother, Paul, preparing to detonate the bridge. Then the air filled with the raining death of the tank rounds fired by the Germans. Andre's arrival had been spotted and his position targeted.

More armored cars and tanks emerged from the woods, an overwhelming assemblage of force.

The Senegalese troops fired back fearlessly, but their small weapons were no match for the cannons and machine guns of the panzers. Forced into a defensive perimeter, they dug themselves into the hillside and prepared to sell their lives dearly.

⟡

Paul helped a pair of Grenadier Guards who reached the north side of the bridge carry their wounded comrade off the roadway. Behind them, knots of British soldiers were running back toward the span. They did not bother firing their weapons at the oncoming German vehicles, knowing that the small arms would have no effect on the steel plating.

Paul retreated to the place where the detonation cords came together. "Prepare to fire the charges," he ordered, realizing as he spoke that he was sealing the fate of Raymond and any of the others who remained across the river.

Suddenly he could see horsemen on the far shore. Behind them shell fire burst among the trees. Paul silently urged them on. He calculated the angle made by the fleeing horsemen and the approaching tanks and knew that the margin was too small, the Germans too close.

Sadly, he turned to the engineer standing by the detonator. "Get ready."

Across the river, Raymond came into view. Paul could tell that the bay was injured; it staggered and pitched against the post of the tower that suspended the bridge. Raymond slewed around in the saddle, almost toppling off. So he was wounded, too. Paul silently urged horse and rider to hurry, imploring them to get clear.

Raymond had barely reached the north end of the span when his mount stumbled again and fell, pinning the young cadet beneath him. Paul started back toward the bridge when the German tank across the river fired again.

"Blow the—" Paul's words were cut off as a high-explosive round landed close beside him.

ᑐ∞ᑐ

Paul lay in a pool of his own blood when Andre reached him. Cradling his brother's head in his lap, Andre stroked the matted hair and placed his fingers on Paul's cheek in a gesture of farewell.

Paul, his body shattered, still tried to talk. "Save my boys, Andre." Then he repeated, "Save my sons."

The fighting had stopped. The bridge, the detonation cables severed, had not been blown.

Gaston staggered up beside his fellow commander, sinking to his knees at Paul's side. "Give me a gun," he cried.

Paul shifted his gaze to the row of German Panzer units covering them from the opposite bank of the Lys.

Gaston clutched Andre's sleeve. "Give me a gun! I want to die with honor like the others!"

Paul reached out with a bloody hand to touch Gaston's arm. "It is enough . . . Gaston. Enough."

Andre looked up at a movement across the river. An officer in the uniform of a Wehrmacht major advanced across the span, carrying a flag of truce.

He stood over Andre and Paul. "I am Major Horst von Bockman, Seventh Panzer. You are the commander?"

"My brother," Andre replied. "Captain Paul Chardon of the Ecole de Cavalerie."

The major removed his hat and used it to shield the eyes of the dying man. "Captain, I salute you. Who were the men defending the town?"

Andre replied, "Not men, Herr Major. Five hundred cadets of the Ecole de Cavalerie."

"*Kavalleriekadetten . . . tapfer Soldaten . . .* brave soldiers." Then to Paul, "Your cadets have resisted the Wehrmacht. You have done all that honor demands. Will you not surrender and stop the killing?"

"No!" Gaston said fiercely.

"Wait," Paul gasped. "Will you . . . let my boys go?"

Andre's eyes seized those of Horst, locked onto them. "I am a colonel. I will guarantee the surrender of the regular forces if you will let the cadets go."

Horst hesitated only a moment, then nodded and said with a wry smile, "The Führer would not approve . . . however . . . honor among soldiers permits me no other course. A pity you were not born German."

"A pity you were not born French."

"I will allow you a two-hour lead to Dunkirk. You will accompany them. Perhaps we will meet again on another battlefield, Herr Colonel."

Paul smiled and raised his chin. Looking up at Andre, he said a last time, "Save my sons for France." Then he died.

⊘

Lining the road out of Lys, five hundred panzer troops stood at attention as eighty surviving cadets rode past the body of Captain Paul Chardon for the last time.

In contrast to the depleted supplies of the young defenders, the Germans had a full complement of ordnance: grenades, ammunition, and MG-34 machine guns. As the departing warriors filed by, the Wehrmacht soldiers presented arms.

At the head of the troop, Andre glanced down at the body of his brother, then at Major Horst von Bockman. A look passed between the two men, and for a moment, the expression of the German officer softened.

39

Miracle of Dunkirk

On the afternoon of his twenty-first birthday, Badger Cross gave up his hope of strawberries, of rescue, and of life.

David also had a growing sense that the Dunkirk miracle would not be a miracle for him and Badger. The defensive perimeter was shrinking as rearguard troops were pulled back and evacuated. As the German lines crept closer to the men on the beach, the Wehrmacht artillery shelled the enclave at will. When the gray skies cleared and the Luftwaffe returned in force, it was rumored that the end of the rescue effort was very near.

For the moment the skies above the sand were empty of hostile aircraft. The shelling fell silent.

David had not mentioned the strawberries to Badger that morning or the fact that it was the fourth of June, his birthday. Maybe Badger would not remember the date, David hoped. If they could get on a ship—any ship—and back to England, David would buy Badger a field of strawberries!

"It's quiet," David said. "They've let up."

"I'm twenty-one," Badger replied. "Interesting thing, that a bloke could die twenty-one years to the day after he is born."

"You aren't gonna die." David's tone was firm, but he was thankful Badger could not see the doubt on his face.

"I'm sure of it." Badger raised his nose as if to sniff the air that smelled of cordite and rotting flesh.

"Sure? All this over strawberries. You're looney; that's all."

"No matter about the strawberries. Today is my day."

"Shut up, Badger!" David said hotly. "It's bad luck to talk that way."

Badger paid no heed to the rebuke. "I saw it. Plain as anything." He paused and raised his right hand in the air as if he could see a plane circling above him. "I wonder what time of day I was born."

"Late," David said gruffly. "Near midnight. Probably it's not even your birthday yet. Probably you still got hours before you have to have those stinking berries."

"Doesn't matter." Badger turned his head toward the low conversations of a large group of French soldiers who sat in the sand a few feet away. "What are they saying?" Badger asked.

"How should I know?" David was angry. Angry at Badger. Angry at whoever was in charge of the evacuation. Angry at himself for being stupid enough to get shot down.

"They're saying something about the panzers moving in on us. The SS shoot anyone wounded. You'd better leave me when they come."

"It would be better if I put my fist in your mouth and smash a few teeth out if you don't knock it off."

"I'm just saying. . . ." Badger exhaled loudly. "You've been good about all this, taking me with you and all. I wish there was some way I could repay you."

"I'll think of something, you putz. When we get back to England, I'll think of something. Now shut your trap. We're gonna make it."

Badger did not reply. He turned his head toward the poilus. "I just wish I knew what they were saying."

At that instant an American voice spoke from behind the two men. "They're talking about women. The women they left at home."

David turned slightly to see an oil-covered, stockily built man wearing the uniform of an American correspondent.

"You American?" David asked.

"Mac McGrath." The man stuck out a sand-covered paw and pumped David's hand as if they were meeting on a peaceful street corner in Paris. "Some mess we're in, huh?"

David jerked his thumb at the press patch on Mac's shoulder. "You're neutral, unless you know something I don't know. Did Roosevelt decide to join our crusade?"

"Not hardly."

"So what are you doing at Dunkirk? You news guys go wherever you want on both sides of the line, don't you?"

"I like it better on this side of things," Mac replied with a bitter laugh.

"You've got a death wish. Is that it, pal?" David brushed the sand absently from his hands. "Or are you here for the story?"

"Just not real fond of Nazis. So, what's your excuse for being here?"

The correspondent's brown eyes were ringed with soot, giving him the appearance of a bandit with a crooked nose.

"I wanted to fly Hurricanes." David shrugged. "This is my pal, Badger Cross. It's his birthday."

"Lousy place to celebrate." Mac shielded his eyes against the glare of the sun on the water.

"I'll say," David said glumly as Mac moved closer. "The army is not real happy with us RAF guys. Can't say I blame them. They put us at the back of the line. But worse than that, they run us all over the beach and the harbor. We may be the last ones out of this dump."

"We're never getting out of here." Badger sighed. "I told you, Tinman. My birthday . . . and no strawberries."

Mac snorted. "Real cheerful fella."

David shrugged again. "Never mind him. He's crazy."

Badger wagged his head. "I'm doomed, Mr. McGrath, and you, too, if you stick by me."

The other solitary souls edged away from Badger at this thought, and shortly Mac, David, and Badger found themselves a very small group indeed.

David explained Badger's preoccupation with strawberries and cream. "I got the tin of milk," he told Mac. "I've been carrying it around with me. But you can't find strawberries anywhere around here. But today is his birthday, and it isn't over yet."

"Would a chocolate bar do?" Mac offered, patting his pockets for the food pilfered from the NAAFI truck. "Or how about . . ." And he withdrew a jar of strawberry jam from his jacket.

It was probably cruel, but David could not resist opening the jar under Badger's nose. The gauze twitched, and the big man said mournfully. "I must be a dead man, mates. Or I'm dreamin'. I can smell strawberries!"

❦

The forty lather-flecked horses from the Ecole de Cavalerie carried double riders. Raymond and Gaston shared the bay gelding that had belonged to Sepp.

Two horses abreast in a column of twenty, the defenders of Lys approached the rubble of Dunkirk. The heads of the last footsore stragglers turned to stare after them.

"Cor! Hit's a lot uv li'l boys! Brought their 'orses fer a bit uv polo wif Jerry!"

Gaston did not understand the English words, but he understood clearly the derisive laughter that followed.

Two sentries at the barricade stepped out in the road as the troop reined to a halt. The dress uniforms of the cadets were torn and bloody, giving mute testimony to the action at the river, but these were still not like any uniforms the sentry had yet seen passing through Dunkirk.

"Cadet Officer Gaston Corbet." Gaston saluted. "Ecole de Cavalerie."

The BEF sentry rocked forward in surprise. Again the words were in English. "Looks like Napoleon's chaps after Waterloo. S'pose we got us a bunch of ghosts, Bobby?"

"Jack! It's those schoolboys who held Jerry off back at the river . . . at the hospital!"

"Ghosts. Like I said . . . thought they was all dead!"

"What do we do with them?"

"We can't stop ghosts. Let 'em pass, I s'pose. Let 'em all pass."

The sentry saluted Gaston smartly; then as the squadron trotted by he remarked, "Right. The new motto of the French Army. *Let them pass* ."

ᆼᄋ

"You have to report your arrival so you can get on the list," a sergeant at the western mole said, turning back the eighty cadets.

Twilight was gathering as the young soldiers of the Ecole de Cavalerie assembled outside the headquarters. While his fellows waited, Gaston was escorted into an office where a short, stocky British colonel was engaged in conversation with a subordinate.

At the sight of Gaston the colonel roared. "Good heavens! What are you supposed to be? Napoleon's cavalry?"

"Cadet Officer Gaston Corbet. Ecole de Cavalerie. Ordered by Captain Paul Chardon to report for duty, sir!"

"The Ecole? I thought you were all dead." The colonel's French was very bad.

"There are eighty of us, sir. We will fight the Boche again if we can get out of here."

The mocking smirk of the colonel vanished. He pulled himself to attention and snapped a salute. "Do you know you are heroes, Cadet Corbet?"

"No, sir." Gaston's eyes brimmed with emotion. "The heroes are the men who are still beside the River Lys."

Minutes later, accompanied by the colonel, the eighty cadets marched to the head of the column of soldiers boarding ships on the western mole.

Small ships were ferrying men from the mole to the larger ships beyond the harbor. Three British fighter planes passed in formation overhead. Seconds later two more followed.

Andre, Gaston, and Raymond stood together silently on this last point of French soil jutting into the oil-coated waters of the Channel.

How long would it be before they could come back to France? When would they face the German panzers again?

All hoped it would be soon. The cadets, conscious of the need to uphold the honor of their fallen comrades, marched proudly aboard the tug that carried them out to HMS *Intrepid* for the Channel crossing.

ᴑꙮ

The high-pitched scream of an incoming artillery shell sent every man on the beach diving for cover.

Every man except Badger Cross.

Clutching his precious jar of strawberry jam, he stood and faced the sea as the wails of the French poilus were drowned by the boom and rumble of the explosion. A hail of sand and shrapnel fell down on the prostrate forms of the soldiers. The angry buzz of hot metal passed close by David's ear to hiss into the dune.

Then silence.

Sounds resumed. The moans of the wounded. Choked sobs and the sounds of men retching with fear.

Then there was Badger.

David rolled onto his back to see who was alive and who was dead.

Badger's shadow fell across his face. "Well, that was a close one," Badger said calmly.

"Idiot!" David pulled Badger down onto the dune.

Badger was nonplussed. "I won't eat it on French soil, and there's an end to it." He stood again and held the jar of berries heavenward, as if to offer thanks for a holy sacrament. "For what we are about to receive, may the Lord make us truly thankful. Amen."

"What's he talking about?" Mac McGrath peered at the blind man suspiciously.

"I told you, he's nuts," David said.

"I won't have my birthday tradition here with these Froggies. Tinman, get me out on the lorries. Out on the jetty there."

"Tide's coming in."

"No matter. I won't have my strawberries on this stinking beach. The roof of a sturdy British lorry. That's the place for tea and cakes."

Mac and David exchanged looks. *Tea? Cakes?* Mac touched his finger to his temple. "Bonkers."

"I heard that." Badger stretched out his hand and began to walk unescorted toward the sound of water. "I'll have my birthday on the lorry jetty. And I'll eat my strawberries and die a happy man. On English trucks. Good English-made trucks. A bit of England. Like a finger in the water pointing to England. To home. Off this bloody French ground. I won't have it anywhere else."

David let him weave toward the shoreline and in the direction of the jetty. Leaping to his feet as the whistle of a shell approached, David shouted, "Down, Badger!" and grabbed the blind man by the arm.

Badger resisted him, strengthened by determination. Shoving David to the ground, he waved his hands and pressed on in the general direction of the makeshift pier. "They can't see me, Tinman," he roared. "I'm invisible. . . ."

The last few words were lost beneath the shriek of the shell.

The sand erupted close by. But Badger walked on, unharmed, through the lethal rain of debris.

David jumped up and followed, suddenly filled with the eerie belief that blind Badger Cross, clutching his strawberries, had indeed become invisible to harm. An instant later they were joined by Mac, who muttered over and over, "Nuts. He's nuts. We're nuts. Nuts!"

David and Mac took Badger's arms and guided him toward the jumble of troop lorries and equipment heaped in the water to make Badger's little bit of England.

Behind them, geysers of soil and pulverized men leaped skyward in a dozen places along the dunes. In front of them was the lorry jetty, deserted and dismal, being swallowed by the returning tide. There were the remains of sunken ships, derelict and abandoned, and the drifting wreckage of men and machines.

A succession of explosions erupted one hundred yards up the beach. While David and Mac ducked and cringed, Badger pressed forward. There was a momentary lull.

"No worries . . . home today." Badger raised the jar toward the Channel. "What's that noise?"

David saw nothing, heard nothing. He looked over his shoulder, anticipating another barrage. "Your imagination."

"No," Badger insisted. "It's there!" He stretched out a gauze-wrapped hand, now ragged and gray with dirt.

David followed the line of Badger's arm along the jetty. Far beyond the end of the tide-washed equipment danced a dark speck.

"There *is* something. . . ." David's voice trailed off.

Mac stripped off his jacket and waved it overhead.

"They're still too far to see it," David warned.

"The boat will come straight here." Badger stepped into the water ahead of his companions.

The boat approached bow on, aimed unerringly toward the wharf. A black hull swelled into view, and a boxy superstructure reared itself above the swirl of the sea.

Far away thunder announced the nearing of another barrage, but David paid it no mind. The three waded into the surf and climbed onto a three-quarter-ton truck. David looked back to see other men staggering after them. Half running, half crawling, they emerged from the dunes until a new queue of several hundred snaked toward the water's edge.

The lashings that secured the lorries were worn by the waves. The nose-to-tail formation of dark green metal beasts swayed with each new surge. A plank walkway, improvised from fence posts and scavenged driftwood, wobbled under David's feet. In constant danger of pitching into the water, he helped Badger as they lurched from roof to roof.

"How many ships?" Badger cried.

David raised his eyes to count the formation of ships that seemed to suddenly materialize on the horizon behind the black hull of a river barge. How had Badger known there was more than one vessel coming? "I count a dozen!"

"How many men behind us?" Badger called the question over the tumult of artillery and the clanking of shifting metal against the tide.

From the veil of smoke wafting across the dunes still more ragged soldiers stumbled out until the number in the queue was perhaps half a thousand. They crept forward, struggling to climb onto the shifting pier.

"Five hundred, about," Mac shouted as he leaped from the hood of one truck onto the swamped bed of another.

"How far to the end of the jetty?" Badger asked as David helped him across the gulf.

"We're almost there. Two more lorries ahead and we're home!"

The jetty groaned beneath the weight and movement of the troops. For an instant the roar of the German guns fell silent, only to be replaced by the more ominous hum of approaching aircraft engines.

A collective moan rose from the jetty. Faces craned skyward in dread. A few men jumped into the water and began to swim back toward the beach.

"Home today, boys!" Badger braced himself on the wood-plank walkway and raised the jar of jam as if it could somehow ward off imminent death.

David crouched and tugged at Badger, who swatted his hand away and faced the oncoming buzz head-on.

"Get down!" Mac cried.

Badger laughed and began to sing:

> "The Son of God goes forth to war,
> A kingly crown to gain!

His blood red banner streams afar:
Who follows in His train?"

Then exclamations of joy resounded up and down the line.

"It's the RAF!" A spontaneous cheer as a trio of Hurricanes roared in low from the sun and dipped their wings in salute as they passed overhead.

Guardian angels with Merlin engines, they circled above the beach as the school of French fishing vessels moved in.

David, Mac, and Badger reached the end of the jetty as hundreds more crammed in behind them.

"Here we are, Tinman. At the head of the line at last!" Badger opened his strawberries, dipped one unbandaged finger in to scoop out the red goo, and sucked it off.

"Happy birthday, Badger," David said.

The three men sat on the half-submerged hood, their legs dangling in the water. "I had this vision." Badger licked his fingers. "It was the ship . . . you know? The boat . . . the Lady of Avalon who carried off King Arthur. Always loved that part of the legend. Now, Tinman, tell me what you see."

"I only wish I had my camera," muttered Mac. "Nobody's gonna believe this." The newsman stood and shook his head.

"I'm not sure I believe it!" David whistled low at the incarnation of Badger's vision.

"Well?" Badger croaked impatiently.

David clambered to his feet. "She's not a magic boat from Avalon. More like *Tugboat Annie*, but she'll do." David waved broadly as a low, broad-hulled barge chugged up to the jetty. It was piloted by a thickset woman with a scowl that would have made the Führer cringe. On her shoulder perched a large white rat, who studied the approach intently.

"Give a hand!" The woman's voice was as gruff as a stevedore's. "You think we've got all day? Lewinski! Step lively with those ropes!"

Tending the bow rope was a gangly, red-haired apparition wearing a gas mask. At the stern was a slim, pretty, sunburned woman who shouted at Mac McGrath, "Where's your camera?"

He shrugged, pointed at the water. "Thought you'd never get here." He laughed with relief, then caught the cable, tying it off to the grill of the lorry.

As the Hurricanes boomed overhead, the faces of a half-dozen children popped out of the hatch. The old woman at the helm scowled down at them until they vanished again, then waved to the assembled troops to begin embarking.

Arthur Badger Cross led the men on board.

⟨��⟩

The Royal Navy MTB 102 cruised slowly by the Dunkirk shore, just as the ninth day of the greatest military rescue in the history of the world was ending.

Over the loud-hailer of the motor torpedo boat the sailors called out in both French and English, "Is anyone still there? There will be no more boats. Is anyone there?"

A pudgy figure emerged from the cellar doors beside a demolished house. In one hand he waved a bottle of champagne. "Here," he said. "Do not forget me!"

When he was hauled aboard, he smelled of brandy, wine, and *pâté de foie gras*. Over his shoulder he carried a bag that jingled suspiciously like silverware. "Poilu Jardin, at your service. I was a guest of the mayor of the town. Perhaps you know him? A great capitalist, but a friend of the common man!"

⟨�⟩

While the others slept in heaps of exhaustion, Gaston and Andre sat quietly together in the stern of the destroyer *Intrepid*.

What disturbed Gaston most were his thoughts about the heroes who remained behind: Captain Chardon, Sepp, the other cadets . . . they would not be remembered long. Perhaps in fifty years the battle of the Ecole de Cavalerie would be a forgotten fragment of the story of Dunkirk—lost in some dusty archive.

"So many . . . who will know them?" Gaston asked bitterly.

Andre sat without speaking for a long time. "Dust of heroes," he whispered at last. "God will know you!"

EPILOGUE

Heaps of bones once moved by the proud breath of life
Scattered limbs, nameless debris, chaos of humanity,
Sacred jumble of a vast reliquary,
Dust of heroes, God will know you!

War memorial at Louvemont

Journalist John Murphy sat beside Mac McGrath in the packed, airless gallery of the British House of Commons as Winston Churchill summed up the Miracle of Dunkirk.

Over 300 thousand troops had been removed from the beaches of France by a heroic civilian navy of little ships.

The *Garlic*, which had carried Josephine Marlow, Richard Lewinski, and a company of assorted refugee children, including Yacov Lubetkin, did not lose even one passenger in the escape from Paris to the haven of England. Piloted by Madame Rose, the survival of the precious human cargo of the *Garlic* was perhaps among the greatest miracles of that day. Now Madame Rose and the children were on their way to the farm in Wales where Elisa Murphy and Lori Kalner and the others lived. Word had even come that Madame Rose's sister, Betsy, and the other orphans of No. 5 Rue de la Huchette had likewise escaped the Nazis' clutches.

Mac considered how quickly their lives had changed. The past days had made it clear that time was too precious to waste.

Richard Lewinski had been shuttled off to an undisclosed British government intelligence site to continue his work deciphering the Nazi codes. The countless Allied victories that would come from his survival were yet to be told.

Josie was reunited with Andre Chardon within hours of her arrival in England. They married the same night in a little chapel in Hampstead.

Mac and Eva likewise determined to marry by the end of the week. Together they would travel to Jerusalem to take Yacov Lubetkin home to his waiting grandfather, Rabbi Shlomo Lebowitz.

Eva had held the child and whispered to Mac, "I will continue to pray for his sister. For his family in Poland. We Jews believe that if even one Jewish life is saved . . . to save even one . . . is like saving the whole world. Could it be that everything—everything—can be changed for the good by even one life? Can it be, Mac? It must be so. That in God's eyes even one is as precious as the universe. Only one can make such a difference in the world that someday evil will be defeated."

Mac had not believed it before Dunkirk, but now? Who could deny that only one person could change the course of history and eternity?

Dust of heroes, God will know you!

And so, lives that seemed so horribly interrupted by tragedy and war paused only long enough to take a breath and then continue on at a more rapid pace.

All these thoughts were fresh in Mac's mind as he listened to the stirring words of the British prime minister.

Winston Churchill praised the heroism of the civilian sailors and marveled at the massive accomplishment but warned that wars were not won by evacuations. Even so, God had given England and the world another chance.

It seemed to Mac that the fate of the free world had somehow turned upon the hinge of Dunkirk's miracle. Somehow, Churchill said, England would survive the storms of tyranny that beat upon her shores. His words of hope and courage in the face of so great a disaster were heard around the world:

"We shall go on to the end! We shall fight in France. We shall fight on the seas and oceans. We shall fight on the beaches. We shall fight in the fields and in the streets; we shall fight in the hills. We shall never surrender!"

Digging Deeper into DUNKIRK CRESCENDO

Will evil always have the upper hand? Why is heaven silent? Does God not care about tyranny? about disasters? about who lives—and who dies?

And how can we find the hope and courage to go on in the midst of seemingly overwhelming odds? What can one person do, if anything, to make a difference?

These questions—and a myriad more—have reigned in men's and women's minds throughout history. Most likely you too have asked at least one, if not all, of them.

In the spring of 1940, people wondered, *Is Hitler unstoppable? Will the Nazis take over the world, reshaping it for their twisted purposes? Will life ever be the same again?*

The people's fear was real. As Madame Rose told Josie, "You know what will happen to the special children if the Nazis lay hold of them. Their fate will be the same as that of the Austrians, my little sons of Abraham. And your little ones as well. It is a fearful thing, this total war of Hitler's" (p. 218).

When would it end? How would it end? The future was as unsure in 1940 as it is for us today.

As the spunky Madame Rose said, "We need a true miracle" (p. 218).

And the miracles came, even in the midst of war.

Josie Marlow rescues little Yacov from the clutches of the Nazis. Her unlikely partners on her mission of mercy are a Wehrmacht major and his wife.

Andre Chardon escapes death numerous times and helps get French soldiers off the beaches of Dunkirk.

"A heroic civilian navy" (p. 303) bands together to rescue 300,000 troops via Dunkirk Harbor . . . when it seems humanly impossible to do so.

The orphans of Rue de la Huchette are granted many miracles: Madame Betsy and some of the orphans escape France by train. Madame Rose escapes with others on the *Garlic*. And when the *Garlic* begins to drift out to sea, the boat is rescued by the fishing fleet of Harfleur (p. 274), bound for Dunkirk!

Then there is the miracle of the longed-for strawberries, just in time for Badger's birthday!

Could these all be coincidence, or are they the hand of God in the lives of men—in both the large and the small details?

Madame Rose is vehement about her perspective: "They've made war on the apple of God's eye, my dear girl. Pity the German nation. They have made war on heaven, and heaven will not be silent forever" (p. 218).

Dear reader, has heaven ever seemed silent to you? deaf to your requests? Josie felt that way—even as she stood in the courtyard of the orphanage, staring at the star-flecked sky (see p. 218).

But Josie began to see the miracles along the way. And that is our prayer for you, too. As we receive your letters, we hear your soul cries. We long for you to see and experience the miracles of God—both large and small.

We know you question how life works. (Who doesn't?) We trust that the following questions will help you as you dig deeper for answers to your daily dilemmas. You may wish to delve into these questions on your own or share them with a friend or a discussion group.

We hope *Dunkirk Crescendo* will encourage you in your own life situations. But most of all, we pray that you will "discover the Truth through fiction." For we are convinced that if you seek diligently, you will find the One who holds all the answers to the universe (1 Chronicles 28:9).

Bodie & Brock Thoene

SEEK . . .

PART I
Chapters 1–2

1. Have you ever had to choose between loving two people, as Mac McGrath had to decide between Josie and Eva (see p. 4)? Which person did you choose and why?

_____

_____

2. France's military and political leaders spent a lot of time arguing about whose fault Hitler's advances were instead of fighting Hitler himself (see p. 9). Think back to a crisis in your life. Do you tend to *act*—be proactive in solving the problem and making changes and decisions? Or do you tend to *react*—blame others for the problem, be passive until the fallout, and then be forced to act? Explain by giving an example.

_____

_____

3. When have you found yourself "incredibly busy with important matters" (p. 13)—so much so that you've missed what is *really* important? If faced with the same situation today, what would you change?

_____

_____

Chapters 3–4

4. Imagine that you are David Meyer, drifting in a parachute toward enemy territory. What are your thoughts and emotions as you land upside down in that tree (see pp. 17–19)? What do you wish you would have done before taking off in that airplane?

_____

_____

5. An unlikely person—a Belgian farmer—offers David refuge in an unlikely place (see pp. 20–22). Horst von Bockman, a Wehrmacht major, is an unlikely person to rescue a Jewish baby. Have you experienced protection from an unlikely person or in an unlikely place? If so, tell the story.

_____

_____

6. If you were Josie and received a phone call about picking up a baby in a war zone (see p. 30), what would be on your list of pros and cons? How would you make the final decision?

_____

_____

7. When the Royal Navy was accused of cowardice, Admiral Sir Roger Keyes said, "It is not a lack of courage with the sailors! It is a failure of leadership in this government!" (p. 35). Do you agree with Keyes? Why or why not? What impact do you believe a government, like that of the United States, has on a person's everyday life?

_____

_____

8. Is there anyone of whom you could say, as Oliver Cromwell did, "You have sat too long for any good you have been doing. Depart, I say, and let us have done with you" (p. 35)? Who, and why? In which parts of your life could you say this of yourself?

_____

_____

Chapters 5–7

9. Years earlier, Andre Chardon had made two mistakes that now hang heavy over his life. He loved Elaine Snow but chose not to marry her because of pressure from his grandfather. He fathered Juliette through Elaine, then chose not to be a father. There is no second chance on the first mistake—Elaine is dead. But now Andre has the opportunity to act as a father to Juliette. However, to do so, he has to overcome tremendous obstacles, including meeting with Juliette's stern grandfather, Abraham Snow.

   What past mistakes shadow your life? What obstacles would you face if you decided to right the wrong?

_____

_____

10. "I am sorry," Horst whispers. "For myself. For you. For this child and ten million others. For everyone. And there is nothing more I can do. There is no changing anything" (p. 51).

Have you felt like Horst? Inadequate? Unable to change things? When? What has happened between then and now?

_____

_____

11. "Each minute evil committed or allowed by ordinary men has evaporated into the air like water in the hot sun. We thought it did not matter. . . . But now it has come back in a cloud to cover us with darkness—with storm and flood and thunder. My little sins? Joined with those of other men, they may now wash us all away" (Andre Chardon, pp. 52–53).

How can "little sins" become a "flood"? Give an example.

_____

_____

12. "'Do not waste pity on a creature like Müller,' Horst said flatly. . . . 'I know it is hard for you to understand, Frau Marlow. Perhaps later you will see it is necessary. When an unpleasant task is necessary, then emotion is a waste of energy. Perhaps even dangerous'" (p. 63).

Do you agree with Horst—totally, partially, or not at all? Why?

_____

_____

Chapters 8–9

13. "You once said you had found something worth living for—someone worth living for" (Josie Marlow, p. 67).

What something or someone are you living for? Why is this so important to you?

_____

_____

14. "The hour has come. . . . Some to fight. Some to say farewell. I will not say which is harder" (Andre Chardon, p. 68).

    When has your "hour" (a time of great crisis or need, when you realized life was going to change somehow) come? Have you fought for what you believe in—or said farewell? What was the result?

    _____

    _____

15. "It is strange, is it not, upon what small hinges great events often turn?" Winston Churchill says (p. 71).

    Identify a few "small hinges" that have led to great events (whether for good or evil) in your nation within your lifetime. Why do you think these small events were so crucial?

    _____

    _____

Chapters 10–11

16. Imagine sitting at breakfast (like Mac, p. 80) or being asleep (like Josie, p. 81) when air-raid sirens go off. What would your first reaction be? Panic? Disbelief? Fear? Why?

    _____

    _____

17. Have you ever misjudged someone, as Sister Mitchell did Paul Chardon, and vice versa (see pp. 83–85)? When did you discover that he or she was different than you thought? How has that experience changed your view of that individual and of others in the same "category"?

    _____

    _____

PART II
Chapters 12–13

18. "'Get out of there, Hewitt!' shouted David.

"There was no response. David never saw the hatch open. No chute appeared as Hewitt's plane dwindled to a falling speck" (p. 97).

As a wartime pilot, David Meyer was familiar with death. But he still got that tightening of his gut every time one of his pilots "bought it." When someone you love is dying or has died, how do you respond? Do you believe this life is all there is? that there is life after death? Or something else? Explain.

_____

_____

19. "Before dawn Josie was awakened by the munching of an abandoned Jersey cow whose udder was swollen with milk. There was a halter on her head, and a lead rope dangled from the leather buckle. What had happened to her owner? . . .

"'And this cow? She is sent from heaven'" (Madame Hasselt, p. 101).

Do you believe God sends miracles from heaven when we need them? Why or why not? If so, what miracle (large or small) have you experienced lately?

_____

_____

Chapters 14–16

20. "You ask, what is our aim? I can answer in one word: It is *victory*. Victory at all costs. Victory in spite of all terror. Victory, however long and hard the road may be; for without victory, there is no survival" (Winston Churchill, p. 110).

How important is victory to you? What are you willing to go through to win in a particular area (sports, career, family, a personal character flaw . . .)?

_____

_____

21. "How long would it be before Josie would feel happiness again?"
    (p. 113).
    In a dark period of life, have you wondered if the light would
    ever shine on you again? What was (or is) the situation? Is there a
    difference between having joy and being happy? If so, what is it?

    _____

    _____

22. "The commander shrugged. 'We have inferior numbers . . . inferior
    equipment . . . inferior methods. . . .' The rest of the sentence
    expired in the air and fell to the floor. This was the response from
    the man who had presided over the training and equipping of the
    present French army" (p. 129).
    When have you been faced with incompetence—your own or
    someone else's? What—if anything—have you chosen to do about
    it?

    _____

    _____

Chapter 17–18

23. David Meyer had a unique opportunity. He could get even with
    his longtime enemy, Badger Cross. Or he could choose to help
    Badger when he was in desperate need (see pp. 133–135). If you
    were David (and you're being honest with yourself), what would
    you have done? Why?

    _____

    _____

24. It's interesting that Badger Cross says in "a very meek voice":
    "Don't kill me, Meyer. Don't let me die. I'm trusting you" (p. 134).
    Think of an enemy in your life right now. Would you place your-
    self in the hands of that person willingly? unwillingly? only when
    desperate? Explain.

    _____

    _____

25. When Josie finally reaches the relative safety of the Ecole de Cavalerie and the comforting arms of Paul Chardon, she cries. The "dam of emotion" bursts (p. 142). Whom do you go to for safety when you are overwhelmed emotionally? Why this person?

_____

_____

Chapters 19–21

26. Why do you think Madame Rose was able to get through to the grieving mother when others could not (see pp. 150–151)? How can Madame Rose's approach assist you the next time you're confronted with someone's grief and pain?

_____

_____

27. Horst von Bockman was certain that not only his career but his very *life* would end because he had taken command of the Wehrmacht attack. He's shocked when Rommel calls his attack "brilliant" (p. 163). Have you ever thought you were going to be in trouble . . . and then unexpectedly something good happened? Explain the situation.

_____

_____

28. "All at once Mac stood up, embarrassed with himself. 'Come on, Corporal,' he said to Castle. 'We've just been attacked by a volley of leaflets'" (p. 168).

  When have you made something larger than it really is? What was the result? How has that humbling experience changed how you view similar issues now?

_____

_____

Chapters 22–24

29. If you were one of the last "original" pilots (as David Meyer was by May 1940—see p. 169), what would be going through your mind as you headed out on yet another mission?

_____

_____

30. "It occurred to Nicholi Federov, the White Russian, that when the pieces of a puzzle finally fall into place, it is amazing how the completed picture leaps out" (p. 177).

    When has a puzzle piece fallen into place for you? What completed picture did you see?

    _____

    _____

31. Why do you think Madame Rose was so effective at what she did? List her character traits. Which of those traits remind you of yourself? Which are different from you?

    _____

    _____

32. The French people at Gare du Nord were indignant about the orphans of Rue de la Huchette getting on the train in a car especially reserved for them. They were even angrier that these orphans included "cripples and foreigners" (p. 187). If you were in that crowd, trying desperately to leave a country that would soon be overtaken by the enemy, how would you respond? Would you consider some people better than others? Would you give up your seat on the train (which might mean giving up your life) to one of the orphans? Why or why not?

    _____

    _____

PART III
Chapter 25

33. Why do you think Andre Chardon was the only one who escaped from the burning barn in the woods (see pp. 195–196)? Was it simply chance? purposed by heaven? Or something else? Explain your theory.

    _____

    _____

34. Put yourself in the shoes of the British and French women: waiting for word from husbands and sons in battle; anxiously reading lists of dead, wounded, or missing and hoping their loved ones wouldn't be on them; watching for ships to return with their men; thinking about sending their children to another country for safety (see p. 197). What concerns and hopes would you have for the present? for the future?

_____

_____

35. "Take me with you, Tinman! . . . Walk me back across the Channel, will you? Point the way. . . . No hard feelings, Yank. Just don't leave me here" (Badger Cross, p. 198).

Life certainly has its ironies. Two enemies, Badger Cross and David Meyer, end up literally linking arms to try to get back to England. When have you "linked arms" in some way with a person you wouldn't normally work with, spend time with, or whom you disliked? What happened because you worked together?

_____

_____

Chapters 26–27

36. "'Whatever you do, you must be ready to leave by midnight the day after tomorrow if you expect to evacuate with my staff.'

"'General,' Andre replied quietly, 'if my countrymen are not provided for by then, I will not be going with you'" (Lord Gort and Andre Chardon, p. 205).

If you and your family had one chance to flee a dangerous area, would you take it? Or would you stay to help get more of your countrymen and women to safety? What facts and feelings would figure into your decision?

_____

_____

37. Andre wonders what he can do "as one lone voice in the face of this 'English ships for Englishmen' attitude" (p. 210). When have you run into this type of attitude? How have you dealt with it (words, actions, etc.)?

_____

_____

38. "Mac glanced at his reflection in the mirror and shuddered as a thought flashed through his mind. What if he did not survive the journey? What if he didn't come back to sweep her off her feet and carry her off into the sunset?

    "He wanted to speak to her. Tell her how he felt. Just in case" (p. 213).

    Make a list of the people most important to you. If something was to happen to you today, what would you wish you would have said to each of them? Write down your thoughts . . . and then find the time and the courage to say those things *now*, while there is yet time.

    _____

    _____

Chapters 28–30

39. In order to get the British leaders to listen to him, Andre used a little "extortion" (see p. 216). Have you ever used a little extortion for a good cause? When?

    _____

    _____

40. "The Lord approves of common sense. And when common sense fails, then there is some other course we are meant to sail" (Madame Rose, p. 217).

    When should we use common sense, and when should we pray? How can you know which to use when?

    _____

    _____

41. If God can use even Madame Hilaire, the Anteater, for good (see p. 219), how might He use you as part of a "perfectly logical miracle" (p. 220)? Is there someone who needs your assistance today?

    _____

    _____

Chapters 31–34

42. "Mac marveled at the way John Galway not only plucked [the soldiers] from danger but lifted their spirits. Mac himself got a boost from listening—a renewed belief that everything would work out after all" (p. 240).

   Who lifts your spirits? How?

   _____

   _____

43. In what ways does the relationship between Sister Abigail Mitchell and Paul Chardon change (see pp. 243–244)? Has your relationship with someone ever changed dramatically? How?

   _____

   _____

Chapters 35–37

44. Would you, like captains Sepp and Gaston, be ready to "die gloriously" (p. 269)? Why or why not?

   _____

   _____

45. "Badger had grown very fatalistic. To counter this despair, David became ever more obsessed with strawberries. He had come to think of Badger's upcoming birthday as a symbol of their survival" (p. 275).

   What is your perspective on birthdays? Do you look forward to yours? try to ignore it? dislike it when you're another year older? How can you celebrate your birthday this year as a symbol of your survival—physically, emotionally, mentally, and spiritually?

   _____

   _____

46. Of what times in your life could you say, with Gaston, "A battle lost, but not the war" (p. 284)?

   _____

   _____

Chapters 38–39

47. Paul Chardon, a true leader, was faithful to his "boys" to the very end. "Will you . . . let my boys go?" he pleads with Horst von Bockman. Right before Paul dies, he says with a smile, "Save my sons for France" (p. 290). If you could say only a few words to someone before you died, what would those words be? What would they reveal about your priorities in life? (There's a wonderful saying: Live the way you want to die.)

_____

_____

48. Why was Badger Cross no longer afraid of the bombers on his birthday? What led to such a change that he risked climbing onto the jetty, to be on British soil when he ate his strawberry jam? (See pp. 295–298.)

_____

_____

49. "Andre sat without speaking for a long time. 'Dust of heroes,' he whispered at last. 'God will know you!'" (p. 299).

When you are only "dust," will others consider you a hero? Why or why not? Do you believe God will know you? Explain.

_____

_____

Epilogue

50. "Mac considered how quickly their lives had changed. The past days had made it clear that time was too precious to waste" (p. 303).

How does your perspective on time, and how you spend it, change as you grow older?

_____

_____

51. Eva tells Mac, "'We Jews believe that if even one Jewish life is saved
. . . to save even one . . . is like saving the whole world. Could it be
that everything—everything—can be changed for the good by even
one life? Can it be, Mac? It must be so. That in God's eyes even
one is as precious as the universe. Only one can make such a difference in the world that someday evil will be defeated.'

    "Mac had not believed it before Dunkirk, but now? Who could
deny that only one person could change the course of history and
eternity?" (p. 304).

    Do you believe as Eva does? Why or why not? How does your
belief or disbelief that one life is as important as the entire universe impact the way you live today? the way you think about the
future?

    _____

    _____

52. "We shall go on to the end! We shall fight . . . .We shall never surrender!" (Winston Churchill, p. 304).

    To you, what is worth going on for? fighting for? never surren-
dering for?

    _____

    _____

Bodie and Brock Thoene (pronounced *Tay-nee*) have written over 45 works of historical fiction. That these best sellers have sold more than 10 million copies and won eight ECPA Gold Medallion Awards affirms what millions of readers have already discovered—the Thoenes are not only master stylists but experts at capturing readers' minds and hearts.

In their timeless classic series about Israel (The Zion Chronicles, The Zion Covenant, and The Zion Legacy), the Thoenes' love for both story and research shines.

With The Shiloh Legacy series and *Shiloh Autumn*—poignant portrayals of the American depression—and The Galway Chronicles, which dramatically tell of the 1840s famine in Ireland, as well as the twelve Legends of the West, the Thoenes have made their mark in modern history.

In the A.D. Chronicles, their most recent series, they step seamlessly into the world of Yerushalyim and Rome, in the days when Yeshua walked the earth and transformed lives with His touch.

Bodie began her writing career as a teen journalist for her local newspaper. Eventually her byline appeared in prestigious periodicals such as *U.S. News and World Report, The American West,* and *The Saturday Evening Post.* She also worked for John Wayne's Batjac Productions (she's best known as author of *The Fall Guy*) and ABC Circle Films as a writer and researcher. John Wayne described her as "a writer with talent that captures the people and the times!" She has degrees in journalism and communications.

Brock has often been described by Bodie as "an essential half of this writing team." With degrees in both history and education, Brock has, in his role as researcher and story-line consultant, added the vital dimension of historical accuracy. Due to such careful research, The Zion Covenant and The Zion Chronicles series are recognized by the American Library Association, as well as Zionist libraries around the world, as classic historical novels and are used to teach history in college classrooms.

Bodie and Brock have four grown children—Rachel, Jake, Luke, and Ellie—and five grandchildren. Their sons, Jake and Luke, are carrying on the Thoene family talent as the next generation of writers, and Luke produces the Thoene audiobooks. Bodie and Brock divide their time between London and Nevada.

For more information visit:
www.thoenebooks.com
www.TheOneAudio.com

THE NEW BEST-SELLING SERIES
FROM BODIE AND BROCK THOENE...

A.D. CHRONICLES®

BOOK ONE

First Light

In their most dramatic historical series to date, Bodie and Brock Thoene transport readers back in time to first century A.D., to the most critical events in the history of the world. // ISBN 0-8423-7507-4 • SOFTCOVER • US $13.99

BOOK TWO

second touch

This moving story will draw readers down the path of discovery to the understanding that we all need the hope of Yeshua's touch upon not only our bodies, but our souls. // ISBN 0-8423-7510-4 • SOFTCOVER • US $13.99

BOOK THREE

third watch

"Who do they say that I am?" From the wilderness of Sinai to Mount Hermon the question of Yeshua of Nazareth's identity resounds across the ancient land of Israel. Even evil waits to hear the answer. It is in the very air, the storm, and the sea. // ISBN 0-8423-7513-9-0 • SOFTCOVER • US $13.99

WATCH FOR **fourth dawn**, BOOK 4 IN THE BEST-SELLING A.D. CHRONICLES SERIES, AVAILABLE FALL 2005!

Unabridged audios are available on CD from Tyndale Audio and Luke Thoene Productions. Performed by actor Sean Barrett for your listening enjoyment.
FIRST LIGHT UNABRIDGED AUDIO CD • ISBN 0-8423-7508-2 • US $49.99
SECOND TOUCH UNABRIDGED AUDIO CD • ISBN 0-8423-7511-2 • US $49.99
THIRD WATCH UNABRIDGED AUDIO CD • ISBN 0-8423-7514-7 • US $49.99

The dramatic audio of *First Light* is also available in cassette and CD from Tyndale Audio and Luke Thoene Productions.
CD • ISBN 0-8423-8291-7 • US $24.99 • CASSETTE • ISBN 0-8423-8292-5 • US $24.99

DISCOVER THE
TRUTH
THROUGH
FICTION™

suspense with a mission

TITLES BY

Jake Thoene

"The Christian Tom Clancy"
Dale Hurd, *CBN Newswatch*

Shaiton's Fire

In this first book in the techno-thriller series by Jake Thoene, the bombing of a subway train is only the beginning of a master plan that Steve Alstead and Chapter 16 have to stop . . . before it's too late.
ISBN 0-8423-5361-5 SOFTCOVER
US $12.99

Firefly Blue

In this action-packed sequel to Shaiton's Fire, Chapter 16 is called in when barrels of cyanide are stolen during a truckjacking. Experience heart-stopping action as you read this gripping story that could have been ripped from today's headlines.
ISBN 0-8423-5362-3 SOFTCOVER
US $12.99

Fuel the Fire

In this third book in the series, Special Agent Steve Alstead and Chapter 16, the FBI's counterterrorism unit, must stop the scheme of an al Qaeda splinter cell . . . while America's future hangs in the balance.
ISBN 0-8423-5363-1 SOFTCOVER
US $12.99

for more information on other great Tyndale fiction,
visit www.tyndalefiction.com

THOENE FAMILY CLASSICS™

✪ ✪ ✪

THOENE FAMILY CLASSIC HISTORICALS
by Bodie and Brock Thoene
Gold Medallion Winners*

THE ZION COVENANT
Vienna Prelude*
Prague Counterpoint
Munich Signature
Jerusalem Interlude
Danzig Passage
Warsaw Requiem*
London Refrain
Paris Encore
Dunkirk Crescendo

THE ZION CHRONICLES
The Gates of Zion*
A Daughter of Zion
The Return to Zion
A Light in Zion
The Key to Zion*

THE SHILOH LEGACY
In My Father's House*
A Thousand Shall Fall
Say to This Mountain

SHILOH AUTUMN

THE GALWAY CHRONICLES
Only the River Runs Free*
Of Men and of Angels
Ashes of Remembrance*
All Rivers to the Sea

THE ZION LEGACY
Jerusalem Vigil
Thunder from Jerusalem
Jerusalem's Heart
Jerusalem Scrolls
Stones of Jerusalem
Jerusalem's Hope

A.D. CHRONICLES
First Light
Second Touch
Third Watch
Fourth Dawn
and more to come!

THOENE FAMILY CLASSICS™

✪ ✪ ✪

THOENE FAMILY CLASSIC AMERICAN LEGENDS

LEGENDS OF THE WEST
by Bodie and Brock Thoene

The Man from Shadow Ridge
Riders of the Silver Rim
Gold Rush Prodigal
Sequoia Scout
Cannons of the Comstock
Year of the Grizzly
Shooting Star
Legend of Storey County
Hope Valley War
Delta Passage
Hangtown Lawman
Cumberland Crossing

LEGENDS OF VALOR
by Luke Thoene

Sons of Valor
Brothers of Valor
Fathers of Valor

✪ ✪ ✪

THOENE CLASSIC NONFICTION
by Bodie and Brock Thoene

Writer-to-Writer

THOENE FAMILY CLASSIC SUSPENSE
by Jake Thoene

CHAPTER 16 SERIES
Shaiton's Fire
Firefly Blue
Fuel the Fire

✪ ✪ ✪

THOENE FAMILY CLASSICS FOR KIDS
by Jake and Luke Thoene

BAKER STREET DETECTIVES
The Mystery of the Yellow Hands
The Giant Rat of Sumatra
The Jeweled Peacock of Persia
The Thundering Underground

LAST CHANCE DETECTIVES
Mystery Lights of Navajo Mesa
Legend of the Desert Bigfoot

✪ ✪ ✪

THOENE FAMILY CLASSIC AUDIOBOOKS

Available from
www.thoenebooks.com or
www.TheOneAudio.com